Ravencliffe

Ravencliffe

CAROL
GOODMAN

Viking

An Imprint of Penguin Group (USA)

Viking

Published by the Penguin Group

Penguin Group (USA) LLC

375 Hudson Street, New York, New York 10014

USA ✳ Canada ✳ UK ✳ Ireland ✳ Australia ✳ New Zealand ✳ India ✳ South Africa ✳ China

penguin.com

A Penguin Random House Company

First published in the United States of America by Viking, an imprint of Penguin Group (USA) LLC, 2014

LIBRARY OF CONGRESS CATALOGING-IN-PUBLICATION DATA

Goodman, Carol.

Ravencliffe / by Carol Goodman.

pages cm

"A Blythewood Novel."

Summary: Seventeen-year-old Ava Hall continues to learn more about herself
and her heritage through her work in a New York City settlement house as well
as through her social obligations with the Blythewood girls.

ISBN 978-0-670-78477-6 (hardcover)

[1. Supernatural—Fiction. 2. Identity—Fiction. 3. Love—Fiction. 4. Social settlements—Fiction.
5. Social classes—Fiction. 6. Boarding schools—Fiction. 7. Schools—Fiction.
8. New York (N.Y.)—History—1898–1951—Fiction.] I. Title.

PZ7.G61354Rav 2014   [Fic]—dc23   2013046780

Printed in U.S.A.

1   3   5   7   9   10   8   6   4   2

Book design by Nancy Brennan

Set in Haarlemmer MT

To Nora, my history muse.

1

WHEN I'D DECIDED to work at the Henry Street Settlement house for the summer, I'd been told that part of my job might entail navigating the Lower East Side tenement houses where our clients lived. But I'd never pictured myself leaping from rooftop to rooftop. Or chasing after an escaped changeling.

I thought I'd left all that behind at Blythewood.

But now that's exactly what I was doing, running hell-for-leather, leaping over the dividing walls between rooftops.

It had started that morning at Henry Street with an unexpected guest.

I was leaning out my office window trying to catch a breeze, watching a gang of boys whose damp and tattered clothing suggested they had been swimming off the piers. I envied them, even if the East River smelled, the currents were deadly, and bloated bodies occasionally bobbed to its slick, greasy surface. It would be worth it to feel cool water on my skin! I pulled the damp, limp lawn of my shirtwaist away from my tightly laced corset and closed my eyes. If only I could sail out this window and wing my way over the tarpaper roofs and water towers, out to the river. If only I could fly. . . .

A memory of a dark-eyed boy who had carried me up into the air on his ebony wings flitted through my mind. *Raven.* The last time I'd seen him he had fled from me, sure I saw him as a monster—but really I had only reacted to him as I did because I had been afraid that *I* was one. Now I might never get a chance to tell him I'd been wrong. The memory of him was so real I could almost feel the beat of his wings stirring the stale air around me and hear the rustle of feathers. . . .

I *did* hear rustling.

I turned around, but of course it wasn't Raven. It was a young girl—a child in stature, but perhaps really a teenager stunted by poor nutrition—in a white shirtwaist that had been much mended but was clean and pressed and a plain brown skirt with a tattered muddy hem that hovered a few inches above the tops of her worn, scuffed boots. Instead of a hat, she wore a faded scarf tied over her hair, as many of the Jewish girls in the neighborhood did. All in all, she looked like many of the young immigrants who filled the Lower East Side tenements surrounding the settlement house. Like Tillie Kupermann, my friend who had died last year in the Triangle fire. As an image of Tillie striding across the smoke-filled factory floor filled my head, I remembered.

"Etta!" I cried. "Etta Blum! You were at the Triangle. You're the girl Tillie—"

"Saved. Yes, although she couldn't have done it without you and that strange young man."

Raven. How much did Etta remember of that day? Raven leading us through the flames beneath a cloak and up onto the roof? A man in an Inverness cape shoving Tillie off the roof?

What about me falling? Or Raven catching me midair and bearing me aloft on ebony wings? Or had she relegated all the events of that terrible day to the realms of nightmare?

"Much was strange about that day," I said, glancing nervously at the door where Miss Corey and Miss Sharp had appeared, drawn by my crying out Etta's name, no doubt. "But I'm so glad to see you. I've thought about you, but I didn't know where to find you." A prick of guilt stung me. I had seen her name on the rolls of survivors; I could have looked for her. I *should* have looked for her.

"I thought *you* were dead," Etta said simply. "I saw you fall. But a couple of days ago I saw you walking on Ludlow Street. At first I thought you might be a ghost. I've seen so many strange things recently. But then I followed you and saw you come here to the settlement house." She turned around and smiled shyly at Miss Sharp and Miss Corey. "It didn't seem a place for ghosts."

"No, of course not," Miss Sharp said, holding out her hand to Etta. "It's a place for girls who need help. Do you need help, Etta?"

"Not me!" Etta said. "It's my sister, Ruth. She's . . . she's . . ." Etta's face crumpled and she began to shake. Miss Sharp grasped her shoulders just before she slumped to the floor. She helped Etta into a chair and snapped at Miss Corey.

"Lillian, don't just stand there! Make the girl some tea. And Ava"—she turned to me—"go see if there's some bread and cheese in the soup kitchen—"

"No!" Etta roused herself to grasp my hand. "I want you to stay. I knew when I saw you that you were the only one who could help me . . . that if you could come back after falling off a ten-story building, you could bring back my sister."

"How long has she been gone?" Miss Sharp asked, handing Etta a cup of tea.

"That's just it," Etta said. "She's not gone—she's just not herself anymore. And the thing that's taken her place . . . it's not *human*."

⤞ ✦ ⤝

We gave Etta three cups of sweet, hot tea, but she still didn't make a lot of sense. A change had come over her sister, Ruth, three weeks ago, but Etta insisted it was more than a change. She insisted that the *thing* sharing the cramped two-room tenement with her and two younger brothers and their parents was *not* Ruth. "It looks like Ruth and talks like Ruth. It's fooled my parents and my brothers, but I *know* that's not my sister."

"When did you first imagine that she had changed?" Miss Corey asked brusquely, holding a pencil to her notebook.

"When did she stop being your sister?" Miss Sharp rephrased the question more gently.

"It was after the Fourth of July Tammany Hall excursion to Coney Island. Papa forbade us to go. He says picnics are for *goyim*." She blushed, looking apologetically at blonde, blue-eyed Miss Sharp.

"But your sister didn't care about the old ways, did she?" Miss Sharp asked gently.

I startled at the phrase. *The old ways* was how we talked of tradition at Blythewood. I'd learned last year that the phrase had a more sinister meaning having to do with breeding and forced marriages. I was surprised to hear Miss Sharp use it in connection with a Coney Island excursion, but I understood when Etta answered.

"No," she admitted with a small, shy smile. "Ruth said we might as well have stayed in the *shtetl* in the old country if we'd only come to America to marry good Jewish boys and shave our heads. . . ." As Miss Corey's eyes widened, Etta went on. "That's what Jewish women do when they marry," she explained. "Ruth didn't care about marrying a Jewish boy. She flirted with the Irish boys on Cherry Street and the Swedes from Bay Ridge."

"She went with all these men?" Miss Corey asked.

"Not *that* way!" Etta cried, bristling. "She liked laughing with the boys and going out to Coney Island to ride the Steeplechase and dancing at the dance halls. She worked hard all week at the factory and wanted to have a good time on her day off."

"There's many a girl who's been led astray in the pursuit of fun," Miss Corey said primly, giving me a knowing a look. Since I'd volunteered to spend my summer vacation working at the settlement house, the Blythewood librarian had kept a close eye on me and lectured me daily on the dangers of the city. "Especially girls who go with strange men."

"Let's not jump to any conclusions, Lil," Miss Sharp said. She cradled Etta's hand in hers and added in a softer tone, "But perhaps, Etta, the change that came over your sister is a result of an attachment she's formed. Young women can sometimes seem quite different when they fall in love. "

"Yes!" Miss Corey said, snapping her pencil in half. "They frequently act like perfect fools!"

"But that's just the thing," Etta said. "She's not acting like a boy-crazy fool. She's become perfectly obedient and suddenly has no interest in boys at all. She does everything Mama and Papa tell her to do—except for the ironing—but she wrings the clothes instead and hangs them all on the clothes rack, which is much harder."

"But she won't use the iron?" Miss Corey asked, looking up from the new pencil she was sharpening and catching Miss Sharp's worried glance. "Is there anything else she won't use or touch?"

Etta frowned, thinking. "The kettle," she said finally. "Ruth used to get up first and put the kettle on the stove, but now she goes to fetch the water from the pump even though it's six flights down and back . . . come to think of it, she doesn't go near the stove either."

"The iron, the kettle, the stove," Miss Corey said. "All made of iron."

"If she can't touch iron," I began, "does that mean she's a fair—"

"It means it's *fair*ly certain we should go see her," Miss Sharp broke in, widening her eyes at me. "Is she home now, Etta?"

Etta nodded. "It's her half day at the factory, but she comes home straightaway now to help me and Mama make silk flowers to sell. Mama will be wondering where I am."

"Well, let's get you home, then," Miss Sharp said, squeezing Etta's shoulder. "Lillian, why don't you take Etta down to the kitchen to see if there are any day-old loaves to be had while Ava and I collect my nursing bag so we can give Ruth a proper exam."

"She's not sick," Etta began to object, but Miss Corey steered her out of the office, explaining to her that coming as a visiting nurse would give Miss Sharp an opportunity to speak with Ruth. When their voices had faded on the stairs, I turned to Miss Sharp, who was bent over her leather valise. It had surprised me that Vionetta Sharp, English teacher at Blythewood, would spend her summer off training as a nurse, but she told me that the world might soon be more in need of nurses than English teachers. The jeweled dagger she pulled out of her bag and slipped into a concealed sheath at her waist, though, did not look like part of the usual nurse's kit. I recognized it as a magical dagger from Blythewood.

"What do you think has taken Ruth's place?" I asked.

"A *Fata mutabilis*," Miss Sharp replied, adding a potions vial to the bag. "Or in common parlance: a changeling."

»→ ✦ ←«

Henry Street was so crowded with housewives buying their dinners from food carts, young women pouring out of factories, and men pouring into the taverns, that we had to walk in pairs. Miss Corey went in front with Etta, while Miss Sharp walked beside me, whispering what she knew about changelings—which wasn't much.

"Little is known about them in their indigenous state, as they are almost only encountered after they have assumed the characteristics of their human hosts. By that time they look almost entirely human, save for certain telltale marks on their skin, which only an expert trained by the Order can recognize. Also there are their habits—avoidance of iron, unusual appetites, insomnia—that give them away. If Etta's sister has indeed been taken over by a changeling, it's quite remarkable that Etta spotted the creature. When this is done, we should conduct an interview with Etta to test for preternatural talents. She might be a candidate for Blythewood."

"I can't imagine Etta wanting to leave her sister. She seems so devoted to her." A sorrowful look from Miss Sharp froze my voice. "We will get her back, won't we? That's how the stories my mother used to read me always ended—once the changeling is driven off the real child returns."

Miss Sharp sighed. "Unfortunately, those really *are* fairy stories. The original host is rarely restored. We're not sure what the changelings do to them—we suspect they kill them to absorb their features and memories." Seeing the look of horror on my face, Miss Sharp pulled me to the side of the street, out of the path of a horse-drawn ice cart, and gripped my shoulders.

"These creatures are dangerous, Ava. I know your . . . *encounter* with the Darkling this past year has predisposed you to look favorably on the fairies, but there are dangerous creatures hiding in plain sight, preying on humans, and as members of the Order we're pledged to protect humanity from them."

Vionetta Sharp might not have looked like a warrioress of an ancient Order, but she and Miss Corey had taken the same oath I had on my first night at Blythewood to defend humanity against the creatures of Faerie. Some of those creatures— trolls, goblins, ice giants—were dangerous and scary, but others, like the tiny lampsprites, were harmless. And then there were the Darklings . . .

"Darklings aren't fairies," I protested. "But yes, Raven did help me to see that the Order is wrong about the fairies. They're not all evil. I thought you agreed. Your grandfather believed they weren't all evil."

"And nearly killed my uncle Taddie trying to prove it!" Miss Sharp snapped in an unusually brusque manner. She hadn't been herself all summer. I'd put it down to the strain of settlement work, but now I saw that something else must be on her mind. "I believe it's true that we have to revise the old ways of the Order, but we can't throw them out willy-nilly. Many of these creatures are truly dangerous—the changelings perhaps most of all. Look at what one did to poor Lillian."

"To Miss Corey? What do you—" Then I remembered what she'd said about the marks that distinguished a changeling. "Do you mean the marks on Miss Corey's face—?"

"Made by a changeling that was trying to take her place. Her father killed it before it could, but it left those marks. So you can understand why Lillian does not feel kindly disposed toward the species. If that is what's up there . . ." She lifted her eyes up to the tenement house where Etta and Miss Corey had stopped. "Then you must let us do what is necessary. You stay with Etta and help her distract her family while Lillian and I draw the creature out and . . . *deal* with it."

I thought of the dagger in Miss Sharp's bag and shivered despite the sultriness of the day. I'd seen Vionetta Sharp mesmerize a murder of shadow crows at Blythewood with that dagger. Her blue eyes were shining now with a cold light that reminded me of the eyes of the Dianas when they went into a Hunt trance. She didn't look as if she would brook any disagreements. I nodded my head.

"Good girl," she said, turning to join Etta and Miss Corey at the door of the tenement, dismissing me as abruptly as a general would dismiss a field soldier. My teacher was already *on the hunt*. I almost felt sorry for the creature waiting for us upstairs.

⇥ ✦ ⇤

Though I was no stranger to the dark, unlit stairwells and strong odors of tenement houses, I felt a lowering sense of dread as we climbed to the sixth floor to face a creature trying to pass as human. Would it go with us peaceably? Or would it fight to keep its place? And how did Miss Sharp plan to *deal* with it?

At the top of the stairs, Etta removed a key from a string around her neck and held it to the lock of a worn and faded wooden door. She turned to Miss Corey. "Are you going to hurt it?" she asked.

"We'll do what we have to do," Miss Corey answered.

"I only want my sister back," she said.

"We'll do what we can," Miss Corey said, not meeting her eyes.

We stepped into a dim and dingy room. The only light came from a window facing an airshaft, inches from a brick wall, and a smoking kerosene lamp on the center of a large round table. Around the table were gathered a circle of indistinct figures hunched over piles of incongruously bright flowers, the only color in the room. The two women at the table wore gray dresses and dark scarves over their heads. The two little boys were so covered with dirt I could only make out the whites of their eyes as they looked up at us. Everyone looked up except for one figure at the far side of the room, who curled herself over the table and tugged her scarf down lower over her forehead.

"Etta!" the older woman cried, and then spoke in a stream of words I didn't understand but recognized as Yiddish.

"Mammaleh, speak English!" Etta replied. "I brought a nurse from the settlement house to look at Ruth. I've heard her coughing at night."

Mrs. Blum switched her gaze from her youngest daughter to her eldest. "Is that true, bubbeleh?" She reached out her hand to touch Ruth's forehead but the girl squirmed away. As she did, her scarf slipped and I caught a glimpse of her face. She had the same dark hair and olive complexion as Etta, but her skin was mottled around her hairline and neck—a faint pattern of spots similar to the ones on Miss Corey's face. And her skin wasn't just olive-toned; it was distinctly green. As soon as she saw us she bolted out the open window onto the fire escape. Miss Sharp raced after her. Miss Corey tried to follow her, but the old woman stood up.

"Who are you?" she demanded. "What you want with my Ruthie?"

I dodged around both of them and ducked out the window onto the fire escape.

The metal structure shook under my feet, reminding me of how the fire escape at the Triangle factory had twisted away from the building, hurtling everyone on it to their deaths. I clutched the rusted metal railing and looked up to see Miss Sharp's blue serge skirt disappearing over the ledge of the roof. I climbed to the roof, wishing my corset wasn't so tightly laced, and swung my legs over the brick ledge just in time to see Miss

Sharp leaping over the dividing wall onto the roof of the next tenement, her petticoats frothing around her legs like feathers. I'd seen girls at the Triangle leap to their deaths, their skirts fluttering in the air like that.

I bit my cheek to banish the image and ran across the rooftop after Miss Sharp, who'd landed safely on the next roof and was chasing the changeling. The changeling was already two buildings away, leaping over the walls between the buildings like the gazelles at the Central Park Zoo. *Nothing human moves like that,* I thought as I vaulted over the wall. I landed hard on the tar-paper roof, my knees and shoulder blades tingling with the impact. Miss Sharp would never catch her, but she wouldn't give up either. She'd kill herself in the chase.

I quickened my pace, catching up with Miss Sharp at the next wall. I leaped over it, my heart hammering against my corset stays—*the damnable contraption!* Surely I could go faster without it.

I reached under my shirtwaist and tugged at the laces to loosen them. Something ripped. I felt a sweet relief as cool air cascaded across my back. *Ah!* The wind felt delicious! I barely touched down on the next roof before I was off again, soaring over the roofs like a seagull skimming the surf, gaining on the changeling who'd reached the end of the row of tenement houses and was teetering on the edge of the last building. She turned to look over her shoulder and our eyes locked. We both knew there was nowhere to go but six stories down to the street.

She turned away and began to step into the empty air. I plunged through the air crying her name—the only name I had for her.

"Ruth!"

She turned, her eyes widening with horror, teetering on the edge of the roof. I somehow cleared the gap between us quickly enough to grab her and got a handful of shawl that began to unwind. I grasped the other end and she flung her arms around me, her sharp fingernails digging into my back. With both my arms pinned to my sides I couldn't counteract the pull of the changeling's weight. We were both going to plummet to the pavement. I felt the empty air beckoning us . . .

Then I felt something else pulling me back—a pressure along my shoulder blades as if someone had grabbed me by my corset and yanked. We both fell backward onto the rooftop, slamming hard onto the sticky tar paper, the changeling's arms still wrapped around my back, her eyes wide with surprise.

"Quickly!" she cried, pulling me up and wrapping her scarf around my back. "I'll hide your secret if you protect me. You of all creatures must know what the Order does to our kind."

Secret? Creatures? Our kind? What was she talking about? I stared at her, but she was looking behind me. Baffled, I reached under the shawl and felt wet, slick skin where my shirtwaist and corset had torn. I must have scraped my back on the roof and started bleeding.

But as my fingers reached my shoulder blades, I felt something else beneath my torn skin: the soft silk down of newly fledged feathers. The wings that had been growing beneath my skin these past few months had finally broken free.

2

I'D KNOWN SINCE May, when Raven told me that my real
father was a Darkling and the pains in my shoulder blades were
fledgling wings, that this day would come. But I had hoped
to forestall the moment with tight corsets and will power. I
certainly hadn't meant to reveal my true nature in front of a
changeling—or my favorite teacher. Had Miss Sharp seen? A
cold wash of horror, as if I'd been dunked into the rank waters
of the East River, swept over me.

But when Miss Sharp reached us, panting, her hair loosened from its bun and whipping around her face, she had eyes
only for the changeling. She withdrew the dagger from the
sheath at her waist and held it up before the changeling's face,
spitting out words in Latin. The carved runes on the blade
floated into the air and hovered over the changeling's head. The
mottled pattern on the changeling's hairline and throat began
to move under her skin, forming into the pattern of the runes.
She moaned and writhed, her skin turning greener where it
wasn't covered by the marks.

"Please make her stop!" she cried, clutching my arm, her
eyes pleading—eyes that seemed to be changing color even as
I looked into them, into a blue-green that reminded me of my

mother's. Her hair was changing, too, turning the same color red as my mother's.

"Let go of her!" Miss Sharp growled, pointing the dagger at the changeling's throat.

The changeling's hand slid off mine. Instantly, her eyes and hair changed back to brown. She had been changing into *me*. Only it had looked like my mother.

"You look like her," the changeling said.

"How . . . ?"

"She was stealing your memories while she was taking your appearance," Miss Sharp said. "Just like she stole Ruth Blum's identity."

"Not stealing," she said, her eyes sliding slyly to mine. "I only borrow. I have not taken your memories away, have I, miss? Your secrets are safe inside you, no?"

I nodded, guessing at her meaning. "She didn't harm me," I said, raising my eyes to Miss Sharp.

"And what about Ruth?" Miss Sharp demanded. "Does she still have her memories wherever she is? What have you done with her?"

"I did nothing to her. She disappeared, so I took her place."

"You're lying!" Miss Sharp cried, moving the blade closer to her throat. "You can only assume a human's appearance by touching them."

"I didn't say I never met her," she said sulkily. "I brushed up against her on the excursion boat to Coney Island. Her memories of her family were very strong, but only because she was planning to leave them. When I knew she didn't mean to go back to her family I decided to go back in her place—"

"That's a lie!"

We all turned to see Etta standing in the middle of the roof with Miss Corey. Her hands were curled into fists, her eyes glaring at the changeling.

"Ruthie would never run away and leave me."

"She felt bad about that," the changeling said, her expression softening at the sight of Etta. "She meant to send for you once she was settled, but I think . . . well, I don't think things turned out for her the way she'd hoped."

"Where did she go?" Miss Sharp asked, pressing the point of the dagger into the changeling's throat. "If you touched her thoughts you must have seen what she was planning."

The changeling frowned. "I saw a man—someone who would be waiting for her beneath a sign—but I couldn't see his face, only the terrible grinning face on the sign." She shuddered.

"A grinning face?" Miss Corey asked.

"Like this." The changeling drew back her lips into a hideous, unnaturally wide smile, revealing two crowded rows of small teeth. That smile was instantly recognizable as the face above the entrance to Steeplechase Park in Coney Island.

"So she was meeting a man at Steeplechase," Miss Sharp observed. "Is that all you know? What was his name? Where were they going?"

"I don't know. When Ruth thought about him, her mind grew dim, as if he were cloaked in shadow. Even the picture she had of him—here—" As she reached into her pocket Miss Sharp tensed, but the changeling only drew out a photograph. "Ruthie carried this with her that day, but she dropped it on the boat."

We all looked down at the photograph. It showed a couple driving in a topless automobile against the backdrop of a great arch that I thought might be the Arc de Triomphe on the Champs-Elysées. Or at least a painted backdrop of the Parisian avenue. I'd seen girls at the Triangle showing off such souvenir photographs. I recognized Ruth as the girl in the car, but the face of the man at the wheel was a blur.

I looked harder at the blurred face of the man and felt a shiver go through me. The face wasn't just blurry; it was veiled by a shadow. As if the man in the car with Ruth wasn't a man but a creature of the shadows.

I looked up to find Miss Sharp and Miss Corey exchanging a look. Last year a man who controlled the shadow demons—the evil *tenebrae*—had gained control of one of the students at Blythewood and attacked the school.

"Yes, I thought the same thing," the changeling said. "The man who took Ruth is controlled by the shadows."

I looked down and saw that her hand had crept onto mine. I snatched it away. "Then why didn't you go and help her?" I demanded.

"How? We changelings have no power over the shadows. We only take the places of those who have gone missing. Luckily many girls go missing in this city."

"*Luckily?*" I cried. "Did you never think to tell anyone of this to help these girls?"

The changeling stared at me, confused. "Who would listen to me?" she asked. "I'm no one."

"Don't you have an identity apart from the one you take?" Etta asked.

The changeling shook her head. "We are not fully grown until we take a human's identity. I haven't just assumed Ruth's form; I've acquired her thoughts and feelings. I know how much she loved you because of how much *I* love you." She reached her hand out to touch Etta, but Etta pulled away.

"You are not my sister!" Etta cried, tears springing to her eyes. "Because of you no one has gone looking for Ruth. We could have gone to the police."

"Do you really think the police would do anything to find a poor Jewish factory girl?" spat the changeling. "Go and ask them—see how many girls go missing every day in this city."

It was true, but I put my arm around Etta's shoulders and said, "We'll go together. My friend Mr. Greenfeder has connections at the police department."

"Lillian and I will also help look for her," Miss Sharp said. "If there are really many girls going missing, the Ord—the settlement house should investigate."

"What will happen to *her*?" Etta asked.

"We could take care of her right now," Miss Corey said, taking the dagger from Miss Sharp.

"No!" I cried, stepping in between Miss Corey and the changeling. "Don't hurt her. She's harmless."

"How do you know?" Miss Corey snapped.

"Because . . ." Because she'd seen what I was and hadn't revealed my secret? She might just be manipulating me. But there *was* something else.

"I don't hear my warning bells," I said, looking into the changeling's eyes. They were no longer the blue-green of my mother's eyes or the brown of Ruth's; they had turned colorless as water. Inside them I saw my own reflection—and the stark fear of losing herself.

"We could take her back to her kind in the Blythe Wood," Miss Sharp suggested, laying a restraining hand on her friend's arm.

I expected the changeling to show some relief, but she cried out in a mournful voice, "No, please, I'd rather die here and now. If I go back to the forest, I'll be no one. I'll lose *Ruth*. I'll lose her memories—*my* memories now—of Mama and Papa and little Schlomo and Eliahu and, most especially, of you, Ettaleh. Imagine, *shvester*, what it would feel like to lose your memory of the time Mama put salt in the Rebbe's tea and he spit it out on the tablecloth and Papa asked if that was his blessing."

Etta laughed, but then steeled her mouth. "You weren't there."

"But I *feel* like I was! Please . . ." She turned to Miss Sharp and Miss Corey. "Let me stay just a little longer. I can help you find Ruth. Her memories are still inside me. Perhaps there is some clue . . ."

"I thought you said everything about the man was shadowy," Miss Corey said suspiciously.

"Yes, but I can try to see through the shadows." She squinted her eyes. "I think I see something now . . ."

Miss Corey snorted. "She's just playing for time."

But the changeling's face was undergoing a transformation. Just as before she'd assumed the grinning face of the Steeplechase man, now her face was changing into a man's face. A familiar face. She was beginning to resemble Judicus van Drood, the man I knew was the Shadow Master.

"Stop!" I cried, terrified at the idea of seeing that face again.

The changeling's eyes flashed open, her features reassuming the features of Ruth Blum.

"What's wrong, Ava?" Miss Sharp asked, touching my arm. "Did you recognize the man she was becoming?"

I shook my head, not wanting to admit it had been van Drood. I had hoped he was dead—drowned on the *Titanic*. But if he were the one who had lured Ruth Blum away, then he was still alive.

"If the changeling could show us the face of the man who abducted Ruth, she could be useful," Miss Sharp said to Miss Corey. Kneeling beside the changeling, she asked, "Do you promise to go peaceably back to the Blythe Wood once we've found Ruth?"

The changeling's eyes shifted away from Miss Sharp's and fastened on Etta. "Yes," she said. "I'll do it for Etta. That's what Ruth would do."

"How can we possibly take her word . . . ?" Miss Corey began.

"We don't have to," Miss Sharp said, laying the flat of the dagger on top of the changeling's head. "I can perform a binding spell to make her keep her word."

Miss Sharp recited a few Latin words I recognized from Mrs. Calendar's Latin class as a promise-keeping spell. The elderly teacher had subjected us all to it to ensure that we returned our Latin spell books in good condition. I recalled that it had made the top of my head ache for days and that whenever I touched my Latin textbook I felt a little shock, but if the changeling felt any pain she didn't show it. She kept her eyes locked on

Etta as she recited the words: "*Do meam verbam tibi in fide.*"

When the spell was done we made our way back to the Blums' apartment. Ruth walked beside Etta, with Miss Corey staying close behind, keeping an eye on the changeling's back. Miss Sharp lingered behind with me.

"I feel sorry for her," Miss Sharp said as we followed behind them.

"Because she'll have to go back to being no one?" I asked, shivering at the thought. I pulled Ruth's shawl more tightly around my shoulders, hoping that Miss Sharp wouldn't notice that it wasn't mine.

She shook her head. "That sort of oblivion might sound awful, but when you think about it, she won't know what she's missing. No, what I pity her for is the life she's leading now. Having to play a part around the people you care for most . . ."

Her voice faltered, and for a moment I thought she *knew*. Although she would be sorry to do it, she would have to turn me in to the Order. I would be exposed as a monster before all my friends, and then I would be killed. If Miss Sharp wouldn't do it, Miss Corey would. I'd seen the merciless look in her eyes. One of these creatures had scarred her for life; she had no pity for them, just as she'd have no pity for me.

But then Miss Sharp gave me a bright, brittle smile. "But you don't have to worry about that, Ava dear. You're so open and honest. . . . I admired the way you stood up for the changeling back there." Then she quickened her pace to catch up with Miss Corey and I followed, wondering why I didn't feel more relieved.

3

TWO HOURS LATER I was staring at my reflection in a gilt-framed mirror while a lady's maid in a starched white cap and lace collar stuck diamonds into my hair. I couldn't imagine a more startling contrast to the tenement flat where we'd left Ruth and Etta.

Nor could I think of anything I wanted to do *less* than get dressed for Georgiana Montmorency's ball. Georgiana was the richest—and haughtiest—girl at Blythewood. She'd made no secret last year of what she thought of a former factory seamstress attending the same school as her. But for her senior year she'd decided to throw a ball for all the "local" Blythewood girls—meaning the ones high enough in society—and because of my grandmother's connections she couldn't *not* invite me. There would be a few girls, like my roommate Helen, whom I'd enjoy seeing, but I didn't feel ready to face the rest of them, not with the threat of my wings unfurling at any moment.

When I'd gotten home I'd looked at my back in the mirror and seen two long rusty gashes running down my shoulder blades. At least they'd stopped bleeding, and the wings had re-treated back under the skin. I'd washed away the dried blood and feathers, bound myself into a new tightly laced corset, and put on a dressing gown before Betsy came into the room to help me get ready, but I didn't know how long I could keep the wings from bursting out. What if they erupted right in the middle of Georgiana's ball?

"Ow!" I cried, the prick of a hairpin bringing me back into the moment.

"I'm sorry, miss, but your hair's frightful short and Mrs. Hall was particular she didn't want you going to the ball looking like a bald goshawk chick."

I pivoted around on the swiveling vanity stool to face Betsy.

"Did she really say I looked like a bald goshawk?" I asked.

Betsy turned crimson. "No, miss! Just that she didn't want you to look . . . what with your poor hair being burned away in the fire . . . not that it hasn't come back in wonderful . . . and it's a lovely color!" Betsy ended confusedly. I turned back to the mirror.

It *was* a lovely color. I was lucky that it had come back at all. Two months ago I'd defeated the *tenebrae* at Blythewood by setting them on fire—and myself in the process. When my hair grew back, it was a brighter shade of red than it had been before. Gillie, Blythewood's caretaker and falconer, had once told me that when a falcon was fledging, its feathers grew faster than normal. My hair had been swiftly growing into fat, glossy ringlets, but it still barely reached my shoulders. I liked how it framed my face, making my green eyes look bigger, and how light my head felt—as if I could fly. But fashionable society demanded a more formal coiffure, and so my grandmother had, without my knowledge or consent, purchased an elaborate hairpiece that sat in Betsy's hands now, looking like Mrs. Rutherford's pet Pomeranian.

"Why don't we save ourselves a lot of trouble and leave it off?" I suggested to the flustered Betsy. "No one will be looking at me with Georgiana strutting about."

"I *did* hear Miss Georgiana's wearing an entire peacock in her headdress, just like that French queen who lost her head!"

"Yes, she's dressing up as Marie Antoinette, and all of us Blythewood girls are supposed to be going as her ladies-in-waiting."

We both turned toward the enormous cerise confection of silk, chiffon, lace, and ruffles hanging from the post of my bed. It looked as if it could walk on its own—and I wished it would. Perhaps there was a spell that could animate it and I could send it to the dance in my stead. All I'd have to do was give it instructions to curtsy and utter polite platitudes—*Of course I'm thrilled to be one of Georgiana's ladies-in-waiting! The cucumber sandwiches are simply divine! I'd be honored to have this dance with you.* . . . It would probably do it all better than I could, despite the hours of dancing lessons my grandmother had paid for. I was so wrapped up in the idea of sending an automaton in my place that I didn't hear my grandmother's secretary come in.

"Land's sake! Is that the dress? It looks like someone murdered a raspberry trifle." Agnes placed a large box down on the bed and stood, hands on slim hips, staring at the hideous dress. "Caroline Janeway said the instructions from the Montmorencys were a bit over the top, but this . . ."

She cocked her head. In her slim blue serge dress and neat

plumed hat she looked like a wading bird listening for fish. Everything about Agnes Moorhen was neat and ordered. Even her freckles adhered to a strict mathematical formula as precise as the social calendar and accounts she kept for my grandmother. Of course she would hate the dress.

"This," she concluded with a decisive shake of her plumed hat, "is a riot of ruffles . . ."

Betsy tittered.

". . . a flummox of foorfaraw. . ."

Betsey snorted and covered her face in her apron.

". . . a lunacy of lace!"

"You're going to give Betsy an apoplexy," I said, stifling my own laughter. It wasn't as funny if you were the one who had to wear the damnable thing.

"Betsy," Agnes said solemnly, "go right down to the drawing room and remove the late Mr. Hall's dueling pistols from above the mantel. Someone must shoot this dress and put it out of its misery."

Betsy fled the room, shrieking like a banshee.

"You really shouldn't tease her," I scolded Agnes. "If she *does* pick up one of those pistols she might shoot herself."

"They haven't been loaded since Throckmorton Hall used them to hold off an invading army of rebel trolls at the battle of Antietam," Agnes said. "And it would take more than them to do away with this monstrosity."

At the word *monstrosity* I broke out in a cold sweat. Agnes had always been kind to me. But if I was discovered as a half-breed Darkling and sent away in shame from my grandmother's house and Blythewood, I'd never see Agnes again—and I wasn't sure she'd even want me to. I'd be an outcast to everyone I loved—maybe even Raven. For all I knew the Darklings would reject me because I was half-human. Perhaps that was why Raven had stayed away from me all summer. I was a monster to humans and Darklings alike.

"What's the matter, Ava?" Agnes asked, narrowing her eyes at me. "You don't look well. Has Betsy laced your corset too tightly?" She laid her hand lightly on my back, but it felt like a brand burning through the silk of my dressing gown. I flinched away from her touch. Her eyes widened in surprise.

"Did you hurt yourself today chasing that *creature*?"

"She's not a creature!" I cried. "She's a person with thoughts and feelings."

"Strictly speaking she doesn't have her own thoughts and feelings, only those of the host she takes over, but I think I understand why you feel such sympathy for a creature of Faerie. It's that Darkling boy you met last year, isn't it? That Raven fellow. You think that if he's good, then *all* the fairies—"

"He's not a fairy!" I sulked, sorry now that I'd ever told Agnes about him. "The Darklings are different. They bridge the gap between humans and fairies. It's all explained in the book my mother was looking for—*A Darkness of Angels*."

"You mean the book that poor Mr. Farnsworth died trying to save?"

I was immediately sorry that I'd brought it up. Last winter I'd written to Mr. Herbert Farnsworth, the librarian of Hawthorn, Blythewood's brother school in Scotland, asking about the ancient book *A Darkness of Angels*. Raven had told me that it would prove the Darklings' innocence, and that it also contained the secret to destroying the *tenebrae*, the embodiment of pure evil. Mr. Farnsworth had written back to tell me he was sailing to America with the book. He embarked on the same boat that my grandmother and Agnes—and Helen's parents— were taking back from England: the ill-fated *Titanic*.

There'd been another passenger on the voyage—Judicus van Drood. Agnes and Mr. Farnsworth had seen him on the deck when the ship ran into the fatal iceberg, and Mr. Farnsworth had used the book to keep van Drood on the sinking ship. As much as Agnes grieved for Mr. Farnsworth, we'd both hoped that van Drood had perished, too.

Now, I wasn't so sure. I told Agnes about the changeling morphing into the likeness of van Drood and showed her the picture of Ruth and the shadow man. I thought she'd be horrified, but instead a glimmer of hope sparked in her eyes.

"If van Drood survived, perhaps Mr. Farnsworth did, too!"

"Maybe he did," I said, thinking it was rather unlikely. If he had survived, why hadn't he contacted us?

"I'll check again with the Seamen's Friend Society," she said enthusiastically, and then added, "I'm sorry I called your friend Raven a fairy. I'm sure if Mr. Farnsworth risked his life for that book, there must be something valuable in it, and real proof that the Darklings aren't evil. Perhaps you could ask Raven to help look for him."

"I would, but I haven't heard from him since the end of school. We had a . . . disagreement. I'm afraid I may have driven him away for good."

Agnes sighed. "Perhaps that would be for the best." Seeing my stricken look, she gestured to the large box she'd laid on the bed. "Why don't you open the box? There seems to be a corsage of violets on top."

I was up and across the room as if my wings had sprung loose. So many people grew violets in Rhinebeck that it was known as the violet capitol of the world. There was no reason to assume they came from Violet House, where Miss Sharp's aunts lived. And certainly no reason to think they came from Raven, who lived there under the disguise of Raymond Corbin, clockmaker's apprentice. But still . . .

I untied the bouquet and lifted the flowers to my nose, inhaling their fragrance. Memories of a wooded grove, a night I'd spent in Raven's tree house hidden in the highest boughs, came flooding back to me, along with a touch of wings that had calmed me, a mouth that had tasted of violets . . . no, the kiss had come later. But it was all mixed up now with the scent of violets. Could Raven have sent them?

"Are you going to open the box?" Agnes asked with amusement. "I think there's more than flowers in a box that big."

The box sprang open as if something alive had been waiting to get out . . . something with feathers.

I stepped back, catching my breath, as delicate, sheer wings unfolded from the box.

"Costume wings," Agnes said, lifting them from the box. "And look—there's a dress to go with them."

I'd never heard practical Agnes utter the word *dress* with such longing in her voice. Her freckled hands gingerly lifted the gown out of its nest of lavender tissue paper. It seemed to catch a breeze as it rose, billowing into the shape of an invisible girl. A girl on fire. The dress was the color of molten gold, embroidered with tiny rubies and blood-red feathers. "Oh!" Agnes said. "It's quite . . . quite . . ."

"Divine," I finished for her, thinking that a girl wouldn't need wings to feel like she was flying in such a dress.

"Try it on," Agnes said with a mischievous grin.

I shucked off my dressing gown and held up my arms for Agnes to slip the dress over my head. It felt like a waterfall spilling down my bare skin. I tingled from head to toe as the cloth skimmed past my breasts, flared over my hips, and swirled around my ankles like a cat. I turned to look in the mirror, the satin moving with me like a second skin, and thought someone else had taken my place. A changeling, perhaps, who had assumed my features and figure but had set them on fire.

The bodice was fitted with tiny pleats and a beaded design at the neckline that framed my throat with a rim of rubies that made my skin whiter, my eyes greener, and my hair an even more vibrant red. The overskirt flared out into a petaled design that swished as I moved. The damask red underskirt clung to my ankles. I looked like some kind of exotic bird rising from the flames.

"Like a phoenix," Agnes said, fixing the gold and ruby wings to my back and then a matching feathered crown to my head. "It's the perfect costume for you to wear tonight."

"But all the Blythewood girls are supposed to go as Marie Antoinette's ladies-in-waiting," I said, glaring at the monstrosity hanging from the bedpost.

"Too bad your dress was never delivered from Miss Janeway's,"

Agnes replied, handing me a pair of crimson satin gloves. "And this came instead. There must have been a mix-up."

She picked up a folded card nestled amidst the tissue paper. "Hm . . ." Agnes said, frowning. "Caroline writes that the instructions and payment for the dress were sent to her and that she was to have it made to your measurements with a note that said that it was from—"

"Yes! Who's it from?"

"It says, 'From a secret admirer.'"

4

THE MONTMORENCY MANSION was only two blocks north of my grandmother's house, and I could have easily walked. Indeed, I would have gotten there more quickly on foot than trapped in the traffic making its laborious progress up Madison Avenue. But my grandmother had scoffed at the idea when I'd come into the parlor to say goodnight, and I was afraid a prolonged argument would draw more attention to my dress, which she was already studying skeptically through the lenses of her lorgnette.

"I thought the theme was the court of Marie Antoinette."

I considered claiming, as Agnes had suggested, that Caroline Janeway had sent the wrong costume, but I didn't like the idea of getting Miss Janeway in trouble, and I certainly didn't want to say anything about the note that had come with it. Every time I thought about it my knees went weak. *A secret admirer.* Who could it be but Raven?

"I like this dress better," I said, lifting my chin defiantly, although part of me wanted to cringe like the ebony Moors crouching on either side of her chair. I sometimes fancied that they—along with all the statuary, stuffed birds, antimacassars, and aspidistras that cluttered the Victorian-style parlor—

had been frozen by my grandmother's Medusa stare.

"Mmmph," she finally uttered, tapping her cane on the marble floor. "Wise girl. I told Albertine Montmorency that wearing Marie Antoinette's necklace to her own ball fifteen years ago didn't bring any luck to Cornelia Bradley-Martin, not to mention what it did for Marie Antoinette. But are you sure this dress is not a bit . . . *revealing*?"

"It's quite similar to the dresses all of Paris wore after Monsieur Poiret's costume ball last year," Agnes piped up, having crept silently into the room. "And doesn't Ava look lovely in it?"

"Of course she looks lovely in it!" my grandmother barked. "We Hall women have always had good figures. Go and have a good time." She waved her lorgnette at me. "Show all those Montmorencys and Rutherfords what we Halls are made of."

I kissed her cool cheek and hurried out before she could change her mind—or before I could. But now I was stuck sitting in a stifling-hot motorcar as Babson the chauffeur jockeyed for position in front of the Montmorency mansion. Staring up at the granite façade, I felt a bit as Marie Antoinette must have felt approaching the Bastille. I could see all my classmates emerging from their carriages and motorcars in frothy explosions of lace and ruffles. There was Wallis Rutherford in a peaches-and-cream pouf that looked like a blancmange. Her hair was piled high on top of her head and powdered white. She was followed by Alfreda Driscoll in a chartreuse confection that quivered like lime aspic in the glare of the photographers' magnesium flash lamps.

But as hideous as the dresses had seemed to me, I saw now what they really were—protective armor. Corset, bustle, and wire hoops sheathed in layers of lace and taffeta and damask formed a carapace that enclosed the girl beneath the costume. These girls—my Blythewood classmates—were clothed in their uniformity, protected by their families' wealth and position. I, on the other hand, was about to stand nearly naked and exposed at the foot of this granite altar of high society.

"Perhaps if we can't get in we should just turn around and go home, Mr. Babson."

"Not a chance, miss," Babson replied, nosing the Rolls into a narrow gap between a Benson and a horse-drawn phaeton. "You're worth ten of them overdressed poodles. I've watched you make your way through streets on the Lower East Side what would make a stevedore quake, Miss Ava, and seen you face down gangs of strikebreakers at them meetings you go to at the Cooper Union. You hold your head up and do us proud."

I met Babson's eyes in the rearview mirror and smiled. Having a chauffeur drive me to the settlement house and union meetings had been the one condition my grandmother had demanded to allow me to do "social" work. It had been embarrassing to be chauffeured around poor neighborhoods, and I had imagined it had embarrassed Thomas Babson to deliver me to such destinations. I'd had no idea he thought well of the work I was doing. It gave me courage.

"Thank you, Mr. Babson," I said. "I think I can now."

"That's all right then, miss," he nodded curtly. "Because here we are. Sit tight till I come around to get the door for you and I'll give you my arm while you make your grand entrance."

I took a deep breath to steady myself as Babson got out. *This is silly*, I told myself, *You've faced down goblins and ice giants. What's a handful of reporters and curious onlookers?*

A flash like lightning greeted my first step on the pavement, followed by a thunderous roar. Behind the flash of the magnesium lamps and the smoke they made was a crowd of spectators pressing against a line of policemen. There were mostly girls in the crowd—young girls like me, in shirtwaists and skirts, shopgirls and factory girls come to see the society debutantes in their fancy dresses. I remembered how Tillie always strained to make out the hats worn by the factory owner's daughters. If Tillie were alive, she'd be in this crowd.

"Don't she look a dream!" I heard one cry. "Like something out of a fairy story."

If only she knew.

"Miss Hall," a voice beside me said, "you're wearing a most unusual costume. Could you tell the readers of *The World* why you're not dressed like the other young ladies tonight?"

I turned to the reporter, hearing my grandmother's voice in my head—*a woman's name should only appear in the paper three times: when she's born, when she marries, and when she dies.* I could murmur some inanity about liking feathers or a mix-up at the dressmaker's, but when I looked at the crowd of young women behind the police line I was reminded of the women who had struck last year for better working conditions, and of the girls who had died in the fire at the Triangle Waist factory. I knew from my work at the settlement house and the union meetings I attended that many were trying to improve working conditions, but I also knew that there were plenty of girls who labored in overcrowded factories or were forced into working at the bordellos. Or who disappeared from the crowded city streets like Ruth Blum, never to be seen again, because no one cared what became of them.

"I'm dressed as a phoenix," I told the reporter in a loud clear voice that carried to the crowd. "It's a bird that rises from the ashes of a fire to be reborn. I'm wearing it in honor of the girls who died in the Triangle fire last year . . . and all the working girls in this city who risk their lives to earn a living."

A great cheer greeted my words, and a dozen magnesium flash lamps exploded around me. Smoke from the flashes filled the air. Silhouetted against the light, the crowd became a cluster of shadows, as if the *tenebrae* had risen up to challenge my proclamation. I turned and walked up the steps of the Montmorency mansion, feeling less like a proud phoenix and more like a newly hatched chick cowering in the shadow of a hawk's wings. The spectacle that greeted me beyond the front door did nothing to soothe my jangling nerves.

The Montmorency mansion, imposing at all times, had been done up to resemble Versailles at the time of Louis XVI. The foyer had been transformed into a formal garden with dusky bowers and fountains lit by floating lamps and scented by a thousand roses and orchids. Footmen in gilded livery and powdered wigs glided across the polished floors with gold trays of sparkling champagne and delicate pastries. My eyes still dazzled from the magnesium flashes, I wandered through the faux greenery in a blur, to the threshold of the ballroom.

The girls in their wide frothy skirts pirouetted around the dance floor like flocks of tropical birds wheeling across a marble sky; the men in their dark velvet costumes and black tails could have been their dark shadows. I recognized Georgiana at the center of the interlocking circles in a brilliant blue dress, peacock feathers quivering in her headdress as she preened over her flock. There were Alfreda Driscoll and Wallis Rutherford—and even the shy Jager twins, Beatrice and Dolores, dutifully following the steps of the waltz. I suspected some of the girls I didn't recognize were the rising class—the new nestlings. They seemed to know the steps as well as anyone. How could I have ever thought I would be able to fit back in at Blythewood after all that had happened to me? I wanted to turn and flee, but a familiar voice stayed me.

"Ava! What a brilliant dress! Is it a Poiret?"

I turned to find Helen, my Blythewood roommate, standing in a robin's egg gown that turned her blue eyes azure and her blonde hair gold. Unlike the overdone confections worn by Alfreda and Wallis, this dress was simple and elegant.

"I should have known Louis XVI would suit you," I said, slipping my arm around Helen's slim waist and hugging her. Beneath the layers of lace and silk she felt thinner than she'd been in the spring—and more fragile—but she embraced me back with the same strength and fierceness I recalled. "But how did yours turn into something so pretty?"

"Oh," Helen replied, twirling her skirts, "I had a word with Caroline Janeway and we made a few alterations. You should have seen the puce monstrosity Georgiana had picked out for me. Puce! With my coloring! It was a deliberate attempt to sabotage my chances of attracting a suitable husband."

"Is your mother still after you to marry?" I asked.

"It's her idée fixe, especially since Daddy . . ." She didn't finish her sentence. She didn't have to. I knew that when Helen's father had perished on the *Titanic*, he had left his financial affairs in a shambles. Agnes and her lawyer friend Samuel Greenfeder had outlined a plan by which Helen and her mother might survive frugally, but from the quality of lace on Helen's dress and the jewels in her hair, I didn't think they were following it.

"Mama sees a rich husband as a way out of our financial difficulties, but you should see the ancient specimens she's put forward." Helen flicked open a silk fan and rolled her eyes. "They lurk around the house like undertakers waiting for someone to die. I'd *rather* die than marry one of them. Or marry a bank teller like Daisy's Mr. Appleby."

"Has Daisy written to you?" I asked. I hadn't heard from our third roommate all summer.

Helen shrugged. "Just some drivel about campaigning for women's votes in Kansas. You see, *Daisy* would be fine without money, but not me. Poverty just doesn't suit me."

I laughed. "I don't really think it suits anyone, Helen. You should see the tenements I go into and the choices that life drives girls to." I thought of Ruth meeting her mysterious stranger under the Steeplechase entrance. Had she thought he was going to deliver her to a better life? "Which reminds me, there's a project I'd like you to help me with."

I began to tell her about how Ruth Blum had gone missing, but I soon saw she wasn't listening to me. Her eyes were focused on the glass doors to the garden, where a tall man in a top hat was leaning jauntily against a fake rose arbor. "Yes, yes," Helen said distractedly, "I'm sure it's a good cause. Put me down for a few dollars."

"Really, Helen!" I stamped my foot. "Are you pursuing

everything with pants on now?" But when I saw who the young man was I quit my scolding.

"Nathan!" Helen cried, then covered her mouth with her fan, embarrassed to have been caught shouting at a boy as if we were on the hockey field at Blythewood instead of a ballroom. But it was too late. Nathan Beckwith had turned and was scanning the crowd to see who had called his name. I'd have recognized those searching gray eyes anywhere, but the rest of him was quite altered.

He'd grown half a foot at least, and his pale silvery hair that always fell in front of his eyes was slicked back. The lines of his face had been set into an immovable coldness I had never seen before—the result, I guessed, of spending the last few months at asylums and hospitals searching for a cure for his sister Louisa's madness after we'd rescued her from Faerie. From the look of his face, I was betting he hadn't found one. Pools of darkness filled the hollows beneath his eyes and under his too-sharp cheekbones, as if he carried a reserve of shadows with him.

But then he spotted us and his smile chased the shadows from his face.

"Look how happy he is to see you!" I told Helen, because I knew how she felt about Nathan. As he crossed the room, though, I saw that his eyes were locked on me with a look that set my heart knocking against my ribcage and made me want to either fly from the room or fly to him. My shoulder blades were itching under my corset, my fledgling wings straining against the metal stays. The movement under my shoulder blades made my wire wings tremble.

Their movement in the light must have drawn Nathan's attention. His gaze moved from my face to just above my head, and his pale gray eyes flashed silver. Had the wings reminded him of catching me and Raven kissing? When he looked back down at my face the shadows had reclaimed him. He stopped a few feet from us, doffed his top hat, and bowed low before us.

"You've learned fine habits on the continent," Helen quipped.

"I've learned more than that," Nathan said as he lifted his head. Up close I saw that his fine blond hair really *was* silver now, as if he had aged a decade in the months since I'd last seen him.

"How is Louisa?" I asked.

"As well as the combined medical knowledge of all the finest doctors in Europe could make her. I left her in an asylum in Vienna where there was a doctor who made some progress with her—at least enough so she's stopped trying to run into the woods and can sit down to tea without playing chimes on the teacups. In her doctor's last letter he informed me that she's learned to repeat a few phrases of polite conversation and doesn't tear her dresses to bits anymore, so I suppose she's as fit as half the automatons here."

He looked scornfully at the dance floor. "Really, where are they sending you girls to dancing school these days? I've seen less complicated maneuvers at the changing of the guard at Buckingham Palace."

"Oh, there's the most brilliant new dancing school up in Riverdale. All the new girls are going there," Helen said with a touch of envy in her voice. The dancing school was too expensive for the van Beeks. In solidarity I had gone to lessons with old Madame Musette in her fusty Stuyvesant Square studio. But Nathan didn't hear the strain of jealousy—or anything else Helen was saying. He was staring at me.

"That's an interesting dress," he said, looking me up and down in a way that made the blood rush to my face. "What are you supposed to be?"

"She's a phoenix," Helen said, "in honor of the girls who died in the Triangle fire."

I stared at Helen, amazed that my interview had traveled so fast and that Helen had paid attention to it. But that was Helen—loyal when you least expected it.

"Oh, so you've become a socialist," Nathan said, not softening at all. Why had he come over here if he was going to be so disagreeable?

"Ava's been working at the Henry Street Settlement House," Helen went on, surprising me by knowing the settlement house's name. "She was just telling me about a girl who's gone missing."

"A missing girl?" The interest made his face human again. "Do you think she's been *taken*?"

I knew he meant taken by the Darklings, whom he believed had taken Louisa. Even though Raven had helped get Louisa back, Nathan still thought the Darklings were evil. Would I ever convince him—or the Council of the Order—that they weren't? Not unless I found *A Darkness of Angels*—which proved the Darklings' innocence and revealed how to end the centuries-old curse that kept them out of Faerie. That is, if it wasn't lying on the bottom of the ocean among the ruins of the *Titanic*.

"The changeling didn't say Ruth was taken by a Darkling," I said. I told them what she had said about Ruth meeting a shadowy man in Coney Island. I didn't say it was van Drood, because I was still hoping she had assumed his features from my memories and not Ruth's. I was still hoping van Drood had died on the *Titanic*.

"Ruth's memory of the man she was meeting might have been obscured by shadows because a Darkling had mesmerized her."

"Nathan's right," Helen said. "Just like that Darkling mesmerized you last year."

"He didn't mesmerize me!"

"How would you know?" Nathan asked coolly. "He could be using this changeling to lure you back to him. You're planning to go look for the missing girl, aren't you?"

As soon as he said it, I knew I was. Nathan knew me better than I knew myself. "I thought I'd go to Coney Island to see if anyone saw Ruth and the man she left with."

"Alone?" Helen asked, appalled. "With all the rabble that frequent Coney Island? Why, I've heard that women show their bare legs on the beach and drink spirits in public and men take improprieties on the carousel rides . . ."

"Why Helen," Nathan said with a grin, "you've done quite a bit of research on the place. It sounds as if you're dying to go there."

Helen turned pink. "I never!" she cried.

"Then you don't want to go with Ava and me when we go investigate?"

"You're going with me?"

"I can't very well let you go alone and get snatched by a Darkling or pawed by a lowlife on the Steeplechase, can I?"

I stared at Nathan, trying to figure out what he was up to. He stared back. Helen looked from one to the other.

"Yes, Nathan's right," she said. "We can't let you go alone. We'll all go. I suppose I'll have to acquire a new bathing costume; my one from last year is horribly out of date. I should have one by Thursday next."

"We'll go tomorrow," Nathan said. "While the trail's still hot."

I began to object that the trail was hardly hot and to think of some other pretext for not going tomorrow. It wasn't that I wouldn't be glad of Helen and Nate's company, but if a Darkling *was* behind Ruth's disappearance . . .

"It's settled then!" Nathan declared. He grabbed Helen's hand. "Now have we come here to dance or what?"

Helen was barely able to suppress the jubilant smile that rose to her face, but she did spare a backward glance at me. "But we mustn't leave poor Ava alone," I heard her whisper in Nathan's ear.

"Oh, I don't think *poor* Ava will be alone for long. I've noted half a dozen gentlemen eyeing her, just waiting for their chance to ask her to dance. You'll be fine, won't you, Ava?"

I wasn't at all sure I'd be fine dancing with a stranger, but I didn't want to deny Helen the pleasure of dancing with Nate. "Of course," I assured them both.

They were instantly sucked into the whirl of the ballroom as if into a cyclone. I stood on the edge of the dance floor watching the swirling couples, moving faster now in steps I didn't recognize—no doubt one of the newfangled dances the girls were learning at that new dancing school. I could no longer make out individual faces in the blur of pastel satin and lace and the dark, upright men whose heads all inclined to their dancing partners, moving to the rhythm of the music as if they were gaily painted automatons in a huge clockwork mechanism—a mechanism I stood outside of. I wasn't sure what I was most frightened of: remaining here on the margin or being taken up into it.

"Of course no one would want to dance with her . . . after all, no one even knows who her father is."

The whisper came from behind me. I turned to see who had spoken, but the edges of the ballroom had been built into dusky green arbors from which onlookers could sit and watch the ball unobserved. I made out dim shapes in the shadows, matrons in subdued dark dresses and older men in black tails, their stiff clothing rustling like wings.

The room seemed suddenly full of whispers and rustlings, my ears tingling with the undercurrent of sound. I had an image of crows roosting in the shadows. The elders of the Order were plotting who would marry whom, which matches would be most advantageous for wealth and property, but also to strengthen the Order's powers. I had discovered last year that the Order kept records of bloodlines going back for centuries that recorded magical traits . . . and flaws. They bred their children as if they were livestock, selecting for desirable gifts and winnowing out the weak and abnormal. If the Order determined there was something wrong with you, you would be condemned to a life of spinsterhood. Which would be preferable, I thought, to being mated to a stranger. I'd far rather stand here alone all night.

"May I have this dance?"

The voice was so low I thought I might have imagined it; it was the voice I heard in my dreams. I turned slowly, afraid a quick motion might dispel the dream, and found myself facing a winged creature.

"Raven!" I cried, my whole body tingling at the sight of him. Black wings stretched out behind him, in full view of the Order. How had he dared . . . ?

But then I saw that the wings were made of wire and feather, costume wings. Like me, he was hiding in plain sight. Only I didn't see how anyone could look at him and think he was an ordinary mortal. His black eyes flashed behind a feathered mask. His skin was the color of fine marble veined with gold. His teeth, when he smiled, were slightly pointed and fully menacing. I could sense the power of muscles flexing beneath the velvet doublet and lace collar and cuffs of his costume.

"They'll kill you if they see what you are," I hissed. "What are you doing here? How did you get in?"

"You mean without an engraved invitation?" he asked with a crooked smile. "I flew into the garden along with a flock of pigeons who weren't on the guest list either. Your Order seems to forget that footmen and high gates can't keep our kind out. As for what I came for—well, to dance, of course. But if you say no, I will have risked the wrath of the Order for nothing."

"Oh!" I should tell him to flee before they recognized what he was—and recognized what *I* was when they saw me with him. The music swelled—a new waltz was beginning. I felt my body swaying with it, swaying toward Raven as if a magnetic force were pulling us together. I put my hand in his and felt a spark of electricity race through my body, my fledgling wings tingling beneath my shoulder blades.

"Yes," I said, afraid I would explode if we didn't move. "I would be most honored to share this dance with you."

5

IT SHOULDN'T HAVE surprised me that Raven was such a good dancer. After all, he could fly. Being in his arms *felt* like flying. My dancing slippers barely touched the marble floor as he swept me into the waltz. A jasmine-scented breeze from the garden ruffled my hair. My wings itched to spread out . . .

"They won't," Raven said.

"How did you know . . . ?"

"I felt your shoulders tense. Just relax. Quit trying to lead."

"I'm not!"

"Is this your first dance?"

"It is," I admitted.

"Mine too," he said, grinning. "I got the Sharp sisters to give me dancing lessons."

I giggled at the picture of Vionetta Sharp's plump aunt Emmaline and tiny aunt Harriet practicing dance steps with Raven. "And they still don't know wha—*who* you really are?"

The smile disappeared from his face and his arm tensed around my waist. "No, poor dears, they have no idea they're harboring a monster in their midst."

"Raven, I never meant . . . when you told me about my father

I was shocked to learn what *I* was. I've never thought of *you* as a monster."

"But you've spent these last few months seeing yourself as one, haven't you? You've been working at the settlement house to appease your conscience. You're dreading the moment your wings will break out . . ."

His voice faltered as I flinched under his accusations.

"Have they?"

"Almost," I whispered, looking around to see if anyone was close enough to overhear us. But each of the couples revolved around the floor in its own separate bubble. All I could hear was the music and the beating of my heart as I told Raven about chasing the changeling over the rooftops and my wings breaking through my skin.

"I could have told you that leaping from high places is often enough to fledge your wings. My father tossed me from the top of a tree when he thought it was time." He twisted his lips in a wry smile at the memory and I pinched his arm.

"You should have told me that! All these months I've had to wonder when it would happen and what it would feel like . . ." I stopped because my voice was hoarse with tears. I hadn't realized until now how angry I was at him for letting me go through this alone. But then I realized I hadn't been alone. He'd known I was working at the settlement house.

"Have you been following me?"

"You needn't make it sound so predatory. I've wanted to make sure you were all right in case you were being pursued by the *tenebrae* and to be there when you fledged . . . in case you needed me," he added. "How *did* it feel?"

I blushed at the intimacy of the question. "Painful, frightening . . . amazing!" I admitted. "Like I was free for the first time in my life! Like I could have kept on going into the clouds . . ."

". . . and straight on till morning."

I laughed at the quote from *Peter Pan*. "Yes! Only the changeling saw my wings."

"I wouldn't worry about the changeling. They're shy, retiring creatures who don't like to make trouble."

"So they *don't* steal human babies?"

Raven snorted, a sound so uncivilized that it attracted the attention of a stout matron on the edge of the dance floor. We had fallen out of step with the other dancers, and people were beginning to stare at us. Raven waltzed us out the open glass doors and into the garden. He put his arm around my waist and steered me away from the crowd. I could feel the warmth of his arm through the thin silk of my dress. My wings quivered at his touch pressing against the corset. I could barely follow what he was saying. Something about the Order spreading myths . . .

". . . a changeling only takes the place of a human baby if it's dying. They've spared many a human family heartbreak over the centuries. I hadn't heard of them taking the place of missing people, but from what you've told me, this changeling spared the Blum family the grief of losing their daughter."

I collected my senses at the mention of the Blums. "But if the Blums had known that Ruth was missing they could have told the police!" My voice had grown so loud that Raven pulled me into one of the secluded bowers at the end of the walled garden.

"Do you have any idea how many girls go missing in this city? And what usually happens to them? I've carried the souls of the departed to your mortal afterworld enough times to know how often they perish alone and unloved in unheated tenements or beneath the icy river." His voice grew husky and he looked away, as if the memories were too painful to share.

"I wish I could make you *see* . . ." He looked back at me, his eyes glittering. "I *will* make you see!"

Before I knew what he meant, he had shucked off his fake wings and unfurled his real ones. My own wings tingled in sympathy against my corset, but they were restrained by Raven's arm tight around my waist.

"What are you doing?" I hissed, but my words were drowned out by the beat of his wings, which seemed to be keeping measure with my heart as he pressed me tightly against his chest and we rose into the air.

"People will see us!" I cried.

"Not if you stop squirming," he snapped back. "Our wings cloak us from human sight, but that dress of yours is awfully . . . *bright*."

I was going to object that he had picked it out, but then I realized I didn't know that for sure—and it seemed a minor point now that we were flying over the city, sailing over rooftops and streets like Wendy and her brothers in *Peter Pan*. We were flying southeast, over rooftops of mansions with statuary and gardens that no one would ever see and, as we flew further downtown, humbler tenements where the occupants had dragged out their mattresses to sleep in the cooler air. An old woman in a head-scarf lifted her head to watch us winging toward the river.

"I thought you said we couldn't be seen," I whispered.

"By humans. Not everyone who lives in this city is human."

"What sort of non-humans . . ." I began, but he hushed me.

"Quiet. We're almost at the river. Do you hear her?"

"Hear who?"

"Use your inner ear," he told me.

I was going to ask what he meant, but suddenly I knew. All summer I'd wondered at my strange new sensitivity to noise, picking up whispers I shouldn't have been able to hear. Now I made out an underground stream running just below the sur-face of the night, full of sighs and clicks and whistles that made my ears tingle and my hair stand on end. Some of the clicks came from a flock of pigeons that had joined us. Raven clucked back to them.

"They've seen her, too. We have to hurry."

He ducked his head and folded his wings. We were sud-denly diving, caught in a current of wind that was rushing us to the East River. I heard the water—and smelled it: the reek of refuse mingled with a tang of salt where the river met the tides from the bay. And then we were caught in those tangled currents of air.

"Hang on," Raven yelled above the roar of the river. "She's there on the pier."

We were fighting the wind to reach the shore where a lone figure stood on the edge of an old rotting pier. Even over the shriek of wind and water I could hear her ragged breath—

because I was *meant* to, I realized. She was a soul in danger and I was a Darkling. I was meant to save her. My wings itched under my skin, my ears burned, I felt my heart beating with hers in fear—

Of what?

She looked over her shoulder, but there was nothing there but shadows.

Shadows that writhed like snakes. *Tenebrae.* She was running from the *tenebrae.* They reached out for her . . .

She screamed and plunged into the river. Raven dove toward the water, but he couldn't reach for her because he was holding me. I stretched out my arms for the girl, but when she saw us she screamed and flailed away. Still I was able to grab her wrist.

"I've got her!" I screamed.

But something was pulling her away from me. She was caught in a current—but no ordinary current. It wasn't pulling her to sea; it was dragging her down into a whirlpool. I'd heard stories of dangerous tides on the East River. The sailors and wharf rats had a name for the river.

"The Hellgate!"

Raven's voice was tight with fear. "It traps souls—even a Darkling's soul. If you're caught you'll spend eternity there! You have to let her go."

"No!" I cried. The fetid stink of the river rose out of the churning maw—all the refuse of the river concentrated here like a foul breath belched from a hungry mouth.

It *was* a mouth, a hungry, gaping mouth that ate souls. I couldn't let this girl sink into it, but Raven was right. We would be trapped if I didn't let her go. I felt her hand slipping from my grip. Her eyes locked on mine. I saw terror in them—and *more*. I saw her life, the glimpse a Darkling was granted of a dying soul. I heard a dying woman say her name—*Molly*—and saw a windowless room where bent-backed women sewed until their fingers bled, and the dirty floor on which she slept. Then I saw a man whose face was blurred by shadows. He had lured her away from her family with promises of a sweeter life, but then he had locked her away into another hell. This hell was pretty and soft, full of satin and velvet and feather beds . . .

The vision became blurry when it moved toward the bed, and I wondered if Molly was trying to shield me from seeing what happened there or if she was too ashamed to let me see.

I'm here with you, I said, not out loud, but inside her head. *You're not alone.*

I felt something relax in her. *You have to let me go*, she told me, *before I turn into a monster.*

I cringed at the word *monster*—and her hand slipped from mine.

"No!" I shouted, reaching for her, but Raven was pulling us back, out of the way of something that shot past us and dove into the water. Raven shouted something as the water broke over us. It sounded like a name: *Sirena*.

"Who's Sirena?" I asked.

"One of our fledglings. She's too young to try to save a soul from the Hellgate whirlpool. She might get stuck there—"

Before he could finish, the girl Darkling broke the surface of the water and rose straight up. In her arms she held Molly.

Only it wasn't the flesh-and-blood girl who'd held my hand, but a luminous transparent phantom. A soul. Molly was dead.

"Can't we try to save her?" I cried.

"Sirena has saved her soul," Raven said. "That's more than we could do." He was already winging away from the churning whirlpool.

"We have to go back!" I cried, pounding Raven's chest with my fists.

"She's gone."

"Molly, her name was Molly. I saw her life, saw what happened to her . . ." I poured out everything I had seen as we flew back over the city. Raven was silent, his arms tight around me. He didn't speak until we lit down in the Montmorency Gardens, in the same bower we'd taken off from.

He put me down on the bench and put his wings around me as I sobbed out the whole of Molly's story for the third time. I would have started a fourth, but he stopped my mouth with a kiss. The warmth of his mouth on mine shocked me into silence. I shuddered all over, aware for the first time of how cold I was. His warmth poured into me. When he pulled away he touched a finger to my lips.

"There," he said. "You can stop now. You were with Molly in her last moment. She knows that her life was seen, her voice heard. You have borne witness. It's what we do. You can let go now."

My whole body began to shake and he folded me back into his wings. When I stopped shaking I raised my head and looked at him. His face was wet—with my tears, I wondered, or his?

"You saw, too?"

"Yes," he said grimly. "I was connected through you. I wish you hadn't had to see . . . *those horrors*."

"But now that I have—now that *we* have—we can't rest until we find the place where those girls are being kept."

"We'll look. I'll talk to Sirena and see if she found out anything more."

"Sirena. She's . . ." I tried to think of a way of asking what she was to Raven, but only ended with "She was very brave."

"And reckless," Raven said shaking his head. "She could have been trapped inside the Hellgate. I should go and make sure she's all right." He stood up and looked down at me. "Are *you* all right?"

I looked down at my limp dress. The silk had been drenched in the water of the East River. I smelled awful. "Well," I said, "it's not exactly how I thought my first dance would go."

He laughed—a short bark. "Me neither. You still owe me another dance."

With a movement fleet as hummingbird wings, he brushed my cheek with his lips. Then he was gone, vanished into the darkness.

I made my way through the gardens slowly, not sure if I was ready to join the bright lights and gaiety of the party after the horrors I had witnessed. How could I make light conversation and eat cucumber sandwiches after what I'd seen?

You have to let me go, Molly had said, *before I turn into a monster.* I had held that girl's hand and given her some comfort. I hadn't felt like a monster then. I had felt . . . *useful.* If that's what being a Darkling meant, then I would gladly be a Darkling. But I hadn't been able to save her. Sirena had. Perhaps I was no good as a Darkling. Perhaps I didn't belong in either world.

I slipped through a side door into a dim hallway lined with dark wood and carpeted with thick Oriental rugs. There was a gilt-framed mirror tucked into a velvet-upholstered niche. I peered into it and was shocked at what I saw there. My hair was standing on end, my costume wings were twisted and crumpled, my dress plastered to me and torn—and I smelled like a garbage heap. I could never go back into the ballroom. I'd have to sneak out the back door and find my way home.

I heard a door opening behind me. I pressed myself into the niche to hide myself.

Male voices—deep and throaty with amusement and content—billowed out of the room on a gust of smoke. This was where the men went to smoke their cigars and talk of matters deemed too coarse for female sensibilities. Through a scrim of smoke I made out the stout, prosperous shapes of three of my classmates' fathers—Alfred Driscoll, president of the New York Bank; Wallace Rutherford, owner of the *New York Sun*; and George Montmorency, councilman and, many said, soon to be the next mayor. There were others—men in dark, expensive evening coats and sleek whiskers, one in a police uniform with medals, another in a cleric's collar, and one, half-hidden in the smoke and shadows, who was looking straight at me.

Impossible! I was hidden inside the niche and he couldn't see me through all that smoke.

But I felt the force of those eyes on me as strongly as if they had pinned me in place—and I heard the bass bell gonging in my head. The last time I had felt this frozen immobility and heard my bell ring so madly was when I'd encountered Judicus van Drood on the streets of Rhinebeck. Was it him?

But then the door to the smoking room closed and the spell vanished. I broke from the niche like a pheasant flushed from the underbrush and ran through the servants' quarters to find the service door, my wire wings trembling behind me and all the clocks in the house chiming midnight as though I were Cinderella fleeing the ball.

6

I MET NATHAN and Helen at the Fifty-Ninth Street station where the Sea Beach Railway embarked for Coney Island. Nathan looked cool and crisp in striped linen trousers, matching jacket draped nonchalantly over one shoulder, and a straw boater tipped rakishly low over his face. I didn't know how he managed it. The walk downtown had left me drenched and limp as last night's violet corsage, which lay on my night table. Helen was also enviably fresh in a frothy lace dress with matching parasol, which looked more suited for tea with the Astors than a train ride with the masses. I wondered if she had ever ridden in public transportation before. She was peering around her at the morning holiday crowd as if she'd just landed in a spice bazaar in remotest India.

"Where's your bathing costume?" she demanded as I joined them.

"I don't plan to bathe," I replied primly. "This isn't a holiday outing. We're going to find clues to Ruth Blum's whereabouts, not to have fun."

The truth was I would have loved to swim. My mother used to take me on Sundays and holidays to the beach. We'd wade in, hand in hand, squealing at the slap of waves so excruciatingly cold I couldn't imagine going an inch farther, but when she cried "*Now!*" I would dive blindly into the swell. My mother would emerge laughing, her hair slicked back like a seal's fur, her face radiant, as if the cold salt water had washed away the sadness that always clung to her like the lingering scent of smoke.

My body ached for that kind of release. But how could I risk even the most modest bathing costumes with my newly emerging wings? Besides, after all I'd seen last night through poor Molly's eyes, I wasn't in much of a holiday mood. But I was more determined than ever to find Ruth.

"Nonsense!" Helen sniffed. "This is my first excursion to Coney Island, and I'm determined to enjoy the full experience. We will ride the Steeplechase, eat fried clams, and bathe in the ocean. I've brought a bathing costume for you." She held up a basket that dangled from her arm and pulled out a red and white striped bathing costume covered with ruffles and ribbons. "I used it at Newport last summer, so it's out of date, of course, but it should do."

"Ava's four inches taller and ten pounds lighter—" Nathan began, until I kicked him in the shin. Aside from not wanting my physical attributes described—had he been paying such close attention?—I'd just realized why this outing was so important to Helen. Last summer—and every summer of her life before that—Helen had spent the season in Newport, but she and her mother could no longer afford such luxuries.

Instead, she had spent this summer in the hot, dusty city helping her mother pack up their Washington Square brownstone and sell their most valuable possessions to move to a dreary suite of rooms at the Franconia Hotel. Mrs. van Beek had let it be known within her social circles that she'd sold the brownstone because she was tired of its dark narrow rooms and was looking about for a grander residence on Fifth Avenue, but what she was really "looking about" for was a husband for Helen who would lift them both out of the encroaching maw of poverty. Poor Helen. She deserved a holiday.

"We'll see," I said, looking doubtfully at the dreadful bathing costume. I would look like a candy cane in it. "You can certainly swim while I show Ruth's picture around."

I showed Nathan and Helen the photograph.

"Oh, how droll!" Helen cried. "It looks like they're driving down the Champs-Elysées. Do let's get our picture taken, too!"

It was rather sweet to see Helen, who had had her portrait painted by John Singer Sargent, so enthusiastic about having our day in Coney Island memorialized in a souvenir photograph, but when I looked at Nathan I saw the color had washed out of his face.

"What's wrong?" I asked.

"The man," Nathan said between tight lips. "He looks familiar."

"How can you tell?" Helen asked. "His face is all funny."

"That's just it. That's how I remember him—the man who questioned me that day in the Wing & Clover. Whenever I think of him—or dream of him—his face is a blur just like that."

"If it's the same man," I said, remembering the day that Helen and I spied Nathan in our local Rhinebeck tavern beside a strange gentleman, "that means the man who took Ruth is Judicus van Drood."

A gust of cool salt air hit us as soon as we got off the train in Brooklyn. It felt delicious but didn't blow away my ominous thoughts. I'd learned last year that Judicus van Drood was Nathan's real father, but Nathan didn't know that. And if I had anything to do with it, he never would.

"What's the plan?" Nathan asked me as we descended the stairs from the elevated platform to the street.

I *did* have a plan. We would start at the entrance to Steeplechase Park, where Ruth was going to meet her mysterious stranger, and locate anyone—ticket takers, buskers, security guards—who worked there regularly and show them Ruth's picture. But I hadn't figured on the crowds. As we descended from the train platform we were swept up into a stream of people and carried along like bits of flotsam and jetsam onto the Bowery, the wide avenue named after the more disreputable street in Manhattan, which led to the amusement parks and was, itself, an amusement park of sorts.

"Hang on!" Nathan cried, linking our arms under his as we plunged into the masses. It was impossible to even hear each other over the cacophony of the laughing crowd, the antic calliope music that seemed to come from everywhere at once, and the buskers advertising the many attractions.

"Look well upon this group of savages, ladies and gentlemen!" one cried. I craned my neck to make out an African tribesman in a fur loincloth, his shaved skull and bare chest covered in tattoos.

"That man is nearly naked!" Helen whispered into my ear.

"See the freak show! See the bearded lady and the ape woman of Borneo!" Out of the corner of my eye I saw a woman dressed in a beautiful lace dress, only her face was covered with fur. She stood with an odd regal dignity, her eyes fixed on a point above the heads of the crowd.

"This way for Delilah of the Seven Veils," another shouted. "The hottest show on Earth! See her dance the hootchy-kootchy! Anywhere else but in the ocean breezes of Coney Island she would be consumed by her own fire!"

A woman with a veiled face but an exposed midriff shimmied by us, clinking finger cymbals and twining one of her scarves around Nathan's neck. An intoxicating scent of jasmine mingled with the aromas of fried clams, salt air, and circus animals. Nathan's eyes followed the dancer as she wove through the crowd.

"How very familiar of her!" Helen sniffed.

The hootchy-kootchy dancer wasn't the only one who was familiar. Twice I felt a stranger's hand on my person, but when I turned to catch the offending party I looked into a sea of laughing faces so distended with hilarity they resembled the grotesque sign the changeling had mimicked. And then I saw the face itself, looming over the crowd like the guiding spirit of the place—a spirit of antic glee that put my teeth on edge but somehow made me want to smile and dance to the crazy tune of the calliope.

"Over here!" I shouted to Nate, who was fending off a mountebank in plaid trousers holding out a handful of playing cards. Helen, wide-eyed, was watching a spooning couple whose limbs were so intertwined they appeared to be one creature. I steered them both to the entrance of Steeplechase Park, where there was a pocket of open space just below the funny-face sign. I saw why when we got there. A giant of a man stood in the center of the empty space. He wore white robes that billowed in the breeze, a white tunic and turban, brilliant red pantaloons, and a matching sash. He stood absolutely still, his dark face immobile as a statue carved out of mahogany, jet-black eyes boring into the crowd of spectators that had stilled around him as though under a spell. I thought he might be a statue until he raised his arm and pointed at a girl in a navy blue swimming costume.

"You!" he bellowed. "Do you not believe in the magic of Omar the Magnificent!"

The girl covered her face with a cheap paper fan and giggled. But when Omar spoke next her giggles stopped and the whole crowd fell silent.

"And why do you not believe? Because it is told to you at Coney Island and in your heart you say . . . what is the word? *Humbug?* But I ask you, why should I come all the way across the oceans, far from my own land where the sun is hot all year and the sacred Ganges flows to the sea from the great hills that wear white turbans of eternal snow and whisper secrets in the ears of the stars—why should I do this if my entertainment is humbug?"

His voice dropped to a low whisper that seemed to tickle the inside of my ears. He seemed to be looking straight at me now.

"And why should you come if not to find the lost one you seek?"

Then, without another word, he turned, his robes billowing around him in a white swirl. There was a flash of blinding light, a puff of smoke, and he was gone. The crowd gasped as one.

"See more of Omar the Hindu Hypnotist at the Golden Pavilion!" a spieler announced.

"Oh, do let's!" Helen cried. "I want to see if he can hypnotize me. I'm sure he can't. I'm much too strong-willed."

"It's a parlor trick," Nathan said dismissively.

I found it curious that my friends who knew magic existed were so doubtful of the possibility that it might exist *here*.

"If he does that little demonstration here every day, perhaps he saw Ruth," I said, getting on the ticket line. I showed Ruth's picture to the ticket seller, but he only shrugged and told me he saw "a thousand mugs a day and they all look alike after a while." I thanked him and asked for directions to the Golden Pavilion. "Just past the Steeplechase and before the freak show. Don't miss the winged woman."

I started, but he was already turned to the next customer on line, and Helen was urging me along.

"Look at the beautiful horses!" she cried, pointing to the mechanical wooden horses on the Steeplechase. "I've missed riding since we sold our stables! Can we ride on them?"

"After we've located Omar," I said, beginning to feel like the dowdy governess to two rambunctious charges. But when we found the Golden Pavilion there was a sign telling us that Omar the Magnificent's next sitting wasn't for another forty minutes. I asked the attendant if we might have a private word with Omar, but he told us that the Great Omar was meditating in preparation for his appearance.

"We might as well ride the Steeplechase in the meantime," Helen pointed out.

Seeing that it was fruitless to argue, I agreed. We went back to Steeplechase Park and selected our horses. For all Helen's horsemanship, she needed quite a lot of assistance from Nathan to mount her wooden steed, and once seated she professed herself terrified of falling.

"Look!" she told Nathan. "Everyone is riding in pairs. There's plenty of room for you, and you can keep me from falling."

"And who will keep Ava from falling?" Nathan asked.

"I'm perfectly capable of holding on to a hobby horse!" I snapped, sure now why Helen had been so anxious to ride the Steeplechase. All around us I saw girls giggling as their young men tightened their arms around their waists. The whole ride was one big excuse for cuddling. I suddenly felt ridiculous riding alone. I would get off and go show Ruth's picture around . . .

But then a juddering of gears and a sudden jolt told me the ride was starting. Helen gave a little yelp and Nathan swung into the saddle behind her with all the ease of a cowboy in a Wild West show. I grasped the pole and hung on as the wooden horse trembled beneath me, swooped down over an artificial stream, and then began climbing a long upward-sloping track. I could see the minarets of Luna Park and the great Ferris wheel and the terrifying Loop-the-Loop. We were rising high above the stultifying crowds into clean, cool air.

Beyond the park lay the Atlantic Ocean, blue-green and vast, seagulls wheeling over the whitecaps. The cold salt air lifted the damp hair off my neck and slid under my fine lawn shirtwaist. I closed my eyes and let the air lap over me. It was like diving into a wave. It was like *flying*. Beneath my corset my wings itched to flex themselves and soar over the ocean with the seagulls. And why not? Here at Coney Island wasn't everything allowed? Men and women held each other in public, women danced bare-bellied on the streets, magicians vanished in a puff of smoke . . . If I spread my wings now and took off, would anyone think it was more than one of the wonders of Coney Island?

I opened my eyes. Ahead of me, Helen had her head buried under Nathan's arm, her arms wrapped rigidly around him. I remembered suddenly that Helen was deathly afraid of heights. She must not have realized that the ride went so high up in the air. Nathan had his hands full—literally—with keeping her from going into hysterics. All the other couples were engrossed with each other. Who would notice my absence?

We had come to the crest of the course. *Now!* my whole body urged. But even as I rose from my saddle, a scrap of conversation floated toward me on the wind.

"But I can't leave my family behind!"

It was a girl's voice, high and querulous. A deeper bass answered her in tones so low I couldn't make out the words, only the low persuasive rumble.

"Well, if I could send them back money . . . and you're sure this job out west will pay . . ."

Another rumble, almost a growl, followed.

"Then I'll do it! Oh, but not today. I'll have to pack a bag. I'll meet you next week . . . yes, under the funny face like always. You always show me a swell time . . ."

The girl's voice was carried away as the ride turned a corner and the wind was coming from the side. I lifted up in my saddle to see which horse the voices had come from, but I couldn't tell. And even if I could, how could I tell if this girl was being lured into a life of slavery or was only eloping with her sweetheart? Still, if I could follow her next week when she went with her beau, perhaps she would lead me to where Ruth was being held.

We were swooping down now into the final stretch. The couples were all leaning forward, urging their horses on as if they were live breathing animals instead of wooden simulacra. The horse with the heaviest load would go fastest and win and I, alone, would come in last. The girl who was planning to elope would get away. I leaned forward and clucked my tongue as if it would make a difference—and to my amazement, it did! My horse sped up and overtook the others.

"Go, Ava!" I heard Nathan cry as I passed him and Helen, then two other riders. Only one horse was still in front of me. The man had already dismounted and was helping his companion down. I heard her giggling voice declaiming, "We won! We won!" It was the girl I'd heard before. She was wearing a sailor suit and a flower-trimmed bonnet. She threw her arms around the neck of her companion, her back to me.

"Yes," I heard him say, his voice a deep rumble. "I always do."

The bass bell in my head clanged as I passed the finish line, as if signaling my victory, but that wasn't why it was ringing. It was because the man in front of me was Judicus van Drood. I recognized the Inverness cape and Homburg hat he habitually wore, looking heavy and out of place in the summer crowds.

Our eyes met and he smiled, a wisp of smoke curling out of his parted lips. Then he slipped from his companion's arms and vanished through the exit.

I jumped off my horse and ran after him, pushing rudely past the girl in the sailor's outfit and through a curtained doorway...

Where the ground gave out beneath me. I was tumbling down into darkness, my arms flailing for purchase on slick walls, plummeting into the abyss.

7

I LANDED HARD on the wooden floor, lights blazing around me like the fires of hell. A face loomed out of the glare, distorted and strange, the eyes circled with shadows, the nose bulbous and red, the mouth stretched unnaturally wide. The creature held out a red-gloved hand to me, beckoning me toward the hellfire. Ignoring it, I got up on my own and found myself towering over a little man. He shrugged and doffed his hat, and marched forward. Was he leading me to van Drood? A gust of hot air shot up my legs, lifting my skirts up above my knees. From behind the glare of lights I heard a low rumble. Laughter. I blinked into the glare and made out the shapes of heads and hats—feathered women's hats and men's straw boaters. It was an audience gathered to watch my humiliation. I pushed my skirts down and strode across the stage, where the little man—a dwarf in clown face—waited.

"Don't be mad!" he cried in a loud falsetto. "Be bad! Join the audience and laugh at our next performers!"

So that was how it worked. They humiliated you, then offered you the chance to laugh at their next victims. Even if I would stoop that low, I had van Drood to find. I rushed past the dwarf.

"Try the fun house," he whispered under his breath. "The humbug went that way."

Had I heard him right? Could I trust him? And what was a humbug? Was he referring to the Homburg hat van Drood wore?

After exiting the stage, which looking back I saw was called the Blowhole Theater, I found myself in a vast vaulted pavilion full of screaming crowds. I looked in vain for van Drood as I passed a ride called the Human Roulette Wheel that spun people around in a mad circle and one called the Barrel of Love that tossed men and women around like bits of laundry in a tub. Then I spied the dark Homburg hat at an arched gateway that looked like the gates of hell. A Hellgate. Yes, that's where van Drood would go. I entered a long narrow corridor that seemed to get narrower and narrower as I went forward. At the end of it I spied a wisp of smoke trailing behind van Drood. I rushed forward and collided with a wide-eyed, frightened girl.

Was it the girl from the Steeplechase? She looked familiar. But when I reached for her, my hand hit glass. I was staring into a mirror at my own frightened reflection. I wheeled around and a dozen Avas turned with me, all with their mouths gaping open and their eyes popping wide.

Foolish girl, a deep male voice chided. *You don't even recognize yourself.*

I spun around again, searching for the source of the voice, and glimpsed the hem of a cloak and the brim of a hat vanishing on the edge of each mirror, as if van Drood had somehow slipped *behind* the mirrors. The thought that he was standing behind the glass watching me was sickening.

Of course I see you, Ava, van Drood's voice purred from behind a mirror. I stepped toward it, staring at my own face as if I could find van Drood behind the glass. *I've always seen you. Since you were a little girl.*

My image in the mirrors wavered, blurred, and another image took its place. I was looking into eyes that looked like mine but weren't. They were a deeper green, older, and shadowed by fear. They were my mother's eyes. I followed them down to a little girl playing on the beach, running in and out of the surf like a sandpiper. My mother was watching me as a child . . . but why were her eyes so fearful? Then I saw *him,* a dark figure standing in the misty verge between land and sea.

I turned back to see my mother's face, but the scene had already changed. I saw myself, older, walking down a street in the city beside my mother, both of us under a large umbrella.

"It's stopped raining!" I cried, springing out from under the umbrella to leap over a puddle and holding my arms out. In my black cloak it looked like I had wings. As I lit down on the pavement I nearly collided with a man in an Inverness cloak.

"You were watching me to see if I was turning into a Darkling," I said.

I wasn't the only one, he replied.

His voice came from behind me. I whirled around and saw another scene from my childhood: my mother standing behind me, brushing my hair. I could almost feel the brush stroking my scalp and the weight of my mother's hand on my shoulder . . .

And her gaze on my back, eyes shadowed by fear.

She was afraid you were turning into a monster.

"No!" I cried, turning toward the voice. A kaleidoscope of images spun around me: my mother measuring me for a dress, watching me reach for a book on a library shelf, her eyes always shadowed with fear, a look that I'd known throughout my childhood but that I'd assumed was from her own demons.

You were her demon.

"No!"

She was waiting to see what kind of monster you would become. That's why she fled from her friends and family, why she hid herself in shame. Knowing that you would become a monster like the demon that ravaged her.

"No! That's not how it happened. She was in love—"

How do you know that? Did she tell you that when you saw her in Faerie?

"No," I admitted. "But Raven told me . . ."

Of course he wouldn't tell you that one of his own kind attacked a defenseless girl. That you, too, are becoming a monster. Look.

The images from my childhood vanished, leaving only my present self. But as I stared at my reflection my wings burst through the confines of my corset and spread out behind me, and feathers began erupting from my skin, not just on the enormous wings, but from my hands and face—rough, ugly feathers that made me look like the bearded lady or the ape woman of Borneo. I turned from the sight, but the image followed me, multiplied a hundred times.

It's a trick, I told myself, *an illusion van Drood is creating.*

But even as I said the words to myself I knew that if I didn't banish the images I would see them forever. I would be trapped forever in this fun house, a hall of mirrors as cracked as my mind.

That was it. I stepped closer to the mirror, cringing at the closer view of the monster in it, and pounded the glass with my fists.

The glass shivered and I heard a faint tinkling sound . . . like *bells*. Why wasn't my bass bell gonging if I was truly in danger?

Once before in the dungeons of Blythewood my bells had failed me. They'd been muted by the *tenebrae*. Were they muted now by the mirrors? Was that why van Drood had lured me here—because my bells didn't work in the Hall of Mirrors?

Where's your power now, chime child? Van Drood's voice mocked me. *Did you think you would keep it while you became a monster? Did you think that the power of Merope would remain in the body of the cursed race that destroyed her?*

"Merope wasn't destroyed by a Darkling," I cried. "She loved Aderyn and he saved her."

Is that what your Darkling lover told you? Van Drood snickered. *Would you like to see what really happened?*

The image of the feathered monster vanished from the glass. A moment ago I would have been grateful to see it gone, but as I turned around, looking into one blank mirror after another, it felt stranger not to see anything. My own reflection had been wiped from the glass. It was as though I didn't exist anymore.

Then the mirrors started spinning, faster and faster, like the Human Roulette Wheel—or like a zoetrope I'd watched once in the nickelodeon, a wheel with images inside it that made a moving picture when you looked inside. Only I was *inside* it, and the pictures that began to emerge of a snow-filled forest were not just pictures. I felt the bite of the cold snow blowing through those woods and heard the howls of the wolves that prowled it.

Shadow wolves.

I knew exactly where I was.

I'd seen this story twice before—once in the candelabellum, a device kept in the Blythewood dungeons, and once in a spinning teacup that Raven had showed me. It was the story of how the Order of the Bells came to be. In both stories the seven daughters of a bell maker set off through the woods to deliver a set of seven bells to a prince at a castle. They were set upon by shadow wolves, creatures possessed by the *tenebrae*. When their cart toppled, the youngest sister, Merope, rallied her sisters to play changes on the bells to keep the shadow wolves at bay. They rang the bells through the night, one by one ceasing as they grew exhausted, until only Merope rang her solitary bell. When the prince and his knights came to rescue them Merope was gone, leaving a blood-filled impression in the snow.

That's where the stories diverged.

The Order believed that Merope was abducted by a Darkling—an evil creature on the side of the *tenebrae* and all the monsters of Faerie. But Raven had showed me a version in which Merope was in love with the Darkling Aderyn, who saved her and then, together with the creatures of Faerie, helped battle the *tenebrae*. What story would van Drood show me in the hall of mirrors?

I watched warily as the shadow wolves pursued the bell maker's daughters and Merope rang her bell to drive them away. Surprisingly, van Drood's story followed Raven's, as the great black-winged creature descended toward her and her face lit up with love. Aderyn gathered Merope up in his arms and carried her into the sky. Together they followed the sisters and the knights back to the castle, fending off the shadows that pursued them. I watched in horror as the prince was set upon by shadow crows and devoured by them—just as van Drood must once have been devoured by the *tenebrae* to become what he was now. Was that why he was showing me this story? Was he showing me how he became a Shadow Master so that I would feel sorry for him . . . or even *save* him?

"Can you be saved?" I asked aloud.

The revolving pictures juddered for a moment as I'd seen moving pictures in the nickelodeon jerk when the film got stuck in the projector—or as I'd seen van Drood himself jerk once before. He had looked then like a broken machine. Was a piece of him that was still human struggling to break free?

But then the pictures ran again all too smoothly. The prince was ripped apart by the shadows, the crows burrowing beneath his skin to eat him from the inside out. I bit my cheek to keep from crying out.

The thing that was once the prince turned to me, face bulging as the shadow crows moved beneath its skin, red eyes glowing, mouth spewing smoke. I watched in horror as the creature ripped open its own chest to extract a writhing crow.

I ducked to dodge the flying missile and heard a thud and cry of pain from behind me. I turned, thinking someone had joined me in the hall of mirrors and been hurt, but the cry came from a creature in the mirrors. Aderyn, the Darkling that had saved Merope, clutched his chest, his eyes wide with pain.

No! Merope's scream rent the air, shaking the mirrors, but not enough to dispel the image of Aderyn ripping the shadow crow from his chest. He tore it out, but a bit of the darkness had already burrowed inside.

Where it remained until his dying day, destroying him and Merope and their children and cursing all the Darklings. Van Drood's voice was very near now. I could feel his breath against my skin.

The shadows are already inside you, his voice hissed, *as they are inside all Darklings since they corrupted Aderyn. His infection cursed all the Darklings. That is why they can no longer enter Faerie. That is what Raven didn't tell you. And that is why you are a monster now. Just like me.*

"No!" I whirled around, flailing my arm out in the direction the voice had come from, but it only hit glass, as did the pocket watch that I wore on a chain around my neck. The bells inside the watch chimed with the impact, faint and tinny, but loud enough that they reminded me of the watch's purpose. It wasn't an ordinary watch. It was an automaton repeater, given to me by Miss Emmaline Sharp to help me focus my own bells. I'd used it once before to dispel the *tenebrae* and once to banish van Drood. Now I grasped the watch in my hand and pressed the stem, praying it would play a tune that would destroy van Drood's hold on me.

The two automaton figures—a woman and a winged man—drew back their hammers and struck the two bells between them, playing, to my surprise, the calliope tune I'd heard before on the Bowery. Perhaps it was just because that was the last music I had heard. I certainly didn't see how the gay, antic tune would do anything against van Drood.

But the figures in the mirror began to move backward in jerky motions, faster and faster, as if they were actors in a vaudeville melodrama performing the parts. And now when Merope played her bells they rang out in the crazy calliope tune, growing louder and louder, the music shaking the mirrors. I stepped away from the glass just in time, before all the mirrors shattered.

As the glass fell all around me, one fragment landed on my hand. I looked down at the shard and saw inside it the image of a crow, its yellow beak just where the point impaled my skin. I flung it from me and looked up, prepared for a murder of mirror crows to descend on me, but the glass had all fallen away, and in its place stood the dwarf from the Blowhole Theater and Omar the Hindu Hypnotist, incongruously flanked by Nathan and Helen.

8

"THANK THE BELLS we found you!" Helen cried, crunching toward me over a sea of broken glass. "Mr. Marvel and Mr. Omar said you'd be in here."

"Mr. Marvel?" I asked as Helen brushed mirror fragments from my skirt and straightened my shirtwaist.

"Kid Marvel," the dwarf said, striding forward and sticking out his hand. "Showman and impresario, entertainer to the crowned heads of Europe, and," he added with a wink, "dwarf. And not just the human variety, if you get my drift."

"Oh," I said, not sure I did, "do you mean you're a fairy dwarf?"

"Right on the nose!" He tapped his own bulbous and painted proboscis. "Or as your folk would say, genus: *Fatus*; species: *dvergar*. I hope you'll excuse the liberties taken back at the Blowhole. Just doing my job, you know. But then Omar here"—the tall Hindu bowed his head—"said you were looking for the girls gone missing, and when I saw you chasing the humbug I knew you'd get yourself in trouble."

"The humbug?" I asked, remembering he'd used the word before.

"A fake, a con, a master of disguise." Kid Marvel rattled off the names. "A gyp, a hoister, a goniff . . . a thing that ain't what it's got up to look like—"

"In short," Omar interrupted, "what my esteemed colleague Mr. Marvel is attempting to establish is that the man you pursued is no longer a man, but a creature possessed by demons. In my land we called such a creature a *pishaca*, a flesh-eating demon wont to haunt cremation grounds and feed on human souls."

I shivered at the description. "We call him a Shadow Master. This one's name is Judicus van Drood."

Kid Marvel and Omar exchanged looks. "Yeah, we seen him here before," Kid Marvel said. "Bloke who's always got a different bleak mort on his arm, spreading the muck around."

"What—?" Helen began.

"He's always got a pretty girl with him and plenty of spending money," Nate translated, and then shrugged at Helen's stare. "A fellow spends time in the gambling hells, he picks up the lingo."

"You'd be well advised not to spend so much time in *hells*, sahib," Omar said, staring sternly at Nathan. Then turning to Helen and me, he added, "Nor should you be allowing these young ladies to chase after dangerous creatures."

"It's not up to him to *allow* us," Helen said, bristling. "And we're not ordinary young ladies. We belong to the Or—"

"Helen!" Nathan and I cried.

"My dear young lady," Omar said, bowing his head to Helen. "We know all about your Order. But I suggest if we are going to talk of such weighty and clandestine matters we repair to the privacy of my pavilion."

Helen, Nathan and I looked at each other. Omar the Magnificent and Kid Marvel were clearly not ordinary humans—or even humans at all. If they knew about the Order, they knew we were charged with destroying their kind. They might be leading us into a trap. And yet they had come to my rescue and they knew about the shadows and had seen van Drood escorting young women around Coney Island . . .

"We shall be delighted," Helen answered for us, as though accepting an invitation to tea. "I've never been to a hypnotist's pavilion before!"

The Golden Pavilion of Omar the Magnificent turned out to be a wooden caravan plastered with theatrical posters parked between the fun house and the freak show. From the outside it looked too small to hold the five of us—even if one of us was a dwarf—but it proved to be surprisingly commodious on the inside. The floor was covered with thick Indian carpets, the walls and ceiling draped with beautiful silk scarves edged with tiny brass bells. We were offered seats on low tufted cushions and served spicy tea from a brass samovar in delicate gilt-edged glasses.

"How lovely!" Helen cried, sampling an iced cake from a brass tray. "I'm going to give my next tea party an Oriental theme."

"We're not here to trade recipes for scones," I said sternly. "We're here to find a girl." I laid Ruth's picture on the brass tea tray. "This is Ruth Blum. She went missing on July fourth. A change—a witness said she saw Ruth meeting a man who matched van Drood's description at the Steeplechase entrance on the day she disappeared."

"Your witness must not be an ordinary mortal if she was able to recall the *pishaca*'s face," Omar said, seating himself cross-legged on the rug. "The *pishaca* is even more adept at the arts of mesmerism than I. To the undisciplined mind his face would appear as a blur."

"*My* mind is quite disciplined," Nathan objected. "And I only recall him as a blur."

"You, sahib, have indeed a fine mind," Omar said, bowing his head to Nathan, "but I am afraid it has been sadly addled by liquor—"

"The blue ruin, eh?" Kid Marvel concurred, tapping his nose. "What a cab moll serves at a flash-panny'll give you the barrel fever in the end. Better stick with the scandal soup." He held up his tea glass, took a sip, and screwed his face up.

"—and by melancholy," Omar continued, leaning forward and pinning Nathan with his glittering black eyes. A fog seemed to rise in Nathan's pale gray eyes, and he swayed like a cobra rising from a snake charmer's basket.

"Stop that!" I cried, snapping my fingers in front of Nathan's drugged gaze. "It's not fair to use your powers on us."

"No more than it's fair for you to wander into our turf without laying all your cards on the table," Kid Marvel snarled back, his voice an octave lower than it had been a moment before. "You know we're madges and we knows you could turn us into the Order of the Ding-Dongs. Your kind has never shown our kind a bit of mercy. You hunt us down and kill us. Why do you think we're hiding out here at the freak show? Where else can we go that's safe from youse ding-dongs? Why should we trust you? Why should we help you?"

"Madges?" I echoed. "Ding-dongs?"

Helen had shrunk back at the dwarf's venomous attack. Nathan was clenching his fists as if he'd like to punch the little man. Omar was silent and watching, his black eyes moving across our faces. When those eyes reached me I felt a pinprick behind each eye and an itching along my shoulder blades.

"By *madges* my esteemed colleague means magical beings, and by *ding-dongs*, well..." Omar spread his hands wide. "While I admit it's not exactly a respectful name for the Order of the Bell, I'm afraid I must agree with Mr. Marvel's assessment. We would be foolish to trust your kind. When your emissaries came to my country they rooted out our gods and ransacked our temples. They combed our ashrams looking for children with magical ability and took those children from their homes, promising their parents they would be raised as equals in their schools."

Omar held up his hand. I heard Helen gasp as she recognized the ring on his finger. It bore the Bell and Feather insignia.

"But we were never equals. They used us to learn our magic and then treated us as servants. Why should we trust you now?"

"He's right," Nathan said. "Their kind and ours can never work together. They don't care if helpless girls are being stolen from their families. They'll never help us." He unfolded his long legs and began to rise stiffly to his feet, pulling Helen up with him.

"It's you who'd sacrifice those poor helpless girls instead of taking help from our kind!" Kid Marvel cried, jumping far more agilely to his feet and jabbing his finger at Nathan's chest, jarring Helen's arm in the process. She dropped her teacup. As it shattered on the brass tea tray it made a sound like a bell ringing. The sound expanded in my head, swelling into a maddening peal that filled the caravan. The tiny bells on the hanging scarves rang and the glasses on the brass tray chimed. The whole caravan was shaking. I looked at Omar, sure he must be making the caravan move, but saw from his wide, surprised eyes that he wasn't. I was the one doing it.

"A chime child," Omar said, with something like awe in his voice. "And an unusually powerful one." He fastened his glittering eyes on me. I felt my wings straining against my corset as if Omar was a wing charmer and he was coaxing them out. Would he reveal my true nature to my friends?

"A ringer!" Kid Marvel cried. "We could use you in the business, kid, if you ever get tired of working for the ding-dongs."

"You never know," I answered, looking at Omar instead of Kid Marvel. "I might need a change of scenery."

Omar bowed low to me. "We would be honored to have you among us, *garuda*."

"Then you'll help us?" I asked, wondering what he'd called me.

Omar nodded at Kid Marvel, who stuck out his hand to shake mine. "Sure, kid, for a ringer, anything you want." I was sure, though, that the reason Omar had decided to help me was because he knew now what I was, and that I couldn't turn him and Kid Marvel in without endangering my own secret. As far as Omar and Kid were concerned I was one of them. Another *madge*. I supposed there were worse clubs to be a member of.

"But I don't know how easy it'll be. These molls that the humbug makes away with aren't just strolling down Fifth

Avenue. He puts 'em in a flash-panny tight as the Tombs."

I knew by "the Tombs" he was referring to the jailhouse, but still the word made me shiver. I wasn't sure what a flash-panny was, so I asked.

"A house of ill repute," Omar said. "This one's called the Hellgate Club."

I shivered at the memory of the churning whirlpool that had sucked Molly down into the river last night. "There's a place in the East River called that."

"Yeah, that's what it's named for. They say sailors who survive the Hellgate come to the club after. And," Kid Marvel added in a lower, more ominous tone, "they say them that *don't* survive frequent it too, if youse take my meaning. It's down on the waterfront—not a neighborhood nice kiddies like yerselves ought to go. It's surrounded by gin joints and hop dens. It looks nicer than those places, but it's not. All them dives are havens of grace compared to the Hellgate. If your friend is there it'll take a pretty big con to get her out."

"Mr. Marvel is correct," Omar said. "The Hellgate Club is protected by the most ruthless gangsters of the underworld, corrupt officers of the New York City police force and demons of the shadow world. The girls are never allowed out and the building is guarded night and day. All who work there—and all who enter—are held in thrall to the shadow demons. It would be easier to extract a prisoner from the Tombs. Only a master confidence man could get a girl out of the Hellgate."

"And luckily," Kid Marvel said, grinning, "you've found one."

9

FIVE HOURS LATER Miss Corey and I were sitting on the rooftop of the Hellgate Club, an unassuming brownstone on Water Street in the shadow of the looming Gothic tower of the nearly finished Woolworth Building and within sight—and smell—of the East River. The odor reminded me that the real Hellgate whirlpool was not far, and that poor Molly had escaped from here to throw herself in the river last night.

Once Kid Marvel had agreed to help us he had outlined his plan—or his *con* as he called it—so speedily I wondered how long he'd been devising it.

"Trick of the trade," he'd confided. "I'm always workin' the angle—how to get in a place, how to get out."

It had been clear right away that we needed more players for the con and he'd agreed to let me enlist Miss Sharp, Miss Corey, and Agnes Moorhen. We'd met at the Henry Street Settlement after it closed for the night.

Once they'd agreed, despite Miss Corey's reluctance to collaborate with "carnies," as she called them, Kid Marvel had laid out the con. Agnes had suggested that her lawyer friend Sam Greenfeder could drive the "getaway" car. Sam had been in his last year of law school attending a lecture in the building next door to the Triangle factory when the fire had broken out. He and his fellow students had helped girls across the roof to safety. He'd met Agnes at the pier where the bodies were laid out and spent months helping her track me down. In recognition of his bravery, Sam Greenfeder had been deputized as a retainer to the Order and entrusted with the rudiments of its mysteries.

Miss Sharp suggested that we also enlist Mr. Bellows' help.

"Rupert Bellows!" Miss Corey had cried. "Whyever would we use him?"

I knew that Miss Corey didn't like our history teacher. I had begun to suspect that she was jealous of the attention he paid to Miss Sharp.

"Because a man has to accompany Nathan into the club, and I don't think Agnes's Mr. Greenfeder will fit the bill."

"Are you saying that Rupert Bellows does?" Miss Corey squawked. "Do you honestly think Rupert Bellows has ever set foot in a house of ill fame?"

Miss Sharp blushed. "I most certainly hope not! But he is a knight of the Order. He is charged with going into hell itself if need be, and I have every confidence he will play his part admirably."

"He looks like a two-bit dandy," Miss Corey remarked now, looking over the edge of the rooftop. "I can smell his bay rum cologne from here."

I looked over the edge of the roof and saw Mr. Bellows and Nathan standing on the club's front stoop. Mr. Bellows, who usually wore muted tweeds, was dressed in a loud plaid suit, spats, and a top hat, which he now doffed, revealing slicked-back hair, as the door opened. A whiff of gin and tea-rose perfume merged with Mr. Bellows' bay rum cologne and wafted up to our perch along with a woman's voice. I leaned farther over the edge of the roof and opened up my inner ear to hear what she was saying.

"You needn't flash your brass at me, Diamond Jim," she purred in a rich, seductive voice. "Only gentlemen with references get past Madame LeFevre."

Nathan, in an only slightly more subdued outfit, stepped forward and whispered something in Madame LeFevre's ear. Even my bird ears couldn't hear what he said, but everyone on the waterfront must have heard Madame LeFevre's throaty laughter.

"Well, why didn't you say you were friends with Big Jim O'Malley right away, boy-os? Any friends of Big Jim's are always welcome here."

"Big Jim O'Malley?" I repeated, sitting back on my heels as Nathan and Mr. Bellows disappeared inside. Miss Corey looked puzzled, and I remembered she couldn't hear what I could, so I explained that I'd heard Nathan say that name.

"Hm . . ." she said, narrowing her eyes at me. "Big Jim O'Malley is a bigwig in Tammany Hall politics. I can't imagine how Nathan knows him, but it was clever of him to use that name to get in. Nathan's a lot smarter than he lets on."

I stared at her, surprised that she thought about Nathan Beckwith at all. "I didn't think you liked any—" I began, but when I realized what I was about to say I clamped my hand over my mouth.

Miss Corey tilted her head and smiled. "Men?" she asked. "Is that what you were going to say?"

"I didn't m-mean . . ." I stuttered, unsure what I *did* mean and feeling as if I'd stumbled on forbidden territory. Blood rose to my cheeks. Luckily the only light on the roof came from the welding torches of the workmen laboring through the night on the Woolworth Building eight blocks to the west.

"I think what you've probably noticed is that I don't like Rupert Bellows," she replied with a strained smile. In the light of the torches I could see how pale she had become. In the daytime she usually wore a veil to hide the marks on her face, but she had left it off for tonight's operation. The marks on her face stood out like constellations of a distant universe. Remembering what Miss Sharp had told me about their origin, I felt a pang for her. Miss Corey had been kind to me at Blythewood. She had gotten me a part-time job as her assistant in the library to augment my allowance and give me independence. The last thing I wanted was to pry into her secrets and make her feel uncomfortable.

"Yes, of course, that's what I meant," I said, grateful for the exit she had offered me.

For a moment I thought she would leave it at that, but then she sighed and said, "Or perhaps you've noticed more than that."

I could have pretended not to know what she meant, but then I remembered what it felt like to keep my own secret. "I suppose I've noticed that you like Miss Sharp very much," I said.

She bit her lip. "Yes, I do like Vionetta *very* much," she rasped in a strained voice. "I like her . . ." She looked away and stared up at the half-built Woolworth Building as if the words for her feelings could be found in the elaborately carved Gothic tower. "I like her more than as a friend. I would like to spend the rest of my life with her, I don't care where or how."

"Does she feel the same?" I asked.

"I don't know!" she cried. "How can I know? If I tell her how I feel it might ruin the friendship we have." She turned to me, her eyes glittering as if the flares of the welding torches had lodged in them. "You understand that the way I feel is not . . . *accepted*. It's not the way I'm supposed to feel."

"I don't *understand* that at all," I replied hotly. "How can anyone control the way they feel about someone else? And how can anyone tell someone how they're *supposed* to feel? The way you feel about Miss Sharp . . . well . . ." I fumbled for what to say. "*I* accept it. Anyone with half a brain and two eyes in their head would have to!"

She laughed hoarsely and wiped her eyes with the back of her hand. "Avaline Hall," she said, "you are quite remarkable. If you ever have a secret burdening you, you know where to come." She leaned forward and squeezed my hand.

"A secret . . . ?" I began, but then a noise drew our attention to the street.

"There's Vi!" Miss Corey cried, leaning over the edge of the roof.

Below us stood a woman, but I was sure it couldn't be Miss Sharp. She was drab and stooped, her head covered by a gray shawl. She looked shorter and older than Miss Sharp, but when she knocked on the door the noise resounded across the waterfront. The door opened and Madame LeFevre's voice wafted up to our perch.

"Have you come about a job, dearie? I'll have to see what's under all them layers if you have."

"I've come for my husband," Miss Sharp replied in a quavering voice that nonetheless carried on the night air. "Mr. Robbins. He's here with his friend, Mr. . . . er . . . Flyte."

It had been Kid Marvel's little joke to assign us all aliases based on birds or flying. I was "Phoenix" and Miss Corey, much to her chagrin, was "Magpie."

"It's not my policy to divulge the names of my clients or to let ladies into my establishment. Go home, duckie, and wait for your husband like a good little wifie."

"Oooh," Miss Corey whispered, "Vi won't like that."

"I most certainly will not!" Miss Sharp announced in the clear loud voice she used to reprimand students who didn't do their assignments. "I will stand here and wait for my husband until he comes out!"

"Suit yerself, pet." Madame LeFevre began to close the door, but before she did Miss Sharp shouted in a loud, commanding voice. "John! John Jacob Robbins! I know you're in there. Come out this minute before you spend another penny on some painted harlot while our three children go hungry!"

A large man came out the door and remonstrated with her. "Ma'am, you can't stay here. You'll raise the whole neighborhood—"

"I will raise the hounds of hell if that's what it takes to get my husband out of the clutches of that she-devil!"

"She could, too," Miss Corey remarked admiringly. "I've seen her raise the hounds of hell."

The front door opened and closed again. Miss Sharp's voice

rose ever higher and louder, raining threats and pleas that convinced *me* that she had three starving children at home. Lights went on in buildings around us and neighbors leaned out their windows to watch the fracas. In the building below us I heard slamming doors and querulous voices. I opened my inner ear and listened.

"Get a load of the bellows on that one!"

"No wonder the poor man came here for a little peace and quiet."

"At least he has someone who cares enough to come looking for him."

This last came from a girl on the top floor in back. I moved toward the back of the building and looked down into the rear alley. A patch of light from a top-floor window illuminated a rickety old fire escape clinging precariously to the crumbling brick walls. In the alleyway below, two large men stood guard smoking cigarettes and listening to Miss Sharp's tirade. I focused on the voices coming from the top-floor window.

"I'm here to help you, Ruth," I heard Nathan say. "I'm here to take you back to your family."

"I told you my name's not Ruth, it's Fanny and I don't have no family!"

"Not even a sister Etta?"

The only reply was a whimper that might have come from a small mouse, then the girl repeated in a monotone. "My name's not Ruth, my name's not Ruth, my name's not . . ."

"There's something wrong," I told Miss Corey. "I have to go down there and talk to her. You keep an eye on Miss Sharp."

Before she could stop me, I was on the fire escape heading

down to the second floor. Each step I took made the whole contraption shake. I was afraid the noise would alert the guards in the alley, but they were too busy listening to Miss Sharp's shrieks, which had now been joined by Mr. Bellows' retorts delivered from a front window. The two of them were shouting back and forth like an old married couple.

"If I'da known you were such a lazy good-for-nothing layabout I'd never have married you, John Robbins!"

"If I'd have known you were such a sanctimonious shrew I'd never've let your father strong-arm me to the altar!"

They sounded like they were enjoying themselves.

I hurried down metal steps filigreed by rust to a lacy thinness, trying not to picture the fire escape at the Triangle. When I reached the window, I paused to breathe and looked through the glass.

I'm not sure what I thought a house of ill fame would look like—gaudy, I suppose, certainly not this well-appointed room with a four-poster canopy bed, lace curtains, and china bric-a-brac on the tables and chests. It looked more like a girl's room in a wealthy home—until I looked at the girl inhabiting it. I recognized her features—dark thick hair, olive skin, high wide cheekbones and large brown eyes—from her photograph, but it was hard to believe she was that same laughing girl. She was wedged into a corner between a wardrobe and night table, her bare arms wrapped around her chest protectively, shivering so hard that her yellow silk dressing gown trembled like a butterfly's wing. She looked so scared I thought one of the guards must be in the room, but when I looked around all I saw was Nathan standing as far as he could from her, raking his hands through his hair and staring at her as if she were an explosive device.

"Please," he was pleading, "I'm here to help you. If you just come with me we'll bring you to Etta."

At the sound of Etta's name, Ruth whimpered as if Nathan had struck her, causing Nathan to tear at his hair and look wildly around the room. When his gaze lit on me he flung his arms up and rushed to the window.

"Thank the Bells!" he cried, helping me into the room. "I thought she would start screaming any minute. She's acting like I'm trying to murder her every time I mention Etta."

Ruth whimpered and cringed as if she had been struck. I took a step toward her, holding my hands out, palms up, as if I were approaching a bating hawk.

"It's all right, Ruth. I'm a friend of Etta's. We worked together at the Triangle factory. My name's Ava. Maybe she mentioned me?"

Ruth only whimpered and slid down the wall with her arms clasped around her knees, trying to make herself small. She stared at me out of eyes so wide and glassy I could see my reflection in them . . . only it wasn't my image. Taking a cautious step forward I knelt down and stared into her eyes. Where my reflection should have been was a ghoul—decaying skin hanging over a hollow-eyed skull. When I opened my mouth smoke poured out.

No wonder Ruth was terrified.

"She's been hypnotized to see us as monsters," I told Nathan, who'd knelt beside me. A twin horror leapt into Ruth's vision: Nathan as he might appear three months dead with worms crawling out of his empty eye sockets.

"She seemed to think I looked all right before. It was only when I mentioned Etta—"

Ruth whimpered and Nathan's reflection bared yellow fangs and spat with a forked tongue.

"Et—her sister's name must be a trigger of some sort to prevent anyone trying to lure her away by promising to return her to her family."

"What a nasty trick," Nathan said with a grimace of disgust.

"That's how van Drood operates," I said, recalling the images of my mother van Drood had shown me in the Hall of Mirrors. "He takes what's most precious to you and makes it horrible."

"Can she be cured?"

"I broke van Drood's spell by using my bells." I took out the repeater from underneath my shirtwaist. "I'm not sure if it will work with her."

I was about to press the watch stem, but Nathan stayed my hand. "Shh. Do you hear that?"

I'd been so intent on Ruth that I'd forgotten to listen with my inner ear, but when I focused now I heard a voice in the hall. "Madame LeFevre says to get all the clients out in case that harridan outside draws the coppers."

"We don't have much time," I said. "We have to hurry."

I pushed the stem of the watch, holding it close to Ruth so the sound wouldn't be heard outside in the hall. She cringed when I got close to her, but when the repeater began playing, her face relaxed and she fastened her eyes on the tiny figures hitting the bells. The watch played a tune I'd never heard before but that reminded me of the folk songs I sometimes heard the Jewish women singing at Henry Street. Ruth's eyes filled with tears that washed away the ghoulish images.

"I think she'll come with us now."

A loud rap on the door startled me so badly I nearly dropped the watch.

"Time's up, boy-o," a loud, gruff voice announced. "Less you wanna end up spending the night in the Tombs."

I nudged Nathan to respond.

"I say, old sport, it's not cricket to rush a fellow. Give me a minute to . . ." Nathan's face turned beet red. "Er, say my fare-wells."

Raucous laughter greeted his remark. "Kiss the girl good-night and be off with you!"

"Keep talking!" I whispered, getting Ruth to her feet and steering her to the window. As long as she looked at the watch she moved docilely. I helped her out onto the fire escape while Nathan declaimed love poetry to the amusement of the men in the hallway. With one hand holding the watch in front of Ruth and the other on her back I managed to lead her up the shaking fire escape. Miss Corey was there to help us onto the roof.

"Thank the Bells! I think the police are on the way. I'll go signal Vi that we've got Ruth while you get her to the next rooftop."

I led Ruth to the roof of a neighboring tenement, down its stairs, and out the back door to a side street where Agnes, Sam

Greenfeder and Kid Marvel were waiting in a car. As soon as we were inside, Sam peeled away from the curb. I kept Ruth's eyes focused on the repeater while Sam navigated the crowded streets of the waterfront to get us back to Henry Street Settlement House.

I was beginning to wonder if there was any way to break the spell for good when the door to the house opened and Etta burst out crying Ruth's name. The minute Ruth heard her sister's voice she looked up from the watch. Would she see a monster when she looked at Etta? I wished I had been able to prepare Etta. No one wanted to be looked upon as a monster, especially by her own sister.

But then Ruth was rushing into Etta's arms and bursting into tears. The spell was broken.

10

WE ALL GATHERED in the downstairs parlor. Agnes went to the kitchen to find Helen, who'd used her time waiting for us to prepare an elaborate tea, while Omar examined Ruth for aftereffects of the hypnotism she had been under. Miss Corey paced nervously until Miss Sharp and Mr. Bellows appeared, laughing at the parts they had played and reprising bits from their roles. Miss Corey paled and turned away, excusing herself to help Agnes with the tea. Kid Marvel congratulated everyone on a con "well played" and Sam asked for details of what cons he'd played in the past. The drab little parlor with its union meeting notices and worn copies of *Girl's Life* and *The United Worker* was suddenly filled with a gaiety more buoyant than the Montmorencys' ball. There was one figure, though, that hovered on the periphery in the shadowy hallway: the changeling. I left the warm circle and went to stand beside her.

"I only came to bring Etta," she said quickly. "I didn't want her walking here alone. But I see I can leave her now. I suppose I'd better before your Miss Corey decides to kill me." She had tied a scarf over her head to hide her features, but I could make out her red swollen eyes.

"Where will you go?" I asked.

"Back to the Blythe Wood. I'll be absorbed back into the forest, into the bark and moss and ferns. Once we're set loose from our human hosts we revert back to our natural state. See, it's already happening."

She looked down at her hand, which was resting on a wooden table. I followed her gaze. Her hand was turning the color and texture of the wood. It was nearly invisible.

"Is that why I've never seen your kind in the woods?" I asked. "Because you're . . ."

"Camouflaged? Yes. Without the human spark we merge with the elements. It's not so bad, really, only . . ." Her voice hitched in her throat. "I think it will take me a long time to forget Etta."

I reached out to touch her hand, but she snatched it away. "No, Ava, I don't want to steal your memories. But will you do me one favor?"

I nodded.

"Will you come to the woods and talk of Etta sometimes? Don't worry if you don't see me—I'll hear you. It will make me feel I belong to something, the way you belong with your friends."

I began to tell her that I wasn't so sure I belonged anywhere, but she held up her hand to stop me. "You *do* belong, Ava. I can feel it. Will you promise to come to the woods and talk to me?"

"I will," I agreed, wishing I could touch her or offer her some comfort.

"Thank you," she said with a sigh that already sounded like wind moving through trees. "Now go back. I'm only going to watch a moment longer before I leave."

I left her standing in the shadows and went to join the warm circle in the parlor. Would I, too, be an outcast once I became a full-fledged Darkling? The circle, though, had become heated rather than warm.

"It's no use," Ruth was arguing. "I can't stay. Madame Le-Fevre told me that if I ever ran away they would find Etta and take her instead."

"They made you think that through hypnotism," Miss Sharp said. "It was how they controlled you."

"That may be, but I know it even now when you've broken my trance."

"She's right," Omar said. "She's no longer under their control. They used her love for her sister as a means to control her, but there's no reason to believe the threat isn't real. Once a man—or woman—is taken over by the shadows, they have no conscience. They are capable of unspeakable atrocities." The grimness of his face suggested he had seen some of those horrors.

"Then we'll hide Etta," Sam Greenfeder said. "I've done it before with witnesses. We can get police protection."

"Because that worked so well for Herman Rosenthal," Kid Marvel said sarcastically. Just last month a man named Herman Rosenthal had been gunned down because he had agreed to testify that Police Lieutenant Charles Becker was extorting protection money from gangsters. The case was in all the papers.

"Then we won't use the police," Miss Sharp said. "The Order will clean out the Hellgate Club."

"Yeah, like the ding-dongs care what happens to a bunch of street girls and madges," Kid Marvel said, sneering.

Miss Sharp bristled. "They certainly will take an interest in a club run by the Shadow Master."

"Some of them girls they've taken ain't exactly human," Kid Marvel said. "Your ding-dongs'll blunder in and round 'em all up together and kill the madges, but the humbug will be long gone before youse bell ringers set foot on the doorstep. They'll just set up shop somewhere else."

"I'm afraid he has a point," Mr. Bellows conceded, looking sheepishly at Miss Sharp. "I did a year on Underworld Operations for the Order and I'm afraid we were less than, er, effective."

"All's your informants got dead," Kid Marvel remarked.

Ruth turned pale and squeezed Etta's hand.

"We can't just leave those girls at the Hellgate Club after—" I'd been about to say "after what I saw in Molly's dying moments," but of course I couldn't say that without revealing I was a Darkling. "After what we know about what goes on there."

"But that's just it," Omar said. "We don't really know what's going on there. If the Order, or even my associates, storm in to rescue those girls, the shadows will just hunt them down again—and their families."

"That's why I must go back," Ruth said, letting go of Etta's hand and standing up.

"*No!*"

The voice came from outside the circle. We all turned. The changeling stood in the doorway, her shawl fallen from her face. Ruth gasped as she recognized her own features. The changeling was staring back at her.

"Ruth is right," she said. "The Shadow Master will stop at nothing to fulfill his threat. If Ruth is discovered missing from the Hellgate Club they'll come for Etta. They'll track her down wherever you hide her and take her as a replacement for her sister."

Miss Corey spoke up, her eyes fastened on the changeling. "She's only saying that so Ruth will go back to the Hellgate Club and she can continue living Ruth's life."

"No," the changeling said, staring back at Miss Corey. "I'm saying it so you'll all see what must be done. Isn't it obvious? I'll go back to the Hellgate Club in Ruth's place."

Of course we all argued with her, Miss Sharp most vehemently.

"We can't possibly let you do it. It would be like . . . well . . ." She looked nervously at me and Helen.

"Acting as her procurer?" Nathan suggested. "Or as they say in the streets—"

"Actually," Ruth said, glancing at Nathan and blushing. "That's not what we were there for. We were supposed to talk to the men and make them feel special. Madame LeFevre said most of them just wanted someone to listen to them. That their wives didn't care about what they did all day and that we should ask them questions."

"What sort of questions?" Sam Greenfeder asked.

"Oh, about how their day was, what was new at their office, had they made any interesting investments if they were stock traders, or how a certain trial was going if they were judges—"

"Judges!" Sam repeated, the tips of his ears quivering with indignation. The idea that a judge might even *visit* a place like the Hellgate Club—let alone discuss his cases there—clearly made him livid.

"Do you know which judges?" he barked. "And which cases?"

Ruth shook her head, her eyes filling with tears. Etta moved protectively in front of her and clutched her hand.

"I can't remember. After the men left, Madame LeFevre would come in and ask me to tell her everything we had talked about. After, it was like I had emptied it all out of my brain. I'd feel drained"—she choked back a sob—"like a tin of beans that's been scraped and tossed on the garbage heap."

"Those scoundrels!" Agnes cried. "To use poor innocent girls like that!"

"They *were* used," Omar said. "They were compelled with an eidetic spell so that they would recall everything they heard but forget it once they relayed the information."

"So they're using the girls to collect information from powerful men," Mr. Bellows said. "But to what end? What are they up to?"

"The *pishaca* is gathering his forces," Omar said. "I have heard from others like myself that they have been approached by shadow creatures and induced to take sides with them against the Order."

"Well, I certainly hope they refused!" Mr. Bellows said. "Surely your friends know how evil the *tenebrae* are."

"My friends," Omar replied, looking down from his great height at Mr. Bellows, "have suffered at the hands of your Order. My dear friend Zao Shen watched his people become addicted to opium brought to his country by your Order. My Irish friends taught your Order the magic of the little people, but when they asked your Order for help during the Great Hunger, they were told the Order could 'not interfere.' My Voudon friend Shango was sold into slavery—"

"Now wait just a minute," Miss Corey interjected. "We of the Order were abolitionists. We fought to free the slaves."

Omar bowed his head to Miss Sharp. "That is true, my lady. Many of you have done good in this world, but not enough good. Yes, you were abolitionists, but are there any Negro students or teachers at Blythewood? Or even any of the Jewish faith?" He bowed to Etta and Ruth.

I mentally searched through the rolls of Blythewood, but Helen got there before me.

"Madame Musette has that funny little whatsit on her doorframe."

"A mezuzah," Omar said. "Yes, Irena Musette is Jewish. And you'll notice that she's never been invited to teach at the school. As you can see, the Order makes use of madges, but keeps us on the sidelines—or worse."

"Yeah, at least the ding-dongs don't hunt you down and kill you like they do to my folk," Kid Marvel said. "They call us *freaks*. Could you blame my kind if we joined the other side? Not that I'd go over to the shades. And I tells my crew to stay away, but they don't all listen."

"I, too, have certainly urged my associates to resist the persuasion of the *tenebrae*," Omar said, "but they offer powerful inducements, and where those fail they make threats that are difficult for even the most valiant to resist. A small group of us have banded together to resist the *tenebrae* and protect our own kind, but we do not have the resources of the Order."

"Well, then," began Miss Sharp, "we'll go to the Council and tell them of this threat—"

"What threat?" Mr. Bellows asked. "All we have is the word of one girl who's been mesmerized and whose memories have been tampered with. Without more information the Council will just as likely think that the Hellgate Club is run by fairies."

"If only Ruth could remember more details," Miss Corey lamented.

"*I* could."

We all turned to the changeling. Her eyes burned fiercely. She no longer looked like she was fading into the woodwork. "Changelings can't be hypnotized or enspelled. And we remember everything. If I take Ruth's place I'll be protecting Etta *and* I can report back to you what I learn at the Hellgate Club."

"It would be very dangerous," Miss Sharp said.

"I want to do it," the changeling said, gazing fondly at the two sisters. "For Etta and for Ruth. At least then when I fade back into the Blythe Wood I'll know I had purpose in this life. I'll know I was part of something."

"But if the changeling takes Ruth's place," Helen asked, "where will the real Ruth go?"

"Ruth can stay at my aunts' house in Rhinebeck," Miss Sharp said. "And Etta . . ." She held out her hand to Etta. "Etta has powers that need to be trained. No matter what you all think of the Order, they *are* good at that. She'll apply to Blythewood. We don't have to tell Dame Beckwith or the Council about the Hellgate Club until we know more. We'll just say we discovered Etta's powers on a home visit to her tenement. And if they object on account of her religion I personally will resign from my post at Blythewood."

"As will I!" Miss Corey said.

Miss Sharp beamed at her friend and then looked at Etta. "What do you say, Etta?"

Etta looked uncertainly at me. "Will you be there, Avaleh?"

I hesitated. For the first time I realized I'd been considering not going back to Blythewood in the fall—and all I'd just learned about the Order didn't encourage me. I was one of the "freaks" that Kid Marvel said the Order killed. How long could I keep that secret?

But here was Etta looking up at me trustingly. True, she could go stay at Violet House with her sister, but then what? Back to working at sweatshops? Keeping what she saw a secret her whole life? Blythewood would train her to use her powers and give her a chance to make something of herself, and she'd be safe there until we found out what van Drood was up to at the Hellgate Club. I owed it to the girls there—all the girls like Ruth and Molly—to stay put at Blythewood until I found a way to help them.

"Yes," I told Etta, "I'll be there with you."

11

"ARE WE REALLY getting on this big train, Avaleh? I've never been on one before."

I gaped open-mouthed at Etta as porters and passengers bumped into us on the crowded platform. Over the last two weeks, Etta had surprised us all. First, she had passed her entrance exams with flying colors. Although she had been pulled out of school at an early age to go to work in the factories, she had spent all her free time at the Seward Park library reading books and teaching herself Latin, which she claimed was much easier than Hebrew. Then she surprised us even more by asking if there would be any strange creatures at Blythewood, like Mr. O'Malley at the tavern, who had pointed ears and cloven hoofs, or Mrs. Golub from across the way, who had sharp teeth and a bone leg.

"The girl's a fianais," Miss Corey had declared one afternoon while we were prepping Etta for her exams.

"Yes," Miss Sharp concurred. Then she had explained to me. "It means a witness. A fianais can recognize the true nature of any being no matter how they are disguised. Let me guess," she said gently to Etta, "you only started seeing these creatures recently, say, when you started your monthly courses."

Etta blushed and nodded.

"A fianais comes into her ability at puberty. That's how you knew Ruth had been replaced by a changeling," she said, turning back to Etta. "And yes, you will encounter other creatures like Mr. O'Malley, whom I suspect is a cluricaune, and Mrs. Golub, who is most likely a Baba Yaga—"

"Vi!" Miss Corey cried. "She's not supposed to know all that until the initiation!"

"I don't think we can keep it from her any longer, Lillian. She sees we're keeping secrets from her, and it's just making her more nervous."

So Miss Sharp had explained that there was a portal to Faerie in the Blythe Wood and that creatures from there sometimes strayed out—fearsome creatures such as trolls, goblins, and ice giants, but also the benign lampsprites and mischievous boggles (although Miss Sharp and Miss Corey had a heated argument about how benign boggles were).

"The Council will be sure to let Etta into Blythewood," Miss Sharp said when she was done. "A fianais is invaluable to the Order. We haven't had one in ages. Who knows what creatures have infiltrated our own ranks?"

I recalled what Omar and Kid Marvel had said about fairies and other magical beings hiding in plain sight in the city—*madges*. And I also remembered Omar's story of how the Order exploited his magical abilities and those of others like him. Were we doing the right thing taking Etta to Blythewood? She looked worried—but not, as it turned out, for herself.

"What will you do with them once you find them?" she asked, her eyes avoiding mine.

"Destroy them, of course," Miss Corey said briskly, slapping her notebook shut.

"*Kill* them?" Etta asked. "But what if they're harmless? Mrs. Golub is certainly up to no good, but Mr. O'Malley wouldn't harm anyone."

"If Mr. O'Malley really hasn't harmed anyone, he'd only be banished back to the Blythe Wood and Faerie," Miss Sharp said more gently. "We've learned that some of the creatures of Faerie—like the lampsprites—are genuinely harmless. We're changing our ways at Blythewood. You needn't worry, Etta; you won't be asked to bring harm to any creature that isn't a danger."

"Good," Etta said. "I would never expose someone with a good heart to harm just because they were a little bit . . . different." I suspected she knew what I was, but we never spoke of it, and I believed that she would never tell anyone what I was. But sooner or later I would have to tell someone at Blythewood before they discovered my secret. Hopefully, the Order would choose merely to banish me rather than kill me.

In the meantime, I owed it to Etta to stay at Blythewood until she was settled and out of danger. I think she clung to me because I'd come from the same place as her—the crowded tenements, the sweatshops, the Triangle factory. I remembered how afraid I'd been last year that the Blythewood girls would disdain me if they knew of my lowly origins. How silly that fear seemed now that I had a much bigger secret lurking beneath my tightly laced corset!

But I also remembered that I'd been as shocked by the trappings of genteel life—the clothes, the manners, the big houses—as by the revelation that there was magic in the world. So when

Etta looked more amazed at the size of the train we were boarding than the fact we were on our way to a school that taught magic, I replied, "Yes! And look, here's Helen. She's not used to taking the train either." That was clear from the number of bags Helen was struggling with. Last year Helen had been driven to school in a chauffeured Rolls-Royce, but of course she couldn't afford that now.

"I'll help her with her luggage while you get us seats on the left side so you can see the river," I told Etta. "It's a lovely view!"

Reassured by my enthusiasm, Etta eagerly dashed into the car, dodging around a group of girls standing in the doorway. I stepped forward to unburden Helen of a large portmanteau and a hatbox.

"I thought you were going to miss the train," I said. "What happened?"

"That ridiculous cab driver made such a fuss about my luggage. The man actually had the gall to suggest I might not *need* so many clothes. Can you imagine? Paulson would never have dared to comment on my wardrobe!"

If someone had reined in Helen's and her mother's clothing allowance, I thought, perhaps they wouldn't have had to let their chauffeur go. To Helen I only said, "Well, I'm glad you made it. Etta's very nervous and I think we need to do everything we can to reassure her—" At just that moment I heard Etta's clear, sharp voice calling our names from inside the train.

"Avaleh! Helena! Come quickly, I've got us seats on the river side!"

"I *told* you the left side was the most desirable," one of the girls blocking the doorway drawled in a Southern accent as we tried to edge around her. "My cousin Georgiana said that if we must take the train we ought to sit on the left. Now that *child*"— she glanced disdainfully at Etta, her pale blue eyes lingering on her plain homespun skirt and scuffed shoes—"has gone and taken the last seat on the river side, and she's not even a Blythewood girl."

"Why don't you think she's a Blythewood girl?" I asked as I attempted to duck under the wide brims of the girls' hats. They were all covered with feathers; the one belonging to the Southern girl sported an entire dead pheasant. She turned on me, still blocking our way, and replied, "Why, she's far too young, bless her little heart."

"I'm fifteen," Etta announced. "I'm just small for my age."

"*And*," Dead Pheasant Girl continued, "she's hardly attired like a Blythewood girl."

"Neither are you," Helen observed, staring pointedly at the mounds of lace around the girl's high collar, her pinched-in waist, hobbled skirt, and thin-soled slippers. "You'll never be able to draw a bow with all those ruffles in your way, and you'll faint from lack of oxygen the first time you try to ring the bells in that corset. Never mind what the falcons will do to that bird on your hat. You'll be lucky to get through the front door without Blodeuwedd plucking you bald."

Dead Pheasant Girl had been growing pink as Helen spoke, while her two friends stared at me as if I had sprouted wings, which I might at any moment do if the girls didn't get out of our way.

"Are you a senior then?" a snub-nosed short brunette asked, her black button eyes going wide.

"Oh," I demurred, embarrassed that I'd been lording it over a group of new girls. "No, I'm a fledgling, that's a—"

"Second year!" the third girl, tall and thin with glasses, shouted out. "I've been studying the handbook."

"Well then," Helen said. "You should know that mere nestlings should defer to fledglings. Please step aside so we can join our friend."

"I don't recall any such rule from the handbook," the studious girl remarked.

"Handbook?" Etta yelped. "I didn't know there was a handbook. There's plenty of room in the seats facing us. Why don't you join us and we can all look at it together?"

"But then we'd be facing backward," Dead Pheasant Girl replied. "I simply can't ride backward; it gives me the vapors."

"Well, I can," the black-eyed girl piped up, cramming into the seat facing Etta. "I've never had the vapors a day in my life."

"Nor I," the studious girl remarked, slipping into the other rear-facing seat. "Although I think you may actually mean vertigo if you're referring to the dizziness caused by the rearward motion of the train."

"I can squeeze in with them because I'm so small," Etta said with a mischievous smile for Dead Pheasant Girl, "and you can sit with Ava and Helen. *Nu*, then we will all be Blythewood girls together!"

Etta hadn't even gotten to Blythewood yet and already she was making friends.

Helen looked at Dead Pheasant Girl as if she would like to pluck every feather off her hat. But with all the grace that decades of Old New York breeding had instilled in her, she simply said, "Would you care to join us? I'm sure we'll all benefit from each other's company."

Unsurprisingly, Dead Pheasant Girl turned out to be a Montmorency—Myrtilene Montmorency of the Savannah Montmorencys, who I gathered from all of Myrtilene's attempts to establish otherwise were rather the poorer side of the family.

"Our plantation was the finest in Georgia—that is, until the Yankees burned it to the ground during the War of Northern Aggression, of course," Myrtilene confided to us.

"You mean the Civil War?" I asked with a strained smile. "The one the South started by seceding? And that ultimately freed the slaves?"

"Is that what they teach y'all at Blythewood?" Myrtilene asked.

Actually, I wanted to say, *what they teach at Blythewood is that slavery was an evil institution instigated by trows and that the Order, vehement abolitionists, fought alongside the North to set things to right.* I recalled, though, what Omar had said to Miss Sharp. Yes, the Order had fought to free the slaves, but there were no Negro students at Blythewood.

Besides, Myrtilene Montmorency, black-eyed Mary Mac-Crae, and studious Susannah Dewsnap wouldn't know about the magical side of Blythewood until the first night's initiation. I'd thought it might be hard for Etta to keep her own knowledge a secret, but she didn't seem to be having any trouble. She appeared far more interested in the everyday lives of her new friends than in the dark secrets she'd been made privy to these last few weeks.

Mary and Susannah, in turn, chatted amiably with Etta and peppered Helen and me with questions about the school.

"Do they have dances at Blythewood?" Mary asked. "I love to dance. I came up weeks early to attend Miss Montmorency's ball and was just dazzled by the new steps."

"That's thanks to the new dancing master Uncle George hired for Georgiana's ball," Myrtilene remarked. "Herr Hofmeister. I understand he's from Vienna. Georgiana has asked Uncle George to have Blythewood hire him."

"Madame Musette was good enough for generations of Blythewood girls," Helen said with a sniff.

I bit back a laugh, recalling how Helen had rolled her eyes at Madame Musette's old-fashioned ways, but was touched by her loyalty to the ancient dancing teacher.

"We've never had a dancing master at Blythewood before," I added. "It's not . . ." I caught myself before saying it wasn't part of the *old ways*. Since when had I become a defender of Blythewood traditions? Those *old ways* had exploited Omar and his kind and would probably get me kicked out.

"I declare! How do y'all prepare for your cotillions, then?" Myrtilene asked with a shake of her head that made the pheasant on top of her hat look like it wanted to take flight.

"I don't know how to dance," Etta said, her brow creasing. "Except for some folk dances I learned in the settlement house."

"Don't worry," I assured Etta. "There are more important things to learn at Blythewood than how to do the latest quadrille." But as I looked at Myrtilene preening at her reflection in the window I wondered if I knew Blythewood as well as I thought I did. Perhaps it really belonged to these new girls more than it did to me.

Any melancholy I felt on the journey, though, was dispelled by the sight of Gilles Duffy.

"Gillie!" I shouted, throwing my arms around the tiny elf-like man.

"Mmph," he said, squeezing me in a surprisingly strong grip and then holding me out at arm's length. "Let me have a look at ye, lass. Aye, you've come out of the fire right as rain." Within the black depths of his eyes I saw a flash of green and felt the air on the riverside platform stir with the scent of the woodland. "But I knew ye would. You're your mother's daughter, all right."

My eyes filled up with tears at the mention of my mother, and I felt a small hand slip into my right hand and the touch of another hand on my left arm. Helen and Etta had come to stand on either side of me.

"Hello, Gillie," Helen said. "You're looking well."

"And you, too, Miss," he said, doffing his shapeless tweed hat. Somehow he managed to convey in those few words his sympathy for Helen's recent loss of her father without embarrassing her with mention of it. Then he turned to look at Etta. "And who's this wee lass?"

"This is Etta," I told him. "We were at the Triangle factory together, and Miss Sharp and Miss Corey discovered she's a . . ."

"Fianais," Gillie said, his eyes flashing a violent shade of acid green. The gentle woodland breeze turned into a stiff gale. "Aye, I can see that."

I looked down at Etta and saw that she was staring wide-eyed at Gillie. Hell's Bells! I'd only discovered by chance last year that Gillie wasn't entirely human. He was a Ghillie Dhu, a sort of woodland elf that protected the creatures of the woods, rescued lost girls, and, I'd begun to suspect, controlled the weather. He'd told me that Dame Beckwith knew what he was, but I didn't think the rest of the Order did.

The other girls—Myrtilene with her nose in the air, Susannah and Mary struggling to keep up with all their bags and hatboxes (and Myrtilene's, too, I suspected)—were approaching, looking curiously between Gillie and ourselves. Would Etta give Gillie's identity away?

"Is this the valet?" Myrtilene sniffed. "Why, he'd have to stand up twice to cast a shadow!"

A sudden gust blew Myrtilene's hat clear off her head and sent it, dead pheasant and all, soaring over the river, which had become suddenly choppy as the ocean.

"He's not a valet," Etta declared. "He's a"—I tried to catch her eye, but she went on—"caretaker."

She invested the word with a significance that went far beyond a job title. Gillie's eyes simmered a mellow green. "Aye, lass, that's what I am and I'm proud of it. I promise to take good care of ye and keep ye from all harm."

Etta had given him his proper name, but without revealing his magical nature to the other girls—certainly not to Myrtilene, who, having given up on retrieving her hat from the river, gave Gillie a dismissive glance and addressed a point a few inches above his head.

"I'm pleased as punch y'all are getting reacquainted, but are you fixing to load up our baggage?"

Gillie looked at Myrtilene as though he'd like to chuck her many bags into the river along with her, but instead he hauled one of Helen's trunks onto his shoulder.

"I'll come back for yers," he said to Myrtilene. "You can wait here with it or come up to the coach. Only . . ." He eyed the river. Although the day was bright and clear, fog was gathering over the water, creeping toward the shore. A fog that hadn't been there before and that I was pretty sure was of Gillie's making. "I wouldna tarry too long beside the water. Ye never know what might be lurkin' in the fog." He gave me a wink as he passed by me. "Or what might come out of it."

12

BY THE TIME Gillie had carried all our trunks up to the top of the station the fog had dissipated and it was once again a fine, clear day. So fine that Gillie had brought the open-air trap instead of the gloomy coach I'd ridden in last year. Etta sat in the back with her new friends Susannah and Mary, chattering as cheerily as the birds flitting through the sycamores above our heads.

"She certainly has adapted quickly," Helen said quietly. I thought I detected a slight tone of resentment in her voice. Helen, after all, had had to adapt to quite a lot in the last few months.

"I think it's part of being a fianais," I whispered back. I glanced anxiously at Myrtilene sitting on the other side of Helen to make sure she wasn't listening, but she was busy trying to pin a new hat on her head—this one festooned with artificial cherries and a dead sparrow—so I went on. "Part of being a witness makes her very sensitive to other people and gives her the ability to ask people just the right questions to open them up."

"Hmph," Helen sniffed. "Where I come from we call that the art of polite conversation . . . although I suppose Etta didn't learn that on the Lower East Side. I'm glad she's making friends," she added grudgingly. "We won't have to worry about her."

"We still need to keep an eye on her to make sure she's safe. If van Drood realizes at any point that the changeling has taken Ruth's place he'll come looking for Ruth and Etta."

"We'd know if that had happened, though. Mr. Marvel and Mr. Omar will be watching the Hellgate Club, and Mr. Greenfeder has promised to bring in his friends at the police force if he thinks anything has gone amiss."

"I still wish we could have done something for those girls," I said.

Helen sniffed. "You can't go around saving everyone. Most of those girls are there because they made the wrong choices."

"How can you say that, Helen? Ruth was kidnapped!"

"She wouldn't have been kidnapped if she hadn't been meeting a man she hardly knew at Coney Island. Honestly, I think it's appalling how girls act these days—even Blythewood girls. Look at this new crop with their newfangled dances. Do you know that there's one called the Turkey Trot? I heard that some young women were fired from their jobs for doing it on their lunch hour. Imagine going around acting like a bird in public!"

"Helen, we go to a school that trains us to hunt like falcons." I shifted uncomfortably to ease the ache in my shoulder blades. "Innocent young girls are being kidnapped from the streets of New York and being held against their will in places like the Hellgate Club. Kid Marvel says there are magical beings hiding all over the city, and Omar told us that the Order has been exploiting people like him for centuries. But you're affronted by a dance called the Turkey Trot?"

"It sounds undignified," she replied, ignoring all my other points. "And I don't like these new girls coming in and changing things before they even know what it means to be a Blythewood girl. I don't like—"

"Change?" I asked more gently, slipping my hand over hers. Helen's home life had changed beyond recognition. Of course she wanted Blythewood to stay the same.

"No." Helen sighed, squeezing my hand. "I expect I don't. Ah, but look, we're almost there."

We'd passed through the tall iron gates inscribed with the motto *Tintinna Vere, Specta Alte*—Ring true, aim high—and were climbing the hill. As we did, the bells began to toll, ringing us home. I saw Helen's face rinsed clean of all the worries and fears of the last few months. Etta, Susannah, and Mary fell silent to listen. Even Myrtilene stopped fussing with her hat and stretched her long neck to catch the first glimpse of Blythewood as we crested the hill.

There it was! As magical as I'd remembered, the worn centuries-old stone glowing gold in the bright sunshine, the bell tower rising against the blue mountains in the distance like a proud battlement standing guard over the valley. The solid castle walls radiated safety and protection just as the bells spoke of home, but the bells evoked something else in me. They seemed to vibrate in my blood. While I felt the longing for Blythewood that the bells were meant to engender in all of our Order, also it came with an unbearable sadness.

Raven had once told me that the bells of Blythewood

aroused a sorrow in the Darklings for all they had lost. I felt that sorrow now. It felt like being *cast out*. And I knew that if I were unveiled as a Darkling and sent away from Blythewood I'd feel this sorrow every day of my life. It was the sorrow my mother had felt, I saw now, that had compelled her to keep an engraving of the castle on her bedside table.

I looked away from the castle and caught Etta's eyes fastened on me. They were wide and brimming with tears. What a burden it must be to feel so deeply what others felt! I gave her a brave smile, hoping to spare her my pain and she, not fooled at all, said, "You will be all right, Avaleh, I promise."

"Of course Ava will be all right," Helen said. "We're back at Blythewood, where nothing has changed in centuries. Look, there's Daisy! She's gotten here early to get us a good room."

I doubted that had been Daisy's sole purpose in coming early. She was wearing a sash—the mark of a warden—and I recalled that she'd said in one of her rare, brief letters that she would be taking a job this term. It was usually something scholarship girls did, and I wondered if Daisy's father, a prosperous Kansas City merchant, had suffered a reversal in fortune. Whatever her motive, it was delightful to see Daisy standing in the thick of the arriving girls, making order out of chaos. In just the time it took us to reach the circular driveway I saw her order Georgiana to remove her luggage from the front steps, tell a chauffeur to move his Rolls-Royce, and rescue a new girl's hat from being plucked from her head by an escaped falcon.

"I see one of the Dianas has lost her falcon already," I said, recalling that the Dianas came early to school and spent their first three days and nights "waking" their birds to train them.

"Is that a new falcon?" I asked, admiring the elegant white hunting bird. "I don't remember it from last year."

"That'll be Georgiana Montmorency's gyrfalcon," Gillie, who'd come around to help us out of the trap, said. "Mr. Montmorency bought special a pair of fine gyrfalcons for her and Miss Driscoll. They're both Dianas this year." From his tone, it was clear how he felt about Georgiana and Alfreda being selected—a choice that doubtless had more to do with their fathers' donations to the school than their talent as huntresses.

"Of course Georgiana's a Diana," Myrtilene said as she edged in front of everyone to be the first to disembark. "We Montmorencys are born sportswomen and natural leaders. Why, I've been riding to the hounds since—"

Myrtilene's discourse on Montmorency excellence was cut short by Georgiana's falcon diving straight at her head and plucking the dead sparrow from her hat.

"I told you to control that bird," Daisy scolded as she came toward the trap, but when she saw Helen and me she threw up her hands and called our names. Helen pushed past the affronted Myrtilene and dove into Daisy's open arms, pulling me with her. I was surprised at how strong Daisy's arms were—and at how good it felt to be enclosed within them. Maybe Etta was right; I *would* be all right here.

"I thought you two would never get here!" Daisy cried, stepping back to look at us. "I've got so much to tell you!"

"You can start by telling us why you're a warden," Helen said. "I know it's not because you're on scholarship. Didn't your father just open up a new store in Saint Louis?"

"Really?" I asked, sounding peevish to my own ears. "Why didn't you write and tell me that?"

"Why, I didn't think it was the sort of thing you'd be interested in," Daisy replied simply. "But Helen kept writing and asking me questions—"

"I was raised to show a polite interest in my friends' affairs," Helen interrupted. "As I am doing now by inquiring why you have become a warden. Is it because they've substituted this attractive purple-and-green sash for that hideous plaid one?"

I noticed now that the sash Daisy wore wasn't the same as the one Sarah Lehman had worn last year. Daisy's had some sort of motto on it as well that did not appear to be the school's motto.

"Don't be ridiculous." Daisy laughed. "It's purple and green because those are the colors of the suffragist movement. I've spent the summer campaigning for women's votes. The Kansas legislature is voting on the referendum in November. I really ought to be home in Kansas picketing, but Dame Beckwith convinced me that I could do more good here—and she let me switch the warden sash for a 'Votes for Women' one. Here—" She dug into her pocket and handed me and Helen each a tin badge with the "Votes for Women" slogan and green-and-violet ribbons. "You can wear them with your sashes."

"What do you mean *our* sashes?" Helen asked, her voice suddenly icy.

"Oh, didn't I say? I suggested to Dame Beckwith that she make you both wardens, too. I thought it would help with Helen's . . . er . . ." she cupped her hand around her mouth and stage whispered, "*tuition expenses.* You'll even be paid a stipend that you can use for pocket money. Mr. Appleby and I agree that a woman should make her own money and be independent—"

"How very thoughtful of you, Daisy," Helen, who had been turning nearly the same violet shade as her new badge throughout Daisy's speech, interrupted in a sugary voice, "to remember me in my impoverished state. But why, pray tell, have you volunteered Ava? She's still rich."

"Oh," Daisy beamed, "that's the best part. Since we're all wardens we get our first pick of rooms on any floor. I chose our old room for us. I thought you'd like that, Helen. What will all the other . . . er . . . alterations you've had to endure."

For a moment I thought Helen might throttle Daisy, but instead she crushed her to her bosom and, eyes shining, said, "That's perfect, Daze. That's exactly what I need."

In the next few hours I saw how right Daisy had been to get us our old room back. It was true that Blythewood had not changed for centuries. The very castle had been brought stone by stone from the Order's first abbey in Scotland; the men's monastery was still there serving as our brother school, Hawthorn. The events of last spring, though—the shadow demons' attack on the castle and the return of the long-lost Sir Miles Malmsbury and Nathan's sister from Faerie—had jarred the school off-kilter, as if one of the ancient cornerstones had been yanked out of its foundations. Daisy filled us in as we made our way up to the fourth floor of the South Wing.

"First of all, Sir Miles and Miss Frost got married."

"No!" Helen cried. "Do you mean to say that Euphorbia Frost is now *Lady* Malmsbury?"

"Oh no, Sir Malmsbury has renounced his title. He says that among the lychnobious people such class distinctions are considered primitive. He and Miss Frost—who has chosen to keep her maiden name in the spirit of progressivism—will be teaching a class on the tolerance and understanding of cultural differences of nonhuman species."

"That *is* a change," Helen said. "Last year she was pinning and pickling lampsprites."

"It's a good change," I added, thinking to myself that if the Order was beginning to accept the lampsprites, perhaps they would someday accept the Darklings.

"Not everyone thinks so. Miss Swift threatened to quit if she couldn't use lampsprite feathers in her arrows after Sir—I mean, Mr.—Malmsbury explained that the lampsprites consider the use of their feathers as weapons a desecration of their most sacred beliefs. The lampsprites came up with an ingenious compromise. They offered to collect stray bird feathers from the forest for Miss Swift. Featherbell came up with the idea," Daisy added proudly. Featherbell was the lampsprite Daisy had rescued last year.

"Featherbell?" Helen asked. "Are you still . . . in touch?"

It was a little hard to imagine how Daisy could have corresponded with a creature who communicated telepathically by dispersing the powder from her wings.

"I saw her as soon as I got back. She had a lot to tell me—as did I her." Helen turned bright pink. "I still haven't told you—oh, you there, new girl, you can't block the hall with those trunks. I don't care if your father owns the Knickerbocker Bank—"

We left Daisy remonstrating with a nestling who appeared

to have brought the entire contents of Ladies' Mile with her and proceeded to our old room at the end of the hall. While I was relieved to have our old room back, I saw now that the disadvantage was that we were surrounded by nestlings. Loud nestlings.

"Were we this . . . *boisterous* last year?" I asked Helen as we threaded through a clot of giggling girls.

"I have never been *boisterous*," Helen replied, scowling at a girl practicing a dance step in the middle of the hall. "I don't know what the Council was thinking this year. Clearly they've lowered their standards. And we'll have to be 'in charge' of this lot. I'm not sure I like Daisy taking the liberty of volunteering us to be wardens."

I was pretty sure that what Helen didn't like was the fact she needed the money from the job. "But don't you see," I said, "it will give us the perfect opportunity to keep an eye on Etta."

As I said her name she flitted by with Mary and Susannah. "Oh, Avaleh, what a wonderful place! Daisy arranged for me to share with Mary and Susannah *and* I even have my *own* bed! Mary and Susannah are showing me the washrooms. They're indoors, on the very same floor!" She disappeared with her new roommates to discover the wonders of indoor plumbing.

"I'd say Etta doesn't need much watching over," Helen said. "Let's hope the rest of them don't. I'm not looking to be nursemaid to a bunch of nestlings. Perhaps there's an aversion spell we can cast over our door to keep them from intruding—as these girls are trying to do. That's our room," she said loudly as we came to the end of the hall and found two new girls peering inside.

"Oh, we just wanted to have a look," a girl in a pink gingham dress and matching hair ribbons said. "It's quite the best room. Do you have to be warden to get it?"

"Not at all," Helen replied haughtily. "For your information my roommates and I performed acts of valor and heroism last year, for which we were rewarded with our choice of rooms. Perhaps when you have ceased wasting your time with silly dance steps and ribbons you will someday do something worthy of such an honor. In the meantime, I suggest you change out of that ridiculous pink dress and try to comport yourself like a Blythewood girl. Now, shoo!"

Helen waved the goggle-eyed girl away and swept into our room. I hurried in behind her, giving the frightened girl an apologetic look. I was hardly in before Helen slammed the door behind her and leaned back against it as if barricading the entrance from an attacking army of goblins and trows.

"What an insufferable ninny!"

"Actually, she reminded me of Daisy last year. Remember, Helen, these girls haven't had their initiation yet. They seem frivolous and silly because they haven't learned what the world's really like. They don't know about the door to Faerie, or the frightening creatures that roam the woods, or that they will be called upon to defend the world from those creatures. Why not let them be silly for a few more hours before they have to face those horrors?"

Helen stared at me for a long moment, during which I imagined she was thinking of a different set of horrors—creditors, unpaid bills, poverty, an enforced loveless marriage.

"You're right," she said. "Let them enjoy their innocence a few more hours. But don't tell me I have to watch it."

Helen glanced around the room and sighed. "At least *this* is the same. Good old Daze, she must have spent hours setting the room up just as it was."

I looked around and saw what she meant. Helen's and Daisy's beds, on opposite sides of the long room, were made up with the same cheerful quilts we'd had last year. A tray with teapot, teacups, tea caddy, cocoa canister, and biscuit tin was laid out by the fireside where we used to have our tea and cocoa parties. Worn but comfy cushions—raided from the downstairs parlor—were strewn around the hearth.

On the mantel were framed photographs taken last year—Helen winning first prize for archery, the three of us, arms linked around one another's waists, in front of Violet House, and one of Nate clowning beside the statue of Diana in the garden, Helen in the background trying to look severe and failing. Helen paused in front of that one with a wistful look on her face. I turned away to give her privacy and carried my bag over to the chest by my bed.

My bed was on the far end of the room, fitted into an alcove below a window with a view of the river. Knowing how I liked fresh air, Daisy had left the window open. A breeze fluttered the lace curtains, letting in the scent of river water, roses from the garden, fresh grass . . . and something else. I knelt on the bed, opened the window wider, and leaned out, sniffing the air. I smelled moss and tree bark and leaf mulch, the wild cresses that grew in the secret forest springs, and the resin of pine needles. *The Blythe Wood.* I not only smelled it, I *heard* it—the wind soughing through acres of pine, the rattle of dry leaves falling from oak and maple and beech, the song of birds calling one to the other, the rustle of small creatures gathering food for winter, even the roots seeking through the soil for water. All of it calling to me, stirring the wings beneath my skin to break free and take flight . . .

"If you're not careful you're going to fall out." Helen's reproving voice called me back from the brink. I drew my head in, untangling a curtain from my hair. My hand brushed against something caught in the lace: a long black feather.

I quickly glanced in Helen's direction to see if she had noticed, but she was turned away from me, contentedly folding her chemises and corsets into a drawer, humming to herself and every so often lifting her eyes to the picture of Nathan, which she'd moved to the top of her bureau. Speared on the sharpened quill point of the feather was a piece of folded paper. I unfolded it.

Meet me tonight in the woods, it read. *There's something I must tell you.*

The note wasn't signed, but there was only one person it could be from. My heart pounding, I folded the note into a tiny square and tucked it into my skirt pocket along with the feather, where, for the rest of the afternoon as I unpacked, they rustled like trapped birds.

13

IT WAS DIFFICULT to get through the afternoon and dinner with Raven's note stirring restlessly in my pocket. What made it worse was that in our new capacity as wardens we were each expected to oversee a nestling table. I managed to get Etta's table with Mary, Susannah, Myrtilene, and two girls whose names I instantly forgot, but I would have much preferred sitting with my friends. I briefly saw Beatrice and Dolores in passing, but only long enough for Beatrice to say they had some momentous news that we'd hear at dinner and for Dolores to give me a silent, but surprisingly firm, hug. Camilla Bennett flew by me on the stairs and quite startled me by announcing she'd gotten her "wings." After a moment I realized she wasn't talking about the kind of wings I was getting. Cam was an aviation enthusiast, so she no doubt meant she had taken flying lessons.

But for now I had to answer an endless litany of questions that ranged from "Why are there so many forks?" (from Susannah) to "Is that bacon in the soup?" (from a wide-eyed Etta) to "Is this what y'all eat up here?" (from Myrtilene) to "What's this initiation all the girls are whispering about?" (from a frightened-looking Mary).

"Don't worry," I told Mary, "you'll be safe. It's just . . ." I found myself unable to finish. What else could I tell her? That everything she thought she knew about the world was about to be cracked in two? That she would be all right? Not everybody survived the initiation mentally intact. Miss Sharp's uncle Taddie had become so agitated during the initiation that he'd run off, gotten lost in the woods, and never been the same again. Some girls became hysterical and left the school. Nathan's sister, Louisa, was so haunted by what she had learned that she was drawn back into the woods and got stuck in Faerie. For all I knew there were girls who never made it back. What was I doing leading these innocent girls into danger? How different was I from van Drood abducting girls into the Hellgate Club?

"Actually, Mary—" I began.

"*Actually*, Mary," a male voice drawled, "you'll be perfectly fine because I'll be keeping an eye on you."

Nathan plucked an apple from the basket on the table, tossed it into the air, and winked at me. Mary MacCrae dimpled and blushed.

"You must be Dame Beckwith's son. We've heard all about you."

"Don't believe a word of it," Nathan said, crunching into the apple. "Rumors fly around here—actually, a lot of things do." Again he winked at me. I shifted uneasily in my seat and heard Raven's note crinkling in my pocket.

"Second years don't normally go to the initiation," I said to Nathan, more to cover up my guilty secret than because I cared about the rules.

"Spoken like a strict warden," Nathan rejoined. "But how could I resist accompanying such lovely ladies?" He gave Mary and Susannah a smile that reduced them to simpering puddles of giggles. Even Myrtilene was stretching her long neck to work her way into Nathan's field of vision. I glanced across the room to where Helen was sitting two tables away and saw her scowling in our direction. Perhaps that was the whole point of Nathan's performance—to make Helen jealous.

Or perhaps not. After a witticism that made the whole table burst into laughter Nathan bent down to retrieve a fallen napkin and whispered in my ear, "I'll be keeping an eye on you, too, Ava." Then he retreated with bows and smiles for the new girls.

"Oh, what a handsome and charming young man!" Mary MacCrae swooned with one hand pressed over her heart.

"And a very brave one," Etta said, looking up from her nearly untouched plate.

Et tu, Etta? I almost said, but then I remembered that Nathan had rescued Ruth from the Hellgate Club. Of course he was a hero to Etta—as he clearly was to the rest of the girls. I had my work cut out getting them to quiet down when the first bell rang.

"Shh . . ." I hissed, pointing to the gold handbell in the middle of our table. "One of you has to ring the bell. It's part of the tradition."

All the girls except for Myrtilene looked toward Etta, who, smiling shyly, grasped the bell in her small hand and rang it fiercely.

The Great Hall filled with the clamor of ringing bells as the teachers of Blythewood filed onto the stage. I told the girls each of their names as they appeared: Vionetta Sharp, Rupert Bellows, Euphorbia Frost followed by Miles Malmsbury, returned from Faerie—both he and Miss Frost wearing elaborate cere-monial headdresses of lampsprite feathers, which I supposed the lychnobious people did not find objectionable—Martin Peale, the bell master, Matilda Swift, the archery mistress, and Mrs. Calendar, the ancient Latin mistress. I was looking out for Professor Jager, our science teacher and Beatrice and Dolores's father, but instead a svelte gentleman in black tails, bow tie, white gloves, and spats glided onto the stage.

"Oh, look!" Mary cried. "It's Herr Hofmeister, the dancing master."

"But where's Professor Jager?" I wondered aloud.

I looked across the hall to Beatrice and Dolores's table. They were both sitting ramrod straight with their hands clasped tightly in front of them, eyes shining. Had something happened to their father? I tried to catch Helen's eyes, but she was rolling them skyward as the elegant dancing master grabbed ancient Mrs. Calendar and spun her around to the delight and amuse-ment of students and teachers alike.

I looked back to the center of the dais, where even Dame Beckwith was smiling indulgently at the dancing teacher's an-tics. She pantomimed a little applause and then turned her gaze on the room, commanding silence with her clear gray eyes. When her gaze fell on me I felt a tingling down my shoulder blades. I suddenly recalled that Dame Beckwith possessed the power of compelling truth with her gaze. What if she could tell merely by looking at me that I was turning into a Darkling? Worse, what if her gaze could draw the wings right out of my back? I could feel them pressing against the tight laces of my corset. I imagined fabric splitting, my wings exploding into the air, the shocked and horrified faces of my friends and school-mates and teachers . . . then the drawn bows of the Dianas and the lethal arrow to the heart.

But then Dame Beckwith smiled at me.

Instantly I felt a peacefulness pervade my soul. My wings subsided, my heart slowed. As she had last year, Dame Beckwith began by acknowledging those who had not returned to Blythewood. I thought of Sarah Lehman, my friend who had turned out to be a spy for van Drood and had perished in the fire during the battle with the *tenebrae*. As Dame Beckwith spoke proudly of our alumnae who'd gone into the world to spread the mission of the school to the four corners of the globe, I thought of the seniors who had graduated last year. It all sounded very inspiring, but I couldn't forget what Omar had said, that the emissaries of the Order had combed through the temples and ashrams of India looking for magical adepts to use their skills—but not to invite them into the Order.

Then I realized Dame Beckwith was talking about Professor Jager.

"...and one of our esteemed professors has also gone into the world on a mission of the utmost importance. Professor Ernst Jager"—Dame Beckwith looked toward Beatrice and Dolores, who sat up even straighter and glowed with pride—"has gone abroad on a diplomatic mission of great delicacy and international significance. It is no exaggeration to say that the very fate of civilization as we know it hangs in the balance. That is how important the Order of the Bell is. You girls are the heirs to that tradition of service. Who knows what missions each of you may be called upon to perform in the difficult times that lie ahead."

Dame Beckwith paused and allowed her gaze to travel around the room. As her gaze fell on each girl she sat a little straighter, and her eyes burned a little more fiercely. "Let us begin, then, as we do each year, by pledging ourselves to the light and pledging ourselves by the bell."

After dinner the nestlings rushed upstairs to their cocoa parties, but I stopped Etta outside the dining hall.

"You didn't eat anything," I said, looking down at her plate. "I know you're excited to be in a new place . . ." I faltered when I saw her blushing, then I blushed myself. "I am a complete idiot! Of course your family keeps kosher. I'll speak to the cook immediately—"

"It's all right, Avaleh. I spoke with my father before coming here, and he said that I should do the best that I could among the gentiles. I had planned just to eat dairy and fish, but then it came all mixed up. . . ."

"We'll speak to the cook," I said, squeezing Etta's hand. "I'm so sorry I didn't make arrangements earlier. If you come to the kitchen now, we'll find something for you to eat."

"I can just have hot cocoa and cookies," Etta said, smiling.

"If you're sure," I said. She nodded, and I let her run upstairs to join her friends. I stopped in the kitchen and talked to Ethel, the cook, about making sure that Etta was only served dairy and fish.

Then I joined the rest of the second and third years in the Commons Room, where my classmates were eagerly catching each other up on their news. Cam Bennett had indeed gotten her pilot's license.

But her news was quickly drowned out by the announcement of several engagements, including those of Alfreda Driscoll and Wallis Rutherford. Helen *oohed* and *aahed* with the rest of us over their enormous diamond rings, but in an aside to Daisy and me said she thought it was *gauche* to get engaged before graduation. Daisy glanced nervously at me, and I, divining that Helen was anxious about her own marriage prospects, hastily changed the subject by asking Daisy to tell us her news.

Daisy looked uncertain for a moment, twisting her hands nervously and glancing from me to Helen.

"Spit it out, Daze," Helen snapped. "It can't be worse than all this engagement blather."

"I've joined the National American Woman Suffrage Association," she announced breathlessly. "Of course, the women in Kansas aren't as *dramatic* as our sister suffragists in England who've broken windows and been arrested, but we did shout very loudly at our demonstration at the state capitol."

This led to a discussion of the movement in England and the news that Blythewood alumna Andalusia Beaumont had been arrested at a demonstration with the radical suffragist Emily Wilding Davison and had engaged in a hunger strike in prison. A debate ensued over whether violence was ever justified and led to talk of other conflicts in Europe and the Jager twins' announcement their father had been summoned to the court of the Emperor Franz Joseph in Vienna to negotiate between the Serbians and the Austrians.

"There are dangerous forces at work in Europe," Beatrice solemnly informed us as her sister Dolores looked gravely on. "Papa fears the shadows are gathering for an assault on the Order. Dolores and I, of course, offered to accompany him to Vienna, but he assured us that we would do the most good here at Blythewood. The dark forces will try to undermine the Order before they dare put their plans for European domination in motion. He told us that we must be vigilant here at Blythewood to guard against intruders."

"There will be no intruders here," Alfreda Driscoll announced, rattling the quiver of arrows on her shoulder. "Not with us as Dianas."

It should have come as no surprise that Alfreda Driscoll, Wallis Rutherford, and Georgiana Montmorency had been elected to the elite squadron of protectors known as the Dianas, but still it didn't make me feel particularly safe to have them running around the house with their bows drawn. I'd seen the Dianas in a hunting craze. Van Drood had told me that their training made them susceptible to being turned to his uses. I'd have to keep an eye on them.

"Come on," Daisy whispered. "We should go upstairs and make sure the nestlings are all tucked in. They'll have little enough sleep before we take them to the initiation."

"I don't remember any wardens going with us last year," I said.

"They didn't. And look what happened—we nearly got eaten by goblins. There aren't enough Dianas to watch over all the nestlings. I suggested to Dame Beckwith that we go along so no one strays from the group."

It was a sound plan, with the sole disadvantage that it would make it difficult for me to get away from the rest to meet Raven. I half wondered if that wasn't Daisy's intention.

She'd been giving me queer looks all evening since Helen had made her pronouncement about early engagements, and when I asked after her beau, she'd turned beet red and said he was "just-fine-thank-you-very-much." Had she broken it off with Mr. Appleby? I'd have to ask her. But first I would have to figure out a way of getting free of my friends' well-intentioned interference.

When we opened our door later that night we saw that the Dianas were already going from door to door rousing the sleepy and confused nestlings. I hurried toward Etta's room and found her helping Susannah and Mary into slippers and reassuring them that everything would be all right. Myrtilene, in a silk peignoir and paper curlers, was loudly complaining that it was terribly uncivilized to roust a lady from sleep in the middle of the night, until her cousin hissed at her to be quiet. When the nestlings gathered, I managed to position myself at the back of the group, just behind Etta and her friends. When Daisy waved me forward I told her that I would take up the rear to make sure there were no stragglers.

We proceeded down the wide stairs, lit only by the lamps the Dianas carried. Although I knew what the initiation consisted of, I found myself awed by the solemnity of the procession. In the flickering lamplight, the portraits of teachers and illustrious alumnae on the walls looked down upon us gravely, as if enjoining us to live up to the Blythewood tradition. In the Great Hall the stained-glass windows depicting women archers seemed to be standing guard against the darkness pressing in on the castle. But then we were passing through the wide-open doors and out into that darkness.

Our lamps cast insubstantial pools of light in the wide expanse of fog-shrouded lawn, the beams carving strange shapes out of the fog, and then shrinking to pinpoints when we passed into the forest. The nestlings, who had been whispering among themselves, went silent as we entered the woods. I opened up my inner ear and listened.

At first I heard nothing. All the forest sounds I had heard today—the sift of leaves, creak of branches, and stir of the wild things that lived there—had vanished. It was as if the wood knew it was being invaded and had gone to ground like a frightened hare. Or like an owl who stalks its prey on muffled wings. The Blythe Wood was listening to us, watching us, waiting . . .

I stopped and let the last girls go on ahead. Into that silence fell the sound of wings swooping down from a great height, heading straight toward me. It took every ounce of nerve in my body not to bolt, but I stayed still until those wings descended and swooped me up into the night.

14

AFTER WEEKS OF longing to fly, it felt wonderful to be winging into the sky, even if the wings that carried me were not my own. The flutter in my chest, though, *was* my own—my heart beating against my ribcage. I wondered if Raven could feel it where he held me pressed against his chest. I could feel his heart keeping time to the pulse of his wings.

We rose for so long I thought he was taking me to the moon, but when we at last touched down on a swaying pine branch and I smelled tea and violets I knew exactly where we were.

"Your lair!" I said happily. "I was afraid you'd abandoned it when you went to live at Violet House."

His lip quirked into a smile. "I prefer to think of it as my nest," he replied, lifting a pine branch out of the way so I could pass into the snug tree house. "And of course I haven't abandoned it. A Darkling might pass among humans, but sooner or later he—or she—must spread his wings and fly."

When he laid his hand on my back to guide me into the nest I felt the warmth of his hand through my cloak and thin nightgown—

And right through to my bare skin! I wasn't wearing a corset underneath my nightgown. I suddenly felt very aware of him, standing close to me in the snug space, his breath hot against my cheeks, his hand resting between my shoulder blades. My wings stirred and I automatically tensed my back muscles to keep them from unfurling. He flinched his hand away suddenly.

I wanted to tell him that I hadn't tensed because I was nervous around him, but he'd already turned away to light a lamp and the little gas stove he used to boil water. I looked around, taking deep breaths to steady my heart. The nest was actually a small round room with a smooth plank floor and woven branches for walls. Violets grew in moss pockets tucked among the branches. There were pots and teacups and bits of clock mechanisms on the cleverly fitted shelves—but more of the latter than when last I'd visited.

"I see you're still working on Thaddeus Sharp's clocks," I said when I trusted myself to talk again.

"Yes. I believe that he was working out a system to control the *tenebrae*," he answered, putting the kettle on the stove. Was his hand shaking? Was he as nervous around me as I was around him?

"Control them?" I asked, trying to concentrate.

"Thaddeus realized that certain patterns of sound waves could repel the *tenebrae*."

"The way the automaton repeater that Miss Emmie gave me repelled van Drood?" I asked, thinking I sounded very normal, as if my heart weren't fluttering like a hummingbird's.

"Exactly," Raven said, pouring boiling water into the teapot, swishing it around, and dumping it out an open window. "Thaddeus designed the clocks at Violet House to cast a protective net over his home so that it would be safe from the *tene-*

brae. I'm trying to figure out if his system can be used to cast a wider protective net. Thaddeus couldn't—so he designed the repeater for Miss Emmaline when he realized that if a chime child could control the bells inside her own head she need never fear the *tenebrae*. Even a Shadow Master would be powerless against her."

Raven looked up and caught me watching his hands as he measured tea into the pot. He blushed and looked down again. "That's why you are so potentially dangerous to van Drood and why he so desperately wants you in his control. Which is why I warned you to stay away from him—and yet you deliberately put yourself in danger by going to the Hellgate Club." His voice was suddenly angry, taking me by surprise.

"How do you know about that?" I asked. "Have you been following me?"

It came out sounding more snappish than I'd intended. Truthfully, I didn't really mind the idea of Raven keeping an eye on me—but I didn't like him lecturing me on what I should and shouldn't do.

"Not anymore," he said, pouring more hot water into the teapot. "You didn't seem to like the idea when I mentioned it at the ball."

The reference to the ball brought back to mind how it had felt being whisked around the dance floor in Raven's arms. *Funny,* I thought. The dress I'd worn that night was flimsier than my nightgown, but I felt more exposed now. I was about to tell him that I didn't really mind, when he added, "I know about your visit to the Hellgate Club from Ruth."

"Oh," I said dumbly, "of course. She's at Violet House with

you. I didn't realize . . . I mean . . . I didn't know you'd become . . . um . . . that she would feel comfortable . . ."

"She was shy around me at first," he said, giving the tea a vigorous stir. "Perfectly understandable given what she'd been through. But then when I explained what I was—"

"You told her you're a Darkling?" I squawked.

"I thought it would help Ruth if she had someone she could talk to about what she'd been through." He handed me a cup of tea with milk and sugar already added. I was tempted to tell him I didn't take it with sugar, but he continued. "Sirena helped explain."

"Oh, so she's met Sirena. I see." I lifted my teacup and took a sip that scalded my tongue.

"Sirena's very compassionate. Ruth told us both about how you and your friends rescued her." He looked up from his own teacup. "It was very—"

"Foolish?" I asked, defensively.

"That too, but I was going to say brave. If you hadn't found Kid Marvel and Omar at Coney Island and tracked Ruth down to the Hellgate Club, she'd still be there. I should have thought of talking to some of the fairies with underworld connections."

"You can't think of everything," I said, willing to be conciliatory now that Raven was praising me. "I just ran into Mr. Marvel, actually, and he came up with the plan to get Ruth out—the 'con' as he called it. And everyone played his or her part. You should have seen Miss Sharp play an angry wife—"

"Yes, and I heard Nathan did an excellent job impersonating a client, although perhaps that didn't require such a lot of acting."

I opened my mouth to defend Nathan, but Raven was going on. "You all put on an impressive show. Too bad you spoiled it by sacrificing one innocent girl for another."

"You mean the changeling? But she insisted!"

"And that makes it all right? If one of your friends—Helen or Daisy—*insisted* on going to live in a brothel, would you let her?"

The blood rushed to my face. "But Ruth said it wasn't like that there . . . and the changeling said that if she was able to do something that protected Ruth and Etta she would know that she belonged s-somewhere . . ." I stammered to a halt, choking on the words, tears stinging my eyes. Had Raven summoned me here just to chastise me? Did he no longer care for me at all? Clearly he didn't think me as "compassionate" as Sirena.

"Changelings are very sensitive creatures. They spend their lives waiting for just the right opportunity to merge with a host and be of use in that host's life. But that doesn't mean you should have let her sacrifice herself."

I stared at Raven, aghast. It wasn't fair. I had done little else for weeks but worry about the girls in the Hellgate Club. At night I dreamed about the things I had seen in Molly's head. I had tried to argue with the changeling. "What should I have done?" I asked at last. "If the changeling hadn't gone back, Ruth would have."

Raven whistled under his breath, a sound like a bird calling to its mate. "That's true. It's just . . . it's so easy for your kind to treat the fairies like something less than human. I thought you were different."

"What do you mean 'your kind'?" I demanded. "What kind

am I? When the Order discovers what I am they'll cast me out. And then where will I go? Will *your* kind take me in? What if I can't fly? What if I'm just a half-breed freak with stunted wings? Of course I let the changeling convince me to let her go back to the Hellgate Club. I believed her when she said she would prefer to die rather than not belong anywhere."

Raven was staring at me as though I had sprouted horns. "Is that what you're afraid of? Not belonging?"

I nodded, unable to speak. Raven whistled under his breath again and turned away from me. My heart was pounding and I was tingling all over, as if every nerve ending in my body was on fire. I'd poured out my heart to him—my deepest fears—and now he was rummaging among his shelves, rearranging some picture frames. When he was done he turned back to me, gave me a baleful glance, and grabbed my hand.

"Stand here," he said gruffly.

He yanked me in front of the shelf and then stepped aside. I stood blinking into my own startled eyes. He'd set up a mirror on the shelf, angled so I could see myself from head to toe—and from wing tip to wing tip. In the heat of my speech my wings had ripped through the back of my nightgown and swept away my cloak. Fully extended, they spanned the width of Raven's nest. They weren't black, though; they were a fiery red-gold, the color of my hair.

"You are, indeed, a rarity," Raven said, his voice hoarse with emotion. "You were caught in the fire just as you were beginning to fledge, and so you became a phoenix, a creature revered by the Darklings. You certainly don't have to worry about being able to fly. Your wings . . ."

He took in the expanse of my wings, his eyes reflecting their red-gold, his skin basking in their glow. I, too, felt myself glowing, as if a flame had been kindled by his eyes.

". . . are aeronautically sound."

I snorted at the dry language and he, startled, laughed too.

"You sound like Cam with her flight manuals," I said relieved to see him laughing. "But if they're so sound, why can't I fly?"

"Have you tried?"

"Well, no," I admitted.

He grinned. "Then I think it's time for your first lesson."

Raven flew me across the river. I rode on his back so I could "feel the wind" in my wings. I closed my eyes. We were moving through a ribbon of air that was warmer than the surrounding atmosphere, gliding along it as though carried by a warm current in the ocean. When I opened my eyes I saw we had crossed the river and were soaring over a terrain of terraced cliffs and deep forest. The bare rock ridges stood out in the moonlight. Above them winged creatures soared, gliding and dipping into the canyons below. I thought they were hawks at first, but as we got closer I realized they were Darklings. I stiffened and drew in my wings.

"It's all right," Raven called. "We fledglings come here to stretch our wings. This range is called the Shawangunks, an Indian name that means smoky air. We think they named it that because of glimpsing Darklings flying here at night."

"I thought you said our wings cloak us from human sight." It felt funny to say *our*.

"From most humans," he replied. "There are always a few—

like Etta, or members of the Order who have been trained to spot magical creatures—who can see beyond the veil of the mortal world. Many of the Indians who lived here were able to see us. In fact, when your Order first settled here they used the Indians to learn about indigenous magical creatures—then stood by while the Indians were massacred or driven west."

"That's horrible!" I gasped. But I wasn't entirely surprised.

"But I didn't bring you out here to lecture you on the Order's history. I brought you out here to fly. These cliffs make great thermals."

I watched a Darkling gliding over a ridge suddenly plunge downward and then, just before he would have crashed on the rocks, somersault in the air. Another Darkling followed and performed a double somersault. I laughed out loud.

"Show-offs," Raven said. "A lot of the fledglings come out here to practice their stunts. I thought it would be a good place for you to test your wings."

"Oh, I could never fly in front of them!" I cried. "I'd be too embarrassed."

"They aren't. Look."

A gawky boy, all clumsy long limbs and tangled brown hair, took a swan dive off one of the ridges. He tried to perform the same elegant maneuver as the two before him, but instead he flipped sideways, careened into the cliff, and skidded down the rock face.

"Is he all right?"

"Marlin? He's lost so many tail feathers since he fledged, the other fledges call him 'Baldy.' Watch Sirena, though, she has a great spin."

Sirena was here? I looked to the ridge and recognized the lithe, athletic Darkling whom I'd seen dive fearlessly into the East River. Her abundant dark hair whipped around her finely carved face. She stretched her arms above her head, stood on tiptoe, and then sailed gracefully down to the next ridge on glossy blue-black wings, where she skimmed close to the edge and then dropped down another ten feet and alit on a narrow rock abutment.

"So graceful!" I sighed wistfully. "I'll never be able to do that."

"Sirena was scraping rock same as Marlin a few months ago. She's just been practicing more. Here." We'd arrived at the cliff, but instead of landing on the ridge we touched down on a narrow ledge a bit below the top, a small niche carved into the rock face. "Why don't we just watch for a while," he said, giving me his hand to steady me as I slid off his back. "You don't have to try it tonight if you're not ready."

I sat down and Raven squeezed in beside me. The niche was just big enough for the two of us if we tucked in our wings. I wrapped my arms around my knees, tenting my nightgown over my legs, and shivered.

"Cold?" he asked.

I shrugged. I wasn't cold—the excitement of watching other creatures soaring through the air had made me shiver—but when Raven stretched his wings over my shoulders I didn't object. Under the mantle of his wings, tucked into a niche in the rock face with the whole moonlit valley spread out before us, I felt completely safe and utterly free in a way I hadn't since I'd discovered I was half-Darkling.

Raven told me the names of the young fledglings as they soared past us. Besides Marlin and Sirena there were also Oriole, who was headstrong and fearless, Sparrow, shy and sweet but always looking after others, and Buzz, who was a bit of a bully. Some of them tilted their wings in our direction and some whistled greetings that Raven returned, but our little niche was only big enough for two, and the other fledglings left us to ourselves. I realized after a little while that they must know who I was. Which meant Raven had talked about me.

I felt like I could have stayed like that forever, but when I noticed the sky lightening in the east, I gasped.

"I have to get back!" I cried. "The initiation's long over, and they'll be wondering where I am."

"Yes, we have to get back to our nests before dawn, too." Raven got to his feet and helped me to mine. The space was so narrow that when I stood our faces were only inches apart. I could feel his breath warm on my face, like the thermal currents we'd flown on. I felt myself riding that current, leaning into the warmth of him, the heat of his skin . . . and then the liquid fire of his mouth as he kissed me. Falling into his arms was like diving off a cliff, like holding on and letting go at the same time, like flying and falling . . .

Then we *were* falling. Raven wrapped his wings and arms around me and spun us off into the void. As we turned I felt my wings spread out, catching the air. I opened my eyes and looked straight into his. They were black as the night, with flares of gold where the sun was rising. He grinned at me . . . and then let me go.

I was spinning so fast I couldn't tell which way was up and

which down. The air whistled through my wings, filling out each feather, tugging against gravity's pull on my flesh. I felt as though I were being ripped apart, as if my two selves—human and Darkling—were battling against each other. If they didn't settle it between them I would be dashed on the rocks.

Then I caught the thermal. It was like a warm hand cupping me, like Raven's arms holding me. I flexed my wings, straightened my back, and rode it up into the higher air where the morning sun was lighting up the sky. I wasn't Darkling or human; I simply *was* . . .

Falling. I hit a pocket of cooler air and, as if I'd caught my foot on a loose paving stone, I tumbled toward the earth.

15

"YOU'LL LEARN HOW to adjust to changes in air pressure," Raven reassured me several times on the flight back across the river. He'd caught me well before I would have hit the canyon floor, so all I'd suffered was a blow to my pride in front of the other fledglings, who were mostly generous in their reactions.

"That always happens to me when I hit an air pocket," Marlin said as he flew by us on our way back. "But you were really soaring there for a moment."

"Your wings are so beautiful!" Oriole told me. "I've never seen a phoenix's wings before!"

"Yes, that was an excellent first attempt," Sirena said a bit more primly. "Best hurry, Raven, the elders won't like it if they find out we've been gunking."

"Gunking" was what the fledglings called diving off the Shawangunks. And apparently I wasn't the only one who had a curfew. I'd thought that Raven in his nest—or at Violet House—was completely independent, but it turned out that the elders kept close tabs on the younger Darklings.

"Does that mean they know about me?" I asked, feeling suddenly shy as Raven let me down on the edge of the woods.

"Not yet. I'm looking for the best time to tell my parents

about you. They'll have objections, but I know they'll love you when they meet you." Then he swept his wing over me so we were hidden from view, kissed me quickly on the lips, and was gone in a flurry of wings.

I stood for a moment, trying to catch my breath. Raven had never mentioned parents! And he wanted me to meet them? Then I heard the matin bells ringing and I bolted across the lawn, my cloak flying out behind me and my stocking feet slipping on the wet grass. Where had I lost my slippers? And was that a tear in my stockings? And what did Raven mean about objections?

I reached the side door breathless and giddy. Thank the Bells it wasn't locked! I swung the door open . . . and found Helen and Daisy sitting on the bottom step of the back stairs glaring at me.

"Well, it's about time!" Helen cried jumping to her feet. "Daisy's been half out of her mind over your whereabouts."

"So were you—" Daisy began, but then she just stopped and hugged me. "Thank the Bells you're all right. What happened to you? You're . . ." Daisy took a step back and looked at me, her eyes going wide. "You look like you've been . . ."

If she had said *flying* I might have burst into hysterics. Instead a voice from behind us piped up.

"She was searching through the forest for me."

I turned and found Etta standing in the doorway. She was in an even more startling state of disarray than I was. Her hair was loose and braided with a hundred flowers and feathers. Her nightgown was torn and grass-stained, her bare feet covered with mud.

"Etta, where have you been?" Daisy asked. "We thought you were with Ava when you both disappeared at the same time."

"I was with the fairies," she told them, and then added, "Ava came to bring me back."

"The *fairies*?" Helen and Daisy both repeated together. I kept my mouth shut. Etta clearly meant to keep my secret. And Helen and Daisy were too upset over Etta's state of disarray to question me. We had to sneak her upstairs to the washroom, get her in a tub, pick the flowers and feathers out of her hair, and convince her that it wasn't wise to tell everyone about her adventure with the fairies.

"But they're so lovely," Etta crooned, hugging her grass-stained knees to her chest as Helen poured water over her head. "I don't know why we can't all be friends."

"Are you suggesting that we befriend goblins and trows and ice giants?" Helen snapped, dragging a hairbrush through Etta's tangled hair with unnecessary force.

"They explained that the goblins are really just a bit . . . *simple*. They only attack if they feel threatened or very hungry. The trows and ice giants are usually quite harmless, but someone's been making them behave worse than usual."

"Van Drood," I said, unbraiding a marsh reed from Etta's hair.

"Yes," Etta concurred, sniffing one of the violets that had fallen into the bath. "The fairies told me that the Shadow Master has been sending *tenebrae* into the Blythe Wood to possess the more vulnerable creatures, the simpleminded ones like the goblins and trows, and making them stir up trouble so the Order will fight against all fairies."

"But why?" Helen asked.

"So we fight each other instead of the *tenebrae*," Daisy answered. "That's what Featherbell told me, too."

"Yes," Etta said. "The lampsprites were on the verge of attacking the school last year because of the horrible way they've been treated by the Order, but when Daisy saved Featherbell they decided we must not all be bad."

"You mean Daisy prevented a war?" Helen asked.

"Oh yes! Daisy is a hero among the lychnobious people." Etta splashed excitedly. "And the lampsprites have been spreading the word among the other fairies—the marsh boggles and brownies, the pookas and cluricaunes—that the Order should be trusted. They want to forge a bond among the Order and the fairies and the Darklings—"

"The Darklings?" Helen cried. "The Order will never go for that. There's too much bad history between us."

"All lies spread by the Shadow Masters to keep us enemies," I said, holding a towel for Etta as she got out of the tub. "If only I could find the book Raven told me about—*A Darkness of Angels*—maybe I could convince Dame Beckwith that the Darklings aren't our enemies."

"That book is at the bottom of the ocean," Helen snapped. "That is, if it ever existed at all. You'll never convince Dame Beckwith that the Darklings aren't evil—and if you try they'll just think you've been mesmerized." Helen gave me a searching look. "And if you disappear again, Daisy and I will be forced to go to Dame Beckwith and have her send out the Hunt."

"But that's what van Drood wants," I objected.

"Well then," Helen sniffed, "you'll both just have to be extra careful not to give us any reason to worry."

We managed to keep Etta's and my disappearance a secret, but it proved to be an ongoing chore to make sure Etta didn't wander off into the woods again.

"I hear them calling to me, Avaleh," she complained one day when I'd caught her wandering off the archery field to the edge of the woods. "Don't you?"

And in fact, I did. With my new Darkling ears I heard the fairies' voices piping in the hush of the afternoon woods or at dusk in the wind off the river. They were calling for Etta, the fianais. Listening to them, I learned that Etta's nature made her not just a witness who could identify fairies, but a witness to all that happened to the fairies. They wanted to tell her their stories. That's why they called for her and that was why she wanted to go to them. It was in her nature.

We were very busy between watching out for Etta and keeping up with our own studies. I had found the first-year curriculum at Blythewood challenging, but the work our teachers expected of us in the second year seemed twice as hard.

Miles Malmsbury, who had taken over the science classes for Professor Jager, and who seemed a pleasant, jovial fellow at first, turned out to be a ruthless taskmaster. He made us memorize every known species and phylum of fairy, and their languages and customs.

"In the field," he lectured, "your life and the lives of your cohorts might depend on being able to communicate with the aborigines. A thorough grounding in the flora and fauna of

Faerie is also an absolute must. Please memorize the first one hundred pages in my new book—a work in progress presently being typed by my dear wife, Euphorbia, entitled *A Field Guide to the Lychnobious Peoples: An Everyman's Journey to Faerie and Back.*"

"It's one thousand pages," Helen hissed when the typescript manuscripts were passed out.

"Just be glad you haven't been recruited to help Miss Frost with the appendices, footnotes, bibliography, and index," Beatrice whispered back. "Dolores volunteered us." Beatrice glared at her sister, who was smiling serenely at Professor Malmsbury. As Dolores never talked I wondered *how* she had volunteered, but from the look on her face I didn't wonder *why*. Clearly she had taken a fancy to Professor Malmsbury.

As if we didn't have enough work, Mr. Bellows assigned us a sixty-page term paper on the progress of military tactics over the last five hundred years.

"This isn't even about magic anymore," Helen complained.

"But it is," Nathan insisted. "If you look at warfare over the centuries, you can see the hand of a malevolent force. Each time mankind has mastered one form of warfare, a new technique evolves—from the longbow to gunpowder—that results in even more slaughter. If we can predict what the next innovation will be, we can get a jump on the competition."

"You make it sound like a game," Daisy said. "Wouldn't it be better not to have any more wars?"

"Never happen," Nathan replied. "Red in tooth and claw— that's what we men are."

He said it almost proudly. Was that true? I wondered. Were humans naturally bloodthirsty, or were the *tenebrae* to blame for the evil men visited on themselves?

I decided I would ask Raven about it on our next night flight to the Shawangunks. We took them whenever I could slip away—usually when Helen and Daisy passed out early over their books. I'd gotten better at short flights, but I still didn't trust myself flying over the river—or at least that's what I told myself stretched out on Raven's back, sheltered in between his wings, the heat of his body keeping me warm as the nights grew cooler. When we neared the ridge I would spread out my wings and, when I felt the warm currents of air that flowed in the canyon, launch myself off his back. We'd fly side by side, wing tip to wing tip. If I caught an air pocket and dropped, Raven would always be there to steady me. It was like dancing with a partner who guides you across the floor with the slightest shift of his weight or touch of his hand. I could feel the change in the air as he moved beside me, the warm currents his body moved touching every inch of my body.

Ghosting, I learned the fledglings called it one night when we were sitting around the fire and Sirena remarked that if Raven kept ghosting me I'd never learn to fly on my own.

"She'll learn when she's ready," Raven had replied curtly.

"Aw, if you want someone to ghost with you, Sirena, you only have to ask," Marlin interjected, bumping into Sirena and then tumbling off the cliff face in an awkward triple somersault that ended in a painful-looking belly flop. Everyone's attention was drawn away from me.

Later, Oriole told me not to mind what Sirena had said.

"She's just jealous. Only pair-bonds ghost each other."

I'd blushed and stammered something about Raven only trying to help me because I was so hopeless at flying, but Oriole just laughed and soared off.

Pair-bond. I wondered if that was a bit like being engaged. But I didn't have a ring like Alfreda Driscoll or Wallis Rutherford, and I still hadn't met Raven's parents. What if their objections had convinced Raven that we could never marry? Did Darklings marry? I didn't care about getting a ring or the orange blossoms and trousseau that went with a society wedding. I just wanted to be with Raven forever. But did he want that? How could I ask him?

So instead, when we tucked into our niche, shoulder to shoulder, with Raven's wings mantled over us for warmth, I asked him there whether he thought the evil that men did came from themselves or the *tenebrae.*

"It's a bit of a chicken-or-egg question," he replied.

"You would bring it back to birds," I teased.

He smiled, but a little sadly. "I'm afraid it comes back to humans. The story our elders tell us is that when humans first appeared on the scene, the fairies watched them carefully to see what sort of creatures they would become. They saw much good in them, but also much bad. They were violent and bloodthirsty, prone to clubbing each other over the head and stealing each other's women and food."

"Oh, so it was the *male* humans who behaved badly."

"No doubt, but the women weren't much better. Some of the fairies wanted to destroy the whole human race, but others argued that destroying them would make the fairies as bad as the humans—in fact, it was argued that the influence of the humans was already making the fairies more violent. At last, the fairies decided that if only they could extract the evil from mankind there would be hope for the race. They performed a rite that drew the evil out of all humans, and they trapped that evil in three huge vessels and hid the vessels in three secret places deep in the earth."

"Were things better then?"

"For a while. Humans created peaceful settlements during this period, but there were humans who felt that they were missing something. Stories about the vessels and their hiding places circulated around the world, some purporting that the vessels contained great knowledge."

"Like Pandora's box," I said. "Or the mirror in 'The Snow Queen.'"

"Yes, those stories are remnants of the stories about the vessels. At last one of the vessels was found and broken. When it broke, all the evil inside escaped in the form of shadows—the *tenebrae*. They latched on to the man who had discovered the vessel and possessed him. He became the first Shadow Master. He wielded the *tenebrae* and drove them to possess others to do his bidding and spread evil in the world. The first thing they did was to search out the second vessel and release those *tenebrae*. Since then evil has been rampant."

"What about the third vessel?" I asked.

"It's never been found. The shadow master has been looking for it. If he found it and released the rest of the shadows, the world would descend into irredeemable darkness. Already the Darklings are barely able to maintain the balance between good and evil. As the world gets more and more crowded with humans it becomes harder and harder for us to exist in it. How many more places like this, for instance, are there for young fledglings to spread their wings?"

He tilted his chin out toward the open air where Oriole and Marlin were spinning parabolas against a pink sky. Dawn came so quickly on these nights!

I nestled deeper into Raven's arms, chilled by the story he had told me. "If the Order and Darklings could join forces, the Order could protect the Darklings."

"I'm afraid any hope of that died when your Mr. Farnsworth sank to the bottom of the ocean with *A Darkness of Angels*."

"We don't know he drowned," I protested, although as the weeks went by without any word from Agnes, I had less and less hope that he was still alive. "And there might be another way to convince the Order that the Darklings aren't evil. I could speak to Dame Beckwith—"

"It's too dangerous," he said quickly. "You think Dame Beckwith and your teachers are your friends, but so did the Indians who lived here and the others the Order has betrayed. They'll kill you if they find out what you are."

He stroked my wings protectively, and I felt a shivery sensation deep inside.

"You mustn't take the risk until . . ." he said hoarsely, his hand traveling from my wings to my face, his touch as feathery and light as the touch of his wings, one of which was cupped around my back and drawing me toward him. I scooted closer, my own wings stretching out and intertwining with his, until we were both entirely fitted within the mantle of our joined wings. It was like being inside a nest. The pink light of dawn shone through our feathers, making the space between us glow, turning his skin gold and his lips rose-petal pink.

When our lips touched I felt his wings fluttering against mine, as fast and light as a hummingbird's wings.

"Until what?" I whispered.

"Until you're ready to leave them and come to me."

16

NEITHER OF US spoke on that night's flight home. Nor was I able to see him for another week. Midterms were approaching, and Helen had organized us into a study group that resembled a military camp.

"What choice do I have?" she asked when I complained. "You'll never pass otherwise. You've failed your last Latin quiz and history exam."

She was right. I had been having trouble focusing on my work. What good did it do to study Latin declensions when there were girls being held captive in a place like the Hellgate Club? How could I enjoy the privileges of Blythewood when the changeling and those other girls endured a life of abject slavery, when girls like Molly were leaping to their deaths? And why study the illustrious history of the Order when half of what we learned in our books was lies masking the reality of the Order's shoddy treatment of half the people on the planet?

I veered between distraction and irritability in most of my classes, unable even to draw a bow correctly in archery because of the unfamiliar strain in my back muscles from flying or to ring the changes in bells because my new Darkling ears made the noise unbearable. I couldn't even pay proper attention in my favorite class, English, where a line of poetry recited by Miss Sharp would remind me of the touch of Raven's lips on mine. If I didn't buckle down I wouldn't need to be revealed as a Darkling to be kicked out of Blythewood. Then I'd have no choice but to go to Raven . . .

But where? Would we live together in his nest? Or at Violet House with him in his guise as Raymond Corbin, clockmaker's apprentice? Would we marry? But Raven hadn't asked me to marry him. And he hadn't said anything more about taking me to meet his parents.

On the day before midterms it occurred to me that I didn't have to wait for a chance to slip away at night; I could go to Violet House to see Raven. And I had the perfect excuse.

"Etta," I said as we gathered in the Commons Room after lunch to study, "you must miss Ruth terribly. Why don't we walk into town today and visit her?"

Helen and Daisy lifted their heads out of their books and looked at one another. As if they'd arrived at an agreement, Helen spoke.

"We're not allowed to leave the castle on Halloween. You remember what happened last year."

Last year we'd been attacked by shadow crows on our way back from Violet House. "What I remember is that *you* instigated our excursion into town last year," I said, getting up and brushing pencil shavings off my skirt. "But Etta and I can go and come back far before dusk. We'll just nip in for a cup of tea and a quick visit. What do you say, Etta?"

Etta was already on her feet and racing for the front hall for her coat. I followed her at a more leisurely pace with Helen and Daisy trailing behind me.

"Don't you care if you fail?" asked Helen.

"Actually," I said, putting on my jacket and straightening my hair in the hall mirror, "I don't. But you two stay here studying if you like. We'll bring you back tea cakes."

Helen and Daisy exchanged another worried look and a nod.

"We'll go with you," Helen announced.

"Suit yourselves," I said, sweeping out of the door.

The walk to town would have been uncomfortably silent if not for Etta's bright chatter. She was so happy about the prospect of seeing Ruth that I felt bad I hadn't brought her sooner—and guilty that I'd only thought of it now as an excuse to see Raven. As we turned down Livingston Street, though, I worried he wouldn't be there. He could be out on a job for Mr. Humphreys, the clockmaker, or in the woods at his nest . . . or who knew where else. I realized that although I had shared many nights—and kisses—with Raven, I didn't really know much about how he spent his days. A man who could fly could be anywhere.

But then a burst of laughter from the direction of Violet House put paid to all my worries. That was Raven's laugh; I would know it anywhere. And that was his rich baritone inter-mixed with a higher soprano . . .

A soprano?

As we arrived in front of Violet House I saw where the voices were coming from. On the front porch, seated in a cozy wicker settee—a rather small settee—Raven and Ruth were having tea. Or at least, the table in front of them was set for tea and Ruth was wearing a very pretty yellow tea dress trimmed with cerise ribbons. But they weren't drinking tea at the moment. I wasn't sure *what* they were doing, only that it seemed to necessitate Raven having his hands in Ruth's hair and both of them laughing quite a bit.

I stopped on the bluestone sidewalk, my heart thudding in my chest, heat flaming in my cheeks. My wings strained against my corset.

"Ruth!" Etta cried.

Ruth looked up, her cheeks pink, her dark eyes shining. "Ettaleh!" she cried, jumping up. A cherry-colored ribbon drifted in the air behind her. Raven stood and caught it in his hand and then, seeing me, turned the same color as the ribbon. I would have turned and fled, but Etta and Ruth were pulling me toward the house. Ruth was jabbering away in my ear about something I couldn't follow, and then she was introducing Helen and Daisy to "Mr. Corbin."

I saw Helen narrowing her eyes at Raven and then looking from him to me and back again. The first time Raven had appeared at Blythewood in the guise of Raymond Corbin, clockmaker's apprentice, she hadn't recognized him as the Darkling she'd glimpsed in the woods. He'd looked every inch the humble workingman then. But he didn't look humble now. His cheeks were flushed, his dark hair tumbling around his face and his loose collar revealing his finely carved throat. He held out his hand to shake Helen's and blushed as he saw he still held the cherry-red ribbon.

"I believe that belongs to Miss Blum," Helen said primly.

"Y-yes," Raven stammered. "She got it caught in the wicker settee. I was helping untangle it."

"Mr. Corbin has the most nimble fingers," Ruth gushed. "Of course he has to in his line of work."

I glared at Ruth, but she was too busy simpering at Raven to notice.

"The Misses Sharp will be pleased to see you," Raven said. "They love unexpected visits."

Something about the way he said it suggested that *he* didn't. Was I not supposed to visit him at Violet House? Or was he just embarrassed to have been caught with his hands in Ruth's hair? But if it was completely innocent, why would he be embarrassed?

I would have given much for a reassuring look or a squeeze of the hand, but instead Raven busied himself picking up the tea tray and ushering us inside.

"We were having tea out here," Raven explained, "because it was such a fine day, but I'm sure the aunts will want us all to join them in the conservatory for a proper tea."

"Oh," Helen said archly, "so what you were having wasn't a *proper* tea?"

Raven blushed, but Ruth laughed. When I'd last seen Ruth she had been a terrified, cowering creature. When had she become this carefree, pink-cheeked ingenue? I should have been happy for her transformation—Etta certainly was—but my suspicion that her interest in Raven—or his in her—had worked this transformation chilled my generosity.

"The aunts are always contriving to get us alone together," Ruth whispered to me. "They're such old dears."

"Yes, they are," I agreed through gritted teeth.

The old dears were bustling out of the conservatory, delighted at our arrival. "I only realized you were coming a half hour ago!" Emmaline cried. "It must have been a sudden decision." She looked from one to the other of us with her bright bird-like eyes. Emmaline was a chime child like me and could usually predict the future, but apparently my behavior had been so erratic that it had thrown off even her prognosticating ability.

"Yes, it was," Helen agreed. "Ava seemed to have been *seized* with a sudden desire to be here."

"So that Etta could see Ruth," I said, glaring at Helen.

"Well, whoever's idea it was, we're delighted you're here," Aunt Harriet said. "There's plenty for tea. Come on in to the conservatory."

We all crowded into the conservatory, where there certainly was *plenty* for tea—finger sandwiches, scones, clotted cream and jam, Victoria sponge cake, and a huge sherry trifle. "The darling aunts have been so kind and made everything kosher for us, Ettaleh," Ruth told her sister. Daisy, Etta, and Ruth tucked in with gusto exclaiming over each delicacy, the two sisters in Yiddish, which they laughingly translated to Daisy. Helen sat back, delicately sipping her tea, and interrogated Raven.

"Where did you say your people were from?" she asked sweetly.

"I didn't," Raven responded sulkily.

And so on. I found I had no appetite. Nor was I able to follow the thread of the Misses Sharp's conversation—until Miss Harriet leaned forward and confided to me in a breathy whisper: "It's so lovely to see dear Ruth getting on so well with Mr. Corbin. It's done the poor girl a world of good to have his company."

At which point I spilled my tea.

Just when I didn't think the tea party could get any more awkward, Uncle Taddie loped in to announce that there were some guests to see Miss Blum.

"More unexpected guests!" Miss Emmaline cried. "My instincts are terribly off today. Who can they be?"

Raven leapt to his feet and inserted himself between Ruth and the door. "We should ascertain who they are before letting them in," he told the aunts.

I knew he was only making sure that none of van Drood's henchmen had found out Ruth, but it was the last straw for me. I got up huffily. "I will go *ascertain* their identities. If they're here to harm Ruth I'll simply throw myself on their daggers."

Before anyone could stop me, I was out in the foyer, where I found a rather abashed-looking Kid Marvel standing with his hat in his hand and a more collected and turbaned Omar staring at the grandfather clock.

"You might as well come in," I told them. "Everyone else has."

Oddly, the addition of Kid Marvel and Omar to the mix seemed to bring the disparate elements of our uncomfortable tea party into some kind of harmony. Ruth was delighted to see the men who had orchestrated her release from the Hellgate Club, Daisy was goggle-eyed to meet performers from Coney Island, Miss Hattie seemed enchanted to encounter a person even smaller than herself, and Miss Emmaline and Omar exchanged looks that seemed to indicate they were having some kind of telepathic communication.

"I believe you would prefer the cucumber to the water-cress" was one of the less cryptic comments she made to him. To which he replied, "Yes, the reason you could not foresee our arrival was that I cloaked our intentions."

Before either man could be allowed to tell us the purpose of their visit, they had to be fed a quantity of tea sandwiches, tea, and tea cakes, which Omar, sitting cross-legged on a cushion on the floor, partook of sparingly, while Mr. Marvel tucked in with a gusto that delighted Miss Harriet. Only when both men had been adequately fed did Miss Sharp ask what had brought them to Rhinebeck.

"It's about Ru—" Kid Marvel began, turning his hat around in his hands. "I mean, er, the *other* Ruth."

Ruth leaned forward and laid her hand on his. "It's all right, Mr. Marvel, you don't have to worry about my feelings. *Raymond*"—she said the name like it was a secret only she was allowed to say, and I barely resisted lobbing the sugar tongs at her—"has explained to me how the changelings work, and I see now it was not her fault. I'm the one who was fool enough to go with that awful man. I'm grateful to her for sparing my parents' grief and sacrificing herself on behalf of Etta and me. I wish you would tell her that when you see her next."

"A most generous and eloquently expressed sentiment," Omar began, bowing to Ruth. "The only difficulty being that the, er, young lady—"

"Call her Rue," Etta said. "It means sorrow and that's what she's spared us."

"Ah," Omar said, "that does seem to fit the young lady. And

I know she would be pleased to hear you give her a name. But as I was saying, the difficulty is that—"

"She's gone!" Kid Marvel blurted.

"Gone?" we all said together.

"But where to?" Etta said, clearly upset.

"That's the problem, ain't it?" Kid Marvel answered. "We don't know. The whole lot of them's up and vanished."

"You mean all the girls at the Hellgate Club?" I asked, appalled.

"That's just what I mean!" Kid Marvel replied. "And not just the dolls. Madame LeFevre, the thugs that guarded the doors, the whole kit and caboodle, vanished—*vamoosed*—without a trace!"

"But I thought you were watching the place," Raven said, getting to his feet and towering over Kid Marvel.

"I done that," Kid said, jumping to his feet. "I kept a lookout myself and had two boys watching the back alleyways. But two nights ago a fog comes up from the river. It weren't no ordinary fog, neither. It stank, for one thing, like week-old fish and rotten eggs. Me and my boys could hardly tolerate it, but we stuck to our post all thought the night. In the morning some of them do-gooders from the settlement house—no offense to your friends there," he said, bowing to me, "comes knocking on the door to preach against the Social Evil. Usually Madame LeFevre comes out and gives 'em the boot, but this time the door creaks right open and the do-gooders go inside hollering, 'Is anybody home?' Not two minutes later they comes running out like their knickers are on fire—begging your pardon, misses.

So we goes inside to investigate and comes to find the whole place is empty. Not a soul in sight."

"How can that be?" Daisy asked.

"We deduced that they must have had an underground tunnel," Omar said.

"Yeah, so we looks the whole place over and we find that there's no tunnel, but there is the sewer and it leads to—"

"The river," Raven said. "And the Hellgate whirlpool. They must use it, somehow, to move the girls."

"Mebbe," Kid Marvel said, "but that don't tell us where they are. They could be in any riverside dive."

"We should never have let Rue go there," Etta said.

"I agree," Raven said with an accusing glance in my direction that made me remember the argument we'd had.

"But if we hadn't," I said, glaring back at him, "what would have happened to—" I almost said *your darling Ruth*, but stopped myself just in time and simply jerked my chin in Ruth's direction. "Ruth insisted she would go back to the Hellgate Club until Rue offered to go in her place. If it's anyone's fault—"

"It is no one's fault," Omar declared, his deep voice, though not loud, making all the tea cups shiver and chime, "but the *pishaca*'s. If we fight among ourselves, if we give in to our anger or"—he glanced pointedly at me—"petty jealousy, we become weak and van Drood will win. This is what he wants: to divide us and turn us against each other. To win more of us to *his* army. The world is picking sides as we speak. Alliances are being formed on the side of evil. If the good do not band together, evil will rule and we will all be destroyed."

We were all quiet a moment after Omar's speech. It was Miss Emmie who broke the silence. "He's right," she said in a small but steady voice. "It's what my father was afraid of. If we don't treat the fairies and other magical beings better, they will turn on us."

"But what can we do?" Miss Harriet asked, wringing her hands.

"We must search for Rue," Omar answered. "I am sure she will find a way to contact us when she knows what the *pishaca* is planning. Mr. Marvel and I think it possible that she will try to contact Ruth or Etta, so you must be on the lookout."

"I can tell my people to look for where the Hellgate girls have been moved," Raven said. "We'll patrol the East River and the Hudson."

"The lampsprites can help," Etta said. "They can go anywhere."

"And Gillie," I added. "If anyone knows how to find a lost girl, it's Gillie. He can send his falcons."

"Good," Omar said, unfolding himself from his cushion on the floor and rising to his feet. "Let us not take this as a setback, but as an opportunity. The *pishaca* would not have moved the club unless he felt threatened by us. He is afraid of us banding together, but that is exactly what is happening. Mr. Corbin here"—he bowed to Raven—"has generously pledged to aid in the recovery of Miss Rue. Etta and Daisy have formed a bond with the fairies that will improve the Order's relationship with them. If we all continue to act as our best selves, then, united, we will defeat the dark forces."

He bowed to each of us in turn, giving his deepest bow of

the day, nearly touching his forehead to the floor, to the Misses Sharp, who both beamed at him and Kid Marvel as they pinned violet boutonnières to their jackets. Omar was right, I thought. Miss Emmie and Miss Hattie were the best of us, giving of themselves generously without petty rivalry or mean-spiritedness. I tried as we took our farewells to give them all, including Ruth, my best wishes.

It helped that when I took Raven's hand he slipped a note in mine, giving my hand an extra squeeze before he let it go. At the touch of his hand, all the memories of our nights together on the ridge came flying back to me. *That* was real. No doubt his note contained an explanation and a request to meet again soon.

I couldn't read it right away, though, because Helen stayed glued to my side the whole way back, at first a glaring presence and then, once Daisy and Etta were far enough ahead of us on the road, a vociferous one.

"You never mentioned that your Darkling boyfriend was the boarder at Violet House," she accused.

"I didn't think it was of any interest to you, Helen. You saw him last year and didn't even recognize him."

"Well, I recognized him today, and I saw the way he looked at you. You've been meeting him secretly, haven't you?"

"That's none of your business," I snapped, all my resolutions to be my best self evaporating under Helen's scrutiny. It was hard to be one's best self when other people weren't theirs. "I don't demand to meet the many suitors whom your mother puts forward for you."

Helen stared at me. For a moment I felt bad, because I knew that Helen dreaded the arrival of her mother's candidates for her husband. But that wasn't why Helen was staring. "You're comparing marriageable men in society to that—that . . ." Helen looked around as if afraid of being overheard, but Etta and Daisy had already rounded the last curve of the road before Blythewood. Satisfied they wouldn't hear, she hissed, "That monster!"

"If he's a monster, then so am I!" I shouted back at her, my wings throbbing beneath my corset. *Why not?* I thought. But before my wings broke free, Daisy was suddenly between us.

"Would you two please stop it! Didn't you listen to anything Mr. Omar said? If we fight amongst ourselves we're lost. And yet you two . . ." Daisy was turning bright pink. "You act as though you're the only human beings on the planet with problems. I'm sorry, Helen, that you lost your father and your mother is trying to marry you off, but that doesn't mean that no one else should have a beau or maybe *want* to get engaged.

"And you, Ava," she continued, turning on me. "It's perfectly obvious that your head has been elsewhere since we got back to school and you've been sneaking off to meet your Darkling boyfriend, but do you think you're the only person who's ever had to keep a secret?"

Helen and I both stared at Daisy as if she were the one who was growing wings. "Daisy," I said, "is there something you haven't told us?"

"Yes!" she cried. Then, looking around her, she worriedly added, "But where's Etta got to? She feels terrible about Rue. She's talked of nothing else during the whole walk back."

"Well then," Helen said, "we've *all* been terribly selfish standing here arguing. Let's go tell Etta we're sorry."

She marched off down the road, Daisy and I at her heels. I wanted to tell Daisy that I was sorry I'd been too preoccupied with my own concerns to notice that she, too, had a secret burden. What could it be? The last time she'd had a secret, she'd been hiding a lampsprite in the dungeons. Was she hiding a troll under her bed? But she was walking ahead too fast, and when we rounded the curve of the road I saw we had another problem. Etta was gone.

17

"MAYBE SHE JUST went on to the house without us," Helen said.

"Then why is the gate still closed?" Daisy asked, wringing her hands and looking up and down the road anxiously.

I looked at the gate. Not only was it closed but a vine with blood-red bell-shaped flowers was coiled around the bars over the lock, sealing it shut.

"That's strange," I said, prodding the vine. "This wasn't here when we left—ouch!"

When I tried to pry the vine away from the gate, it lashed out at my hand, its flowers chiming like alarm bells.

"It's a clavicula," Daisy said, her eyes going wide. "A locking vine. It's used to seal in a castle under siege. I read about it in *Sieges and Campaigns of the Dark Ages, Volume II*."

"That's not assigned until next semester," Helen said.

"Some of us read ahead," Daisy replied.

"Some of us have a life," Helen quipped.

"Please, you two, not now!" I cried. "Is there a way to let the vine know that we're not the enemy so it will let us in?"

"There's a secret code that's only entrusted to the Dianas…"

Helen groaned.

"But that I luckily overheard Georgiana mentioning to Wallis Rutherford," Daisy concluded with an unusually smug smile. It occurred to me that sunny, cheerful Daisy actually had a talent for espionage. "But what about Etta? If the castle has gone into a siege lockdown, there must be a threat. We can't leave her out here."

"Maybe Etta knew how to get past the vine," I said doubtfully. "We have to get to the castle and see if she's there." I didn't say what we would do if she wasn't. If Etta wasn't in the castle, there was only one place she'd be: the Blythe Wood. No doubt she'd taken Omar's speech to heart and gone to rally the fairies to find Rue. But she couldn't have picked a more dangerous night. I could tell from Helen's and Daisy's grim looks they were thinking the same thing.

Daisy turned to the vine and recited a long string of Latin words that I couldn't imagine consigning to memory. Perhaps Daisy had a future in codebreaking as well as espionage.

The vine coiled back, its blood-red blossoms chiming a peal that sounded like a doorbell. We quickly opened the gates and squeezed through. As soon as we were on the other side, the gates clanged closed behind us, the flower bells chiming another distinctive peal. We hurried up the drive between the rows of tall, stately sycamores. Glancing from side to side, I noticed flashes of red among the golden leaves. The clavicula had twined itself around the trees, its flowers clattering as we made our way to the castle.

"It seems to know we're here," Helen said anxiously.

"It does," Daisy said. "The clavicula puts out feelers over the entire defensive area. It can sense intruders and send alarms back to its roots. Whoever is commanding it will be able to sense that we're coming."

"Well, that's not creepy at all," Helen said with a shudder.

"It's all right, because we belong here," Daisy reassured her.

But did I belong here? Was the clavicula even now sending a message along its creeping tendrils that I was an intruder? Would I find the castle barred to me? Would the vine strike out and strangle me before I could get to the castle?

The clavicula had formed a thick archway over the door, its bells hanging like a canopy. I didn't like the idea of passing underneath it. As I reached for the doorknob one of the tendrils detached itself and coiled around my wrist. A needle-thin thorn pierced my skin and bit into my vein. The vine pulsed and turned red. It was drinking my blood.

I screamed.

The door flung open and Nathan appeared. "Where the hell have you been?" he barked, grabbing my wrist. When he saw the vine he shouted at it in the same tone. "*Desisto!*" The vine lashed back like an angry cat's tail and retreated.

"We were at Violet House," Helen began, staring reproachfully at Nathan's hand on mine. "We didn't know the place would be overrun by ill-mannered shrubbery in our absence."

"My mother's idea," Nathan said, pulling us into the Great Hall. "She's heard rumors that tonight will be an especially bad Halloween in the Blythe Wood. Once this infernal vine has finished searching the grounds it will seal us all in. I was afraid you'd be sealed out."

"Did you see Etta?" I asked.

Nathan shook his head. "No. I've been watching the front door for the last hour."

"Maybe she came in through the back door?" Helen suggested hopefully.

"I don't think so," Nathan said. "But we can ask Miss Corey. She's reading the clavicula. Come on." Nathan led us through the Great Hall and into the North Wing, toward the classrooms and the library. I supposed it made sense that Miss Corey, the librarian, would be reading the vine in the library. But how did one read a vine? I wondered as we hurried down the darkened hallway.

It wasn't night yet. But when I looked at the windows I saw that the vine had grown over them, blocking out the late-afternoon light. Tendrils snaked in underneath the windowsills and ran along the walls and ceiling. They seemed to be growing thickest around the door to the library.

"Is your mother sure she knew what she was doing when she summoned this thing?" I asked Nathan.

"That's what I want to know," a woman said inside the library. The voice was so icy I almost didn't recognize it as belonging to Miss Sharp. She was standing beside the central reading table, her blue eyes blazing, one hand on the shoulder of Miss Corey, who was seated at the table. Mr. Bellows stood on the other side of Miss Corey, his face pale and drawn. But not as pale as Miss Corey's. She was seated at the head of the table, both arms lying on the table with the palms turned up. It was a strange position that reminded me of something.

I moved closer and saw that Miss Corey's veil was thrown

back and her eyes were staring straight ahead of her, but they didn't seem to see anything. They were covered with a light film as if she was unconscious.

That's what her pose reminded me of. When I did rounds with Miss Wald at the Henry Street Settlement we sometimes had to bring a patient to the hospital. One woman had lost so much blood when her husband stabbed her that she needed a blood transfusion . . .

I looked down at Miss Corey's hands. The clavicula snaked around her arms, thorns sunk into her veins at wrist and elbow crook. More tendrils clung to her forehead, dime-sized suckers plastered to her skin.

"It's draining her!" I cried.

"No," Miss Sharp said in a cold voice, "it's *feeding* her."

I looked again and saw that fluid was pulsing through the vine and pouring into Miss Corey's veins.

"But w-why?" I stammered, feeling sick to my stomach.

"Someone has to filter the intelligence gathered by the vine." Miss Sharp touched Miss Corey's face, and gently stroked her hair away from the thorny vines. I thought of what Miss Corey had told me about her feelings for Miss Sharp and her fears that they weren't reciprocated—and knew suddenly that those fears were groundless. But what would that matter if this blood-sucking vine ate her?

"You have to stop it!" I cried, moving forward and reaching to tear away the vine. Before I could, Miss Corey grabbed my wrist. Her blank eyes fixed on me.

"No," she said in a voice that didn't sound like hers. "I'm bound until sunrise. I can feel and see everything in the forest, and I see Etta running toward the Rowan Circle. You must go and bring her back before . . ."

Her voice faltered and her grip loosened.

"Before what?" I cried.

But Miss Corey had gone limp, her sightless eyes rolling up in their sockets.

"I should think that would be obvious," Helen said. "Before she gets eaten by a troll. Come on."

"You can't!" Mr. Bellows barked. "No one can leave the castle on All Hallows' Eve. You'll be killed."

"We can't leave Etta alone out there," Nathan said.

"He's right," Daisy agreed. She was already opening a chest that contained bows and arrows and handbells against fairy spells, all the equipment for a field expedition. "We've gone into the wood before."

"On the winter solstice," Nathan said, hoisting a dagger from the trunk. "How much worse can Halloween be?"

Mr. Bellows insisted on leading our expedition. Miss Sharp would not leave Miss Corey. Our first problem was getting out the French doors that led from the library to the garden and were covered with vines, but when Miss Sharp whispered something in Miss Corey's ear, the vines drew away and let us out.

"I hate that thing," Helen said as the vines snapped behind us and we strode across the lawn, our shadows stretching out long by our sides. Across the river, the sun was setting behind the Catskills. Daisy, still angry, apparently, had gone on ahead with Mr. Bellows.

"I bet that's her secret," Helen muttered.

"What?"

"Daisy's big secret. I bet it's that she's in love with Mr. Bellows."

"That's hardly a secret," I pointed out. "I've never seen her so angry at us before. Have we really been neglecting her?"

"*I* haven't neglected anyone. *You* are the one who's been mooning about—"

"I have *not* been moo—"

"Shh!" Mr. Bellows hissed at us as we caught up to them at the edge of the woods. "The woods have ears. We must pass silently until we get to the Rowan Circle."

I stared at the trees on the edge of the lawn, half terrified that I would actually see fleshy earlobes budding from their branches. Instead I saw something much more frightening. Every branch, from heavy limb to tiny twiglet, was trembling as though rocked by a great storm. Only there wasn't a breath of air on the lawn. The trees were quivering on their own, pulsating like the nerve endings of the frog we'd dissected in science class last week. It was as if the entire forest was an organism and the trees its nervous system. I had the distinct feeling that stepping into it would be like being swallowed. Mr. Bellows must have had the same thought.

"Perhaps it would be better if you students went back to the house. I can go in to find Etta."

"No." The answer came from Daisy. "Etta's in there. I was supposed to be keeping an eye on her when she vanished. I'm going to get her back."

"Me too," Nathan and I said together.

"Well," Helen said, "what are we waiting for? An engraved invitation?"

It was meant to be a joke, but as we stepped between the trees I had the distinct impression that we had been invited. The tree trunks creaked and moaned as if making room for us.

Branches brushed against my face like a blind person touching my features to know what I looked like. I heard the same branches snapping behind me, and when I turned once to look back I saw that they had plaited themselves into a thick thatch preventing us from going back. Even the trees seemed to have stepped closer together to cut out the last lingering light of the sunset and to bar our retreat. There was no way to go but forward, and even that direction had been narrowed to a tight path only wide enough for one of us at a time. We went single file, Mr. Bellows leading, then Daisy, Nathan, Helen, and me.

"Why do I have the feeling that the woods are funneling us to where they want us to go?" Helen asked, batting at a branch and ignoring Mr. Bellows' direction that we remain silent. I didn't blame her. The quiet was unnerving.

"Maybe the woods want us to find Etta," I said. "The fairies all love her. Perhaps the woods do, too."

"Maybe it's your boyfriend who's controlling the woods," Helen said. "The trees are going to pick us off one by one and then he'll have you to himself."

"Don't be ridiculous, Helen. Raven doesn't control the trees, and even if he did he wouldn't hurt my friends or make me do anything I didn't want to do."

"How do you know?" Helen asked. "He could be mesmerizing you into believing you're doing what you want. He could be leading you into a life of slavery just like those poor girls at the Hellgate Club."

"It's not like that, Helen . . ." I faltered, unable to explain what it was like being with Raven. How could I tell her how it felt to fly with him, without telling her that I could fly? How could I tell her that I knew he wasn't a monster because I was the same as him? "I just can't explain," I finished lamely.

"It's because you think I'm a silly society girl who only cares about clothes and dances, isn't it?" she asked in a shaky voice. "That must be why you and Daisy are keeping secrets from me."

I grabbed her arm to make her stop. She halted, but remained facing away from me. Her whole body was trembling. I had to forcibly turn her to me. In the gathering dusk, I could just make out that her face was wet with tears.

"It's what everyone thinks of me, isn't it? It's certainly what Nathan thinks. The irony is that I'd give anything to be that girl again—that silly, selfish girl with a head full of dresses and social engagements instead of bills and debts and marriage settlements. This is what my life is now!" She held her hands up, palms out, pressing against the thick vegetation on either side of us. "An ever-narrowing path leading to one destination—a loveless marriage to settle my mother's debts. So don't think I don't understand the desire to run off with some wildly inappropriate lover and live in a treetop—I do! It's just not an option for some of us."

I stared at Helen, realizing finally why she so hated the idea of me being with Raven: She was jealous of my freedom. It almost made me laugh. Helen felt hemmed in by her choices, but I was the one who had to lace in my wings every morning before she and Daisy woke. My own body was a cage narrower than the path we were on.

I looked over Helen's shoulder and then wheeled around to look behind me.

"What's the matter?" Helen asked.

I was so horrified I couldn't answer. Instead I turned her around to face the direction we had been moving in. Instead of a path there was a wall of thicket. The forest had swallowed up the path and our friends, trapping us in a leafy tomb.

18

I LET HELEN thrash at the thicket until I saw that she was hurting herself.

"Stop that," I said, grabbing her scratched and bleeding hands. "We're not getting out that way."

"And just which way *are* we getting out?" she demanded.

"I would suggest up."

The voice came from above us. I looked up and saw Raven perched on a branch just over our heads. Marlin was sitting next to him, his wings mantled over his head.

"There are two of them," Helen hissed, clutching my arm.

"It's okay, that's Marlin," I explained. "He's a friend."

Even in the diminishing light I could see the whites of Helen's eyes. "You've been consorting with more than one of them?"

"Now is not the time, Helen."

"I would have to agree," Raven said, dropping down to a lower branch. "Though I would like to discuss later just why you think I'm a *wildly inappropriate lover*."

"*That* was a private conversation," Helen snipped. "It is not polite to eavesdrop."

Raven laughed. "The whole forest could hear your private

conversation. And I'm afraid it's drawn more than Marlin and me. Listen."

I'd been so busy arguing with Helen I hadn't been using my Darkling ears. Now that I did I could hear branches creaking, the soft thud of stealthy feet . . . and my bass bell ringing a danger signal. "Raven's right," I told Helen, pushing her toward a tree trunk. "We have to climb."

"It's a trick to make us go with them," Helen objected. "I don't hear—"

A long high-pitched squeal silenced her.

"What was that?" she whispered.

"Goblin, I think," Marlin said, cocking his head to one side.

"Sounded too warbly for a goblin," Raven said. "Sounds more like a flesh-eating ghoul to me."

Helen fitted her boot into a notch in the tree, grabbed an overhanging branch, and hauled herself several feet up into the tree. Raven gave her a helpful push toward Marlin and reached for me just as the shrubbery behind me exploded.

The thing on the ground might once have been a goblin, but now rotting flesh hung in shreds off its bony skull and clawed hands. Yellow teeth snapped at the hem of my dress as Raven hoisted me up to a higher branch. The thing—the *ghoul*—let out an ear-splitting screech and scratched at the base of the tree.

"Climb!" Raven yelled at me.

I tore my eyes away from the creature and pushed at Helen, but she was frozen on the branch above me, looking down at the ghoul in horror.

"We never studied *that* in Miss Frost's class," Helen whispered as I climbed up next to her.

"There are more things in heaven and earth than are dreamt of in your philosophy," Marlin said as he dropped below us.

"Did he just quote Shakespeare?" Helen asked.

"They're not illiterate, Helen, they're just . . ." I looked below us to see Marlin leap onto the back of the ghoul.

"Brave," Helen finished for me, her voice tinged with surprise and admiration.

"Yes," I said, watching Raven worriedly as he attacked the ghoul. "Let's hope not foolishly so." My wings itched to break free and fly to Raven's aid, but I knew I had to get Helen away from danger.

"We have to climb." I put my hand on Helen's back to urge her, but as soon as I felt how rigid her muscles were I remembered her fear of heights.

"I c-can't . . ." she stammered.

"You managed on the Steeplechase," I said. "And your life didn't depend on it then."

She shook her head. "I only managed because Nathan was there. He took my mind off it." Her eyes were riveted to the ground where Raven and Marlin were battling the ghoul. They were using their wings like toreadors used their red capes, to bate the creature, wearing it down. But I had no idea if they'd be able to kill it—it already seemed dead.

"You have to get higher," Raven yelled as he feinted around the ghoul's charge. "We can only wear it out and then fly higher than it can climb."

"I can't get Helen to move," I called. "She's afraid of heights."

Raven and Marlin spared a moment to look at each other in blank surprise. I don't suppose they could imagine such a thing.

"You take care of her," Raven snapped at Marlin as the ghoul charged again. "I'll take care of this one."

Marlin looked like he wanted to argue, but Raven barked at him to go, and Marlin instantly sprung off the ground into the air. He landed on the branch next to Helen, grabbed her around the waist, and launched them both upward. I looked back down at Raven. The ghoul looked less weary than angry. Drool was dripping from its mouth, its eyes glowing red in the dark. It made a leap for Raven's throat, which he deflected with his wing, but the ghoul took a clawful of feathers with him.

"Follow them!" Raven shouted at me.

Instead I jumped down to the ground between Raven and the ghoul. Its red eyes fastened on me, glowing with a dead malice that chilled me to the bone. I saw it tensing to leap, but before it could I depressed the stem of the repeater, which I'd taken out of my pocket, releasing a tinkling melody.

"Do you know what you're doing?" Raven whispered in my ear.

"Not really," I admitted, "but it seems to have distracted it. I'm not sure for how long—"

Before I could finish my sentence the ghoul leapt for us. Raven grabbed me around the waist and sprang up, carrying us out of reach of the ghoul's snapping jaws. But it was clambering up the tree, following us, and Raven, exhausted by distracting it, was barely able to fly fast enough to evade it.

"Let me go!" I cried. "I'll fly on my own."

"No," he said, holding me tighter. "You don't know how to navigate through the trees."

I certainly hadn't ever flown as Raven was flying, dodging

over and under tree limbs, zigzagging through the woods to evade the ghoul until we finally burst through the canopy into open air. The ghoul made one last desperate leap for us. I felt its claws clamp onto my ankle. Raven lashed at it with his wing and it fell, jaws snapping, into the forest below us. We heard it crashing through the trees, shrieking with pain and frustration as we landed on top of a pine tree where Marlin and Helen waited for us.

"Good show!" Helen cried when we landed. "You trounced that boorish creature with great élan!"

I stared at Helen, not sure what to be more surprised at—that she was paying Raven a compliment, or that she was sitting on a tree branch a hundred feet above the ground seemingly unperturbed by the height. Then I noticed Marlin's wing over her shoulder and remembered the soothing effects of a Darkling's feathers. Perhaps they had provided a cure for her acrophobia.

"Yes," I said, smiling at Raven. "Good trouncing! But what about Nathan, Daisy, and Mr. Bellows? They're wandering through the woods unprotected—and Etta's still out here somewhere."

"Actually, the rest of your expedition was led out of the forest," Raven said, sitting down on a limb across from Marlin and Helen. "The Blythe Wood channeled you all into a narrow path to keep you from the ghouls, but when you and Helen got separated, the rest of your party was ejected and a ghoul managed to slip through a crack in the forest's defenses."

"The trees were protecting us?" Helen asked incredulously.

"The forest is alive. It possesses a guiding spirit—a genius loci—that protects its own creatures."

"But we're not its creatures," Helen said.

"Every innocent life belongs to the woods," Marlin told her. "We all come from the Great Forest originally."

I saw Helen blinking at him. I expected her to tell him that the van Beeks hailed from Washington Square and Hyde Park, not a forest, *thank you very much*, but she only smiled and said, "Why how very kind of the forest!"

"But what about Etta?" I asked. "She's still in the woods."

"Etta is in the Rowan Circle with the changelings," Raven replied. "She's in no danger. If you like, we can take you there."

"Would we have to fly again?" Helen asked.

"It would be quickest," Marlin told her.

"Then by all means, let's," Helen said, tucking one of Marlin's feathers behind her ear and holding out her arms to him. "I think I'm getting over my fear of heights."

⇥ ✦ ⇤

Helen may have conquered her fear of heights, but there were many things to be frightened of in the Blythe Wood that night. As we flew over the treetops, we could see by the light of the newly risen moon all sorts of creatures wandering through the woods—the horrible ghouls, goblins, trows, and some sort of long serpent that wound its way through the tree roots. There were less horrible creatures, too: lampsprites hanging amidst the pine boughs like paper lanterns; diminutive green boggles that squatted frog-like on tree branches, emitting a clear, sweet piping; and diaphanous floating fogs that Raven told me were the souls of departed humans.

"It's not just the door to Faerie that opens on All Hallows'

Eve," he explained. "The threshold to the human afterworld is thin tonight as well."

We flew through one of the clouds of mist. It felt cool and tingly on my face and summoned images in my mind—an old woman's face, sere brown fields, a child rolling an old-fashioned hoop down a small-town street—memories from someone else's life. When we flew out of the cloud my face was wet, but whether from the mist or tears I wasn't sure.

Finally we came to the Rowan Circle—a wide-open glade bordered by rowan trees. Earlier in the year, the trees had been full of white flowers and red berries, but now the branches were nearly bare and bone-like in the moonlight, a white thicket barrier against the creatures roaming though the woods. The Order used the Rowan Circle for its initiation because it could be held against the fairies unless they were invited in. Etta stood at the center of the circle now. She appeared to be alone.

"What is she doing?" Helen asked as Marlin let her down on a branch. "Did she come all the way out here to stand alone in a circle?"

"She's not alone," Raven said, alighting on a branch above the circle. "Look carefully."

I lay down on the branch and studied the circle. The moon was directly above us now, filling the whole glade with shadowless light. There was no place for anyone to hide—and yet Etta seemed to be talking to a large group, turning to address one and then another invisible presence, her face registering interest, sadness, even amusement as she listened to each one. I heard a low murmur filling the circle as though it contained a multitude. But I couldn't see anyone but Etta. I turned to tell

Raven that, but as I moved my head I caught a flicker of movement out of the corner of my eye.

I looked back—sideways—at the edge of the circle and noticed that the air in front of the rowan trees rippled like water, as if there was a waterfall rimming the circle that reflected back the moonlit trees. And in that waterfall were shapes—roughly human, but ever shifting.

"It's how the changelings appear when they're *unhosted*," Raven whispered in my ear. "They exist in a separate dimension, reflecting their surroundings as camouflage."

"So you're saying that Etta is surrounded by changelings?" Helen asked, squinting at the circle. "What if one tries to assume her identity?"

"They're not going to hurt her," Raven said. "She's called them together to help. No one's ever done that before. Listen."

Etta was talking now, addressing all of the changelings. "Thank you all for coming and for all your kind words. It's not me you should be praising, though, but your brave comrade, Rue, who has so unselfishly sacrificed herself on behalf of my sister and myself by taking my sister's place at the Hellgate Club."

A ripple moved around the circle—a wave stirring the shimmering surface and an echo of the words *unselfishly sacrificed*, which the changelings seemed to savor like a fine wine.

"I am afraid, though, that she has put herself in great danger. She and all the girls at the Hellgate Club have vanished. My friends are doing what they can to find and help her, but I have come to ask you to help, too."

The watery shapes shimmied and bobbed like buoys in a

rough sea. "What can what can we we we do?" They spoke in an echoing chorus. "We are noth-noth-nothing on our own own."

"But you're not nothing," Etta said, smiling. "Rue has shown me that. She's a person in her own right. We must find her—and no one is better able to find her than you, her sisters. You can move through the city crowds unseen and unheard, you can hear every whisper and read every thought. Somewhere in those multitudes someone will know where the girls from the Hellgate Club have been moved."

The changelings were bubbling now with excitement. One surged forward from the mass and assumed a roughly human shape. "We can do that," it said. "But once we find our sister and the others, what will we do?"

"All you have to do is send a message. The lampsprites have volunteered to be our messengers."

She held out her hand, and a light drifted down from one of the trees and alit on her open palm. The light resolved into a tiny winged figure that I recognized as Featherbell, the lampsprite Daisy had befriended last year. She brushed her wings against Etta's face, dusting her cheeks with iridescent powder. That was how they communicated with humans.

"Featherbell says that she and her friends will accompany you to the city to look for Rue and the other girls. They will carry any message you have for us and let us know if you are in any danger."

"The light-things have never helped us before," the changeling said. "And we don't know how to speak to them."

Featherbell chatted animatedly to Etta. Since I hadn't been touched by her wings I couldn't understand her, nor could the changelings. They shifted restlessly around the circle, splashing and sloshing, their forms merging with each other.

"Their types of magic are opposite," Raven whispered in my ear. "That's why they've never had anything to do with each other before. I'm not sure Etta's plan will work."

But even as he spoke a dozen lights were drifting down from the trees. A conflagration of lampsprites fluttered around the glade, each one brushing past Etta, touching their wings to her face and then looping around the circle, swooping and gliding like mad barn swallows, each one leaving a trail of bright streamers, like kite tails, which braided together into a multicolored skein. It made me dizzy to watch. I blinked . . . and saw that the changelings were moving, too, their watery shapes dancing around the circle like girls around a maypole—girls in bright dresses. The changelings were no longer made of colorless water; the lampsprites had imbued them with their own colors.

"I've never seen anything like this," Raven whispered. "Changelings always take the features and memories of their hosts. I've never seen any creatures freely give of themselves to the changelings before."

I thought of what Omar had said about alliances being formed and felt a defiant thrill. Van Drood might be amassing the shadows, but if we could harness light and water together like this, we could stand against him. And if the changelings and lampsprites could form such an unlikely bond, why not the Darklings and the Order?

Perhaps Raven was thinking the same thing. He squeezed my hand, his dark eyes shining in the reflected glow of the fiery dance below us. The changelings and lampsprites had come to a standstill. Each changeling had assumed a shape and color now. One pirouetted, its amorphous shape gaining definition, as a blob of clay becomes a pot when it's turned on a wheel. The shape was now distinctly female.

"Let us do what Etta has asked," the female changeling said.

"Let let let us us us!" the multitude excitedly echoed back. But they were no longer a faceless multitude. The circle was now ringed with a dozen Ettas.

"No one has ever entrusted the changelings with a mission before," Raven said. "Etta is their new hero."

"That's all very well and good," Helen said, raising her voice so Etta could hear her. "But she'll also be in trouble if she doesn't get back to the dorm now!"

A dozen Ettas lifted their heads to look at Helen. When the real Etta laughed the laugh rippled through the circle, the lampsprites flocking around Etta like a rainbow cloak. I had a feeling that neither the changelings nor the lampsprites would ever let Etta fall into any trouble.

19

ETTA, HELEN, AND I made our way back through the forest by foot, following a path that the Blythe Wood opened for us, while Raven and Marlin flew overhead. I'd only been able to say a hurried farewell to Raven, but he'd squeezed my hand again and asked if I'd read his note. I told him I hadn't had time to, and he looked hurt and left hurriedly. I opened the note as we walked. "Don't go in the woods tonight," was all it said. *Well, that wasn't very helpful,* I thought, as the clear moonlit sky above us opened up and let down a torrent of rain.

"It's the changelings," Etta told us, smiling through the downpour. "They move through water when they're unhosted. The rain will take them to the river and the river will take them down to the city to look for Rue. The lampsprites will fly with them."

"Couldn't they have caught the morning train from Rhinecliff?" Helen asked, regarding her mud-soaked boots ruefully.

Etta's response was to hug Helen and thank her for coming to find her. Helen gruffly told her to quit the *sentimental bosh* and get back to the dorm or we'd all catch our deaths of cold. But I noticed that she was smiling when Etta turned away to hurry along the path—and still was when we got to the edge of the woods where Nathan and Mr. Bellows were waiting for us.

"Thank the Bells," Mr. Bellows said, tearing at his already rumpled hair. "I thought the wood had devoured you."

"What took so long?" Nathan demanded.

"*We* were rescuing Etta," Helen replied haughtily, "while you gentlemen were being led on a merry chase by a bunch of trees."

I waited to see if she would mention Raven and Marlin coming to our aid, but instead she looked around and asked, "Where's Daisy?"

"She's back in the library with Vi and Lillian—she was so upset that we thought it best she stay there."

"Oh," Helen said, looking more miffed than relieved. "She must be worried about us and sorry we had that silly fight. But you would think she'd have come looking for us."

Nathan and Mr. Bellows looked at each other and shrugged, as if to say they weren't about to enter into the internal workings of girls' friendships. Then they both turned to walk back to the castle, with Etta between them excitedly explaining the plan she had initiated with the changelings and lampsprites. When we reached the library Miss Sharp and Daisy already knew about the plan from Miss Corey. Helen looked uneasy for the first time since we'd left the Rowan Circle.

"Did she tell you anything else?"

Miss Sharp looked at her quizzically and shook her head. "She only spoke of the changelings—and then once you were safe she went into a deep trance. Is there something else we should know, Helen?"

"Yes, Helen," Daisy said. "Is there anything else? We all know how much you despise keeping secrets."

I stared at Daisy. Although her eyes were pink from crying, she hadn't gotten up to greet us. Was she really still angry with us? And would Helen, in her pique, reveal our encounter with the Darklings? But Helen only shook her head. "Of course the experience of seeing the changelings and lampsprites communicate is not possible to convey. You had to be there."

Daisy turned pale and bit her lip. "It was clever of Etta to think of including the lampsprites." Then she busied herself pouring tea for us all while Miss Sharp built up the fire.

We sat around it talking through the night, filling our teachers and Nathan in on everything Omar and Kid Marvel had told us. It was clear that the news weighed heavily on Nathan. I had thought that rescuing Ruth from the Hellgate Club had done something toward relieving his grief over his sister Louisa's condition, but now I saw that the situation was an uncomfortable reminder of his limitations. He had rescued Louisa from Faerie, but part of her still lingered there; he had rescued Ruth from the Hellgate Club, but her changeling self had been lost, and now all those other girls were gone, too. I wondered if finding Rue and the others would dispel the shadows from his soul. Or would there always be one more girl he couldn't save to haunt him?

"I'm glad the changelings are looking for Rue and the other girls," Miss Sharp said, "but I'm afraid it's not enough. We have to go to the Council. We should have gone to them right away."

"I'll go to Dame Beckwith and tell her it was my idea to keep the whole thing secret," Mr. Bellows offered gallantly.

"We'll *all* go to Dame Beckwith," Miss Sharp said.

"Us too?" Daisy asked, wringing her hands. "Do you think they'll expel us?"

"I meant Mr. Bellows, Miss Corey, and me," she said, laying a hand on her friend's shoulder. Even in her trance, Miss Corey stirred at her touch. "As for you three . . ." She blinked at us in the early-morning light as though she'd just remembered something. "Don't you have midterms today?"

⇥ ✦ ⇤

We could have gone to Dame Beckwith and asked to be excused from midterms, but none of us wanted to be around when she found out the secret we'd been keeping from her. Instead we sat through our exams. When I looked up from my own paper I saw Nathan, Helen, and Daisy hard at work at theirs. Daisy looked grim and determined, as though she had decided to best us all by getting the highest grade. Helen looked energized and fresh. Even Nathan looked serious. When had *that* happened? I wondered, lowering my eyes to the blank page in front of me. Last year Nathan had been the one in danger of failing; this year it was me. Perhaps if I hadn't been up all night I would have managed to summon a few random facts to put down, but I had to admit there were few enough of those facts rattling around in a head full of lost girls and menacing shadows, midnight flights and feathery kisses. I wasn't all that surprised to be called in to Dame Beckwith's office the week after exams.

I approached her office with dragging steps, sure that I was about to be asked to leave. I had seriously considered not coming back to Blythewood this year. I had told Helen and Daisy that I didn't care about failing my exams. Raven had told me he wanted me to come to him when I was ready. So why was I so afraid of being asked to leave?

Was it because I wasn't sure Raven would have me . . . or because I wasn't ready to go to him yet?

Well, you should have thought of that before you botched your exams, I chided myself as I lifted a heavy hand to knock on Dame Beckwith's door.

"You musn't blame yourself!"

The words would have been reassuring had they been directed at me, but as they came from behind the closed door, they clearly weren't. Besides, I recognized the voice as that of Miss Frost, who would have been the first to tell me that my problems were my own fault—and to point out that it was rude to be eavesdropping on a private conversation. I lifted my hand again just as Dame Beckwith replied, "Who else should I blame? Jude?"

My hand froze. *Jude?* Could she possibly mean Judicus van Drood? I lowered my hand and opened my inner ear to listen.

"Well, yes," Miss Frost replied, "Judicus van Drood *chose* to become a monster."

"Do any of us make that choice, Euphorbia? I saw what was happening to him. I saw that he loved Evangeline"—my heart quickened at the sound of my mother's name—"but I forbade him to speak to her."

"Of course you did!" Miss Frost cried. "She was his student. It would have been most improper! You directed him to the correct procedure—to apply to the Council for approval of the match when she came of age. And they did approve—"

"Until he lost his fortune. And by that time Evangeline was in love with another."

I waited, scarcely daring to breathe, to see if Dame Beckwith would reveal the identity of my father. Did she know who he was? But if she had known he was a Darkling, she would never have allowed me at Blythewood.

"He's not the only one to ever lose a beloved. When I lost Miles—"

"You spent the next twenty years overindulging in drink," Dame Beckwith snapped. "And allowed the *tenebrae* to possess a student right under your nose." The silence that followed made it clear how mortified Miss Frost must be from the remark. When Dame Beckwith spoke next her voice was gentler.

"Your loss weakened you, Euphorbia, just as Jude's weakened him. It made you vulnerable to the shadows, just as it made him."

"It was because I was jealous of other people's happiness," Miss Frost said. "I see that now that I have him back. Surely you understand."

Dame Beckwith sighed.

"Yes. I think for a time I, too, was preyed on by the shadows. I was happy to go along with the Council's decision to delay Jude's betrothal to Evangeline, and I was happy when they revoked their permission to wed. I allowed myself to believe he'd forget Evangeline, that we could be together. Me, a married woman!"

"Your marriage to Daniel Beckwith was not exactly a love match."

"No." Dame Beckwith laughed ruefully. "It certainly wasn't. But at least he allowed the world to believe Nathan was his child, despite knowing otherwise. And after Nathan was born I understood that I must renounce Jude. I saw what he'd become. I tried to save him, but the shadows had already taken over. And now—to think that he's luring young women to their ruin! I feel as if I am personally responsible for the fates of those poor women!"

"You must not think that, India. You have our own girls to consider. How did the council react when you told them about the Hellgate Club?"

"Not well. They accused me of not having control over my own teachers and students, and they expressed a concern that Blythewood girls have grown too aggressive. They're afraid our girls have turned into bluestockings like the British suffragettes, tossing bricks through windows and planting bombs. What do they expect? They train us to kill and then expect us to be equally comfortable pouring tea and beheading goblins."

"Well," Euphorbia said, "a few additional decorum lessons won't hurt the girls."

Dame Beckwith was silent for a moment. When she spoke, it was lower, and I had to strain to hear. "They said if we didn't demonstrate that our girls were being trained in the feminine arts they will close down the school."

"They wouldn't!"

"I believe they would . . . Oh dear, please don't weep, Euphorbia."

"But where would Miles and I go if the school closed?" Miss Frost said in a quavering voice.

"We'll just have to do our best to make sure it doesn't. Now, please compose yourself. Haven't you a class at this hour?"

The sound of Miss Frost's petticoats rustling gave me ample warning that she was approaching the door. I quickly scurried around the corner and waited until she passed by, so busy sniffling that she didn't notice me. I felt like crying myself. Could the Council truly be thinking of closing Blythewood? I couldn't be kicked out now! I had to find a way to save the school.

I paused, once again, on the threshold of Dame Beckwith's office. Miss Frost had left the door partially open. Dame Beckwith was sitting behind her desk, her chair angled so she could look out the window that faced the lawn, the gardens, and the Blythe Wood, but the windows were fogged and obscured by the rain that had been coming down since All Hallows' Eve. As I watched I saw her lift a hand to wipe her eyes.

It had been shocking to hear Dame Beckwith talk about her love for Judicus van Drood, shocking to hear her talk about the Council trying to close Blythewood, but all of that was nothing to seeing strong, indomitable Dame Beckwith reduced to tears. I almost fled, but she must have heard me.

"Oh, Avaline," she said, turning from the window and squaring her shoulders. "Come in. I was just wondering what this rain would do to the lacrosse field."

It was such a mundane concern that I almost laughed, but then I realized this was how Dame Beckwith was able to face all those problems and go on. Just as she had gone on after she lost her beloved to the shadows and her daughter to Faerie.

"I know you have a lot on your mind," I said, choosing my words carefully. "If there's anything I can do to help . . ."

"As a matter of fact, I have a job for you."

"Anything," I told her, thinking I'd be happy to slaughter goblins or comb the streets of New York City looking for the Hellgate Club.

"I knew I could count on you. The Council has suggested we have a Christmas dance."

I wasn't sure I'd heard her right. "A . . . dance?"

"It's exactly what we have to do right now," she said firmly. "I've already spoken to Herr Hofmeister about it. He's full of ideas and he asked me to assign him an assistant. I suggested you."

"Me? But I don't even like to dance."

"Life is full of doing things we don't enjoy, Avaline," she said grimly. "The discipline will be good for you and keep you out of trouble." She raised her eyes to mine. They were clear and sharp, all sign of tears gone. "Unless there's something else you're doing with your evenings you'd like to tell me about."

I swallowed hard, willing myself not to think about Raven and our moonlit flights lest she divine them with her penetrating gaze. "No," I said, "just studying. I'm afraid I'll fall behind—"

"You did brilliantly on your exams," she said. "I always find that the busier I am the more I can get done. I know you'll do a good job. In fact, I'm counting on you to make this dance a success. The future of Blythewood depends on it."

⇢ ✦ ⇠

I left Dame Beckwith's office in a fog as deep as the one outside on the river. I wasn't sure what to be more befuddled by—that the Council in all their wisdom had responded to the news of an underworld racket of abducting girls by suggesting we throw a dance, or that I'd aced my exams. At least I had a suspicion about the solution to the latter.

"Yes, we replaced your exams," Helen readily admitted when I confronted her and Daisy.

"I used a forgery spell to fake your handwriting," Daisy said proudly. "Helen snuck into Dame Beckwith's office."

At least they seemed to have made up with each other for the purpose of this caper.

"What else could we do?" Helen asked innocently. "You would have gotten thrown out otherwise."

"B-but we'll *all* be thrown out if Dame Beckwith finds out."

"Dame Beckwith has bigger fish to fry," Helen said. "A dance! How completely absurd. And run by that silly man!"

"He *is* rather dotty," Daisy concurred. "But rather sweet. He reminds me of my uncle Gustav. I wonder if outsiders will be invited?"

"I certainly hope not!" Helen cried. "My mother would jump at the chance to send her ancient bachelors. We'll all look like perfect fools. I personally will have nothing to do with it."

"Well, *I* think it sounds like fun," Daisy said, glaring at Helen, their truce apparently at an end. "I'll help you, Ava. Just let me know what I can do."

I would have liked to send Daisy in my stead, but I didn't want to get her in any more trouble than she'd already risked on my behalf. So that evening after dinner I reported to the large room on the second floor that had been converted into a dancing studio by rolling up the old rugs, polishing the hardwood floors, and installing a wall of mirrors.

"Ah, Fraulein Hall!" Herr Hofmeister simpered, clicking his heels together and bowing. "I was wondering when I would have the pleasure of your company. Your absence from my dance classes has not gone unnoticed."

"Well, er, I already took dancing classes with Madame Musette."

"Ah, Madame Musette," he murmured, shaking his head sorrowfully. "A quaint old dear, but unfortunately hopelessly out of date and too blind to see what her students need. Take you, for example." He tucked his stick beneath his arm and, before I quite knew what he was up to, whirled me around to face the mirrors and put his hands on my shoulders. I gasped aloud. Would he feel my wings beneath my bones?

"Look at yourself in the mirror, Fraulein." It was an order, not a request. I half expected to see myself revealed as the winged monster I had seen in the Hall of Mirrors at Coney Island, but all I saw was a nervous-looking redhead cowering beneath the foppish dancing master's gaze.

"See how your shoulders are hunched over as though you were hiding from someone?" He pressed his hands on my shoulders, forcing them down. "And your shoulder blades." He lowered his hands and I flinched, sure now that he would feel the wings. "They are as tight as bow strings. You must stand up straight, but remain relaxed and flexible, like a willow bending in the wind, lest you *snap*!" He rapped his stick against the floor, making me jump.

"You will learn all this in my dance class."

"Actually, I just came to say that Dame Beckwith has put me in charge of the Christmas dance."

"*Ach du lieber!* But then you must certainly attend my classes. How else will you understand what I am attempting to achieve?"

I conceded he had a point.

"Excellent! We will discuss the program and necessary arrangements for the Christmas dance after class, and I will provide you with extra lessons to make up for the time you have missed. You will not regret it, Fraulein. You shall see a marvelous transformation by Christmas. I will have you flying around the ballroom!"

⇥ ✦ ⇤

Although it made me feel disloyal to Madame Musette, I had to admit that Herr Hofmeister's dance classes did transform me. It wasn't just that my posture improved—he was right, I *had* been hunching over—but that my state of mind did, too. Perhaps I had been inwardly cowering, so afraid of being revealed as a monster that I had begun to see myself as one. When I was dancing in Herr Hofmeister's class, though, I did not think of myself as a monster. I didn't think at all. The complicated steps and the hundred and one instructions (*chin up, tummy in, we're not on the hockey field, Miss Bennett*) chased every thought from my brain. It was a welcome respite.

In addition, Herr Hofmeister had decided that it wasn't enough to have a dance; we had also to put on divertissements from a ballet as the evening's entertainment. He chose a Viennese ballet called *Die Puppenfee*, which was about a fairy doll in a toy shop and her troupe of dancing dolls. This meant we needed costumes for Chinese, Spanish, Austrian, Japanese, and harlequin dolls, and it fell to me to take the girls' measurements and send them to Blythewood's dressmaker, Caroline Janeway, in the city.

When I thought about Rue and the other girls at the Hellgate Club I felt guilty that I was using my time planning a dance, but Dame Beckwith had said the Council was looking for them. And Raven—on one of the rare nights I was able to get away—promised me that he and the other fledglings were combing the waterfronts searching for the new location of the Hellgate Club. The constant rain that beat at the ballroom windows assured me that the changelings were traveling back and forth on the river also looking for Rue, but after a while the thrum of the rain merged with the music and the steady beat of Herr Hofmeister's stick, and I didn't think of Rue or Raven anymore. Even when I wasn't in class the music was in my head, driving out every other thought. If I forgot the music for a moment, some other girl humming it brought it back.

The only ones *not* humming Herr Hofmeister's dance tunes were Helen and Nathan—Helen because of her staunch loyalty to Madame Musette and continuing feud with Daisy, and Nathan because he was afraid of being swarmed by partnerless females.

"We all take turns being the boy," I told him one day in November.

"Oh and how is *that* going to work at the Christmas dance? All those girls dancing with each other hardly seems festive."

"Maybe some girls like to dance with other girls," I suggested.

"Oh!" he said, looking surprised and then awkward. "Do, er, you?"

I thought about it for a moment. I actually had been enjoying dancing with my friends. Cam had turned into an especially graceful lead and Daisy, although still chilly with me and Helen, followed as if she could read my mind. But I had not experienced anything like the thrill I got flying wing tip to wing tip with Raven. Not that I would tell Nathan that.

"I don't really care," I told Nathan, "but I suppose some of the other girls would. I'll talk to Herr Hofmeister about it at our next meeting."

"*Ach du lieber!* Of course we need men!" Herr Hofmeister exclaimed when I asked. "I've already discussed the situation with my patron, Mr. Montmorency, and he has agreed to come to the dance with a few of his associates."

"Oh," I said, recalling the smoke-filled room I'd glimpsed at Georgiana's summer ball, "but they're so . . . *old.*"

Herr Hofmeister looked surprised and slightly affronted. "No older than I! And they are all excellent dancers. But have no fear, I will ask Mr. Montmorency to organize some of his younger acquaintances, perhaps some of the junior officers at Mr. Driscoll's bank."

"Hm . . ." Bank clerks sounded only minimally more fun than old men. "I have a friend who is a lawyer—Samuel Greenfeder. Perhaps he'd invite some of his friends."

"Best to check with Dame Beckwith," Herr Hofmeister said. "We don't want any of the wrong element."

I bristled at the idea that anyone would consider Sam Greenfeder *the wrong element*, but when I went to Dame Beckwith she distractedly told me that it was fine with her if I invited some of my friends from the city. As I left her office I heard her humming one of Herr Hofmeister's tunes. Apparently she, too, had been taken over by the dance craze.

I bumped into Daisy outside Dame Beckwith's office. "Oh," she said, turning pink. "Did Dame Beckwith say we could invite friends to the ball?"

"Why? Is there someone you want to invite?"

She went from pink to beet red. "No . . . maybe . . . what business is it of yours if I do?"

She ran off in a flurry of petal-pink petticoats that were definitely not regulation school wear. I considered following her to find out what was going on, but then thought better of it and, humming the Chinese polka from *Die Puppenfee*, waltzed my way back to the dance studio.

20

SAM GREENFEDER WROTE back to me that he would be honored to attend the Blythewood Christmas dance and so would a dozen of his young lawyer friends. He also added that he had some information I would be interested in that he did not feel comfortable imparting in the mail, but that he would tell me when we next saw each other in person. Intrigued, I decided to take the train into the city the first weekend of December. I had to approve the costumes for the dance at Miss Janeway's anyway, and since my schoolwork was finally back on track (Dame Beckwith had been right—having more to do had only made me more efficient) and preparations for the dance were shaping up nicely, I thought a weekend in the city seemed like a perfect reward.

I asked Helen and Daisy if they wanted to go with me, but they both declined, Daisy because she was supervising a nestling tracking hike and Helen because she'd volunteered to go along—which seemed suspicious to me, considering they were still hardly speaking to each other. As I rode out in Gillie's trap I saw the troop of nestlings entering the Blythe Wood under the watchful supervision of Professor Malmsbury and two armed Dianas. Helen was trailing behind the group, scanning the treetops. Since Halloween she had been looking longingly at the woods and asking me a lot of questions about the Darklings.

"No Darkling is likely to provide you with a townhouse on Fifth Avenue and a summer cottage in Newport," I had told her.

"There are more important things," Helen had shocked me by replying. Now I saw why she had volunteered to go into the woods with the nestlings.

"Thank the Bells we don't have to tromp through those nasty old woods!" Myrtilene Montmorency giggled to Susannah Dewsnap and Mary MacCrae. The three girls had tagged along to the station.

"And just how did you get out of it?" I asked.

"Don't you remember? We're to do a divertissement for the Christmas dance—the Spanish doll's dance from *Die Puppenfee*. We've been traveling to Herr Hofmeister's private studio in Riverdale for special instruction on weekends."

"Oh," I said, trying to recall if Herr Hofmeister had mentioned this to me. It seemed that the preparations for *Die Puppenfee* were getting entirely out of hand. "Couldn't Herr Hofmeister teach them to you at school?"

"Oh," Mary gushed, "but we get to dance with his star pupils, and the Riverdale studio is so marvelous. It's in a mansion. I only wish that this confounded rain would stop! The view from the grand ballroom is so lovely when it's clear."

I listened to all the many wonders of Herr Hofmeister's Riverdale mansion all the way to the station and then all the way to the city. Apparently the ballroom floor was paved with multicolored marble so polished you could see the reflection of your dancing shoes in it. When the sun hit the crystal chandeliers they sent rainbows spinning around the room. The other students wore the most marvelous silk dresses and came from all over the world. By the time the girls got off at the Spuyten Duyvil stop in Riverdale my head felt stuffed full of mazurkas and castanets. The bustle of New York City was a relief when I left Grand Central Station and caught a streetcar to Miss Janeway's dress shop in Stuyvesant Square.

Caroline Janeway greeted me warmly, if a tad hurriedly. "Your Herr Hofmeister has been keeping us all up to our eyebrows in tulle."

"I'm sorry if he's giving you too much to do. He tends to be a bit . . . *fussy*."

"He's like a bride with her trousseau! He has insisted we import the embroidered trim for the Austrian doll from Vienna even though I have a perfectly good embroiderer, Frau Schirmer, here in the city. And the Japanese doll must have a hand-painted kimono from Kyoto, the Spanish doll real Spanish lace from Seville . . ." Miss Janeway pulled out lengths of the fabric as she talked. "It's costing the school a fortune. I was shocked that Dame Beckwith would approve such lavish expenditure, especially now."

"Why *especially now*?" I asked.

Miss Janeway looked around the shop, even though there were no customers. She sent her assistant Cosette downstairs to bring up the fairy doll costume. When Cosette was gone, Miss Janeway leaned over the counter.

"I've heard some of my clients—Council members—

talking," she whispered. "The school's endowment was badly reduced last spring because of a failed investment."

"Oh," I said, surprised. "I never thought about Blythewood having an endowment."

Miss Janeway laughed. "Did you think the place runs on fairy dust?"

I blushed. "I guess I never *thought* about what it runs on. Everyone seems so rich."

"Even the wealthiest must put their money *somewhere*, and someone convinced the Council to put it into some risky investment that failed. Of course, there's still money, but what concerns me is . . ." She looked around the shop again nervously and lowered her voice even lower. "I overheard one of the alumnae talking about a financial plan to recoup the losses by investing in a new building downtown. She said it was supposed to be a sure thing and they had gotten in 'on the ground floor,' but it also sounded as if all of the endowment had been sunk in this one investment—as well as the fortunes of our wealthiest alums."

"Well, they wouldn't have invested all the school's money if it wasn't a sure thing, right?"

Caroline Janeway shook her head. "I'm afraid wealth doesn't last forever. My family lost our fortune in the crash of ninety-three. Oh, don't look so sorry for me. I'm quite happy with my lot, but look at the van Beeks. Who would have thought their fortune could vanish as it did?"

"Yes, Helen said poor Mr. van Beek had made some unwise investments—" I looked up from the lace on the counter. "Oh!

I wonder if the same advisors who led Mr. van Beek into ruin also misadvised the Council. Mr. Greenfeder has been investigating Mr. van Beek's affairs. I'm having tea with him and Agnes later. Shall I ask him to look into the investments the Council is making now?"

Miss Janeway bit her lip and considered the question as though it were a crooked seam. "Only if he can be very discreet in his inquiries. If it gets out that the investment is shaky . . . well, rumors like that can start a panic."

"I'm sure Mr. Greenfeder would be most discreet."

"Yes," she said, smiling mischievously, "except in his affection for our Miss Moorhen. Anyone can see he's besotted with her—except for her. Do ask him to look into it. If the school is being compromised, well . . ." She looked up as Cosette came in all but drowning in mounds of pink satin and tulle, humming a refrain from *Die Puppenfee*. *"The Fairy Doll* will be Blythewood's swan song."

»→ ◈ ←«

After giving instructions for the costumes to be shipped to Blythewood, I walked west on Fourteenth Street toward the Jane Street Tea Room mulling over all that Miss Janeway had told me. I had not grown up with money. My mother had made a sparse living as a seamstress and hat trimmer. If a client didn't pay on time we would subsist on meager fare—day-old bread soaked in warm milk and sprinkled with sugar was one of my mother's favorite "hard times" meals, which she claimed tasted exactly like the baked Alaska at Delmonico's—but we always managed somehow. Up until the last months of my mother's life, when she was haunted by her fear of van Drood, we had been happy together in our various little apartments near the river. In fact, as I neared the Jane Street Tea Room, I recognized the streets we had lived on and smelled the salt breeze coming off the Hudson. *I could come back here,* I thought. If Blythewood lost its endowment I could get a job as a seamstress and a little apartment near the water and at night Raven and I could fly up the dark river to the Shawangunks—or perhaps we could live in one of the little farmhouses in the valley beneath the Gunks. We could raise cows and sell milk to people in the city . . .

I might be able to manage, but what about all the other girls at Blythewood? What about those like Etta, for whom Blythewood was a chance to better themselves? I couldn't quite see girls like Alfreda Driscoll and Georgiana Montmorency living in tenement flats or rustic Catskill dairy farms. And while I wouldn't grieve too hard for Georgiana, there were other girls at Blythewood I would hate to see reduced to poverty, not to mention the teachers. And if Blythewood ceased to train girls, who would protect the world against evil?

By the time I reached the Jane Street Tea Room I had worked myself up into a proper tizzy. Only the sight of Sam Greenfeder, dressed in his best Sunday suit with his unruly red hair brilliantined into submission, and Agnes Moorhen, trim and spruce in navy serge with a bright yellow feather nodding from her hat, brought me to my senses. *They would stop it,* I thought. Agnes and Sam would not let Blythewood founder.

"Oh, Mr. Greenfeder," I cried as he got up to pull out a chair for me. "Do tell me you've found out who ruined Mr. van Beek. I think the same person must be trying to ruin Blythewood and we must stop him!"

Sam looked to Agnes, who gave him a curt nod that made the yellow feather bob. "Yes," he said, pushing my chair in and taking his own seat across from me, "you may be right. I'll tell you all that I've discovered about Mr. van Beek's affairs, but first . . ." He looked nervously toward Agnes again and she sighed.

"Oh, for Bell's sake, Sam, I'll tell her. We've found Mr. Farnsworth. And we think he knows where your book is."

»→ ✦ ←«

Agnes insisted I have my tea before they told me the story of finding Mr. Farnsworth. "You're looking too thin," she said. "Are they working you too hard? I hear this new dancing master rules the girls like an Austrian regimental sergeant."

"Herr Hofmeister?" I asked through a mouthful of watercress sandwiches. I was cramming in as many as I could to satisfy Agnes's concerns and get to Sam's story. "He's more like an anxious nursemaid than a military sergeant, but please, tell me about Mr. Farnsworth. How did he survive the *Titanic*? And what do you mean he knows where the book is? Does he have it?"

For answer Agnes handed me a scone slathered in clotted cream and raspberry preserves. Only when I had jammed it in my mouth did she nod to Sam to proceed.

"Well," he said, holding up one finger as if he were presenting a case to a jury, "I began by examining the records of survivors and looking for any who had suffered from exposure and required medical attention. I found that several crew members had been remanded to various sailors' rest homes throughout the Northeast. I tracked down each one—"

"He traveled from Cape May, New Jersey, to Portland, Maine," Agnes broke in, looking proudly at Sam. "On his days off, he interviewed over twenty seamen."

"All of whom had lost their memories," Sam said, glowing with Agnes's praise. "The doctors all thought their conditions were caused by the psychic trauma of the ship sinking or guilt over the deaths of so many passengers, but I began to suspect that some of them had been tampered with."

"Tampered with?" I asked, feeling a chill. I recalled the weeks I had spent in the Bellevue Pavilion for the Insane, drugged into a hallucinatory stupor, convinced by Dr. Pritchard that I was insane. "Who was tampering with them?" I asked, the clotted cream turning sour in my mouth.

Sam looked over at Agnes. She reached across the table and took my hand. "The same man who imprisoned you, Ava. That horrible Dr. Pritchard from Bellevue. Sam found that he had been called in as a consultant on all of the cases. That's when we knew we were on the right track."

"What do you mean?"

"We knew that van Drood had used Dr. Pritchard to keep you . . . *subdued* after the Triangle fire. So we reasoned that he was looking for Mr. Farnsworth, which meant that Mr. Farnsworth was alive. He had tampered with the memories of these sailors, to find out where Mr. Farnsworth was and then to destroy their memories so they wouldn't tell anyone what they had seen on the *Titanic*."

"But then how could you be sure if their memories were gone?" I asked.

"Because we had someone who could retrieve their memories even after they were buried," Sam said. "And for that we have you to thank."

"Me?"

"Yes, you found the gentleman who helped us."

I thought for a second and then saw it. "Omar?"

Sam nodded. "He's quite remarkable. I wish I could do what he does when I'm deposing a witness on the stand. He traveled to each of the hospitals with me and was able to reach each survivor's buried memories. Through them we tracked down Mr. Farnsworth. He was being kept in an insane asylum in Boston. He'd lost all his toes and two of his fingers to frostbite. He didn't remember who he was or what had happened to him, but Omar was able to dig into his memories and ascertain that he was Herbert Farnsworth and he had been on the *Titanic*."

"Poor Mr. Farnsworth!" I said, noticing how pale Agnes was. "Was Omar able to cure him and restore his memories?" I wanted to ask if he had *A Darkness of Angels*, but I didn't want to seem callous after all the poor man had suffered—and all on account of my writing to him about the book .

Agnes and Sam exchanged a look. Agnes nodded and Sam answered. "Omar hasn't been able to completely reverse the damage done to his brain, but he has hopes of reaching him eventually. He's with him now."

"Where?" I looked around the tearoom, half expecting to see the tall Hindu mesmerist hiding among the aspidistras.

"Not far," Agnes replied. "That's why we asked you to meet us here. We brought him to the Seamen's Friend Society Sailors' Home. It's only a block away. Omar thinks that you might be able to jar his memory."

"Why me?" I asked, brushing crumbs off my shirtwaist in preparation of leaving.

"Oh," Agnes said, looking guiltily at Sam. "Didn't we say? He's been asking for you."

21

THE AMERICAN SEAMEN'S Friend Society Sailors' Home was located at the end of Jane Street on the corner of West Street in a handsome red brick Georgian-style building. Fittingly, it faced the river, and in the distance, New York Harbor with the Statue of Liberty. A polygonal corner tower gave it the look of a lighthouse. The Cunard Line piers were just across the street. Seeing them reminded me of the awful night last April when Helen and I waited with a huge crowd to see who had survived the sinking of the *Titanic*—and the horror of learning that Helen's father had not. Glancing over at Agnes, I guessed from her pale countenance that she, too, was recalling that night and her own experiences of the doomed ship.

We passed through a plain but pleasant lobby in which several gentlemen in nautical garb sat in wicker chairs reading newspapers or dozing beneath framed prints of famous ships. The nautical décor was continued in the rope trimming in the elevator and the teak paneling and framed seascapes of the upstairs corridor, which was so narrow it resembled a ship's corridor. Small rooms were strung along it like berths. Sam knocked at one and a shaky voice told us to "come aboard."

The tiny room, perhaps seven feet by seven feet, was so

like a ship's berth that I half expected the floor to rock when I stepped inside. A narrow bed was built into the teak-paneled wall. Drawers and small cubbies were fitted beneath it. The single window, affording a view of the river and harbor, was shaped like a porthole. Omar sat cross-legged in a rope chair that was suspended from the ceiling. A thin, pale man, wisps of sand-colored hair sticking up from his head, sat on the edge of his bed, his hands clasped tightly together. He smiled when he saw Agnes.

"Oh, Miss Moorhen, how lovely of you to visit my stateroom. Is this another passenger? I don't believe I've seen her on board."

"This is my friend, Ava," she said. "She's been kept to her berth since we embarked by a bad case of *mal de mer*."

"Ah." He smiled at me kindly, the lines around his eyes crinkling like cracks in a china teacup. "It took me some time to get my sea legs, but now I hardly feel the motion of the ship at all! And look!" He pointed out the porthole window toward the Statue of Liberty. "We're almost there. We'll be docking by morning, I wager."

"Yes," Omar said in a silky voice. "We ought to start packing, don't you think, Herbert?"

"Yes, yes, you're so right, my dear friend." He knelt on the floor beside his bed and began rifling through the drawers. He pulled out a worn leather portmanteau.

"It's the one he had with him on the *Titanic*," Agnes whispered in my ear. "But it's empty. We hope that he'll remember what happened to the book when he goes to pack it, only . . . he often gets distracted at this point."

He was indeed holding up the leather satchel, blinking as he peered into it. He looked up from it and noticed me. "Oh, Miss . . . Ava, was it? Have you met Mr. Omar? He has traveled all the way from India. He's on a worldwide tour, demonstrating his remarkable talents. I have met such interesting people on this voyage . . ." His voice faltered again and he looked down at the empty satchel. "Though a few rather unpleasant, I'm afraid. If you run into a man in an Inverness cape, for instance . . ." He shivered and then began to shake so hard he dropped the satchel. Sam picked it up for him and Agnes helped him sit back down on his bed. Agnes sat down beside him and motioned for me to sit down on the other side.

"It's all right, Mr. Farnsworth," Agnes said in a soothing voice. "You don't have to pack right now. We're not docking until morning."

"Oh, that's good," he said with a sigh of relief, "because I'm afraid I've misplaced something." He stared at the satchel, which Agnes now held in her hands, and then back at me. "What did you say your name was, dear?"

"Avaline," I replied. "Avaline Hall."

It was as if I'd thrown icy water in his face. He sat up straighter, his vague watery eyes snapping into attention, and grabbed my hand.

"He remembers," I heard Omar whisper to Sam, and then in a louder voice to Mr. Farnsworth. "You mentioned Miss Hall's name to me several days ago. You spoke of a letter you had received from her."

"Yes, yes, Miss Avaline Hall of Blythewood. I had a letter from a girl of that name." Still holding on to my hand, he began patting the pockets of his jacket with his other hand. From inside a breast pocket he withdrew a much folded and faded sheet of paper and unfolded it with a shaking hand. I gasped as I recognized the pale blue shade of my own stationery with the embossed Bell and Feather Blythewood insignia.

"Yes," he said, nodding over the page. "A Miss Avaline Hall of Blythewood School wrote to ask me about a book . . . a very old, rare book. Only I can't quite make out the title. Can you?"

He held the page for me to see. I stared at it, my throat thickening at the sight. Pale wavy blue lines ran across the sheet where there had once been handwriting, but the page had evidently been soaked in water and the words had all run together. Staring at my own blurred handwriting I felt the icy chill of the North Atlantic where the *Titanic* had gone down and heard a bell tolling in my head. It was an entirely new bell I'd never heard before, a distant gong that sounded seven times, in three pairs and then singly.

"Tell him you can make out the title," Omar whispered in my ear over the sound of the bell, which once again rang seven times, this time closer.

"Yes," I told him, "I can read it. The book was called *A Darkness of Angels*. I wrote to ask you if you had a copy at Hawthorn."

"And I wrote back to say I did!" he said with childish glee. "And I told you I would bring it on my voyage . . . only . . . only . . ." He looked around the tiny room. He knelt back on the floor and began going through the drawers. The seven-beat bell rang again. "Only I knew the shadow man was looking for it, so I hid it."

"Did you hide it in your stateroom?" Agnes asked gently.

We were all thinking the same thing. If Mr. Farnsworth had hidden the book in his stateroom on the *Titanic*, the book was now most likely at the bottom of the ocean. Mr. Farnsworth looked at me and clutched my hand harder.

"That man followed me onto the ship because of the book." His voice was as cold and flat as a frozen sea. As cold as the bell tolling seven.

"Yes, that's most likely correct," Agnes said gently, "but that wasn't *your* fault, dear Mr. Farnsworth."

"But I knew he might," he said, his voice swelling with agitation, the lethal ice cracking, the seven-part toll ringing louder now. There was something that the bell was trying to tell me, something Mr. Farnsworth was trying to tell me. His hand in mine was beating time to the peal—three pairs and a single, three pairs and a single. He was making the bell ring inside my head. But why? I looked into his eyes but saw only confusion and fog there. Then I closed my eyes and listened to the bells.

Ding-dong, ding-dong, ding-dong, ding—

The air around me grew colder with each toll. The floor pitched and swayed. I opened my eyes and found I wasn't in Mr. Farnsworth's room at the Sailors' Home anymore. I was standing on the deck of a ship at night. In front of me were Mr. Farnsworth and Agnes, both bundled in heavy wool coats—because it was cold here in the North Atlantic. So cold that enormous icebergs floated in the sea. One was coming toward us right now—or rather, we were heading toward it on a collision path. And standing on the foredeck of the ship, his arms spread out as if he were conducting an orchestra, was Judicus van Drood.

"He's summoning the iceberg," I heard Agnes say just before the ship lurched. "And no ordinary iceberg—look!"

I followed Agnes's trembling finger and stared at the iceberg. Inside the ice a creature writhed—a hoary giant trapped in the ice. Van Drood had summoned an ice giant to ram into the *Titanic*.

The ship was turning. The crew had spotted the iceberg and were steering away from it. I found I was holding my breath, waiting to see if we would be able to avoid the iceberg, as if the *Titanic*'s fate might be avoided, but then I heard the awful screech of metal against ice as the hull of the ship scraped against the giant berg.

"It's breached the hull!" Mr. Farnsworth cried, grabbing Agnes's hands in his. I heard him telling her to go get Mrs. Hall and then go straight to the lifeboats.

"But what about you?" Agnes cried.

"There's something I must do," he said solemnly. "But I will see you again." And then he kissed her—rather passionately, I thought, for a librarian. Agnes, her cheeks flaming, rushed past me as though I were invisible. I watched her go but didn't follow her. I knew now why and how I was here. The bells I'd heard were the seven bells signaling the last half hour of the last watch, which rang ten minutes before the ship collided with the lethal iceberg. He had used his memory of the bells to transport me back to the moment of the ship's sinking, so that I could see what he did with the book. When Mr. Farnsworth turned I followed him, but I wasn't the only one.

I let van Drood go first, not wanting even in a vision to have van Drood behind me, and followed them both below deck, past cabins where sleepy passengers were being woken and summoned to report on deck in their lifejackets. With dawning horror, I realized that many of the people I passed were going to die. Mr. Farnsworth saw it, too, but he went deeper into the ship, to his second-class cabin. When he reached it he paused, looked behind him, and then quickly made a hand motion over the door before going inside. Van Drood was staring at the door. Then he stepped back behind a corner to hide. I slipped past him, holding my breath as though he might hear me breathing, and slipped into Mr. Farnsworth's cabin.

As I crossed the threshold I felt a prickle of energy, like electric static, and noticed a glowing sigil on the doorjamb. Mr. Farnsworth, mild-mannered librarian, was, after all, also a knight of the Order. He had placed a ward on his cabin so that van Drood couldn't follow him and see what he was doing.

He was searching through the built-in drawers beneath his bed just as he had been at the Sailors' Home in New York, muttering under his breath. Was he looking for the book? But he already had the portmanteau strapped across his chest. Agnes had said he carried it with him always. So what was he looking for?

He was scrabbling through a stack of books now, holding up one and tossing it aside, holding up another and rejecting it. Finally he found one that seemed to please him. I peered over his shoulder to read the title.

Some Problems in Archival Record Keeping.

That was the book he'd come back to rescue? Had poor Mr. Farnsworth already been deranged?

He placed *Some Problems* on his berth and then removed

the book from his portmanteau. I gasped aloud when I saw it. It was bound in thick leather the deep blue of a midnight sky engraved with an intricate gold pattern of wings and an ancient runic script that read *A Darkness of Angels. This* was the book that my mother had spent years looking for, that Raven had said possessed the secrets of the Darklings. The book that could heal the rift between the Darklings and the Order and lift the curse from the Darklings. Here it was in Mr. Farnsworth's hands on a sinking ship.

He opened the book to the first page, on which there was an engraving of a Darkling poised in mid-air over a sleeping woman. Mr. Farnsworth ran his hand lovingly over the ancient illuminated illustration . . . and then ripped the page out of the binding.

I cried out at the sight and lunged to stop his hand, but my hands passed through his flesh like water. I could only watch as he ruthlessly tore the pages of the ancient book out of its binding. When he was done, he picked up *Some Problems in Archival Record Keeping* and did the same thing. While he worked, icy water began to fill the cabin. The ship was sinking fast, but still Mr. Farnsworth worked like a medieval monk removing the binding of one book and then the other.

He placed the pages of *Some Problems* into the binding of *A Darkness of Angels*, and then took the original pages and slid them into an oilcloth pouch, which he tied securely and stuck under his shirt. Then he put the fake *Darkness of Angels* back into the portmanteau, secured the clasp, and stood up. He took one look around the cabin and at the rising water. Then he lifted his chin, squared his shoulders, and said aloud, *"Tintinna vere, specta alte!*" He marched out of the cabin as though he were marching into battle.

I saw his eyes flick toward where van Drood had been hiding in the corridor, but he turned the other way down the now-flooded hall, with van Drood following. Mr. Farnsworth stopped to help a woman carry her children out onto the deck and van Drood stayed behind, watching, waiting for his opportunity to seize the portmanteau. I wondered why he didn't just grab it, but then I noticed that there was a shining light surrounding Mr. Farnsworth. He had armored himself with some sort of ward.

I followed Farnsworth and Drood to the deck to a scene of utter chaos. Passengers in life vests were crowding around already-full lifeboats, screaming and pushing to find a seat. When one lifeboat was lowered the crowd surged, looking for the next one. In the midst of this chaos, one figure shone like a beacon. Agnes Moorhen, feathered hat perched jauntily on her head, was guiding my grandmother and Mrs. van Beek through the roiling crowd. Mrs. van Beek was weeping, but my grandmother's face was steely.

"For heaven's sake, Honoria," she cried, "remember you are a lady of the Order and get a grip on yourself!"

"But we'll drown!" Mrs. van Beek wailed as a half-full lifeboat was lowered to the water.

"Stop this instant!" Mr. Farnsworth cried, striding forward. The crewmen stopped lowering the boat. Without another word, Mr. Farnsworth bodily lifted my grandmother into the lifeboat, then Mrs. Van Beek, and then Agnes. As he placed Agnes in the boat she begged him to join them. He seemed to consider it, but then glanced behind him. I followed his gaze to where van Drood stood still among the surging crowds—then I looked back at Mr. Farnsworth. He gave Agnes a tender kiss, whispered something in her ear, and ordered the crewmen to lower the now-full lifeboat down. Then he turned to join the seething crowds on the deck.

I plunged back into the wild melee that now filled the deck of the *Titanic* and followed Mr. Farnsworth. I saw him stop again and again to help others onto the lifeboats, never taking a spot for himself. He kept heading for the prow of the ship, which was now the highest spot as the great vessel began to tilt toward the bottom of the sea. Anything loose was sliding down the deck, careening into the struggling passengers, while Mr. Farnsworth and van Drood made their inexorable way to the prow of the ship.

When he reached the prow, Mr. Farnsworth calmly stepped over the railing. The ship was almost vertical now. I was only able to keep from sliding down the deck by holding on to a stanchion. Drood, though, had no such difficulty. He walked straight up the tilting deck like a praying mantis climbing a stalk of wheat. As he passed me I saw his face, his lips stretched into a horrible grin, smoke curling out of his mouth. He was feeding off the horror of the crew and passengers, and now he intended to swallow Mr. Farnsworth and take the book.

Mr. Farnsworth regarded him stoically as he approached, his lips mouthing silent words that I thought might be a prayer or perhaps a curse. Whatever it was, he was powerless to stop van Drood. I saw van Drood reach for Farnsworth. He grabbed the portmanteau. Farnsworth let go of the railing and spread his arms out wide, like a diver preparing to do a backward somersault, held up only by the straps of the portmanteau . . .

Van Drood jerked the portmanteau, snapping the straps, and Farnsworth fell backward. I screamed and was suddenly airborne, my wings breaking through my corset. I flew over the prow of the ship, which was now plummeting into the sea, and dove down, following Mr. Farnsworth into the sea.

The shock of the frigid water nearly made me lose consciousness. Would I die back in New York if I died here? *This* felt horribly real, the water cold as death. The pull of the sinking ship was dragging me down into the depths of the sea. I remembered what Raven had told me about souls caught in the Hellgate—how even a Darkling could be caught forever in that deadly whirlpool. I could feel the souls of the drowning all around me, their lives pulling me down with them, a bit of my soul going with them . . . and then I was rising up toward the surface, borne up by something winged.

It was a Darkling—a male Darkling with a face carved with lines of grief and a streak of white in his dark, wet hair. His eyes regarded me sadly as he brought me to the surface—eyes that were somehow familiar.

"Even in dreams you can lose your soul, dearling," he said to me. *Dearling.* My mother had called me that.

He helped me onto a stray bit of wood bobbing in the sea where Mr. Farnsworth lay.

"You can see me here?" I asked.

"I could see you anywhere." He touched my face, and I could feel the warmth of his worn hand. "But I cannot stay. There's something I must do for this one."

He turned to Mr. Farnsworth, who was watching the older Darkling with wide, stunned eyes. One hand clasped the edge of the float, while the other pulled out the oilcloth packet that contained the book.

"Take it," he rasped. "Keep it safe. It tells how you can save your kind—and ours."

The Darkling took the packet and slipped it underneath his shirt. Then he gathered up Mr. Farnsworth in his arms. "Come with me, dearling," he said as he sprang into the air.

I followed him into the sky and over the wreckage of the *Titanic*—over the dead and dying in the frozen water. There were other Darklings here—a whole flock—swooping down and flying up again with pulsing light in their arms. They were carrying the souls of the dying away, so they wouldn't be sucked down into the whirlpool created by the sinking ship.

Then we were flying over the lifeboats full of terrified, wide-eyed survivors. I saw Agnes and my grandmother with their arms around Mrs. van Beek as she wept for her husband. And I saw van Drood crouched in the hull of another boat, his cloak drawn low over his head, the portmanteau clutched to his chest. As we flew over him, he tore open the portmanteau, took out the book and rifled through the pages. When he saw that he'd been tricked, he roared, and out of his open mouth poured smoke, and the smoke turned into a murder of crows that followed us.

We flew faster, pursued by the shadow crows, through the cold dark night. I wasn't sure how long I'd be able to keep up the pace, or what we were flying toward . . . and then I made out in the distance the light of a ship steaming toward the wreckage of the *Titanic*. It was the *Carpathia*, the ship that rescued the survivors of the *Titanic*. We flew toward it with the murderous crows at our heels. They came so close I could smell their burnt breath and feel their sharp beaks pecking at my skin. One tore into the Darkling's shirt, scrabbling at the unbound book, and ripped a page away. The Darkling kicked at it savagely and plunged down toward the *Carpathia*. He lit down just long enough to lay Mr. Farnsworth on the deck. "He will be all right here," he told me, "but I must lead away the shadow crows. As for you—" He touched my face so lightly and quickly it was a like a feather brushing against my skin, and bent his sad eyes down at me. "It's time for you to wake up."

"But—" Before I could protest I was no longer on the deck of the *Carpathia*, but back in Mr. Farnsworth's room at the Sailors' Home. I was safe and warm, but I wanted to be back on the freezing sea. I stared at the faces of the four people in the room, even Mr. Farnsworth, who had regained the spark of reason in his eyes, my eyes filling with tears. "I saw him," I said. "I saw a Darkling take the book." What I didn't tell them—couldn't tell them—was that the Darkling who had taken the book was my father.

22

EVEN IF I had told them, I wouldn't have been able to explain how I knew. I just knew. The way he looked at me, how he called me *dearling*—the same thing my mother called me in just the same tone of voice—his eyes, which were familiar because they were so much like my own eyes.

"He saved Mr. Farnsworth," I said instead. "And took the book. He was trying to lead van Drood's crows away. But I don't know if he survived." Could I have been given that vision of my father because I would never see him again alive?

"But he had the book?" Agnes asked.

"Yes." It was Mr. Farnsworth who answered. Omar had been right that recovering his memories would help cure him. His vagueness and confusion seemed to have fallen away. His eyes were clear and sharp. "I gave the book to the Darkling. I knew he would keep it safe from van Drood, only—"

"Where is he keeping it?" Agnes asked the question for all of us. "If this Darkling did indeed escape with the book, and it contains the secret of healing the rift between the Darklings and the Order, then why hasn't he brought it to anyone in the Order?"

She was looking to me for an answer. I didn't have one, but I had an idea who might.

⇥ ✦ ⇤

Agnes and Sam took me in a cab to Grand Central Station. On the way Sam told me all that he had discovered about the financial ruin of the van Beeks.

"Mr. van Beek had invested heavily in the *Titanic* itself," he told me. "He was sure it was a safe bet because the ship was supposed to be unsinkable."

He paused, and we were all silent in the cab, absorbing the awful irony. "Did you find out who talked him into the investment?" I asked.

"Yes, a Mr. Arnold Arbuthnot of the First National Investment Firm. But we can't pin the blame of the Order's present financial blunders on Mr. Arbuthnot. I'm afraid he died right alongside Mr. van Beek."

"Oh! How awful! I suppose he couldn't have been deliberately trying to ruin Mr. van Beek then."

"No, but I did discover that one of the largest shareholders in First National is Judicus van Drood. What I'm beginning to suspect is that van Drood uses hapless minions to do his dirty work."

"He no doubt controls them with the *tenebrae*," Agnes said.

"The way he controlled Sarah Lehman," I said with a shudder, remembering Sarah at the end, smoke writhing out of her mouth even before she burst into flames.

"Yes," Agnes said. "And after they've done his bidding he disposes of them and moves on to his next victim. It will make it difficult to make a connection between Mr. van Beek's financial ruin and the Order's present investment scheme."

"But not impossible," Sam said, lifting an admonitory finger. "The thing to look for is the underlying *pattern*. An investment in one huge project that—should it fail—will ruin the Order. I'll get on it right away."

"Thank you, Sam," I said, squeezing his hand. We'd reached the station, and the cab was having difficulty jockeying in the crowded queue to drop passengers off. It was raining again, and Agnes insisted he get me close to the covered entrance. "And thank you for finding Mr. Farnsworth. I'm so relieved he didn't die on the *Titanic*. I felt so responsible since I was the one who asked him to bring the book..."

My voice faltered as I realized that while I might not be responsible for Mr. Farnsworth's death, I was responsible for the deaths of all those who had died on that ill-fated ship. I saw Agnes's face crease with concern, but before she could waste her breath reassuring me I stepped out of the cab into the driving rain, which felt as frigid and pitiless as the North Atlantic.

$$\twoheadrightarrow \quad \diamondsuit \quad \twoheadleftarrow$$

I felt cold all the way back to Blythewood, huddled in my window seat watching the rain fall into the Hudson, its dark gray water a reminder of the icy chill of the Atlantic. I barely looked up when Myrtilene, Mary, and Susannah got on a few stops into the ride, humming Viennese waltz tunes. I'd been blessedly free of *Die Puppenfee* for several hours. How had I ever thought I liked it? The sound of it made me feel sick now. I pretended to fall asleep after they joined me so I wouldn't have to engage in their chatter. I soon slipped into a deep doze and dreamed myself back to the wreckage of the *Titanic* and that icy sea. All around me I could hear the cries of the drowning and then the beat of wings above me. Looking up, I saw my father's face.

"I've come for you, dearling," he said, taking me in his arms. We rose above the icy water, but its chill didn't leave me. Looking down I saw why. My body still lay on the floating plank. As I watched, it sank into the sea—

I startled awake on the train, the conductor's call of "Rhinecliff!" mingling in my ears with the cries of the drowning. Myrtilene, Susannah, and Mary were all staring at me.

"Are you all right?" Mary asked. "You look like you've caught a chill. You don't want to get sick before the big dance."

"Blast the dance!" I cried, getting shakily to my feet. I *was* chilled. I didn't think I'd ever be warm again. I stepped off the train into a cold wet wind blowing off the river and hurried up the steps with Mary and Susannah twittering behind me.

"Ava!" Susannah called. "Gillie's over here. Where are you going?"

"Into town," I called over my shoulder.

The tromp into Rhinebeck was a good mile and a half, but I couldn't bear the idea of being shut up with those girls going on about the dance and humming those grating waltzes. I walked through the rain all the way to Main Street, turned left, and then right on Livingston Street and up three blocks to Violet House. When Ruth opened the door, she gasped. I must have looked like a drowned woman who'd dragged herself up from the sea. At least that's what I felt like.

"Ava! You're soaked clean through! Come on in by the fire."

She dragged me through the foyer, where I left puddles of water, and into the conservatory, where a cheery fire crackled in the grate and a tea tray was laid out on the table.

"I-I-I n-need R-r-ray—" I stuttered through chattering teeth.

"Mr. Corbin?" Ruth asked. "I'll go get him. Sit down by the fire and put this over you." She draped me in an Indian shawl and disappeared. The aunts appeared in her stead, twittering and tsking over me like birds pecking at crumbs.

I heard Raven's voice saying my name when he entered the room. I tried to get up, but my legs had gone numb. Then he was at my side.

"What happened?" he demanded, his voice harsh as a crow's caw.

"I—I s-saw . . ." My lips couldn't form the words.

Raven turned to Emmaline and Hattie, who loomed over us (even tiny Hattie looked miles tall standing over me, as if I were at the bottom of the sea looking up) wringing their hands. "Leave me alone with her," he barked.

The aunts stared and gaped, but they fluttered obediently away. I heard the door click behind them and then Raven was taking off his jacket. I thought he was going to put it over me, but instead he drew me into his lap and encircled me with his wings. I tried to tell him that it was too dangerous—anyone could come in and find us like this—but I was shaking too hard to speak. As his feathers touched my skin, warmth came back into my body, dispelling the awful cold in great shuddering waves. I nestled deeper into his arms, clinging to him as if the waves might pull me away, but he held onto me.

"I've got you," he said again and again. "I've got you."

When the worst of the convulsions were over, he turned my face up to his and asked again what had happened. I told him about entering the vision with Mr. Farnsworth and all that I had witnessed on the *Titanic*. Then I told him about my father coming for me and carrying me out of the icy water. When I got to that part he looked grave.

"I'm afraid a bit of your soul was trapped in the whirlpool," he said. "Your father saved you, but . . ."

"Not soon enough?" I finished for him. "Are you saying I've lost part of my soul? Will I ever get it back?"

"I—I don't know. It's dangerous for Darklings to vision travel. If your father hadn't been there you might have been lost entirely."

I narrowed my eyes at Raven. "You don't seem surprised that I saw my father. Did you know he was on the *Titanic*?" Raven looked away. "Do you know where he is now?"

He sighed and looked back at me. "I'm sorry. I should have told you earlier, but the Elders forbid us to talk about him. He was banished many years ago."

"It was because of my mother, wasn't it?"

Raven nodded and stroked my damp hair back from my brow. "We're not allowed to love human women—it's how we were cursed in the first place. Anyone breaking that rule is banished from the flock. There's talk of a community of exiles in Europe, but no one knows if that's just a myth. Perhaps your father was traveling with the *Titanic* when it sank and he tried to save the souls of the dying passengers."

"He saved Mr. Farnsworth," I said, a defiant touch of pride stealing into my voice. "And he saved the book. We have to find him. Would these Elders of yours know where he is?"

"They might, but they won't like being asked."

"Too bad," I said, shivering again. The cold was stealing back. "Will you bring me to them?"

Raven wrapped his wings more tightly around me. "Yes," he said, "but not until you're well. You'll need all your strength to face them."

I tried to tell him I was well enough to face them right now, but before I could make my argument I fell back into the darkness—and into that icy sea—again. I dimly sensed being moved from Violet House and riding to Blythewood in Gillie's trap, wrapped in blankets and an old moth-eaten fur rug. Nothing seemed to keep me warm as Raven's wings had. Where had he gone? I wondered. Why would he leave me?

When Dame Beckwith saw me she sent me straight to bed with a cup of tea and a hot water bottle. I fell into a deep sleep—and into the deep, icy sea. I could hear the screams of the drowning and see the great ship *Titanic* sliding into the water, sucking everything down with it, pulling me under. The force yanked me straight into the frigid water. As I sank I saw I was surrounded by the other passengers, their faces distended in horror as they were sucked down into the maelstrom. I looked down and saw the whirling water beneath me, a black pit like an open mouth . . .

It *was* an open mouth. It had rows of razor-sharp teeth that turned like a grindstone. That's what waited beneath us . . . beneath *me.* It was wrapping its tentacles around my legs, sniffing at me because it smelled something on me it liked. It was pulling me down into its ravenous mouth—

I awoke screaming, flailing at the bedclothes twined around me like tentacles. Dimly I heard Helen's and Daisy's voices trying to soothe me, then Helen telling Daisy to run and get Dame Beckwith. "She's burning up," I heard her say. I tried to explain that, no, I'd burned up once before and survived it, but now I was freezing to death. Van Drood had been right: there was darkness inside me. The kraken smelled it and wanted more. It wouldn't be satisfied until it ate me whole. They had to keep me awake, I explained to a wide-eyed, pale Helen, or else the kraken would eat me.

"She's delirious," I heard Helen tell Dame Beckwith when she arrived. "She must have caught a chill in the city in all this damnable rain. I should have gone with her."

"*I* should have gone with her!" Daisy said. "It's all because of this silly argument we've been having."

"Well, now that you mention it—"

I lost consciousness while Helen and Daisy bickered, and I fell back into the sea, where I wrestled with the kraken's many tentacles. When I awoke again I was in a clean white room. For a moment I was afraid I was back in the Bellevue Pavilion for the Insane, but the faces that floated over me like balloons were familiar—Miss Sharp, Dame Beckwith, Miss Corey, Helen, Daisy. They told me I was in the infirmary, that I had caught a fever but I was going to be all right. I tried to tell them they were wrong. I'd been eaten by the kraken, I'd lost my soul, I would never be all right again. I asked Helen to find Raven—at least his wings would keep me warm—and I heard her promise that she would look for him before I fell back into the sea and the arms of the kraken.

The creature was fighting me for my soul. That's what it did with prey. I saw the other drowned passengers struggling in its tentacles, and then finally going limp and letting themselves be eaten. I saw one woman climb right into the maw, plunging into the circle of teeth with a kind of wild, manic glee, as if glad to finally win an end to her struggles.

And why not? a sly voice inside my head asked—van Drood's voice. *Why keep struggling, Ava? Your own father abandoned you when you were a baby, and now he's done it again—he's left a piece of your soul stuck in the kraken's teeth like a stray bit of spinach. And your Darkling boyfriend—where's he? Even your friends would rather bicker and fight than take care of you. Your father cared more about saving that book than you. Your boyfriend's too afraid of the wrath of his Elders to come for you. And if they don't care enough to save you, why should you keep struggling? This is where you belong, Ava, in the darkness, with me, warm inside the kraken's belly.*

I came close, several times, to giving in, but then I would startle awake and find Helen or Daisy or Miss Sharp holding my hand.

"Hang on, Ava," they would say. "Just hang on."

And so I did. But each time I struggled with the kraken I grew a little weaker and I knew it was only a matter of time before I gave myself to those snapping teeth.

It was a snapping sound that woke me. A sharp crack like gunfire; then another.

I woke in the infirmary and stared at the moonlit room. Helen was snoring in the chair beside the bed, so worn out by keeping vigil that the sound hadn't woken her.

There it was again—a series of sharp cracks. Was Blythewood under attack? The sounds were coming from outside the window. I struggled to sit up to see better, failed, and settled on sliding off the bed and crawling to the window. But when I finally dragged myself across the floor and clawed my way up to the windowsill and looked outside, I saw a magically peaceful scene.

The rain that had been falling steadily for weeks had turned to ice. Every blade of grass on the lawn, the urns and statues, the shrubs in the garden, and every branch and twig in the Blythe Wood was coated with a sheath of ice that glimmered like opals in the light of a full newly risen moon. The cracks came from branches snapping off as they succumbed to the weight of the ice. What did it mean? Had the changelings completed their search for Rue? Had they found her? Or given up? Or been stopped by van Drood?

I heard a great volley of crackling explosions—like firecrackers going off on the Fourth of July. Something was coming through the woods, crashing through the upper branches, scattering icicles like shards of crystal from a shattered chandelier. It burst from the woods and flew across the lawn, its great winged shadow etched on the white ice like an ebony cameo laid over ivory, straight toward me.

I fell back from the window as he landed—and then he was beside me. For a moment I didn't recognize him. His hair and wings were rimmed with ice, turning them white. Even his eyebrows were hoary with frost. He looked like a winged ice demon, but when he took me in his arms I knew it was Raven.

"What—? How—? Where have you been?" I finally managed. Even though his wings were limned with ice, they were bringing warmth back into my body.

"To find your father, of course," he replied. "He's with the Elders now. I'm taking you to them."

23

RAVEN BUNDLED ME into my coat and boots before we left, buttoning my buttons and tying my laces as if I were a child. I wouldn't have been able to do it myself; my fingers felt weak and clumsy.

"When I saw how sick you were I knew I had to find your father. Only the Darkling who rescued you from the water could restore the bit of soul you lost," he told me as he gathered me in his arms and launched us into the air. It was too difficult to talk while we were flying, so I snuggled into his arms, soaking up his warmth and watching the frozen woods beneath us. We flew north over the Blythe Wood. Looking down, I was shocked at the damage the ice storm had caused in the wood. The weight of ice had felled hundreds of branches and even whole trees. The entire forest looked like some enormous beast had ravaged through it.

At the northern edge of the forest I saw the little village of Tivoli, looking with its glaze of ice like a diorama of a Christmas village in a store window. Just before the village on the edge of the woods stood a stone castle with a tall octagonal tower facing the river. Raven lit on the frozen lawn beside a statue of a winged angel.

"W-what is this place?" I asked, teeth chattering the moment I wasn't in his arms anymore.

"Ravencliffe," he said. "This is where the Elders live."

I stared at the massive stone castle. It was almost as big as Blythewood but, I saw when the moon struck the stone façade, not as well maintained. Some of the windows were boarded up, and many more were broken. Chunks of the stone cornices were missing from the roof. A double flight of once grand stairs had crumbled to the ground. With its layer of ice, the house looked like it could be a fancy ice cream cake that had begun to melt.

"It looks abandoned," I whispered.

Raven replied with a rueful smile, "I'm afraid we Darklings don't have the Blythewood endowment to maintain the property. Most of us fledglings prefer to live in the forest and think Ravencliffe should be sold, but the Elders want to hold on to it. They're rather old-fashioned."

Raven took my hand and led me under a crumbling porte cochere and through a door into a dark room. He lit a match and touched it to an oil lamp standing in a recessed niche. When he held up the lamp I saw we were in a high-ceilinged oval room paved from floor to ceiling in an elaborate mosaic, pieces of which had fallen off and littered the floor, making it difficult to see the pattern in the dim lamplight. When the moon appeared in the skylight, though, I saw that the design was of hundreds of birds of every sort imaginable, from tiny hummingbirds to great eagles, brightly hued parrots, flamingoes and dark-winged ravens. As I turned around in a circle I had the impression of them flying—and I heard a flutter of wings and realized that some of them were. The broken skylight had let in real birds that roosted in niches throughout the dome.

"This is called the Aviary," Raven told me in a hushed voice. "The Elders believe that we are kin to the birds and should revere them as our ancestors, but," he added in a less respectful tone, "it's a bear to keep clean. Come on. They're waiting for us in the library."

We passed through a dark corridor lined with glass cases holding stuffed birds, their glass eyes shining in the light of Raven's lamp.

"If you revere the birds, then why—"

"It's considered a way of honoring our brethren after they're dead. Personally I think it's creepy. I'm always afraid that I'm going to come across a stuffed Darkling somewhere in this mausoleum." He shuddered and laughed when he saw me staring at him. "Only Darklings dissolve when we die."

"Oh," I said, hardly reassured. "Is that what will happen to me?"

We'd reached a pair of large sliding doors, their dark wood inlaid with a wing pattern on each side, meeting in the middle. Raven stopped and turned to me.

"No one really knows what will happen to you," he said, holding my gaze. "There hasn't been a mixed bloodling since the daughter of Merope and Aderyn."

"Oh," I said, not sure I liked being called a *mixed bloodling*. "And what happened to her?"

He gave me a reassuring smile. "She lived to a ripe old age of two hundred ninety-six. We Darklings are quite long-lived. But"—the smile faded from his face—"the Elders believe that it was Merope's blood that banished us from Faerie. So they outlawed marriage between Darklings and humans on pain of exile. That's why your father had to leave after you were born. He was exiled from the flock."

"I suppose he had no real choice then," I said, although the sly insidious voice of my nightmares was back asking why he couldn't have found a way to at least get a message to me. Something else bothered me about Raven's story . . . something about Merope and Aderyn . . . something van Drood had shown me in the Hall of Mirrors . . .

"No, no real choice," Raven said with a grimace. "The punishment for returning from exile is death."

»→ ✦ ←«

Raven slid open both doors at the same moment, separating the two inlaid wings with a *whoosh* that sounded as if they had taken flight. The sound was repeated in the high-vaulted tower room we entered, a sound of many wings rising to the high-domed ceiling above us. This was the tower I'd seen from the front of the house, only I hadn't imagined it would contain only one room. Looking up, I saw there were ledges around the top where huge birds roosted—only they weren't birds, I realized as my eyes adjusted to the light. They were Darklings— dozens of them. I saw Marlin among the flock and he gave me a tentative smile.

I looked away quickly lest I get him in trouble—and was sorry I had. There were no smiles for me on the ground floor. The three figures that sat on the far side of a long table in the center of the room might have been statues carved of ivory and ebony for all the expression on their rigid faces. Only the stir of their wing feathers in the draft that came through the open skylight told me they weren't statues.

As I walked toward them I was reminded of my admission interview for Blythewood, presided over by three crow-like old women. This triad, though, was made up of one woman and two men. The man who sat in the center of the table had long white hair and a deeply lined face the color of old ivory. As I got closer I realized that some of the lines were scars, including one dreadful one that ran across a sightless, milk-white eye. His other eye was riveted on me. To his left sat the woman. Her hair was gray and also long, but piled high on her head in an elaborate braid. I thought I saw a flicker of sympathy in her large hazel eyes, but that might have been a trick of the lamplight. There was certainly no sympathy in the jet-black eyes of the small-boned, hawk-nosed Darkling sitting on the right side of the table. He reminded me of the kestrels in the Blythewood mews, his bright eyes tracking my movements as if he might spring on me at any moment.

Only when I was directly in front of the table did I see the fourth figure. He was kneeling on the floor in front of the table, his wings mantled over his head. I'd taken him for a statue, he was so still, but as I drew level to him he lifted his head and gazed at me from under his long dark hair and I recognized the Darkling from my *Titanic* vision. It was my father.

I gasped and drew closer to him, but a rustle of wings from above—and Raven's hand on my arm—stopped me.

"You will not approach the prisoner," the white-haired

Darkling barked in a voice that echoed in the high tower.

"Prisoner?" I looked again and saw that heavy chains weighted his hands and feet. Worse, his wings had been nailed to the floor.

"Why is he chained like this?" I cried. "What has he done?"

"Falco knew the punishment for breaking his exile," the white-haired Darkling answered.

"But he's only come to help me—"

"His reasons for breaking the law are not our concern," he began, but when the gray-haired woman lightly touched his hand he turned to her.

"Merlinus," she said in a soft, musical voice, "if Falco has come to save his daughter, perhaps we should show leniency."

"You are too forgiving, Wren," the short hawk-nosed man said in a high, grating voice. "If we show leniency to one exile, how will we maintain our authority?"

"Authority is not won by fear and intimidation, Gos," the gray-haired woman named Wren responded. "It may be earned by mercy as well."

"But he broke one of the cardinal rules—fraternizing with a mortal woman. He even produced a half-bloodling." The man named Gos pointed a sharp-nailed finger at me. Next to me, Falco's pinned wings rustled against their bonds.

"He fell in love," Wren said gently, with a look at Merlinus, who had remained silent and stone-faced throughout the argument between Gos and Wren. At her look something softened in his face that made me suspect they were husband and wife. He didn't put a stop to the argument, though. Wren and Gos went back and forth debating between mercy and punishment until I grew dizzy swiveling my neck back and forth between the two of them and I began to teeter on my feet and lose my balance.

As I fell I heard something tear—and then I was caught by strong arms and surrounded by a flurry of feathers. I looked up into storm-gray eyes. Falco had caught me, tearing his own wings as he leapt for me. His loose feathers fell around us like a gentle snowfall. One touched my face, and I felt a melting warmth spread through my chill limbs. Dimly I heard a voice—Gos's—barking, "Restrain him!" but another voice, gentler but no less commanding, ordered, "Let them be. He is restoring her. Whatever we choose to do with him, the fledgling need not suffer while her bondling is here to heal her."

"Bondling?" I repeated weakly. "Does that mean father?"

Falco smiled at me sadly. "No, dearling, bondling is what we call a Darkling who saves a soul from dying but keeps a bit of that soul enmeshed with his. I did not know that I had kept that bit of soul when I saved you. Now I can give it back to you."

He spread his wings around me until I was cradled in their warmth, a warmth that seeped down into my bones. The chill I'd felt these last few weeks was finally banished, the piece that had been missing finally restored. I looked up at him and saw that his face was etched with pain.

"Does it hurt you?" I asked, alarmed that he was injuring himself to heal me.

He smiled again, but his eyes remained sad. "No, dearling, to restore your soul gives me great joy. I only wish I could restore the time we've lost in the same way. I had no idea when I left that your mother was—that you were—I didn't know about you. I only agreed to leave without Evangeline because I thought it would be safer for her. I thought she would go back to her own kind. If I had known that she was going to have a child, I would never have left, no matter what the Elders threatened to do to me."

I felt tears sting my eyes. How many times had I wondered why my father had abandoned me? It was a grief so deep I had long ago closed it up, like a door to an unused room. Now that door opened and I felt the sadness in his eyes fill it. "When did you find out about me?" I asked.

"When your mother died. I felt her passing, all the way in the frozen North, and came to carry her to Faerie. She told me about you then. I wanted to come to you, but she told me I needed to find the book *A Darkness of Angels*, first. She said that you would never be safe without it. I traced it to the place where it all started—to Hawthorn in Scotland—and saw that Mr. Farnsworth was bringing it to you. I followed him to make sure it made it to you safely, but of course it didn't. Farnsworth gave it to me when I saved him, but van Drood set his *tenebrae* on my trail. I've been running from them ever since, afraid to lead them back to you, but then a few weeks ago I had a dream that you were on the *Titanic*, too. I thought it was only a dream until Raven found me and told me you were soul-sick. I came right away—"

"Even if it meant they might kill you for returning," I finished for him.

"What would that matter if you died?" he asked simply. "I would do anything to make up for the time I've missed with you."

I wanted to tell him that he had, but I knew that nothing would ever make up for my not having grown up with my father—for either of us. But at least I knew now that it wasn't his fault. It was the Elders' fault.

I stood up, fully restored now, and Falco let his wings fall away from me. I turned to face the three Elders. Wren's face was soft with compassion, but Gos looked like he wanted to spring across the table and throttle Falco and me. Merlinus's face was stony and impassive. "How could you send him away from my mother when his only crime was loving her?" I cried.

I heard a rustle above me and saw Raven inch closer to me so that I was between him and Falco. I had a feeling that this was not the way one was supposed to address the Elders, but I didn't care. They had deprived my mother of the man she loved. They had deprived me of my father throughout my childhood.

"You're just a bunch of dried-up old crows," I fumed, "jealous of other people's happiness."

"He broke the law," Gos spat at me.

"It's a stupid law!" I cried. Someone hissed above me. Gos braced his arms on the tabletop, his tendons straining, his wings flexing behind him. "Why shouldn't a Darkling and a human love one another? Merope and Aderyn did—"

"And cursed us to an eternity of banishment," Gos hissed. "We can never return to Faerie. Do you know what it's like to ferry the souls of humans to their afterworld and the souls of the fay to theirs, but never have our own rest? When we die we dissolve into dust. And all because a Darkling loved a *human*." He spit the word out of his mouth as if it tasted bad.

"No," I said, recalling what had bothered me before about the story of Merope and Aderyn. "You weren't cursed because they loved each other; it was because a shadow crow pierced Aderyn's chest. A bit of shadow entered his soul."

"The darkness that entered his soul was his love for a human woman!" Gos snapped back at me.

"Why do you hate humans so much?" I asked.

"We don't hate them," Merlinus said with a stony glare at Gos. "We are charged with their care. If we allow ourselves to fall in love with them, we risk infecting them with our curse. Your mother, for instance, would not have been allowed into the mortal's afterworld because of her love for a Darkling. Falco broke the laws to bring her to Faerie. And you, fledgling—" He gave me a sad look. "You are now subject to the Darklings' curse. You won't be allowed in your own afterworld or Faerie."

"I've already been to Faerie, thank you very much," I snipped back at him.

I hadn't thought those marmoreal features could register surprise, but they did now. "You have?" he said. "How did you get in and come back in your own time without a Darkling to hold the door for you?"

Too late I realized my temper had implicated Raven. Before I could think how to answer, Wren spoke.

"What's important is that she was able to pass through the door at all. It might mean a weakening of the curse."

"She hadn't fledged yet," Gos said. "And even if she can cross over, it only means a half-bloodling can. What good does that do the rest of us?"

A chorus of hoots, accompanied by rustling, came from the upper tiers. Apparently Gos had his following. Encouraged by this response, Gos went on. "And why should we expect any help from her? She's part of the accursed Order that lives to exterminate us. How do we know that her being here now isn't part of a plot to infiltrate our ranks and then lead their Hunt to us? They might be on their way now."

The rustling above our heads grew to a roar, the hooting low and ominous. At the same time Raven and Falco extended their wings over my head as if they expected an attack from above. For the first time I felt frightened. Not just of what might happen to me, but of what might happen to Raven for bringing me here. I realized now what he had risked by being with me. But when he spoke he did not seem frightened; he sounded angry.

"How dare you suspect wrong of Ava? She has risked her life—her very soul—to find the book that will end our curse."

"Then where is it?" Gos demanded, getting to his feet and flexing his wings behind him. "All this talk of a precious book, but I personally searched the prisoner when he was taken and he had no book on him."

I glanced at Falco. Had he lost the book? Perhaps he had only hidden it somewhere. His lips curled back slowly, more a snarl than a smile.

"I was prepared for a search more thorough than any you

would perform," he said coldly. "And so I hid the book here."

He flexed his wings to their widest span—nearly fifteen feet across, wider than I knew wings could stretch. At first I thought he was threatening Gos, but then I looked closer and saw what Falco meant. Stitched to his wings, in between each feather, were pages. Each page was covered with a tiny runic script and beautiful gem-colored illuminations that gave Falco's wings the gloss of a peacock's tail. *A Darkness of Angels*—the book my mother had spent her life looking for—was stitched into my father's wings.

24

A CLUSTER OF Darklings flocked around Falco, edging me away and hiding him from my sight. I could see why a flock of Darklings was called a *darkness*. Together they formed a clot of darkness that hid everything else from sight. After what seemed like a long time, the darkness thinned, leaving one gray-haired old Darkling examining Falco's wings with a magnifying glass.

"What do you think, Master Quill?" Merlinus asked the gray-haired Darkling.

As Master Quill raised his head I saw that his long gray hair and beard were braided with feathers. He plucked out a long goose feather that had been sharpened into a quill and used it to point to the pages stitched into Falco's wings.

"I've never seen anything quite like it," he said. "He hasn't just attached the pages to his wings, he's stitched in every word and picture. His own feathers have bonded to the pages. I don't believe we could separate the pages from his feathers without severely damaging his wings."

"That's his own damned fault," Gos sneered. "I say we lop off his wings right now and take the book."

"You can't do that!" I cried, trying to push through the crowd surrounding my father.

"The girl's right," Master Quill said, his eyes glittering. "It would be a terrible shame to ruin such a masterpiece. The book has become a living thing. I believe it was meant to bond with a Darkling's wings in just this way. It says so here." He touched his quill to one of Falco's feather and read aloud from it: "And so shall the page become the wing, and it shall lead us home."

"What does that mean?" Raven asked. "Is it all written in riddles like that?"

"Oh, that's one of the clearer lines," Quill said, chuckling. "It will take me days—weeks!—to read it all."

"But you *can* read it?" Merlinus asked. "And transcribe it?"

"Yes, yes, yes!" Quill answered, all the feathers stuck in his hair trembling in his excitement. "It would be an honor—the opportunity of a lifetime."

"We don't have a lifetime, Quill," Wren told the old man firmly. "If the Shadow Master wants this book he'll have his *tenebrae* searching for it. The wards of Ravencliffe will conceal Falco and the book for only so long. If there's something in this book that will lift our curse and defeat the Shadow Master, we must learn it before he finds it and destroys us all."

Wren's speech cast a somber pall over the room. I looked around and saw the fledglings looking nervously at each other. But then my father spoke up, his voice ringing clear in the vaulted tower.

"The book will tell us how to lift the curse and much more. Although I could not read it because I am not gifted in the old languages as Master Quill is"—he bowed his head to the old scribe, who quivered with delight at the compliment—"since the book has bonded with my wings, I have had dreams. I can hear it speaking to me. I believe that the end of our curse lies in its pages, and much more." He looked toward me, and I felt the sadness in his eyes echo in my heart. "I believe that the book will heal the rift between us and the Order."

I saw Gos begin to object, but Merlinus silenced him. "We must see about that," he said. "First, let you and Master Quill repair to the scriptorium"—he pointed up to the very highest ledge of the tower—"to transcribe the book. When it is done we three will read it and consult to reach a decision together."

"You won't hurt him?" I asked, pushing my way through the flock to stand in front of the scribe.

Master Quill tore his eyes away from Falco's wings and gave me an appalled look. "Hurt him? Of course not! Your father has become the living repository of our most precious lore and history. I will treat him with the same respect with which I treat our oldest tomes."

I wasn't exactly reassured by this. "He's a person, not a book," I told Master Quill. "He's my father, and I've just gotten him back."

Falco's eyes glittered at my speech, and he stepped forward to touch my hand. "It will be all right, dearling. I trust Master Quill, and this is something I must do for my people and for yours. The rift between them must be healed, or else you will be torn apart." His gaze traveled from me to Raven, and I blushed, guessing his meaning. "I do not want you to suffer the same fate that befell your mother and me."

I squeezed his hand and then looked up at Merlinus. "Can I at least visit him while he's being . . . *transcribed*?"

Merlinus surprised me by looking to Quill. "Will it disturb your work?" he asked the scribe.

"Not at all. I have always welcomed young people to my scriptorium. Few enough"—he cast a disparaging look up at the fledglings—"darken its ledge."

"Very well, then," Merlinus said with finality. "Raven will bring the half-bloodling to the scriptorium once a week. And," he added with a stern look at Raven, "to our chambers afterward for dinner. It's about time I became better acquainted with my son's flying mate."

※→ ✦ ←※

"You didn't tell me Merlinus was your father," I complained to Raven on the flight back to Blythewood.

"Would it have made a difference?" he asked.

I thought about it. "I suppose it would have made me even more nervous meeting him."

"Exactly. He's not . . . an easy man. But I think he liked you."

"Really? How could you tell?"

"He didn't order your wings clipped and toss you in the dungeons, for one thing."

"Oh," I replied, trying to swallow. "I suppose that's a start. Is Wren your mother?"

"Yes." Raven smiled. "She definitely liked you. She told me so when we were leaving."

"I didn't hear—" I began, but then I recalled that she and Raven had exchanged a series of whistles when we left that must have been their way of communicating. "At least we know *my* father likes you. Thank you for finding him."

Instead of responding, Raven dipped his wings and landed us on a sturdy, ice-limned branch near the top of an old oak tree. He turned me toward him and cupped my face in his hand. In the moonlight his face looked different—older than it had a few weeks ago.

"When I saw you suffering with the soul-sickness, I felt . . ." He paused, looked away, his dark eyes glittering fiercely. He squeezed my arms. "I felt as though a piece of *my* soul was missing. I had no choice but to find your father and make you whole again, because"—he looked back at me—"I would never be whole without you."

I stared at him, taking in the force of his words. "I feel the same, only—"

"*Only?*" He pounced on the word, his voice making the whole tree quake, shaking icicles loose and scattering them to the forest floor.

I forced myself to go on. "*Only*, you could be banished for loving me, Raven. Are you sure you want to take that risk?"

"To lose you would be a worse exile," he replied without hesitation. "If I am banished I would take you with me . . . that is, if you would be willing to share my exile."

He said the words with a formality that made me feel that we had both grown suddenly older. The trees of the forest arching above us, their branches filled with milky white moonlight, felt like a chapel. I felt as if the whole woods had stilled to listen to my reply. Before I could answer, though, I heard a shriek coming from below us—a girl's voice. Raven instantly tensed and crouched on the branch to look down through the tree limbs.

"It's Etta," he said. "Stay here while I see what's wrong."
He flexed his wings and dove . . . and I followed him. He'd just
told me that he'd go into exile for me; I wasn't about to sit on a
tree branch while he plunged into danger. I was still too weak
to use my wings, but I scrambled down the tree, nearly sliding
off the ice-slick branches, and falling the last dozen feet to land
in a tumble beside him. I saw that we were in the Rowan Circle.
Raven had his arm around Etta, who was weeping. I whirled
around, searching for an attacker, but the circle was empty and
still, sealed by icicles that hung from the rowan trees so thickly
they formed a sort of jagged circular portcullis. No one could
have passed through it unless they were as tiny as Etta.

"What is it, Etta?" I asked. "What are you doing out here
alone at night?"

"I—I heard the branches br-breaking and saw the ice
storm," she stammered, shivering and sobbing. "I started
thinking about what it would mean for the changelings."

Guiltily I remembered that I had wondered the same
thing—and then quickly forgotten about them. But Etta hadn't.

"I knew they were still traveling back and forth on the river
looking for Rue. One told me just yesterday that they were infiltrating a mansion on the river that they thought might be where
she was hidden—and then this ice storm came out of nowhere!
The temperature dropped thirty degrees in less than an hour.
It didn't feel natural. So I came out here to talk to them—there
are always a few here in the woods keeping a circle the others
can come back to—and this is what I found!"

She pointed at the icicles hanging from the rowan trees. I
stepped closer to look . . . and gasped. Each icicle had a shim-

mery red glow, like a flame behind glass, only these flames had faces flickering at their hearts.

"It's the changelings," Etta said. "They're trapped inside the ice."

⇥ ✦ ⇤

We stayed in the Rowan Circle for nearly an hour trying to communicate with the trapped changelings. A few lampsprites appeared, beating their wings against the icy shrouds, but when they brushed their wings against our faces we heard them say, "We cannot hear them, nor they us." Featherbell tried blowing flames onto the ice, but instead of melting, the ice sprayed over her wings and she dropped to the ground with a dull thud. Etta grabbed her and held her in her hand until she recovered.

"This is no ordinary ice," Raven said, picking up one of the shards that had fallen to the ground. As he lifted the shard I saw a shadow flickering inside it, reminding me of the shadow crow I saw inside the splinter of broken mirror inside the fun house—the crow that had *bitten* me.

"Drop it!" I cried. "There are *tenebrae* inside the ice."

I looked around at the ice-covered woods with a new horror. I thought I could see shadows moving under the surface of the ice, like dark water under a frozen stream.

"We have to get out of here," Raven said.

"But I can't leave them!" Etta cried.

"You can't help them now," Raven told her sternly. And then in a gentler voice, "You'll be frozen yourself if I don't get you back. And Ava's still weak."

Etta looked worriedly between me and the changelings, but

then Featherbell brushed against her face. She listened to her chatter and then nodded solemnly. "Featherbell says the lamp-sprites will stay in the circle guarding the changelings."

Without waiting for her to change her mind, Raven gathered Etta into his arms and carried her up into the trees to cross over the frozen barrier around the Rowan Circle. As I waited for him to come back for me, I saw something out of the corner of my eye—something dark. I turned to catch what it was, but it moved as I moved. I spun around, following the movement. It looked like the edge of a cloak trailing behind a fleeing figure—like the figure of van Drood I'd glimpsed in the fun house. He was here, his consciousness moving through the ice. I could hear him in the chime of frozen branches clattering together.

Ava, he called, his voice brittle as cracking ice, *I see you survived the kraken. Do you think you emerged with your soul intact?*

"Yes!" I cried. "My father—"

The excited clatter of ice made me stop. I couldn't give away my father's location to van Drood.

Aahh, he crooned, an icy breath lapping against my face. *So your father's come back to you, has he? Has he told you why he abandoned you?*

I bit back a reply. I couldn't tell van Drood about my father. A mist had risen in the grove. Where it touched my skin it turned into ice crystals that spread over my arms and face, creeping its way inside me. *How?* I wondered. *The Rowan Circle was supposed to be protected—*

Against fairies, Drood's icy voice whispered inside my mind. *Not those of us trained in the Order.*

He was inside my mind, creeping in with the ice. I tried to shake off the glaze that was spreading over my skin, but I couldn't move.

Ah, he told you he didn't know about you, that he stayed away for your mother's own good—and you believed him! Poor little Ava, so happy to have her daddy back she'll believe anything.

Tears pricked my eyes, but they froze before they could fall. I had to find a way to break van Drood's spell over me before he found out where my father was and I became a frozen statue like the changelings. I fumbled numb fingers over my coat looking for my repeater, but it wasn't in my pocket—Raven hadn't put it there when he dressed me. All I found was one of his feathers clinging to the wool.

But if he really loved your mother, would he have been able to stay away? I know I couldn't. The Order exiled me, too, Ava, but I returned. Doesn't that mean I loved your mother more?

I squeezed Raven's feather in my hand to keep from shouting out at him—and felt a bit of the ice melt. I remembered how I had used a Darkling feather mixed with lampsprite dust to start a fire—could I use it now to break van Drood's hold on me?

Can a Darkling really love with all the darkness inside them? he was asking now. *Can you love, Ava? Why didn't you answer Raven when he declared his love for you?*

The thought that van Drood had been listening to us in the trees made me feel sick—and then angry. I gripped the feather tighter and felt the ice begin to melt.

"We were interrupted," I said through gritted teeth. "I was about to say that I'd follow him into exile—"

As your mother would have. Why didn't Falco take her? No,

Ava, he abandoned your mother. He abandoned you, as he will again. But I never let your mother go, as I will never let you go.

"You abandoned your own son!"

The words were out before I knew I meant to say them. A great stillness came over the forest; the clatter of frozen branches stopped, the creak of ice shushed. I knew suddenly that van Drood did not know that Nathan was his son.

Until *now.*

I tried to clear my mind of all thought, but he'd already found it.

Nathan.

A gale swept through the woods, coming straight toward me. I wrenched up the feather and willed it into flame.

"You can't have him!" I screamed at the ice gale rushing toward me. The crystals formed into a face—van Drood's face, eyes black caverns, mouth open in a horrible scream.

"I *will* have him—and you, and everything you hold dear. I will bring the Order to its knees for everything it stole from me!"

I felt his icy breath on my face; worse, I felt his mind touching my mind. Smoke gushed from the cavernous maw and rushed into my mouth and nose. I felt the stealthy tentacles of the *tenebrae* squirming into my brain, searching for the tender spots to cling onto. *There,* they sighed when they found a spot of envy. *Ah,* they cried when they latched onto a barb of jealousy. *Yes!* van Drood crooned inside my brain. *Who do they think they are, lording it over you because you were once poor?*

I was swept into a vision of swirling color and gay laughter. I was at a grand ball like the one at the Montmorencys'. I was seeing the dancing men and women through van Drood's eyes, and he was seething with anger and resentment. *Yes,* I found myself thinking, *they think they're better than us because they still have their riches. We'll show them, won't we?*

Suddenly, the music changed to the all-too-familiar strains of *Die Puppenfee.* The dancers' movements became jerky, like automatons, and their expressions were glassy. I saw a woman who looked like Dame Beckwith clutching her partner's hand so tightly her fingernails had sunk into his skin and blood was dripping down their joined arms. Tears streaked her face. I looked down and saw that blood dripped from her dancing shoes.

They'll dance to my tune, van Drood hissed inside my head, *until they run out of time.*

Beneath the dripping shoes, the dance floor was designed to resemble a giant clock face. I could see the gears moving below it, controlling the pattern of the dance, counting down the minutes . . . but to what?

I couldn't see that far into van Drood's mind. I hadn't wanted to see into his mind at all. I had braced against his intrusion, but now I pushed further.

I felt his shock—he hadn't known I could do that!—and saw a glimpse of clock gears and then a blast of fire that annihilated everything.

Then I was on the forest floor alone—no, not alone. Raven was beside me. I had banished van Drood from my head, or he had banished me, I wasn't sure which. But it didn't matter now.

"Come on," I said to Raven. "We've got to stop van Drood."

25

RAVEN TOOK ME to the edge of the woods where Etta was waiting. On the way I told him about my encounter with van Drood and what I suspected he was trying to do, before we bid each other a hasty good-bye.

Only when he had turned to leave did I remember that I had not answered his question. I wanted to call him back to tell him that I would gladly share his exile, but somehow it felt as though the moment had been marred. Besides, I had to get Etta back to the castle to warn Dame Beckwith.

The sun was coming up, turning the frozen lawn into a sheet of fire. Jagged icicles hung from every eave and window-sill of the castle, giving Blythewood the appearance of a fortress bristling with bloody spikes. It looked like it was armed for battle. I hoped it was.

We slipped in the side door unobserved.

"I have to go to Dame Beckwith's office," I told Etta. "You should go straight to your room and get out of your wet things."

"So should you, Avaleh. You're covered in ice."

I looked down at myself and saw she was right. I remembered van Drood blowing icy mist at me. It had clung to my clothes and skin. I suddenly wanted very badly to get out of these clothes and into a hot bath where I could scrub all residue of the encounter away. Dame Beckwith might not even be awake yet, and if I woke her up looking like this she would think I was still hallucinating.

Maybe I was, I thought as Etta and I climbed to the fourth floor. The vision I'd seen inside van Drood's brain was crazy. Dancers moving to a tune of his making like puppets, dancing until their feet bled, dancing even to their deaths . . . that couldn't happen here at Blythewood. We were too strong, the school too powerfully protected. Dame Beckwith wouldn't let it happen!

I left Etta at her room and went on to mine. Halfway down the hallway I heard someone humming the waltz from *Die Puppenfee* and my blood ran cold. I ran down the hall and wrenched open the door just as Helen was going out.

"Thank the Bells!" she cried when she saw me. "When I woke to find you gone I thought you'd run off with Raven for good."

I gave Helen a hug that surprised both of us. "We have to tell Dame Beckwith to cancel the dance."

"It's too late," Helen said. "It's tonight."

"Tonight? How long have I been ill?"

"Too long!" Helen snapped. "The entire school has been possessed by a dance mania. Even Dame Beckwith. She cancelled exams."

"Cancelled exams? But that's—"

"Crazy? Exactly my point. And all the stodgy old board members have been invited. They're staying at the Beekman

Arms in town. I'd hoped perhaps this ice storm would keep them away, but they got up here yesterday before the storm began. Unfortunately, Mr. Greenfeder and his friends were supposed to arrive today, and I suspect they won't be able to get through. Gillie says the trains are stopped and the roads from Poughkeepsie to Rhinebeck are impassable. Even the phone lines are down."

"We've been cut off—" I began.

I was interrupted by Daisy swinging open the door. "Ava!" she cried. "I thought I heard your voice. Thank goodness you're better."

"Yes, Helen's been telling me everything—" Behind Daisy's head Helen was waving her hands and mouthing something I couldn't understand.

"Fiddle-dee-dee!" Daisy cried, pulling me into the room. "Helen's become such an awful worrywart while you've been ill. Don't listen to a word she tells you about the dance. It's going to be marvelous. Did you know I'm going to be one of the Spanish dolls? Come see my costume—oh, and yours arrived from Miss Janeway's yesterday. You're to be a Tyrolean doll."

I stared at Daisy as she pulled a green dirndl skirt embroidered with Alpine flowers, a matching embroidered bodice, a white puffy-sleeved blouse, green hose, and a black felt cap out of a box. It was worse than the dress I'd been meant to wear to the Montmorency ball.

"I am not wearing that, Daisy. I'd look like a . . . a . . . marionette!"

"You're meant to look like a doll, silly! We all are. Don't you remember? *Die Puppenfee*, 'The Fairy Doll.'"

"I thought the dance was a party where we danced with boys," I said. "The ballet parts were just little in-between entertainments—divertissements."

"Oh, that's still the plan, but once Georgiana took over after you became ill, she and Herr Hofmeister agreed that we should all dress as dolls and carry the theme through the whole dance. It will be *très charmant*—and perfect for meeting eligible bachelors!"

Dolls. That's what the figures in van Drood's fantasies had been. Dolls that he controlled.

"Daisy," I said, taking her by the shoulders. "Come to your senses! Besides, you don't need to meet eligible bachelors—you have Mr. Appleby."

"Don't be silly, Ava," she answered, wiggling out of my grip and slapping my arm with her Spanish fan. "I've broken off my engagement with Mr. Appleby!"

"Engagement?" I echoed. "You're engaged?"

"*Was* engaged," Daisy said, twirling around. "I've broken it off."

"That was Daisy's big secret," Helen said. "She didn't tell us because . . . well, because I was so awful about engagements in general."

"Silly Helen," Daisy said, "that wasn't the *real* reason! I must have known I wasn't meant to marry Mr. Appleby. The Order will pick a suitable husband for me."

"Don't look so glum!" she cried as we gaped at her in horror. "Maybe you two will find husbands, too!"

※→ ✦ ←※

At breakfast I discovered that all the girls, with the exception of Helen and Etta, were as excited about the dance as Daisy. As I made my way through the dining hall the talk was of dancing slippers and dance steps and costumes.

"I wish I were in the mazurka!" one girl said, sighing wistfully.

"Oh, but the most beautiful costume is the fairy doll. I want to try out for that part next year!"

Next year? Had the winter dance already become a tradition? As far as I knew, Blythewood had never had one before, but when Dame Beckwith addressed the dining hall she began with, "This year's winter dance promises to be the most spectacular in Blythewood's history!"

My hopes of seeking Dame Beckwith's help were dashed as the girls exploded in applause. She went on to say that while the weather had prevented some guests from coming, there was no cause for alarm. Herr Hofmeister had commissioned a fleet of horse-drawn sleighs to convey our honored board members and their guests from the Beekman Arms in Rhinebeck to Blythewood for the dance. "It will be like a real Viennese ball!" she exclaimed, her usually placid gray eyes glittering.

The nestlings at my table sighed and swooned. "I'd love to go to Vienna one day," Mary confided to Susannah. "Herr Hofmeister says that the very best dancing schools are there. And they have balls for everything!"

"Yes, even at the lunatics' asylum," Helen, who had pulled a chair over to our table, remarked to me dryly. "Which is what this is turning into."

"It's van Drood's plan," I whispered. "Is everyone under this . . . spell?"

"Not everyone," Nathan, who'd followed Helen over, said. He'd grown thinner and more drawn during my illness, and his silver hair had turned a duller shade of gray. I shivered, remembering van Drood's threat. Nathan didn't look like he could withstand a strong wind, let alone van Drood. "Are you . . . I mean, why aren't you waltzing around humming *Die Puppenfee*?" I asked him.

Nathan gave me an appalled look. "I've steered clear of Herr Hofmeister ever since he asked me to dress up as a tin soldier. I told him the only kind of soldier I would be dressing up as was an American one if things remained so unsettled in the Balkan States."

I shuddered at the image of Nathan dressed as any kind of soldier. "Who else has remained untouched?" I asked.

Nathan slid his eyes to the other nestlings at the table. They were so busy gabbing about the dance that they didn't seem to be listening to us, but I took Nathan's point that it might be better to talk elsewhere.

"I have so much work to make up," I said, taking a gulp of tea and grabbing a roll. "Would you two come to the library to help me study?"

We hurried through the empty North Wing, where the classrooms looked deserted and forlorn.

"Haven't you all been having classes?" I asked.

"They were suspended last week so we could have more time for rehearsal," Helen said with obvious disgust. I'd never imagined I'd hear Helen complain about missing classes.

"What do the teachers think about it all?" I asked.

"Most of them have been swept up in the madness as much as the students," Nathan replied. "Mr. Peale is playing a bell ringer in a Swiss cuckoo clock. Miss Swift is dancing a polka. Miss Frost and Mr. Malmsbury are doing a tango." Nathan grimaced. "They're actually quite good. Even Mrs. Calendar has a minor part as a granny doll. Only Miss Sharp, Mr. Bellows, and Miss Corey have resisted the allure of the dance."

Nathan knocked on the library door, which I was surprised to see was locked. I saw Miss Corey's face appear in the glass pane, and then the door was unlocked and she pulled us in.

"Oh, Ava, thank the Bells you're up and better! Hurry!" she whispered. "Herr Hofmeister is trying to find Vi and get her to try on a Chinese doll costume."

"He tried to get me to play the puppet master," Mr. Bellows, who was sitting by the fire with Miss Sharp, said with a shudder. "But I refused."

"The puppet master?" I repeated. "I don't recall there being a puppet master in *Die Puppenfee*. There's a toy maker who makes the fairy doll, but he doesn't control her."

"Herr Hofmeister has made alterations to the plot to give the dance more *drama*," Miss Sharp said, rolling her eyes.

"He does have a point that *Die Puppenfee* is a rather insipid ballet, but then why do it in the first place?" Miss Corey asked. "He's borrowing elements from other ballets and Hoffmann's tales, mostly to make the ballet parts longer and more complicated. The poor girls are rehearsing noon and night. I begged

Dame Beckwith to rein him in, but she said it was good for the girls to experience discipline and that it would make them more marriageable."

"The whole thing is insidious," Miss Sharp said, shaking her head. "I'm afraid it might be part of a larger plot."

"It's part of van Drood's plot to destroy the Order," I said as the pieces fell into place. I told them what I'd seen in the Rowan Circle. "He blames the Order for destroying his chances of marrying my mother."

"How like a man," Miss Corey said, "to blame his romantic failures on some outside cause and flail about making everyone else suffer for his disappointments."

"I'm afraid this looks more serious than a spurned lover's revenge," Mr. Bellows said. "This ice storm has all the earmarks of spelled weather. It's halted the changelings' search for Rue *and* isolated us for this damned dance. We're under siege—have been under siege all these past few weeks without us even knowing it. Herr Hofmeister's dance has worked a kind of mind control on the students and teachers and even on Dame Beckwith."

"But Herr Hofmeister is such a . . . a . . ." Miss Sharp began.

"Ninny?" Miss Corey finished for her. "Yes, he hardly seems capable of staging an attack on Blythewood."

"Van Drood can take over a person if he's weak—or she," I said. "Remember how he took over Sarah Lehman last year? She was vulnerable because of her resentment and jealousy. Herr Hofmeister must have a similar weakness that van Drood is preying on to make him his slave." I thought of how van

Drood had tried to make me distrust my father and to see myself as a monster. "He almost got me."

"Is that why you've been sick?" Miss Sharp asked.

I told them about my experience with Mr. Farnsworth, leaving out the part about the Darkling who saved me being my father.

Miss Corey was more interested in the library I described. "We've been searching through all the books here to find a cure for this dancing fever, but we haven't found anything. Maybe the Darkling library has one."

"We could ask," I said. "And I think we should tell the Darklings what's happening here. The last time van Drood got control of the Dianas he tried to make them kill the Darklings."

"You want to go to the Darklings for help?" Nathan asked.

I returned his look levelly, steeling myself for his disapproval. "Yes," I said. "Who else are we going to go to? We can't reach anyone else."

To my great surprise Nathan nodded. "You're right," he said. "Let's go. I'd like to see this Ravencliffe."

It was decided that Nathan, Miss Corey, and I would go to Ravencliffe, leaving Miss Sharp, Mr. Bellows, and Helen to 'keep watch' over Blythewood. We decided that the quickest and safest way to get to Ravencliffe, given the number of trees that had toppled in the Blythe Wood, was to skate on the frozen river.

Miss Corey took off down the frozen sloping lawn like a speed skater. She and Nathan were so enthusiastic that I hadn't the heart to tell them I'd never been on skates before in my life. I imagined, though, that it couldn't be harder than learning to fly.

I was wrong. My ankles wobbled like aspic as Nathan and I made our way down to the river.

"You'll be better off when we get on the river," Nathan assured me, gliding easily over the frozen lawn. His cheeks were pink, and he was wearing an enormously long striped woolen scarf wound many times around his neck and a black wool cap that made him look like the illustration of Hans Brinker in the story my mother used to read me when I was little. It was good to see him with some color in his cheeks. If van Drood was coming for him he'd have to be strong.

"I'm glad you didn't succumb to the dancing fever," I said, linking my arm under his.

"Ugh, I heard quite enough Viennese waltzes last summer while waiting around with Louisa in sanatoriums. I suppose I lost my taste for the music. When I hear it now I think of her stuck in that dreadful place while doctors prod at her 'subconscious' trying to unearth the source of her 'trauma.'"

"I'm sorry," I said. "I wonder if there might be something in the Darkling library that will help her."

"Yes," he said, steering me onto the river, "I'm rather hoping there is. Now hold on. We'll never get there if you totter like an old woman." He tightened his grip on my arm and propelled us both forward, taking long gliding strokes that forced me to do the same. I soon fell into the rhythm and felt the sharp wind sting my cheeks. When I looked down at my feet I noticed dark shapes moving under the ice.

"Fish," Nathan said when I pointed them out. "They're following us." I laughed and looked up. The river was a glittering expanse of clear ice between the blue riverbanks. On the west side of the river the snow-covered Catskills stood white against a gentian blue sky. On the east side we passed stately mansions and formal gardens all glazed in ice. It was like skating through a toy Christmas village from the Woolworth windows. I'd nearly forgotten our mission until I saw the looming tower of Ravencliffe ahead of us.

"There it is," I told Nathan, pointing out the tower.

"That old place?" Nathan asked. "I've seen it from the river before and always thought it was deserted. Your Darkling friends aren't much on upkeep, are they?"

I was about to quip back that they had more important things to concern themselves with—like ferrying souls to the afterworld—but I noticed how tense Nathan's arm was and realized he was nervous. He still considered the Darklings his enemies, but he was going into their territory to help the girls at Blythewood. That was Nathan all over—no matter how cynical his manner, he was always ready to sacrifice himself for someone else. Perhaps too ready.

"It will be all right," I said. "Raven won't let any harm come to us."

But as we walked up the steep bank to the house, I wondered if Raven could really stop the Darklings from hurting us if they thought we were a threat. And Miss Corey, striding on ahead, looked like a fierce ice maiden. Before she could reach the front door, two Darklings—a man and a woman—dove down from the tower and landed directly in front of her, their wings snapping in the frigid air.

"What's your business here, human?" the male Darkling—a huge man with shaggy white-blond hair and a scary-looking scar across his face—demanded. He towered over Miss Corey, his wings casting a shadow over her on the icy ground. Miss Corey straightened her back and tilted her head up toward the menacing giant.

"I am Miss Lillian Corey, head librarian of the Blythewood School and lady of the Order," she said in a clear, ringing voice. "And I have come to consult a book in your library. Please inform your librarian of my request."

The giant Darkling looked perplexed. I whispered to Nathan, "Is there some secret diplomatic immunity among librarians?"

"Not that I know of," Nathan answered, "but Miss Corey seems to think so."

It was clear from the giant's expression that he wasn't sure either. He must have decided not to take a chance.

"Come," he roared at Miss Corey. "I will take you to Master Quill."

We followed the giant into the tower room I had been in the night before. Without the crowd of Darklings roosting in the upper tiers I could see that the entire tower was lined with books and ledges where Darklings sat over desks reading or writing.

"Master Quill is in the scriptorium on the top level," he said. "I will carry you up."

He made a move toward Miss Corey, but she nimbly evaded his grasp. "I will walk," she said indignantly.

"There are no stairs," he pointed out.

Undeterred, Miss Corey studied the honeycomb of shelves and ledges that lined the tower walls. "That shouldn't be a problem," she replied, sitting down on the lowest ledge and removing her ice skates. She then nimbly climbed barefoot up the bookshelf onto the next ledge and from there to the next level. Nathan and I looked at each other and quickly took off our skates to follow her. It was surprisingly easy, as if the tower had been fitted out to accommodate nonwinged guests. Perhaps, I thought, stepping over a shelf of books with English titles on subjects that ranged from philosophy to agriculture, there really had been a time when the Darklings and the Order were friends—and perhaps there could be such a time again.

When we arrived, a little breathless, on the top tier, we found Master Quill warmly greeting Miss Corey.

"Ah," he said, "you have been in a Darkling library before, haven't you?"

"No, but I've studied the architecture of all the great libraries of the world," she replied. "We were taught how to do research in all kinds of libraries . . . but I've never seen anything like *that*." She was staring at my father, who was sitting on the far side of the upper ledge, his wings stretched out across a high shelf. Two scribes were seated beneath him writing in large ledgers, their eyes moving from my father's wings to their pages.

"Nor have I," Master Quill answered. "It's like having a master index that can speak. You can ask him where anything is and he'll tell you the exact page number and line."

"Remarkable," Miss Corey said, her eyes shining. "May I?"

Master Quill nodded, but before proceeding, Miss Corey turned to me. "Would you introduce us, Ava?"

I swallowed. I hadn't thought about whether I would reveal my father's identity to Miss Corey and Nathan, but I saw now that Miss Corey had guessed.

"How long have you known?" I asked.

"Since the night on the roof of the Hellgate Club, when we talked about secrets."

I glanced at Nathan and saw him looking confused. I could, I supposed, find an excuse to send Nathan away, but I didn't have the heart to. I led Miss Corey and Nathan along the ledge to where Falco sat patiently, his grave eyes watching me.

"These are my friends," I said to him, "Lillian Corey, head librarian of Blythewood, and Nathan Beckwith."

Falco bowed his head to Miss Corey and then held out his hand to Nathan.

I took a deep breath. "Miss Corey, Nathan, I'd like you to meet my father."

26

NATHAN'S EYES WIDENED, but he took my father's hand and said in a firm voice, "I'm pleased to meet you, sir."

"And I am pleased to meet a friend of my daughter's," he said, giving Nathan's hand a squeeze that made Nathan grit his teeth. Then he turned to Miss Corey. "And to meet a learned librarian, as well."

I explained to him how I had found Blythewood when I returned there this morning. As I spoke, a flock of fledglings gathered on the ledges around us, including Raven, who listened with growing concern in his face. When I finished, Master Quill nodded.

"It sounds as if your friends have been placed under a musical mesmerism. They're very hard to undo, but I believe we might have something in the music section." He snapped his fingers and a young Darkling appeared. "I'll have one of my pages show you the way. And you, young man," he said to Nathan. "I can tell by the way you're scanning the shelves you're also looking for something. Perhaps . . . ah, yes, here's someone who might be able to help you."

I looked around to see Raven approaching. I glanced nervously back at Nathan, expecting him to make a scene, but instead I saw him whisper something in Raven's ear, and the two of them went off together. I looked back at my father, who was smiling at me.

"It looks as if your friends are finding what they are looking for. Why don't you sit down beside me? Perhaps I can help you find what you are looking for."

I sat down on a stool between the two scribes who were transcribing my father's wings. The scratch of their quills on paper was peaceful, like the sound of pigeons on the fire escape in the apartments I shared with my mother. Where we had lived all alone, cold and often hungry . . . the thought brought to mind the insidious questions van Drood had placed in my mind—or had he placed them there? Wasn't there a little part of me that was still angry at my father for abandoning me and my mother, no matter what the reason?

I looked away from him, afraid he'd see the doubt in my face, but then I felt his hand cover mine. I relaxed as the warmth of his hand seeped into my limbs, and I fell into a sort of daydream in which he was there at various times of my childhood—when I had the flu, when my mother was out late delivering hats and I was alone in the cold dark apartment, or when I stood at the service entrance of a Fifth Avenue mansion afraid to ring the bell—there by my side with his hand in mine.

"You'll never have to be alone like that again," he said. I knew that he had been there with me in my daydream, and some of the loneliness that had clung to me since my childhood was dissipated. I wiped my eyes as Miss Corey came back clutching a heavy book to her chest.

"I think I've found what I need, Ava," she said to me, her eyes on my father's wings.

"Please," Falco said, "you are welcome to look at the book. Perhaps you would like to look at the introduction." He ruffled his feathers, unveiling a richly illuminated page. Miss Corey leaned forward and peered at the page, her face shining. She read for several minutes and then looked up.

"This is remarkable," she cried. "Dame Alcyone was Merope's sister and a founding member of the Order. She says she will tell here the true story of how the Order began and how the Darklings were cursed." She looked up from the book at Falco and then at the small crowd of fledglings who had gathered around us. The crowd included Raven, who had come back with Nathan. The glow from the skylight lit up their faces. "I believe she wrote the book to show how our powers, yoked together, could defeat the shadow creatures, and how together we could release you from your curse. If this is true, we must put our enmity aside and join forces. I pledge to do my best to represent your case before the Council and recommend that we negotiate for peace."

I saw Raven nodding to Marlin, as if what Miss Corey had said confirmed something they had been speaking about—and then I saw them both look at Nathan. Surprised, I saw Nathan nod back at both of them and then extend a hand to shake theirs.

"I am glad that my archive has been of assistance to you, Lady," Master Quill said, bowing his head to Miss Corey. "And I, too, pledge to urge my flock to join with yours. When a great darkness threatens, the small birds must flock together."

At his words the assembled fledglings beat their wings to-gether and whistled a low note that sounded like wind moving through trees. I felt the hair on the back of my neck stand up and my wings strain to break free, but then I saw Nathan star-ing at me and I realized that even if he knew I was half-Darkling I wasn't ready to spread my wings in front of him yet. So in-stead I turned to say good-bye to my father.

He took my hand in his, and again I felt a weight fall from me, as though his hand lifted me up. He drew his wings around me, and I heard the fluttering of all the pages of the book as he wrapped me in their mantle.

"We are still bonded, dearling," he whispered in my ear. "If you need me you have only to call for me and I will come."

Then he unfolded his wings and stepped away from me. Even when I turned to go, though, and I climbed down the tower and left Ravencliffe, I still felt the mantle of his wings' protection around me.

⇥ ✦ ⇤

On the way back to Blythewood, Miss Corey explained what we had to do. "It's really quite simple," she said between swift strokes of her skates. "Musical mesmerism works by inserting a series of commands within a musical score. It's rather like hav-ing a song stuck in your head, only the song is telling you to do things you're not conscious of. What we have to do is disrupt the musical score in their heads by substituting other tunes. It's similar to how we use our bells to dispel fairies and other crea-tures. The book lists a series of tunes that are most effective in dispelling musical mesmerism, only . . ."

"Only what?" I asked, gasping to keep up with her.

"Only a well-crafted mesmerism spell will contain fail-safes to prevent anyone from dispelling it. We'll have to try different tunes on individuals until we discover which one will work. Once we find the right tune, we can use it to de-mesmerize enough of us to ring the Blythewood bells to free everyone in the castle."

"I can program my repeater to play back the tune," I said.

"Excellent," she replied. "The rest of us can hum it. Nathan, you have perfect pitch . . . right, Nathan?"

Nathan had been curiously quiet since we had left Ravencliffe, his eyes on the ice below his skates. Now he knew my father was a Darkling. What if my being half-Darkling was one more thing that pushed him into the shadows? What if his stubborn silence was his way of shutting me out, and he was never going to talk to me again?

But when Miss Corey called his name once more, he pointed to the ice below his feet. We both looked down and saw that there were dark shapes following our passage across the ice—only they weren't fish. There were shadows beneath the ice—*tenebrae*—and they were following us back to Blythewood.

We skated faster, racing the shadows under the ice. I hadn't realized how long we'd been at Ravencliffe until I noticed the sun going down over the mountains. By the time we reached Blythewood the shadows of the western mountains stretched across the river and crept up the lawn toward the castle. The last rays of the setting sun caught the icicles hanging from the battlements and turned them red so that it looked as though the castle were dripping blood. As we skated across the frozen lawn, I looked back at the river and saw the *tenebrae* under the ice. Waiting. But for what?

Mr. Bellows was at the library doors, pacing back and forth and tearing at his hair when we arrived. "Thank the Bells!" he cried. "I was afraid something had happened to you."

"Where's Vi?" Miss Corey asked. She was trying to look around Mr. Bellows, but he kept placing himself in front of her.

Mr. Bellows raked his hands through his hair. "I only left her for a minute."

Miss Corey pushed Mr. Bellows aside and strode across the library, her skate blades clattering loudly and scarring the parquet floor. Miss Sharp was standing by the fire—or rather, not standing but twirling—in a long white satin and lace gown. She was also wearing a long veil and carrying a bouquet of pink rosebuds and baby's breath.

"Vi!" Miss Corey cried. "Why are you dressed like that?"

"Oh, Lillian, there you are! I wanted so much for you to see my dress. I'm to play a bride doll. Isn't it lovely?"

So many emotions passed over Miss Corey's face it was like watching a lake during a summer shower, ruffled by wind and alternately darkened by clouds and lit by sunshine—relief that Miss Sharp wasn't really getting married, horror that she had succumbed to the mesmerism, and then anger at Mr. Bellows.

"How could you let this happen to her?" she said, whirling on him.

"I told her to lock the library doors. Someone she trusted must have gotten in—I'm afraid it might have been Helen."

"Helen!" I cried.

I started across the floor, remembered I was still wearing

skates, and stopped to unlace them. Nathan was already tearing at his laces and shucking off his skates.

"Let me try some of the tunes on Vionetta first," Miss Corey said, laying her hand on my shoulder. "Then we'll know which one works."

"Tunes?" Miss Sharp said, her blue eyes widening. "Do you mean like wedding songs?" She hummed a bit of the wedding march and twirled around, holding her satin train in one hand. "Oh, I do wish this wasn't only a costume. I would so love to be a real bride!"

Nathan turned to me. "Are there any bride dolls in *Die Puppenfee*?"

"No," I said. "But Herr Hofmeister's been adding all sorts of extras. You don't think—"

I was interrupted by a jingling of sleigh bells. Nathan and I went to the window. Coming up the drive were a dozen horse-drawn sleighs trimmed with holly and ribbons. The first one stopped at the door, and several men in fur coats disembarked. Gillie was holding the bridle of the lead horse. I recognized Mr. Montmorency and Mr. Driscoll, but there were a number of younger men—in their thirties, I guessed—whom I didn't recognize.

"Who are all these men?" I asked.

"They're investors," Miss Corey answered. "Dame Beckwith announced a few days ago that they'd be coming."

"Oh!" Miss Sharp cried, jumping to her feet and rushing to the window. "Do you think they're married? They must be rich to invest so much money in the school. I do wish Gillie wasn't giving them such an awful look."

Gillie was indeed staring at the men as if he'd like to haul them back on their sleighs and send them packing. At least Gillie hadn't been mesmerized. When the last man disembarked from the sleigh I saw Gillie's face turn a shade of menacing green, and the sky, which had been clear a moment ago, turned dark. I recognized the last man as the clergyman I'd seen at the Montmorency ball.

A clergyman who could perform a marriage ceremony.

"They can't . . . they wouldn't . . ." I sputtered.

"I wouldn't put it past them," Nathan muttered grimly. "They might be planning to marry off our girls to the highest bidder. We have to stop this."

I wondered if he was worrying about Helen; I knew I was. Miss Corey drew Miss Sharp gently away from the window and back to the chair by the fireplace, where Mr. Bellows urged her to sit down.

"Oh, but I'll crease my dress!" she complained. "Will you carry my train for me, dearest Lil? Oh, you can be my bridesmaid!"

"Over my dead body," Miss Corey muttered. But in a louder voice she said, "Whatever you like, Vi, but first I'd like you to listen to some tunes. They're—"

"Samples of wedding marches?" Miss Sharp asked.

"Yes," Miss Corey bit off between gritted teeth. "So listen to each one carefully."

Miss Corey hummed a tune.

"Oh, I think that's a bit too funereal for a wedding, don't you, Rupert? What would you like for your wedding?"

Mr. Bellows blushed from his starched collar to his scalp. "Let's try another," he said, his voice cracking.

Miss Corey hummed another tune, which Miss Sharp pronounced "charming but better suited for a summer wedding," and another that was for a "younger bride."

"I am, after all, over thirty. I thought I'd die a spinster because the Order said I couldn't marry," she prattled as Miss Corey tried one tune after another. "Because of Uncle Taddie being crazy, you know. But now . . . oh now! I think everything has changed and I'm hopeful . . . hopeful . . . hope . . . full . . ."

She stuttered like a wind-up toy that had been wound too tight, her head tilting from side to side, a puzzled look in her eyes.

"That last one seemed to have knocked something loose," Mr. Bellows said. "Try it again."

Miss Corey hummed the previous tune. I listened to it carefully, as did Miss Sharp, her blue eyes focused on Miss Corey's face growing suddenly clear.

"Lillian!" she cried. "You're back! . . . What . . . ?" She looked down at the bouquet in her lap and fingered the satin of her dress. "Why am I dressed like this? What nonsense have I been spouting?"

"It's all right, Vionetta, you were mesmerized."

"But I thought I was really going to be married . . . to some stranger! It didn't even matter to whom."

"It was the spell," Miss Corey said more firmly. "Don't upset yourself."

"But how could I have even *thought* such a thing"—she

leaned forward and took Miss Corey's hand—"when the only person I ever want to be with is you?"

Miss Corey turned pink and began to stammer her friend's name, but Miss Sharp stopped her mouth with a kiss. Which, after a moment, Miss Corey returned.

I turned away to find Mr. Bellows and Nathan gaping at the two women. "Let's memorize that tune to make sure we have it right," I suggested. "I've got it right here on my repeater."

"Oh . . . y-yes," Mr. Bellows stuttered.

I peeked back to steal a glance at Miss Corey and Miss Sharp, holding hands and beaming at each other.

"Right," I said, turning to Nathan and Mr. Bellows with a broad smile of my own. "Let's get to work."

27

OUR TEACHERS WANTED to go straight to the bell tower, but Nathan insisted on finding Helen and the rest of the girls first.

"I'm not leaving my friends alone with those . . . bounders," he said.

Miss Sharp suggested that Nathan and I go to the ballroom while they went to the bell tower. "We'll de-mesmerize whomever we find along the way until we have enough to ring the bells. But you two stay together. I was converted in an instant. Once you've cured Helen you can break off into pairs, but always make sure you work with a partner and instruct whomever you cure to do the same."

We looked into the Great Hall, which was full of arriving guests. Long tables were set with steaming punch bowls fragrant with liquor and spice and silver trays loaded with roasts and mincemeat pies. But despite the good smells of food, the room was full of the smoky fug from the men's cigars. The seven bell maker's daughters looked down from their stained-glass windows with sadness and shock. But they didn't look as angry as Nathan.

"How dare those men come into Blythewood with evil intent toward our girls? The bells ought to be pealing out at their presence!"

Why *weren't* the bells ringing? I wondered as we went up the narrow back servants' stairs, Nathan following me so closely I could feel his breath on the back of my neck.

"I'm not going to turn into a monster and fly away," I hissed at him when he trod on my feet.

"That's not what I'm worried about," he said. "Raven said you might still be weak from your . . . sickness. He said to stick close to you."

I was about to snap back that I was perfectly fine, but then, looking at him more closely, I saw that he wasn't. In the dim light of a flickering wall sconce his skin was a sickly yellow and his hair a dead gray, and his eyes glittered like a fever patient's. The shadows lurking in Nathan's soul were rising to the surface, flushed out by the presence of the visitors. That's why Raven had told him to stay near me—for his protection, not mine.

"Okay," I said, squeezing Nathan's hand. "I'll stay close." Before I could finish, we both heard something growl at the top of the stairs. Nathan squeezed past me. I followed close on his heels to find a snarling, razor-fanged, green-skinned imp. Nathan drew out his dagger, and the creature lifted its shaggy dark head and glared out of acid-green eyes.

"No, wait," I cried, "it's Gillie!"

Nathan stared at me with disbelief, but I crouched down and held out my hand, speaking in the firm voice Gillie had taught me to use with the hawks. "It's all right, Ghillie Dhu, we're not here to steal your girls, but to help them."

The creature growled low in its throat, but I saw a flicker

of recognition in his eyes, which changed now from the acid green of pond scum to the soft green of moss. He stood up, and resumed a more human cast to his features.

"Hell's Bells, it is Gillie!" Nathan swore. "What did they do to him?"

"No time to explain," I said. I suspected that the threat to the Blythewood girls had triggered a defensive reaction that had turned the peaceful Gillie into a snarling monster. "Are you okay now, Gillie?"

The caretaker nodded and grunted. "Aye, lass. I don't know what came over me."

"It's the guests," Nathan said. "The board members and the investors. We think van Drood is controlling them."

Gillie muttered something in Scots that I suspected was a string of curses, finishing in English. "I should never have let them in, but the Dame insisted. But she's no' herself, is she?"

"No, Gillie," I said. "The girls are all under a spell. We can break it, we think. Can you guard the front door for us and make sure no one tries to take the girls away?"

"Aye," he growled. "Those bastards will take my girls o'er my dead body!" He lurched away down the hall toward the front stairs. I watched him go worriedly, hoping that focusing on a mission would keep him from transforming back into a Ghillie Dhu.

Just then three girls in matching doll costumes flitted out of the dressing room, humming the winter polka from *Die Puppenfee*, and headed toward the ballroom. The sound of hearty male voices was rising up from the stairs along with that awful stench of smoke. The orchestra was tuning up. The dance was about to begin. I took a deep breath and, repeater in hand, dove into the dressing room.

For a moment it called to mind the Triangle factory at closing hour on the day of the fire: girls in rows chattering together, running back and forth in a frenzy. Instead of smoke the air was full of tulle swathes billowing out from the girls' costumes as they spun around and around. Just watching them made me dizzy. I found myself humming the polka . . .

I pressed the repeater to my ear and looked around for Daisy and Helen. Fortunately they were standing together comparing their costumes. Helen was wearing a shade of lavender I knew she wouldn't be caught dead in. I marched over to them and grabbed them each by their arms and started pulling them toward the door. They both squawked, but I told them we were going to the ballroom because it was time for their dance. That seemed to satisfy them both so well they began dancing as we left the room. I handed Helen over to Nathan and waltzed with Daisy around a corner and whisked her into an alcove. I held up the repeater and played the tune.

"That's not my part," Daisy said, frowning.

"It's a new piece that Herr Hofmeister wants you to learn," I said. "You must concentrate, Daisy." I played it again for her. She tilted her head back and forth and began to shake. Terrified that I'd somehow broken Daisy, I screamed for Nathan. He came running with Helen.

"It's all right," Helen cried, putting her arm around Daisy. "This happened to me, too. In my case I think it was the shock of finding myself in *mauve*. Daisy is no doubt just realizing—"

"I broke off my engagement with Mr. Appleby!" she

wailed, pulling a lace handkerchief from her bodice.

Helen straightened her back, took Daisy by the shoulders, and looked her in the eye. "I will personally explain everything to Mr. Appleby and you *will* marry him if that's what you want, and Ava and I will be your bridesmaids in whatever dreadful dresses you choose."

Daisy flung her arms around Helen and pulled me into their embrace. "I was so afraid to tell you both because Helen was so angry at the other girls getting engaged and Ava—well, I know you might never get married because you love a Darkling."

That was why she'd kept her engagement from me?

"Ahem." Nathan cleared his throat. "Far be it from me to interrupt your wedding planning, but we have a school full of girls to de-mesmerize."

"Right," Helen said in a businesslike way while wiping a tear from her eye. Daisy handed Helen her own handkerchief, which Helen quickly passed to me, as if I were the one in need of it. "Let's memorize this tune," she said to Daisy.

Nathan and I left Helen and Daisy practicing the de-mesmerism tune and headed back to the dressing room. As we rounded the corner, though, we ran into Mrs. Calendar waltzing around the landing, humming the Chinese mazurka from *Die Puppenfee*. "Ah, there you are! Why aren't you children dancing? You, Nathan Beckwith, you've always been a lazy, ne'er-do-well. If you don't apply yourself you'll break your mother's heart."

As Mrs. Calendar berated Nathan I saw the shadows rising in his eyes. I grabbed hold of the Latin teacher and held the repeater up in front of her face. At first it had no effect. Years of memorizing Latin declensions and conjugations had given her a mind like a steel trap. Once I got through to her, though, she sprang into action. "We must rescue Dame Beckwith first. She's in the ballroom."

As we approached the ballroom, a flock of girls in pink gauze and tulle flitted past us, twittering like sparrows. Nathan tried to grab the last two in the troop, but they leaped nimbly out of his grasp and joined their cohorts. We'd only managed to de-mesmerize a handful of girls, whom Daisy was trying to corral back into the dressing room. The rest of the girls were streaming into the ballroom. We were caught up in the flow. The ballroom seemed to be spinning like the Hellgate, with colorful bits of flotsam and jetsam caught inside it. I pulled Mrs. Calendar off to the side so I could get my bearings.

The whirlpool was made of dancing couples spinning around the polished marble floor, the girls' dresses bright as tropical fish. The orchestra was playing on the balcony, which was swathed with evergreen boughs. The walls had been draped in heavy garlands of evergreen and sprinkled with some white dust to look like snow. In the corners of the room the pine boughs had been arched over sleighs, their benches upholstered in red velvet and dripping with furs. Here the board members and the older women of the Order sat, the women sipping cider, the men puffing their cigars, the smoke from which hung in the air over the dancing couples.

I looked again at the dance floor. The girls' partners were all young men, handsomely attired in black evening coats and smart red ascots, sprigs of holly pinned to their lapels. They were moving so fast, though, that I couldn't make out the men's faces. They all blurred into one featureless face . . .

I tottered on my feet and Mrs. Calendar—frail little Mrs. Calendar—righted me with a firm shake.

"Get ahold of yourself, girl!" she snapped. "Now's not the time to swoon. There's Dame Beckwith."

As we made our way around the edges of the ballroom I kept my eyes on Mrs. Calendar's ramrod-straight back and grasped my repeater in my hand. When I tried playing it, though, it repeated the waltz that the orchestra was playing, so I recited Latin declensions and kept my eyes off the dance floor, not wanting to look at those blank faces.

I tripped over the leg of a man sitting in one of the sleighs. He grabbed my arm and I felt his whiskers brush my face and smelled the reek of tobacco on his breath. "Watch yourself, girl."

I stared at the old man. His face was fat and red, rimmed with white muttonchops. His eyes were clouded over by cataracts. He looked like someone's harmless old grandfather, but then I saw, swimming beneath his cataracts, smoke-gray shadows like the *tenebrae* I'd glimpsed beneath the ice.

"Leave her alone, Winthrop Clay," Mrs. Calendar said, pulling me away. "Everyone knows you drove your own wife into the madhouse."

"You know these men?" I whispered as we left Winthrop Clay puffing on his cigar, eyes vacant as his empty punch glass.

"I grew up with most of them. Played croquet with Winty Clay in Newport. Thought he was sweet on me." She smiled up at me, her wizened old face looking for a moment youthful. "But the Order had other ideas for us. Married me off to a man twice my age."

"That's awful!" I said.

"Yes," she agreed. "It was. When he died I wasn't allowed to remarry because I'd had no children."

"I'm sorry," I said, not sure what else to say.

"I was too, for a while, but then I was allowed to go back to my studies and teach. I've come to think of you girls as my children. As for this lot," she snorted, "look at Winty now. His wife, Elvira, wound up in the Hudson River State Hospital for the Insane down in Poughkeepsie. And look at Maunsell Livermore." She pointed to a cadaverous gentleman lurking behind the refreshment table. "Lost all his money in the crash of ninety-three and has been knocking around his old mansion like a ghost ever since. In fact, the men of the Order have been going downhill since the crash. No wonder they want to marry you all off. They need new money to shore up the endowment."

I followed Mrs. Calendar to the refreshment table, where Dame Beckwith was chatting with Maunsell Livermore and a portly gentleman whose enormous girth was barely restrained by a scarlet cummerbund.

". . . all of good stock," Scarlet Cummerbund was saying as we drew up to them. "Young men of good families—wealthy families . . . er, p'haps not *old* families like us, if you take my meaning."

"No, not *old* families," Maunsell Livermore drawled. "But wealthy ones. And that's what we need right now."

"Infusion of new blood, don't you know," Scarlet Cummerbund puffed, smoke billowing out of his fat red lips.

"Infusion of new money," Livermore echoed. "Just the ticket. Never mind your fancy breeding charts. What the Order needs now are financial resources."

"I suppose so," Dame Beckwith said uncertainly, tucking a strand of silver hair behind her ear—I don't think I'd ever seen a single strand come loose before. "But where did you say you found these young gentlemen?"

"Found *us*," Scarlet Cummerbund said, bellowing forth more smoke . . . but when had he taken another puff of his cigar? "Enterprising lads. They want to raise their stock by marrying into the old families. Sound reasoning, I say."

"The soundest," Livermore purred, smoke dribbling down his chin. "Good investment, what?"

"I suppose so," Dame Beckwith said, blinking in the smoke. "Oh, here's Mrs. Calendar. You know her, of course."

Both men blinked at the Latin teacher and then simultaneously said, "Junessa Calendar," and bowed.

"And here's Miss Avaline Hall, one of our brightest students and from a very old family indeed."

"Hall?" Livermore said. "Ah yes, believe I played snooker with your grandfather, Throckmorton. Good stock, the Halls. You should be dancing."

"Yes, you should be dancing," Scarlet Cummerbund echoed, blowing smoke rings up into the air. He wasn't even holding a cigar, I realized with a chill. Worse, the smoke rings summoned one of the black-clad young men. He clicked his heels together as if he were in a military parade and bowed to me. As he lifted his head I braced myself to look at his face—terrified that he had none—but the man had the requisite, if bland, features: brown hair, brown eyes, thin nose, brown mustache, red lips.

"Would you care to dance, Miss?" he asked in a smooth, polite voice.

"Oh, thank you, but no, not now—"

"Nonsense, Ava," Dame Beckwith said. "You *must* dance."

"Yes, you must," Livermore and Cummerbund said in unison.

"No, really—"

But the polite, bland-featured gentleman had already taken my elbow and was leading me onto the dance floor. I tried to free myself, but his grip was like iron. I looked back at Mrs. Calendar, who was leading Dame Beckwith into one of the sleighs. She would free Dame Beckwith if anyone could. I'd put up with this one dance and then rejoin my friends.

My partner put his arm around my waist and spun me deftly into the whirl of dancers. I let out a little gasp at the speed and he said, "Don't worry, Miss, I've got you."

That was exactly what I was worried about. His arm around my waist felt like an iron manacle. I looked into his bland face, searching for malice in his brown eyes, but saw nothing there but polite expectancy. He was humming along with the music like a child.

"Who are you?" I began, and then, recalling my manners, amended, "We haven't been formally introduced. My name is Avaline Hall."

"It's a pleasure to meet you, Miss Hall," he replied. "I'm . . .

I'm . . ." For half a second he lost the rhythm of the dance and we nearly collided with another couple—Myrtilene, I saw, and her dance partner. Then my partner laughed.

"Well, ain't that the darndest thing. I seem to have forgotten my name. But don't you worry your little head about that. I do remember that my father owns the largest chain of dry good stores east of the Mississippi and I went to all the best schools. I'm sure my name will come back to me by the time we're standing in front of the altar."

"I have absolutely no intention of marrying you, Mr. . . . Whoever-you-are."

My partner laughed. "That's what all the girls say, but they don't mean it."

"Well, I *do* mean it. Please take me off the dance floor now."

"Look, it's time for one of those divert-i-ments you gals are so good at. Come, let's watch it together."

Still gripping my waist, my partner pulled me off the dance floor. A troop of dancers dressed like China dolls pirouetted out and began to perform a jerky ballet. I saw Herr Hofmeister standing in the doorway waving his baton, directing the girls' movements, plucking the air with his gloved hand as though playing an invisible harp. One of the Chinese dolls—could that be Cam Bennett?—moved at his direction as if connected to him by strings. I felt my partner's arm twitching to the same rhythm.

"That's what all the girls say," he murmured. "Pleased to meet you. All the best schools. But they don't mean it." I looked around and saw that all the young men were mouthing similar inanities. And it didn't seem to bother the girls—*our* girls.

There was Beatrice Jager beaming at her partner as if he were reciting Plato, when all he was saying was "I do love croquet" over and over again. And there was Wallis Rutherford goggling at a chinless specimen prattling on about wanting at least a dozen children.

On the fringes of the crowd I spied Nathan and Helen and Daisy working to separate out our girls to de-mesmerize them, but their dancing partners wouldn't let them go. When Nathan tried to pry Susannah Dewsnap out of one man's grip he back-handed Nathan in the jaw without a change of expression and calmly remarked that he preferred yachting in Oyster Bay to Nantucket. And all the while the men kept their eyes on Herr Hofmeister's twirling baton.

That was it—Hofmeister was controlling *them*. We had to stop Hofmeister. We needed the bells. What had happened to our teachers? Had they been caught?

I squirmed against my partner's arm, but he only tightened his grip.

"Let me go!" I screamed.

He turned to me, his face blank as paste, and said, "That's what all the girls say, but they don't mean it."

My blood turned cold at his words and then curdled when each and every one of the young men turned toward me in unison and spoke in van Drood's voice. "That's what your mother said, but she didn't mean it." Then like clockwork the young men swept their partners onto the dance floor.

As I struggled against my captor's grip, the ballroom doors slammed open with a bang that disrupted the flow of the dance.

For a moment the girls, arrested in their movements, stumbled like automatons whose clockwork had broken. Their partners also stopped and looked toward the door to see what had caused the disruption, their bland, plump faces registering the annoyance of men used to getting their way. Who—or what— had come?

I turned to see the wide doorway darkened by a cluster of cloaked figures. They stood in a V formation, the tallest figure at the point, their cloaks dripping with icicles as though they had swum here beneath the frozen river. I thought of the *tenebrae* under the ice—but then the lead figure took a step forward and whisked his cloak back over his shoulders with a sound like . . . *wings*.

"Raven!" I breathed.

"We heard you were having a dance," he said in his clear, rich voice, sweeping his plumed cap off his head. Under his cloak he was dressed in black leather pants, a black leather vest, and a flowing white shirt. He looked like a pirate from one of Mr. Pyle's illustrated adventure books. "I guess our invitations were lost in the mail."

28

"DARKLINGS!" DAME BECKWITH hissed.

"They're here to help," I said, trying to wrench myself out of my captor's arms. When Raven saw me struggling he crossed the dance floor in two strides and loomed inches from my captor's face.

"*Let her go*," he growled in a barely human voice.

"I lost her mother to one of you." My captor spoke in van Drood's voice. "I won't lose her, too. Now why don't you leave. Your kind aren't welcome here."

Raven seemed momentarily taken aback by van Drood's voice coming out of the rosy lips of the bland-faced man, but he recovered quickly. He looked around the ballroom at the coterie of well-dressed young men frozen like players in a tableau vivant. Then he turned back to the one who still gripped my arm. He stooped his head within a hair of the man's ear and growled. "You're not even brave enough to show yourself in person, van Drood. No wonder Evangeline Hall chose Falco over you."

The man holding me made a hissing sound, like air leaking out of a pneumatic tire, and his hands fell from my arms. Raven swept me away from him onto the dance floor. The orchestra had begun to play again—but a completely different tune from the syrupy strains of *Die Puppenfee*. Glancing up at the balcony I saw that a group of Darklings had taken the musicians' places. The music had a rhythm that made my feet skip over the dance floor. As we spun around the room I saw the Darklings shouldering away the investors, who huffed and puffed but retreated. Around me girls came awake, their cheeks turning pink beneath the pasty doll makeup, their limbs loosening and breaking free of the puppet master's strings.

"*This* is what you planned with Nathan," I said.

"Yes," Raven admitted. "And I wish I could dance all night with you, but your Nathan has another plan."

"He's not *my* Nathan," I objected.

"You may have to tell him that," Raven whispered in my ear, the heat of his breath sending shivers all the way down my spine. "But right now it looks like he wants you to go with him."

He'd danced me to the door, where Nathan, Helen, and Daisy waited for me. Nathan took my hand, but his eyes were on Raven.

"Can you handle things from here?" he asked.

"Yes, I think my friends have got things under control," Raven replied, surveying the room.

"Maybe for now," said Nathan, "But we have to get to the bell tower. The others must have run into a problem." He, too, was looking around the room. When his eyes came to rest on the investors, his brow furrowed. They were clustered together now, looking disgruntled. "I do wonder what *they're* planning, though."

"Oh, let me go find out," Daisy cried. "I've always wanted to be a spy."

"Be careful, Daisy," I said. "Van Drood is channeling himself through them. They might try to mesmerize you again."

"And you be careful," Raven said. "All of you. They'll have placed guards on the bell tower."

I turned back to say good-bye to Raven. "Thank you—"

He raised my hand to his lips and kissed my fingers. "It's always a pleasure to dance with you, Miss Hall," he said formally. "I hope we shall have many more dances." Then he swept away.

I turned back to find Nathan's eyes on me. I expected him to say something about Raven, but all he said was, "Let's go."

We hurried to the North Wing and found Miss Sharp, Miss Corey, and Mr. Bellows on the last landing before the belfry. Seven Dianas were standing guard in front of the door, bows drawn, eyes glazed. *Their training makes it easier for me to get inside their heads*, van Drood had once told me. I had no doubt that they would shoot us if we tried to get past them, and there wasn't any room to navigate in the narrow passage.

I held the repeater in my hand and pressed the stem. All evening I'd had it programmed to play the de-mesmerizing tune, but now it played a refrain from *Die Puppenfee. It must be picking up the tune inside the Dianas' heads*, I thought. Hastily, I stopped it before it mesmerized the rest of us.

I stepped toward Georgiana, who stood in the center of the line, and heard the vibration of her bow string as she pulled it a fraction tighter, adjusting her stance so the tip of her arrow was aimed directly at my heart.

I heard the deep bass bell tolling in my head, signaling danger. Not just for me, but for all of Blythewood. I knew that if I couldn't get past the Dianas something terrible would happen.

Something terrible *was* happening. Beneath the tolling of the bell I heard the orchestra playing *Die Puppenfee* again. Then I heard a loud crack—as if the very stones of the castle had snapped under the strain of the ice holding us captive.

"Gunfire," Nathan said. "We should go back—"

"Wait!" I said, even though every fiber of my being ached to go to Raven. "We have to get to the bells. And I think I know how."

I closed my eyes. Inside my head the only sound was the bass gong of my danger bell, banishing everything else. I could feel its vibrations deep in my belly and in the tips of my fingers and toes. I could taste the metallic tang of the bell's clapper on my tongue. I concentrated on the ringing of the bell and let myself hear all the fears that went with each toll. Fear of being exposed as a monster, fear of losing my home, my friends, Raven . . . fear of making a choice and having it be the wrong one . . . I let myself feel each one of those fears until I thought I would explode with the weight of them.

And then I drove the bell out of my head. I felt it rise out of me and move up into the belfry, where the bells of Blythewood began to ring out—only the sound they made was muted. They had been muffled. They were loud enough, though, to get through to the Dianas. Georgiana was blinking as though she wasn't sure where she was.

"Now!" I cried, reaching for her bow. I plucked it out of her now-limp hands. Helen yanked Alfreda Driscoll's bow, screaming, "Ha!" My friends were able to disarm the other Dianas and then we were racing up into the belfry. We ripped off the cotton batting that had been wrapped around the bell clappers to mute the bells—that was why they hadn't rung out!—and then each took a rope while Nathan called out the changes to muster the bells into order. We rang the de-mesmerizing tune again and again. As we did, the ice clinging to the castle cracked and fell to the ground.

Then I heard someone scream.

I peered over the battlement to see who had been struck by the falling icicles. I was hoping it was Herr Hofmeister, but it was one of the investors. He was lying on the flagstones, flailing his arms like a cockroach. Herr Hofmeister stood above him yelling to "be quick about it—the sleighs are leaving!"

I looked up at the drive. The sleighs were pulled up to the door, where they were being loaded . . .

With *girls*.

I heard Daisy's voice rise up. "Oh, a sleigh ride, what ripping fun!" Then I heard Beatrice Jager cry, "I've never been on a sleigh!"

"No!" I screamed. "Don't go with them!"

But the bells drowned out my voice. Shouldn't the bells have banished the spell by now?

"Oh," I heard Daisy again, her voice less gleeful now. "I say, perhaps another time."

But she was silenced by a man in a beaver coat who shoved her into the sleigh. I heard other girls objecting now, but it was too late. The sleighs were moving out, their bells jangling madly as they raced, not to the drive as I expected, but down to the river. The sleighs slid onto the ice, where they were swallowed by a cloak of shadows—the *tenebrae* rising from under the ice to flock around the sleighs—and then disappeared into the night with the stolen girls.

When we got downstairs we found the Darklings held at gunpoint by a gang of tough-looking men—the sleigh drivers, I realized. Behind the Darklings were a group of girls and teachers huddled in a mass. The Darklings had spread their wings to keep the sleigh drivers from taking the rest of the girls, but they couldn't attack the drivers without getting shot themselves. When the sleigh drivers saw us, their leader yelled, "Let's go, boy-os!" and with a volley of pistol shots aimed at the ceiling, they fled outside into the last remaining sleigh. Mr. Bellows, Nathan, Raven, and Marlin ran after them. I joined them.

"We'll follow the sleighs," Raven yelled, his wings spread out for flight. "You stay here and make sure there's no residual spell. Don't worry; we'll find them." He took to the sky with Marlin and two other Darklings following. My wings itched to go with them, but the sounds from inside—moans, shrieks, hysterical crying—told me I was needed here.

I went inside and found a scene of utter chaos. Dolores Jager ran past me, looking for her sister, until Cam grabbed her and told her that Beatrice had been among the girls taken in the sleighs.

"But she can't have gone without me!" she cried. They were the first words I'd ever heard from her.

A crowd of students was huddled around a small body on the floor. I thought it was a girl at first, but as I got closer I saw it was Gillie. Dame Beckwith crouched over him, pressing her shawl to the wound in his chest. She was calling for Mr. Malmsbury to help her carry him to the infirmary.

Seeing me, she demanded to know where the rest of the

girls had gone. When I told her that they had been taken in the sleighs, her face fell. She seemed to age ten years in ten seconds.

"But Raven and the others are following them," I said, trying to sound more optimistic than I felt. "They're sure to find them and rescue them."

A strangled sound came from Gillie. Dame Beckwith leaned down, angling her ear to Gillie's lips, which were working to form words. I knelt beside him and listened with my Darkling ears.

"Send . . . the . . . hawks."

"He wants us to send the hawks after the girls," I said.

"Of course!" Dame Beckwith cried, her eyes shining. "You've trained them to track the girls, haven't you? Is there a command?"

He shook his head, his eyes on me. "Ava . . ." he gasped. "Ava . . . knows . . ." Before he could finish, his eyes rolled back and he passed out.

"What did he say?" Dame Beckwith cried, staring at me.

"That I know how." I saw Dame Beckwith's eyes widen. The only creatures other than Gillie who knew how to speak to birds were Darklings.

"I, er, heard him practicing with the hawks once. I think I know the command."

"Then go," Dame Beckwith said, freeing one hand from Gillie's to clasp mine. She was looking at me as fiercely as a hawk. "Do whatever you have to do to get our girls back."

I nodded, got to my feet, and ran up the stairs.

On the fourth-floor landing I went out the window to the fire escape that led to the roof. As I crossed the roof to the mews

I heard the hawks beating their wings in their cages and crying out shrilly. They knew that something was wrong.

When I opened the mews door I was shocked at what I saw. The usually clean and ordered pens were filled with feathers and blood. The birds were flinging themselves against their wire cages, so frantic to get out they had bloodied themselves in their efforts.

I stood in the doorway, panting from my sprint up the stairs, their panic infecting me. I was a Darkling. I should know how to talk to birds. I'd seen Raven do it, but I had no idea how.

I tried English first.

"Blodeuwedd," I said, addressing the great horned owl who was Gillie's favorite.

At the sound of her name she stopped the frantic beating of her wings and turned her huge yellow eyes on me.

"Gillie's been hurt," I said, feeling foolish talking to the great solemn owl, but then I poured it all out. "Men possessed by shadows have taken our girls!" She swiveled and tilted her head as I talked. I opened her cage and put out my hand, though without a glove, her powerful talons could snap off my fingers. She was still in an excited state; if she didn't understand me, she might claw my eyes out, too. But she hopped obediently onto my hand. Emboldened, I opened all the cages.

The hawks and falcons hurtled out—kestrels, peregrines, goshawks, and lastly, the two prized gyrfalcons that Mr. Montmorency had bought—a mated pair named Eirwyn and Gwynfor. I feared they might fly in a dozen directions before I could command them, but instead they followed me as I walked to the edge of the roof and stood at the parapet with Blodeuwedd on my hand. Below us the frozen lawns gleamed in the moonlight, but the Hudson was covered with a thick blanket of fog. Our girls had vanished into it. I felt the sting of tears in my eyes. Digging in my pocket for a handkerchief, I came up with Daisy's, which she'd given me earlier. I held it in front of Blodeuwedd, as I'd seen Gillie do with the feathers of smaller birds he wanted the the hawks and falcons to hunt. "Find Daisy," I told Blodeuwedd. "Find them all and tell us where they are so we can bring them back."

Blodeuwedd turned her yellow eyes on me. Their glow warmed something inside me. Then she opened her hooked beak and uttered a shrill cry. The falcons echoed her. "Go!" I cried, only what came out wasn't a human's voice but a wild bird's cry. I watched the birds rise into the night until the white feathers of the twin gyrfalcons faded into the night sky like stars at dawn.

I went downstairs, checking first on the fourth floor to see that the remaining nestlings were all right. Cam and Myrtilene had them all crowded into one room, wrapped in shawls and sipping hot cocoa. Then I went down to the library, where I found Helen, Miss Corey, and Miss Sharp.

Unable to face going to our room without Daisy, we sat the rest of the night in the library, sitting by the window, watching the fog lighten to a pearly gray. My eyes were beginning to droop when Helen grabbed my hand. I startled awake and saw a figure appearing out of the fog—a winged figure, black against the gray, one wing dragging along the icy lawn.

I jumped up and ran out the door, my feet slipping on the ice. I heard Helen running behind me and calling my name, but I didn't listen to her. I just had to reach him.

It wasn't Raven; it was Marlin. I skidded to a halt. Helen rushed past me and caught Marlin's arm as he fell to one knee. His face was as gray as the fog. Blood dripped on the ice from his broken wing.

"What happened?" I cried, taking his other arm.

"We followed them down the river nearly to the city. We had just caught up with them . . . there's a spot where a creek feeds into the river. The currents are tricky there. The ice began to break up. The sleighs . . . they just vanished! We tried to follow them but the ice suddenly . . . *exploded*! It was like a volcano erupting. The water was churning in a whirlpool, the force so strong that it would have sucked us all into it. Raven shouted for us to get back . . . and then . . ." Marlin shuddered, unable to speak for a moment. Helen stroked his arm. I wanted to shake him.

"And then?" I prompted. "What happened to Raven?"

"It grabbed him."

"*It?*"

"The . . . monster in the whirlpool. It was huge, with dozens of tentacles. They wrapped around Raven. I attacked it, stabbed it, but it wouldn't let go. I saw its mouth . . . a giant maw full of razor-sharp teeth . . ." He shuddered and I shook, recalling the kraken from my nightmare.

"It struck me, broke my wing, then tossed me onto the riverbank. I couldn't move. I watched while . . ."

"What?" I screamed. "What did it do to Raven?"

"It dragged him under the ice."

29

THE PARENTS OF the remaining girls sent sleighs for them the day after the party. They left in a dead hush, with none of the shouts and cheerful farewells of last year's end-of-term leave-taking. Dame Beckwith stood on the steps to speak with the drivers and the few parents who came themselves, but most would not even look at her—except for Mr. Driscoll, who shouted at her for a full fifteen minutes and then turned away in disgust.

"They invited those men," I complained to Helen as we stood at the second-floor-landing window watching the exodus. "How can they blame Dame Beckwith for what happened?"

"Because otherwise they'd have to blame themselves," Helen replied. Then she turned away and went to the infirmary, where Marlin lay, bandaged and ashen faced. I went down to see off the last sleigh, which Nathan and Mr. Bellows were taking back to the city to look for the girls. As I approached I saw that a white bird was perched on Mr. Bellows' shoulder. Her wings looked ragged, as if some creature had pecked at it, but I recognized her as the female gyrfalcon, Eirwyn.

"She's the only one that came back," Mr. Bellows explained, smoothing the gyr's feathers. "She showed up at your grandmother's house last night pursued by shadow crows. Agnes sent her back with a message from Sam Greenfeder. He says his inquiries have led him to a property in the Bronx, which is also where the sleigh left the river."

"We'll search every house in the Bronx for the girls . . . and Raven," Nathan said through gritted teeth. "He might have been taken by them when he came out of the maelstrom."

I nodded. We both knew it was unlikely that Raven had survived, but it was kind of Nathan to pretend that he might be alive. Especially since he looked half-frozen himself. His face had taken on that shadowed look again, the brief flush of happiness I'd seen yesterday wiped clean by the night's events. I knew that our girls being taken had prodded the open wound of what had happened to Louisa.

"Don't you get lost, too," I said.

"We won't," Mr. Bellows said with a wistful look at Miss Sharp, who had come with Miss Corey to see him off. "You take care of her," he said to Miss Corey. As he turned to jump on the sleigh runner, his red scarf fluttering in the breeze, Eirwyn leapt onto my shoulder, emitting a plaintive cry. I didn't need to understand bird language to know she was lamenting her lost companions.

When the last sleigh bell faded in the distance, the castle was left in a pall of silence. Miss Sharp and Miss Corey headed to the library, where they planned to comb through the books for any mention of a hellgate. I brought Eirwyn to the infirmary, where Dame Beckwith was sitting beside Gillie's bed. The gryfalcon instantly flew to the iron bedstead and perched above Gillie's head, mantling her feathers as if to protect him, even though it was too late. Gillie lay as though dead, his skin a sickly green, the color of pond scum. When I told Dame Beckwith that Nathan and Mr. Bellows had gone to the city to look for the girls, she paled.

"Am I to lose my son, too?" she asked, looking down at poor Gillie. "The only one who could find our lost girls lies here dying because of me. Mr. Driscoll was right—I was a fool for letting those men near our girls."

"But Mr. Driscoll was one of the Council who invited those men to Blythewood!"

"He says he and others were bewitched, but that the bells of Blythewood should have rung out against their evil intent—just as they should have rung out against Herr Hofmeister."

"I think," I said slowly, putting together what I'd seen last night, "that van Drood has found a way past our defenses. He controls his puppets from afar. They get past our wards and bells because the puppets are empty of ill intent until he activates them."

"Jude always said our defenses were weak," she said ruefully.

"But it's *his* weakness that he can't show himself here in the flesh. And he can only control those who are weak. He has to find a way in—a vulnerability to prey on. He can't control us if we stay strong."

Dame Beckwith's eyes flashed, and I was afraid I'd insulted her. Who was I to lecture her about strength? But then she squared her mouth and replied, "Yes, you're right, Ava. We must stay strong for those who depend on us."

I left her and Helen sitting by their patients. Eirwyn came with me, perching on my shoulder as I climbed up to the bell tower. From the top of the tower I could see in all directions: north to the Blythe Wood, east to River Road, west to the Catskills, and south along the frozen river that led to the city. All approaches to the castle lay frozen and wrecked, and standing at its summit, I felt as though I were stranded on an iceberg in an arctic sea, watching the horizon for rescue.

I stood there each day with Eirwyn until my lips turned blue from the cold and I could no longer feel my fingers and toes. I told myself we were waiting for the other hawks and Blodeuwedd to come back, but only when I was close to the sky did I feel close to Raven. I remembered what he'd said to me that night in the woods—that when I'd been in my trance he'd felt like a part of himself was missing. That's how I felt now, as if the very wind that touched my face was empty because he did not ride upon it.

At night we flew down the river together, both looking for our missing mates. I followed Eirwyn, surer of her instincts than mine, as she swept low over the great houses beside the river, but she always came back alone, crying her bereft cry.

When the new term started, only a dozen or so girls came back. Unsurprisingly most of the parents withdrew their daughters from the school. Luckily, my grandmother was not one of them. She remained staunch in her defense of Dame Beckwith and intended to speak in her defense when the Council met to decide whether she should be relieved of her duties and whether the school should be closed.

Dame Beckwith valiantly tried to keep the school going as though nothing had happened. We had classes even though there were only a handful of girls in each class and two of the teachers, Miss Swift and Mr. Peale, had "taken sabbaticals."

"Cowards!" Miss Corey remarked one night in early February when we were all gathered in the library. "Like rats fleeing a sinking ship. I hear Martin has applied to teach at Hawthorn and Matilda has applied to Miss Porter's—a *civilian* school!"

"They're scared," Miss Sharp said. "No one knows whom to trust anymore. The whole structure of the Order has been compromised."

"At least we know we can trust each other," Miss Corey replied, laying her hand on Miss Sharp's shoulder. "And we know that Nathan, Mr. Bellows, Mr. Greenfeder, and Agnes are doing everything they can to find the girls."

"Don't forget Omar and Kid Marvel," I said.

"And the Darklings," Helen added. "Sparrow came to visit Marlin the other night and told him they're looking for Raven and our girls. In fact, Marlin and I have been talking and we have an idea."

"Is that what you've been doing all those hours in the infirmary?" Miss Sharp asked teasingly.

Helen blushed. "I'm not the only one who was affected by the generosity of the Darklings who came to rescue us on the night of the winter dance—or the only one touched by their valor or"—here she looked pointedly at me—"who wants to honor those who sacrificed themselves for our safety. I've been talking with some of the girls as well, and we all think it's time we did something other than sit around waiting."

I wanted to say that Eirwyn and I were not just sitting around, but I couldn't tell her that.

"What do you suggest?" Miss Sharp asked, no longer teasing.

"We want to form a group of Darklings and Blythewood girls."

"I've already spoken to Master Quill about the same idea," Miss Corey said. "But I'm not sure it'll work."

"You've been in touch with him?" I asked, surprised. I had seen her skating on the river once or twice, but hadn't realized she was going to Ravencliffe.

"Yes, I've been back to the library several times to read more of *A Darkness of Angels*. Falco asks for you, by the way," she said, with a pointed look to show me she hadn't given my secret away.

"I don't think Merlinus wants me there," I said. "Not after what happened to Raven."

"No," Miss Corey admitted. "He blames the Order for his only son going missing. That's why I don't know if your idea of forming a collaboration with the Darklings will succeed."

"That's how the Elders think," Helen replied sharply, "but not how the fledglings feel. Marlin thinks they would be open to forming an association with us."

"Oh," Miss Sharp said, her blue eyes lively. "They must really have enjoyed dancing with our girls."

"Must you make everything a romance?" Miss Corey chided, but with a smile.

"It's not just the boy fledglings," Helen said, leaning forward in her chair and looking earnest. "Oriole and Sirena and a few other girl Darklings want to join, too. In fact, they complain that their Elders don't take girls seriously enough and they'd like to go to a school like Blythewood."

"I don't know if Dame Beckwith would endorse that," Miss Sharp said. "Or any of this. She's in enough trouble with the Council as it is."

"So we don't tell her," Helen replied, leaning back in her chair. "She has enough to worry about. It's time we did something. And you," she said, turning on me, "you need to spend time with people and not stand all day on the bell tower with that bird."

I opened my mouth to tell her that it was easy for her to say—she hadn't lost *her* beloved—but then I closed my mouth. She was right. Standing all day like a captain's wife pacing her widow's walk—or even flying along the river with Eirwyn— wasn't going to bring back Raven or Daisy or the other girls.

"I think it's a good idea," I said. "If the Elders and the Council are both so out of touch, then it's time we young people joined forces."

"I'm glad you agree," Helen said, smiling. "Because Marlin says you're the perfect one to lead us."

⇥ ✦ ⇤

So on a frosty night in February I led a group of Blythewood girls on a skating expedition to the Ravencliffe boathouse. We took pains to sneak out, but without a full force of Dianas on patrol and with Gillie still in the infirmary, it was remarkably easy to evade our teachers' notice.

There were seven of us, including Helen and me, Etta, Cam,

Mary, Dolores Jager, who hadn't spoken again since the night Beatrice was taken, and, shockingly, Myrtilene Montmorency, who'd shown up at the school a week ago saying she was bored at home and was coming back to school no matter what Daddy said about it.

"Are we sure she's not a spy?" I asked Helen when we set off.

"I don't think we can be sure about anything, but I saw her dancing with a Darkling that night."

"Oh," I said. "I hope all these girls realize this is serious business and not an excuse to flirt with boys."

"Don't be such an old maid," Helen sniffed, and then, seeing my appalled look, added more gently, "We'll find him. He was swinging at that kraken when he went under the ice. Marlin says Raven wouldn't give up when he has so much to live for."

"He said that?" I asked, feeling the blood heat my face despite the freezing night.

"Yes," Helen said, linking her arm in mine. "Now come on. It's a lovely night for a moonlight skating party."

It was indeed beautiful on the frozen river. The ice was no longer clear as it had been that first morning I skated to Ravencliffe, but a frosted white that glowed with an opalescent sheen in the light of the full moon. The only sound was the scrape of our skates, the creak of the ice shifting beneath our feet, and the shrill whistle of Eirwyn flying above us. But when I opened up my Darkling ear I could hear the river running below the ice, like a live electric wire connecting us to the sea, and to the lost girls and Raven—if he were still alive.

The boathouse was a ramshackle affair of rotting clapboard and pebbledash. As we approached, Helen startled me by whistling the refrain from a popular song called "By the Light of the Silvery Moon." I thought it an odd choice for Helen, but then I heard an answering refrain from the shore and realized it was an arranged signal.

"They're here," Helen said, and then she skated faster, singing the refrain of the syrupy romantic song under her breath.

"Helen," I whispered, catching her arm, "are you falling in love with Marlin?"

Helen shook her curls at me. "I don't see that it's any of your business, but what if I am?"

"Well, for one thing, he doesn't have any money—and for another the Elders strictly forbid marriage between Darklings and humans. The punishment is exile."

"That hasn't stopped you and Raven from spooning, has it?"

"Oh!" I cried, glad it was too dark for Helen to see me blush. "I wouldn't describe what we did as . . . *spooning*." But as I recalled the way Raven would hold me in his wings it occurred to me that it was exactly what we had done—and perhaps would never do again. "Besides, it was different for Raven and me."

"Why?" Helen asked, staring directly in my eyes. "There's something you aren't telling me, isn't there?"

"Why do you say that? Has Marlin told you something?"

"No, he won't. He says it's yours to tell or not. But I would have thought we'd had enough of secrets. I think it was keeping her engagement secret from us that made Daisy so vulnerable to mesmerism. So you might want to think about whether it's such a good idea to stay mum about whatever it is you're hiding from me. And while you're at it, ask yourself what's more important—

keeping your precious secret or keeping me as a friend."

She turned sharply and skated for the boathouse, where a whole chorus greeted her, all whistling the refrain from that ridiculous song. I followed Helen up the ramp, awkward in my skates, with tears stinging my eyes. Eirwyn landed on my shoulder and uttered a bereft cry that I echoed in my heart.

By the time I got to the boathouse, Marlin and Helen were introducing the Blythewood girls to the Darklings. I already knew Marlin, Sirena, Oriole, Sparrow, and Buzz. Now I met Heron, a tall gangly boy with a shock of white-blond hair, and Pythagoras.

"Pythagoras?" I queried, shaking the slight, owl-eyed boy's hand. "I thought you were all named after birds."

"Actually," Pythagoras said to a series of groans from his friends, "the tradition of giving avian names is rather recent. My family prefers to honor philosophers, human and Darkling, who contributed to intellectual progress. The philosopher Pythagoras—"

"We don't have time for one of your lectures, Gus," Buzz said, clapping the boy so heartily on his back that he stumbled. "Especially with such pretty girls here. Say, would you like a drink?" He offered a flask to Dolores, who, much to my surprise, took it.

"*Buzz*," Myrtilene said haughtily. "Is that supposed to be short for Buzzard?"

Unoffended, Buzz laughed. "Yep! My folks say I ate like one from day one. They weren't about to name me after some old fart Greek guy."

"Actually, Pythagoras believed that he could communicate with birds and was an early advocate for the rights of animals. So his is a perfect name for a Darkling."

We all stared at Dolores, from whose usually silent lips this surprising speech had issued. She finished with a dainty burp and smiled at Gus, who smiled back. "Now," she continued, "let's get down to business and talk about how we're going to find my sister and the other girls."

⊁→ ✦ ←⊰

We talked well into the early hours of the morning. We considered forming a raiding party of ice boats or posing as a traveling vaudeville act looking for jobs as dancing instructors. Myrtilene offered to provide the funds to hire a Pinkerton detective. Cam wanted to rent a plane to fly over the city.

"The problem isn't flying," Marlin pointed out. "We've been flying over the area for months. The mansion must be camouflaged by some sort of spell."

Eirwyn squawked at that, and I wondered if that was why we hadn't been able to find the place.

"Oh, you mean warded," Helen said. "Yes, it probably is. Have you tried using any de-warding spells?"

Marlin tilted his head and looked at his fellow Darklings, who all tilted their heads together like a flock of wild turkeys. "We don't know anything about wards or de-warding spells."

"We don't rely on that sort of magic," Sirena added defensively.

"Whyever not?" Helen asked. "It's awfully convenient. No wonder your lot hasn't found the mansion."

"Neither has your lot," Sirena snapped back.

"Girls," Marlin said, holding up his hand. "I think it's clear why working together is such a good idea. We can fly and you can detect wards. I suggest we search the area again in pairs—one Darkling, one human. We'll work through all the river mansions from Riverdale on up."

"You mean you'll carry us on your backs?" Cam asked, delighted.

"I'd be happy to carry you," Buzz said gallantly.

"I'm not sure I'm happy to carry *anyone*," Sirena sniffed.

"You're not strong enough?" Helen asked, batting her eyelashes innocently.

"Eirwyn and I will go with you," I told Sirena.

She opened her mouth, intending, I was sure, to give away my secret—that I didn't need anyone to carry me—but closed it just as quickly.

"Very well," she snipped, "you look skinny enough—and the gyr will come in handy." Eirwyn ruffled her feathers as if pleased by the compliment.

There were a few awkward moments while the rest of us paired up. Dolores rather boldly asked Pythagoras if she could travel with him so they could "discuss philosophy," and Sparrow shyly asked Mary. Myrtilene, seeing that she might end up with a girl, quickly latched onto a startled-looking Heron, while Oriole and Etta shrugged at each other. No one questioned that Marlin and Helen would join up. I felt a pang thinking that would have been Raven and me a few months ago, but I comforted myself with the thought that now we'd at least be doing something to find him.

"And since you've become such a chatterbox," Helen said to Dolores, "you can be our secretary."

"I've already committed the entire proceedings to memory," she said smoothly. "I'll transcribe the minutes—in cipher, of course—when we return to the castle. But we haven't decided yet what to call ourselves."

Marlin and Helen exchanged a look, which suggested to me that they'd already discussed this point.

"We thought . . . well, since you call yourselves this in your second year . . ." Marlin began.

Helen finished for him. "We thought we'd call ourselves the Fledgling League."

30

FOR THE REST of February and into March the Fledgling League flew missions south to Riverdale to search for the Hellgate Club. Only one pair flew each night so we wouldn't risk attracting the attention of the Darkling Elders or Dame Beckwith and the other teachers who didn't know about the league. If we needed to communicate during the week, Eirwyn carried the message between Blythewood and Ravencliffe. Once a week we all met at the boathouse to report on our findings and, inevitably, share stories and gossip. The Darklings were fascinated to learn about the customs of Blythewood. Oriole was jealous that we got to study literature and history, Heron that we could choose to work if we liked.

"I'd like to study the law," Heron confided.

"Raven was serving as a clockmaker's apprentice," I pointed out.

They all looked at each other awkwardly until Marlin explained that Raven was rather a maverick and used to getting away with things because he was the head Elder's son.

"Many of us would like to lead a normal human life," Heron said.

"I'd trade a 'normal human life' to be able to fly," Cam said.

"I'd like to get inside one of your aeroplanes," Buzz countered. "Just think how useful it would be to have a Darkling pilot. If the engine died the Darkling could bail out and save the passengers."

"Perhaps it would have saved Miss Quimby," Cam said wistfully. She'd been sad about her heroine's death last summer when she was ejected from her plane for unknown reasons.

"At least your women are making some progress in gaining equal rights," Oriole complained.

"Progress!" Mary shrieked. "We don't have the vote and we have to marry whomever our fathers want us to."

"That's not actually true," Heron pointed out. "I've been studying your laws . . ."

And so it would go on. We talked about politics, fashion (the craze for feathered hats was roundly denounced), philosophy, books, popular music, and our hopes and dreams for the future. Before dawn Dolores would give us our assignments for patrol and then we would skate back to Blythewood.

It was an unusually cold and long winter, the ice thick on the river all through March and well into April. When Sirena and I came back from our patrol I always stopped by the Rowan Circle to check on the changelings, but they remained frozen and silent.

"I say we crack one open," Sirena suggested on one visit.

"We could kill it," I protested.

"And Raven could die while we're searching for this confounded house," she pointed out. "They might be able to tell us where it is. Your de-warding spells certainly aren't doing the trick."

She was right. The de-warding spell had failed to reveal the

Hellgate Club's location and was very time consuming. It required that the de-warder walk around the perimeter of the house sprinkling a trail of salt and ash while reciting a long Latin spell. We'd encountered all sorts of obstacles, from guard dogs to thorny hedges and even one estate that was populated by free-roaming elephants that tried to stampede while Dolores was walking the perimeter. It had taken us six weeks to cover all the riverside mansions in Riverdale, Yonkers, and Westchester. Now that we'd gotten as far as Tarrytown, I wondered if we'd missed it.

"You're right," I surprised Sirena by saying. "I think we have to start over and try a new spell. I'll check with Miss Sharp and Miss Corey to see if there's a stronger one."

When I went to the library the next day I found that the women had anticipated our problem. They had received a letter from Mr. Bellows saying his and Nathan's search through Riverdale was proving equally fruitless and they suspected that the mansion was under an especially powerful ward.

"They did hear an odd rumor," Miss Sharp said, reading from the letter. "Some of the river men have reported unusual activity on the river at night—tales of boats vanishing in the vicinity of Spuyten Duyvil."

"Spuyten Duyvil?" I asked. "That's a stop on the train, isn't it?"

"Yes, it's the southern-most neighborhood of Riverdale," Miss Sharp said, "named for the creek that flows into the Hudson, which in turn—"

"Is named for the treacherous currents that occur where the creek enters the river," Miss Corey continued. "In Dutch it means 'spouting devil.'"

"A fitting name for the entrance to the Hellgate Club. It could be the whirlpool that swallowed the girls and Raven."

"There *are* peculiar legends about the area," Miss Sharp said. "In the seventeenth century a man died trying to swim across the river. A witness claimed that the devil, in the shape of a giant sea monster, seized the man and dragged him beneath the water."

"Just as Raven was dragged under the water by the kraken," I said, feeling suddenly chilled although I was standing by the fire. "And now Mr. Bellows says there are rumors of boats vanishing in that area?"

"Yes," Miss Sharp said, looking back at the letter. "And yet, when Mr. Bellows checked with the river authority he found that no boats had been reported missing."

"So perhaps the boats that are vanishing mean to go into the whirlpool," I said.

"But that's—" Miss Sharp began.

"Utterly possible," Miss Corey finished for her, jumping to her feet and crossing to a shelf. "There was a case like it in the mountains of Romania."

"Ah," Miss Sharp said, "the Scholomance?"

"The what?" I asked. It was sometimes hard to follow Miss Sharp and Miss Corey when they started finishing each other's sentences.

"It's a legendary school of black magic in the Carpathian mountains," Miss Corey said, plucking a book from a high shelf and flipping through it.

"Run by the devil," Miss Sharp said, looking over Miss Corey's shoulder. "There are only ever ten students at a time and they spend ten years there learning the black arts. At the end of ten years one of the students is claimed by the devil to do his bidding and guard the school, which—"

"Is in the middle of a lake," Miss Corey said, slapping the book down on the table open to a page that showed an engraving of a ruined castle on a mountain lake. "It can only be reached through an underwater passage. The castle appears to be a ruin to anyone who tries to approach it by boat. In order to see it as it really is you must go through a whirlpool that is guarded by the tenth student and his dragon."

"So the Hellgate Club could be any one of the mansions we've looked at, but we wouldn't see it as it really is unless we go *through* the whirlpool?" I asked.

"Yes," Miss Corey said. "Only you probably wouldn't live through it if you didn't control the monster."

"Unless you were a good fighter," I said. "Raven could have gotten through and been captured. He could be there now. All our girls might be there. We have to find a way to go through the whirlpool."

"I know how."

The small, shy voice came from the doorway of the library. A tiny figure was standing there, dripping water onto the parquet floor and covered in pine needles and wet leaves. For a moment I thought it was a forest sprite, but when she stepped forward I saw it was Etta.

"My dear!" Miss Sharp cried, jumping to her feet and drawing Etta to the fire. "What's happened to you? Did you fall through the ice skating?"

"That's just it," Etta explained as she allowed herself to be draped in shawls. "I've been to the forest to see the changelings. They've finally thawed! And they know where Rue and the other girls are!"

⋙ ✦ ⋘

Only when Etta had changed her clothes and drunk three cups of hot tea would Miss Sharp allow her to bring us to the woods.

"We can't all go," Etta explained. "They're still recovering from being frozen all winter. They say it's never happened to them before—they usually hibernate under rivers and streams before the first frost comes—and they'll be frightened by a crowd. They want to see Ava and—"

"I'll go," Miss Sharp said firmly. "There should be one adult."

"Yes," Etta said meekly, "but it will need to be Miss Corey. They especially asked for her."

"Me?" Miss Corey said, blanching so that her mottled freckles stood out lividly on her skin. "But they must know how I feel about them."

Etta shrugged. "I said you might not like it, but they insisted."

Miss Corey looked at Miss Sharp and then sighed. "Oh, very well. I've gotten used to Darklings; I suppose I can get used to changelings, too."

"That's the spirit, Lil!" Miss Sharp said, patting her friend on the back. "I'll go get your galoshes. It will be muddy in the woods."

⋙ ✦ ⋘

It was, indeed, prodigiously muddy. The thaw had come as quickly as the frost had, dissolving the winter's accumulation of ice in one wet swoop. Pools of slush stood on the lawn, and the trees dripped in the woods, the ground soggy and tender. Our feet sunk into the newly released earth and churned up mud. It smelled rich and loamy and sucked at our rubber boots with loud rude squelches and smacks that all but drowned out the song of a thousand birds celebrating the end of winter.

By the time we reached the Rowan Circle, we were daubed in mud head to foot, but we were nothing compared to the changelings. They appeared to be wholly sprung from the wet earth. They lounged in the circle, scantily clad in moss and long grasses, stretching their glossy limbs in the sun. As they moved, their skin changed from brown to green to the blue of the sky overhead, as if they were absorbing all the colors of the awakening forest. Lampsprites flitted through the clearing, casting their own warmth and radiance over the thawing changelings.

"They barely had bodies when I saw them earlier," Etta whispered.

"Ah, we felt so cramped by a winter spent bodiless, we needed legs to stretch," one said, approaching us. She—or he, I really couldn't tell and I had a feeling neither could she/he—raised long arms to the sun and stretched like a cat. Then, in a flash of sunshine, the changeling was a cat—a tawny mountain lion arching its back—and as the creature passed into the shade, she/he became a green-limbed boy with elfin features and a mischievous glint in his dark green eyes. The changeling was as fluid as the water dripping from the trees and as mercurial as the spring sky. She/he was sheer possibility.

"Sheer," the changeling whispered, apparently hearing my thoughts. "I like that name. Call me that while we talk today. It might keep me . . ." She/he laughed and rippled like a stream moving over rocks. "Stable long enough to tell you what I need to."

"Thank you, Sheer," Etta said, and then under her breath to me and Miss Corey, "We'd best follow along; they're hard to understand while they're in this changeable state."

We each pronounced Sheer's name and she—for she had decided for the moment at least to settle for a feminine air— grew more solid. She motioned for us to sit on some toppled tree trunks in the center of the circle. The other changelings gathered around us, their shapes changing as they moved. It made me dizzy to watch them, so I focused on Sheer, who sat on a log and crossed her long legs.

"Ah," she sighed, "the sun feels so good on my flesh. How can you bear to go about so . . . covered?"

"Yes," Miss Corey said impatiently, "we'll consider becoming nudists when this is all over. In the meantime, Etta says you know where Rue is being kept. We think our girls are there, too. If you tell us where it is, we'll go get them—"

"You'll never get through without us," Sheer said, with a shudder than made her skin ripple. "The only entrance to the house is through the water—through a hellgate."

"Do you mean the whirlpool?" I asked.

"Yes," Sheer said. "A hellgate is a whirlpool that a wizard may use as a doorway to a fortress."

"Like the Isle of the Scholomance in Carpathia," Miss Corey said.

"Yes," Sheer agreed with another skin-rippling shudder. "That one was guarded by a dragon. This one is guarded by something far worse—a kraken."

This time I was the one who shuddered. "I saw it in a vision I had of the *Titanic* sinking."

"Yes, the Shadow Master found the monster in the North Atlantic and brought it here to guard the hellgate to his castle. That's where he's keeping Rue. We found her last winter, but before we could tell you, we were frozen. Rue would not come with us because she said she must stay with the other girls to protect them. She said their minds were being bent to do terrible things." She shuddered again, this time so violently that she melted into the log where she sat.

"Sheer!" Etta called. "Stay with us. Did Rue tell you what the girls were being used to do?"

"No," Sheer said, reassuming her shape. Her features had changed, though, to a face that looked familiar. I saw Etta pale as we both recognized Ruth's face—or Rue's, I supposed, as the changeling told the rest of the story in Rue's voice.

"We are kept in a gilded palace like birds in a cage, made to dance all day and night, never to rest or eat or speak—only dance."

"It's Herr Hofmeister's dancing school," I said. "I knew it! But why—"

"We only know the steps, not where they are leading us," Sheer said in Rue's voice, and then in a voice that was neither Rue's nor Sheer's but a dozen girls all shrieking from one mouth that bulged as if all those girls were inside trying to get out. "You must stop us!"

For a moment I saw the faces of a dozen girls flit over the one changeling's features. Among them I recognized Beatrice and Susannah and lastly Daisy, her face drawn and thin, her eyes sunken in their sockets. "Ava," she whispered, "they are going to make us do a terrible thing, please—"

But by the time I had moved the few feet to where she sat, Daisy's face had melted away and only the bland, mud-colored eyes of the changeling blinked up at me.

"We will take you, but you must know that the journey could kill you," Sheer said. "Few survive the kraken."

"Did Raven?" I asked.

Sheer shook her head. "I don't know."

I sank back down onto the damp log, which nearly crumbled beneath my now leaden weight. "I'll go with you."

"I'll go, too," Etta said.

Sheer shook her head. "Van Drood has put a spell on the gate to keep humans out—only a Darkling can get through— or a changeling."

"Ava's only half-Darkling," Miss Corey said. "What if half isn't enough?"

Sheer tilted her head and looked curiously at me. "We won't know until we try."

"That's not good enough!" Miss Corey cried. "Ava, I can't let you take the risk. We'll get one of the Darklings to go."

"I have to go," I said, turning to Miss Corey. "The Darklings have already lost one of theirs. If the Darklings and the Order are ever to work together, they must see we're willing to take equal risks."

"That's a fine speech," Miss Corey said with a sniff. "But you're going because of that boy."

"Maybe," I admitted. "If Miss Sharp was there, wouldn't you go?"

"That's not . . . oh, Hell's Bells, I suppose I would. But then I'm going with you."

"But you can't," Etta began, "Sheer said—"

"I said only changelings or Darklings." Sheer stretched her arm out to Miss Corey and placed her hand on her face, her fingers tracing the mottled marks there. Miss Corey flinched but remained still, so pale the marks stood out more lividly—a pattern that appeared on Sheer's face.

"A changeling did this to me," Miss Corey said, tilting her chin up and staring defiantly at her mirror image. "Does that give me the power to go through the Hellgate?"

"No, Lillian, that would not give you that power, but you *can* go through the gate. A changeling didn't do this to you. You *are* a changeling."

31

"NO," MISS COREY said, swatting Sheer's hand away. "A changeling was trying to take my shape. My father stopped it and killed it, but it left these marks on my face."

"We don't make marks on the faces of our hosts. Did you see any on Ruth's face?"

"No," Etta answered for her. "But I saw them on Rue's sometimes."

"When we take on a host's personality, there's a period of transition. Rue had not completely transformed into Ruth—and you had not completely transformed into Lillian Corey when her father found you. He probably would have killed you, only his daughter died first."

"I—this thing—killed her!"

"No," Sheer said gently. "Sometimes we come to take the place of a dying human. It's always dangerous, because if the host dies before the transformation is complete, the changeling might die, too. You nearly did."

"My father said I almost died from the attack."

"But he nursed you back to health. He loved you—first because you had tried to save his daughter, and then because you *became* his daughter. His love—his belief that you were *his* Lillian—saved you."

There were tears streaming down Miss Corey's face. "He lied to me."

"He was afraid that you would hate yourself—that you would have felt . . . *different*."

"I always have." A scarlet flush swept over Miss Corey's face. "Is this why I'm . . . why I . . ."

Sheer laughed. "Why you love whom you love? Don't be silly. Vionetta Sharp loves you, and she's wholly human."

"Oh," Miss Corey said, a small smile appearing on her face. "How do you know all that?"

"Because when I touched you, I felt how beloved you are." Sheer looked sad for a moment; her glossy limbs lost a bit of their shine, their sheen turning chalky as dried mud. "That's what we all dream of." She turned to me. "I felt it in you, too, Ava. Raven loves you, and so do your friends, Helen and Daisy and Nathan. They love you, not a Darkling or a human. Just you."

I nodded, wiping tears from my face. "Then I'd better go find Daisy and the other lost girls. I'm ready."

"And so am I," Miss Corey said.

⇥ ✦ ⇤

I spent the afternoon exchanging information with Nathan and Mr. Bellows, who had returned from the city. They told us there were three mansions in Spuyten Duyvil owned by new investors brought in by the Council to replenish funds lost by the *Titanic* disaster.

"And now they've tied up their funds in some secret invest-ment," Nathan said. "They claim that no one can know what it is until the 'big unveiling,' whatever that means." Nathan swore and flung himself out of his chair to pace across the library floor. Helen followed his movements worriedly.

"I just can't believe we're sending Ava and Miss Corey alone to defeat van Drood's monster!" he continued in frustration.

"There's no reason the other Darklings can't go with them," Miss Sharp pointed out, consulting a manual of wards. "Lillian and I and Nathan can go in the boat, too. Once you're all in the mansion, Ava can disarm the wards and send the Darklings for the rest of us. We just have to wait close enough to see a signal."

"I don't like to wait for a bunch of birds to come fetch me," Nathan said, scowling. "The second I see the house unwarded I'll be there . . . with *this*."

He drew a dagger from under his coat jacket. It was like the one I'd seen Mr. Bellows carry, but it had a different pattern on the hilt.

"Is that a knight's dagger?" Miss Sharp asked. "I didn't think—"

"I gave it to him," Mr. Bellows said—rather defensively, I thought. "I know he hasn't had the full training, but in times like these . . ."

"You did the right thing," Miss Sharp said, her eyes shining. "We can none of us be slaves to the old ways while those dear to us are threatened." She withdrew a dagger from the folds of her skirt. "I'll be standing at the ready, too, waiting for the signal."

»→ ✦ ←«

That night, we set sail from the Ravencliffe boathouse. Miss Corey and Miss Sharp came, and the Fledgling League. Nathan said he had "borrowed" the boat from the Astors' boathouse. I remembered that Helen had told me once that she and Nathan had played pirates on the river as children. I had always pictured them on dinghies, but it now was apparent that they both knew very well how to sail.

It was a thirty-foot teak yacht called *Half Moon*. Nathan gave orders for hauling this and raising that, which Helen followed quickly, telling us all what rope—or "line," as I learned they were called—to hold and where to sit. At first Marlin looked baffled, but when the main sail was raised and it caught the air like a silver wing in the moonlight, his face lit up. As the boat leaned into the wind and picked up speed, the light of the full moon turned the froth from the prow white and shone on the silvery shapes of the changelings swimming beside us. One leapt through the air like a dolphin. Miss Sharp, who was sitting beside Miss Corey in the cabin, laughed aloud at the sight and whispered something into Miss Corey's ear that made her smile. I gathered that Miss Corey had told her about being a changeling. I didn't see that it had made any difference in Miss Sharp's feelings, except to make her even fiercer in her affections.

"Why, it's just like flying!" Marlin cried.

"Yes, isn't it?" Helen beamed at him, but with a wistful look in Nathan's direction. "Go sit with him," Helen whispered to me. "He's all alone."

Nathan did look grimly solitary standing at the helm, piloting the *Half Moon* down the river like the Ancient Mariner. The first thing he said to me was, "I'm not happy about you going into that Hellgate."

"I know," I said. "But Miss Corey and I are the only ones who can do it. And the other Darklings will be right behind us."

Nathan looked to where Marlin sat with Helen. "*They* certainly look like they've become good friends."

"Jealous?" I asked.

He began to object, but then laughed at himself. "Yes, I suppose I am. I've always taken Helen for granted. She's just always . . . been there. But seeing her like this, well, she's different."

"We're all different," I said. "How could we not be after all we've seen and been through?"

"You most of all," he said. "How did you explain to Helen how you can get through the Hellgate?"

"I told her it's because I'm a chime child. I didn't like to lie, but . . ."

"You're still not ready to tell her you're half-Darkling?"

"No," I admitted.

"Do you really think it would make a difference to her now?"

I looked at Helen laughing with Marlin and trading quips with Sirena. Cam was standing at the prow of the ship with Buzz, her face turned into the wind, her short hair ruffling in the wind. Dolores and Gus were deep in conversation, probably plotting the geometry of sails. Miss Sharp had accepted that Miss Corey was a changeling, and my friends had accepted the Darklings. Why wouldn't they accept me?

"Maybe," I said, "it's because when they know what I am,

I'll have to make a choice between Blythewood and—"

"Raven?"

"Yes," I said. "But I may already be too late. If he's gone . . ."

"He's not," Nathan said with surprising certainty. "I don't believe he let that monster eat him when he had you to live for. He's in there—and we're going to get him out. And when we do—" He looked at me. "If you choose to be with him, I'll understand. But he's not the only one who loves you."

I stared at him open-mouthed. Was he telling me he loved me? Before I could speak, he barked a sharp order to "come about" and Helen flew into action, ordering everyone to "watch the boom" and hauling on various ropes. The yacht tacked into the wind and leaned toward the left—or port as Helen called it. The changelings struggled to keep up with us in the choppy water.

"We're at Spuyten Duyvil," Nathan cried, pointing to a cleft in the cliffs on the eastern bank. I could see the moonlight shining on a stream rushing into the river from between the steep cliffs. This was where the Spuyten Duyvil creek fed into the river. The whirlpool must be near.

The boat suddenly shuddered and keeled sharply to port.

"Strike down the mainsail!" Nathan screamed.

There was a flurry of confusion as Helen barked orders and she and Marlin and Buzz struggled with handfuls of flapping canvas. Nathan ordered the anchor to be thrown over. The boat righted, but it was still moving.

"We're too close to the whirlpool!" Helen cried. "It's sucking us in!"

I stared over the prow at the water. About thirty feet in front of us was a circular patch of churning froth where the current of the Spuyten Duyvil intersected with that of the Hudson River. I smelled salt, and guessed that the ocean tide was exerting its own force—a force stronger because of the full moon. The water spun in a circle, looking like a giant mouth, which now opened.

The boat lurched toward it, throwing everyone hither and thither. Mary nearly went overboard, but Sparrow grabbed her. We were being sucked into the swirling maw, which opened and shut with a wet smacking sound like lips, hungry for its next meal. A long wet tongue slithered out of the whirlpool. The salt smell of the ocean mingled now with the stench of rotting fish. Somebody shrieked. Above us Eirwyn let out a high-pitched screech. I heard Gus soothing Dolores by citing the Latin classification—*Microcosmus marinus*—given to the kraken by Carolus Linnaeus.

Marlin screamed an order, and the Darklings drew their swords and flexed their wings.

"We'll attack it," Marlin yelled at Nathan. "You get the boat away and save yourselves."

But the boat suddenly wasn't moving. I looked down and saw the changelings swarming around the boat, their arms straining in the moonlight. They were holding the boat back—but they wouldn't be able to hold it for long.

Miss Corey came to stand next to me. She had stripped down to a slim, stylish bathing costume. She took my hand. Miss Sharp stood next to her.

I stripped off my dress. Underneath I wore the silly bathing costume Helen had brought for me on our outing to Coney Island. With its ruffles and bows, which hid my wings, it seemed a strange outfit in which to meet a monster, but I found it oddly comforting.

I took a deep breath, expanding my lungs as the Darklings had taught me, and, hand in hand with Miss Corey, dove into the maelstrom.

32

REMEMBERING THE SEA around the *Titanic* I was braced for the cold, but the water inside the whirlpool was bathwater warm. Somehow that was more shocking, as though we'd dived right into the hot, slobbering belly of the beast.

I opened my eyes, struggling to see through the stinging salt water. At first all I could make out was Miss Corey's face alternately lit by flashes of light and blurred by roiling foam. Then I saw that the flashes of light were the Darklings' swords as they slashed at the writhing tentacles of the kraken—

Which was right below us.

It was crouched on a rocky outcrop, its flashing silver eyes large as dinner plates. Although it flailed its tentacles at the Darklings, it didn't move its bulbous body. It didn't have to. One tentacle wrapped around Sparrow and drew him toward its gaping mouth, but Marlin hacked the tentacle clean off, releasing Sparrow. The kraken writhed at the shock of losing its appendage and pulsed forward to attack Marlin. Miss Corey jabbed her finger down toward the rocks, and I saw that where the kraken had sat was an opening. Marlin saw, too. He dove forward, jabbing the kraken with his sword and then darting back, using his wings like giant fins to backstroke in the water and draw the kraken away from the gap.

We dove toward the moonlit opening. As we reached it I felt something wrap around my ankle. I kicked out and saw a flash of silver as Miss Corey used her dagger to stab the tentacle that was holding onto my leg. When it released me I plunged head-long into darkness.

I could feel that I was in a narrow rock passage, but no moonlight penetrated here. It was too narrow for me to turn and see if Miss Corey was still following me. All I could do was scrabble forward, feeling my way with my hands, every second terrified that I would run into a wall and suffocate before I could get out. The passage seemed to be getting narrower as I went farther, but I reminded myself that full-grown men had gotten through it before me . . .

Unless this was the wrong passage, and it was a trap meant to drown me and Miss Corey below the Hudson River while our friends were slaughtered above me and the lost girls were used in some nefarious scheme and Raven rotted in a dungeon wondering why I never came for him.

Raven.

As if his name had conjured it, my hand touched something soft stuck in a crevice. I drew it out and felt the silky plume of a feather slip through my fingers. I knew it belonged to him. He had survived the kraken and come through the passage. If he could survive it, if I knew he was waiting for me at the end of it, I could make it through.

I swam faster, pulling myself through the tunnel, which

widened and then began to tilt upward until I saw a glimmering light above me. My lungs now burning as though they would explode, I raced upward until I burst through the surface. I nearly blacked out from the shock as air rushed into my lungs. When my vision cleared, I was lying in a shallow fountain beneath a marble statue of a giant man—or at least he had the upper torso and head of a man. His lower body was scaled and cloven-hoofed. He brandished a spear in one hand and a conch shell in the other, through which he spit a stream of water, which arched up and then trickled down into the fountain. A spouting devil—a Spuyten Duyvil.

I looked around and saw that I was in a terraced garden that rose from the riverbank up to a marble mansion that glimmered in the moonlight as though it were carved out of spun sugar. Marble statues stood in rows, as though they were guarding the mansion. There was something strange about them . . .

A loud splash drew my attention back to the fountain. A head burst through the surface of the water—and then another and another. I dragged a gasping Miss Corey out of the fountain and then went back to help Sirena and Marlin, whose arm, I saw, was badly wounded.

I tore one of the ruffles off the skirt of Helen's bathing costume and wrapped it around his arm to staunch the bleeding, tying it with a ribbon from the bodice. When I was done he looked at it and grimaced.

"I look like a blasted Christmas present," he swore.

"We'll find you a more masculine dressing when we get back to Ravencliffe," Sirena snapped, surveying the garden, her sword drawn. Miss Corey also held her dagger ready. "I don't see any guards, but they could be hiding behind any one of these creepy statues."

"They *are* creepy," Miss Corey said. "There's something *wrong* about them." As we walked cautiously up the hill I noticed that their beautiful faces were chipped and marred, as if they had at some time fallen. There were chips in their drapery, too, and some were missing hands or even whole arms—again, as if they had fallen and tried to catch themselves with their outstretched hands.

I heard Sirena gasp. I wheeled around, expecting an attack, but she was standing alone behind one of the statues, running her hands over its marble back. I stepped closer and saw that she was tracing two rough broken ridges in the statue's back, where something had been broken off.

I checked another statue and another. They all had the same rough ridges on their backs where once there had been wings.

"They're angels," Miss Corey said in a whisper. "But all their wings have been broken off . . . why?"

"As a warning," Marlin snapped, his voice edged with anger. "To our kind. Van Drood's declared war on the Darklings, and this is his graveyard."

I looked over the whole hill. The broken angels glimmered dully in the moonlight like a stack of bones. At the foot of the hill stood the muscular devil, spitting from his shell and brandishing his spear—but no, it wasn't a spear. From this angle I saw that it was a broken wing, and what I'd thought was a conch shell was a broken-off angel head, water spitting out of its gaping mouth.

"Come on," Marlin said, tugging my arm. "He means to

scare us; we can't let him. There's an open door here."

He led us through a pair of French doors that opened into a long shadowy room. Moonlight poured in through the glass doors and windows onto a floor that gleamed like water lapping against the dark banks of the far walls, where I saw a flicker of movement. I startled—and the figure across the room made the same motion.

"Mirrors," Miss Corey said. "There's no one here."

"Or out here," Marlin, who had gone out into the hall, came back to tell us. "Sirena's searching the rest of this floor. As soon as you de-ward the house I'll go alert your friends."

We followed Miss Corey across the mirrored hall, our reflections in the mirrors dark twins, and into a foyer dominated by a sweeping grand staircase and mirrored walls lit by a domed skylight. She walked across to the front door, opened it, and stood outside.

We'd rehearsed this. It was the simplest of de-warding spells but required two people to perform. One stood outside of the threshold while one stood inside. We joined hands over the threshold and recited the words *Venite, amici.* Come in, friends. I felt a shiver of energy as we performed the spell, and then that shiver seemed to go through the whole house, like a cat shaking water from its fur. For a moment I saw the house as it would appear to anyone entering it from the front door—an abandoned ruin. But then it reappeared as the gleaming mansion.

"There," Miss Corey said to Marlin. "That should do it. You can bring back the others." Marlin was already out the door. Miss Corey watched him go with a worried look on her face.

"Why don't you go down to the street to see if they're coming," I said, guessing that she would be anxious to see if Miss Sharp was all right.

She smiled at me and then was gone, slipping fast and silently into the shadows. I turned back into the foyer . . . and heard a tiny *plinking* noise that might have been rain falling. Only it was a cloudless night, and the plinking had a rhythm to it—a familiar rhythm. Sirena was standing at the foot of the stairs listening to it, too. Wordlessly she started up the stairs and I followed, the sound growing stronger. I recognized it as one of the waltzes from *Die Puppenfee*, only it was being played slowly, as if on a broken player piano. I pictured a corps of tired ballerinas, their feet bloody, dancing to the broken tune. The whole mansion smelled like cold ash, and the mirrors that lined the stairway were clouded as if stained by smoke. Our reflections looked like wraiths in the smoky mirrors, as if we were already dead.

I drove the thought away and followed Sirena down a long mirrored hallway (thinking that the owner of this house must be very, very vain). The music was coming from the room at the end. The other rooms off the hall were empty. Glancing into them I saw scraps of clothing lying on the floors, as if the place had just recently—and suddenly—been abandoned. The stink of ash was stronger up here.

Sirena checked each room, dagger in hand. I wished I had my repeater with me, but I hadn't been able to bring it through the water. When Sirena came back she confirmed that the rooms were empty.

"They've been burning papers in the fireplaces—to conceal clues to where they've gone, I wager."

We moved down the hall toward the tinny music. It came from the last room on the right. As we entered it I noticed a ribbon lying on the floor and smelled the ash in the fireplace. The music came from an open box on a table by the window. I crossed over to it and saw that it was a music box, the kind that had a tiny ballerina inside that pivoted with the motion of the musical mechanism. It was twirling slowly now as the mechanism wound down, its motions jerky and somehow sickening to watch. I moved to close the lid to put the poor thing to rest, but my hand brushed something soft inside the box. I withdrew a downy black feather.

"That's Raven's!" Sirena said, snatching the feather from my hand. "I can smell him. What's it doing here?"

As much as I disliked her taking the feather from me—and how did she know his smell so well?—I was more interested in the folded note in the bottom of the box.

He's in the dungeons, it read in Daisy's handwriting.

Then I was running back through the mirrored hallway and flying down the grand staircase, its slick steps too many to bother with. As I ran I heard a high-pitched keening. For a moment I thought I was making the sound, but when I reached the foyer I saw it was Eirwyn, who had flown into the house and was battering her wings against a closed door. I wrenched it open and we plunged into dank blackness, Eirwyn diving straight down and me hurtling behind her so fast I tore my feet on the rough stone. Instead of calling out in pain I screamed Raven's name, which echoed in the vaulted space, mocking my desperation. But when I paused for breath I heard that the echoes weren't saying "Raven"; they were calling "Ava." I ran toward the voice—which was so weak and broken I could only hear it because I'd opened my Darkling ears. Even then it was only a whisper. *A dying whisper.*

No. He couldn't die just as I found him. That would be too cruel—but then I knew that was what this place did—what van Drood did. He broke things. He broke people. And if he wanted to break me—which he did—what better way than to have me find Raven just in time to catch his dying breath?

Only it had been Daisy who led me to him, Daisy who had remained whole enough—unbroken enough—to leave me that message.

"Raven!" I called for him. There was no light, so I had to feel my way across each foul, slimy cell, my hands brushing cold metal implements embedded in the walls that made me shake with horror. But he wasn't in any of them. I stopped and called his name again. Something brushed against my face. I screamed out, but then I heard Eirwyn's cries echoed by another falcon's call. It was Gwynfor, her mate. I felt along his matted feathers and found that he was tethered to an iron ring in the floor. He was squawking and beating his wings so frantically I was afraid he would injure himself.

"Be still," I murmured, "and I'll let you free."

In reply he squawked again and suddenly I understood him.

Buried, he was crying over and over, *buried.*

I sank to my knees and crawled over every inch of the cell, tearing at the rough stones until my fingers bled. Finally I found a stone that rocked loose in my hands. I clawed it up, releasing a foul stench, but also a whisper.

"Ava?"

I reached down and touched mangled flesh and bone and feather. I wanted to scream, but instead I took a steadying breath and spoke with all the calmness and strength I could muster. "Raven, I'm here. Marlin and Sirena are here, too. We'll get you out—I just can't . . . see . . ."

He made a noise that I thought for one horrifying moment was a death rattle, but then realized was a chuckle.

"That . . . may . . . be a b-b-blessing," he stuttered. "I d-d-don't b-believe I am a . . . pretty sight."

"Oh, neither am I!" I cried, prying loose another stone. "Would you believe I'm wearing one of Helen's bathing costumes?"

Another gurgle—and the sound of footsteps, and two voices calling my name.

"We're here!" I shouted to Sirena and Marlin. "Raven's here. I need help . . . and light."

"T-tell me . . ." he croaked, his voice as creaky as rusted iron.

"Tell you what?" I asked, finding his hand and grasping it. "How much I love you? How I plan to spend the rest of my life with you, no matter where we have to go?"

"'S good," he spluttered, "but wh-what I really . . . want to know is . . . what Helen's bathing costume looks like."

I made a sound that was half sob, half laugh. Marlin and Sirena were behind me, and then Sirena was on the other side of the cell, shining a lamp into the sunken crypt where Raven was held. I couldn't see him from where I sat, but I saw her face and knew it was bad. "We'll have to cut him loose very carefully," she whispered to Marlin. "Or he'll lose his wings."

I braced myself on the edge of the pit and looked down. The hole was a V-shaped gash gouged out of the rock. Raven was suspended upside down, his wings pinned to the walls. His face was streaked with blood, but his eyes were open and I could see the pulse of his vein at his throat. When Marlin used his dagger to pry loose a link of the chain, a tremor of pain passed over his face.

"Keep talking to him," Marlin whispered to me. "It will take his mind off the pain."

"Well," I said, taking a deep breath. "Helen's bathing costume. It's striped red and white like a candy cane and has three tiers of ruffles—"

"Two," Marlin corrected. "You tore one off to bandage my arm."

"H-have you b-been f-flirting . . . with . . . my . . . g-girl?" Raven asked.

"Absolutely," Marlin answered, wrenching free a steel pin and making Raven gasp in agony. "So you'd better get out of there and get her back."

"Y-yes," Raven managed in a barely audible whisper. "I'm p-planning to do that. Only . . . if . . . I . . . am . . . detained. . . ."

"No worries, old chap, take as long as you like."

"But the girls!" Raven gasped. "Are they . . . ?"

"Gone," Sirena answered. "But the others are searching the grates for clues. The place will be swarming with humans in a moment."

"It already is." I heard Nathan's voice coming from the cell.

"Thank the Bells!" I cried. "Is everybody on the boat—"

"Safe and sound," Nathan replied, kneeling beside me. "And searching the house for clues to where all our girls have gone."

"I couldn't s-save them," Raven rasped.

"No, I don't suppose you could from down here," Nathan said, not unkindly. "Now, why don't we quit the jabber and get you out of here?"

Nathan and Marlin held up Raven's weight while Sirena and I untangled his wings from the chains. When we got him loose we were able to haul him out of the dreadful pit. In the dim light it was impossible to tell how serious his injuries were, but at least he was alive.

"We can take him back to Ravencliffe on the boat—" Sirena began, but Raven cut her off.

"First find the girls!"

"But we have no idea where they are," I pointed out.

"Yes, we do." It was Helen's voice, coming from the doorway to the cell. We all turned to look at her. At first I thought she was standing in shadow, but as she stepped into the light of our lamps I saw that she was covered head to toe in ash. She had been searching through the grates. She was gripping a half-burnt sheet of paper in her hands. We all stood to meet her as she came forward, even Raven, who struggled to his feet, clutching Marlin and Nathan, and looked down at the paper she held.

It looked like a brochure or program of some sort—perhaps for a church service, because the building depicted looked like a grand cathedral with a single soaring tower.

I'd seen that tower somewhere before.

Helen's hands were shaking so much it was hard to read the print. I caught "Spectacular" and "Grand opening" and "Musical enter—" and "Tallest building in the world!"

"It's a program for the grand opening of the Woolworth Building. It says there's to be program of dance performances by the girls of Blythewood School led by the Viennese dancing master Herr Hofmeister and . . ."

A dance atop a towering building? An image came back to me of dancers moving like automatons, the dance floor shaped like a ticking clock . . .

Pythagoras's voice broke into my vision. "We've found gears and wires and a package for blasting powder." And then I heard van Drood's voice again—*They dance to my tune until they run out of time.*

"It's a bomb," I said. "Van Drood is planning to use our girls to set off a bomb at the opening of the Woolworth Building. We have to stop him!"

"Then we'll have to move fast," Helen said, shaking the program so hard flakes of ash fell from it. "The opening's tonight."

33

"IT MAKES A sort of awful sense," Sam Greenfeder said a few hours later, when we had convened in the ballroom. Raven was resting in one of the upstairs bedrooms with Wren, whom Sirena had sent for, and his Darkling companions flocked around him for support. I'd spent the early hours of the morning helping her and Sirena set Raven's broken wings. In those hours my teachers and friends had searched the house for more clues, coming up with handfuls of burnt programs for the Woolworth opening ceremony, discarded packages of blasting powder, and snippets of wires and clock gears. They also found Blodeuwedd and the rest of the hawks caged and half-starved in the dungeons. Nathan had vanished for several hours and come back with Omar and Kid Marvel and blueprints of the Woolworth Building, which he said he'd "finagled" out of the offices of the architectural firm. Agnes and Miss Corey had gone downtown to see what they could discover at the Woolworth Building, but they had returned with frustratingly little information.

"The event's under the strictest security due to the important personages to be present," Agnes told us. "U.S. senators, congressmen, European nobility—I heard a rumor that Archduke Ferdinand was going to be there!" She reported that there were already crowds gathering in City Hall Park to watch, and the whole area was cordoned off by the police.

"It's a huge project," Sam told us. "The tallest building in the world—and one of the most expensive ever built. It's just the sort of investment I've suspected the Order has been sinking their money into. I've heard talk on Wall Street that canny investors are buying shares of the building. Frank Woolworth claims it will be the most profitable in the world and, after all, he's made his fortune by knowing where to put his five-and dime stores and understanding what the average buyer wants."

"It *sounds* like a good investment," Mr. Bellows said, tugging his hair.

"So did the *Titanic*," Sam said.

"But this is a huge building in the middle of Manhattan," Miss Corey said. "It can't sink."

"No," Sam said grimly, "but I hear on the street that Woolworth's sunk all his money into the building but not insured it. If the building is blown up, Woolworth's whole dynasty will go with it, and so will the Order."

There was a moment of silence during which we all looked at each other. We were not a prepossessing group: two teachers, a librarian, a lawyer, one personal assistant, a Hindu hypnotist, a carnival performer, seven schoolgirls, and one schoolboy— all of us exhausted and covered with ash.

"We have to stop him!" Miss Sharp cried.

"But how?" Miss Corey asked. "Who will believe us if we tell them a bunch of hypnotized schoolgirls are planning to blow up the Woolworth Building? And how will we get into the opening? I certainly haven't received an invitation. And you heard what Agnes said—the police have cordoned off the whole building."

"They won't be guarding the upper windows."

The voice came from the doorway where Marlin stood with Sparrow and Oriole. I got to my feet at the sight of them. "Is Raven—?"

"Healing," Marlin said. "And sleeping. He'll be all right. We have to stop this—and we can do it together. Our people can carry you to the rooftop and we can go inside from there."

"We don't even know when he's planning to blow up the building," Miss Corey pointed out. "Or how."

"I think I know when," Sam said, holding up a newspaper that Agnes had brought back with her. "It says here that at seven-thirty tonight President Wilson will push a telegraphic button on his desk in Washington, D.C., that will close an electrical circuit to activate the electricity-generating dynamos in the basement of the Woolworth Building, lighting up eighty thousand incandescent light bulbs all at once. 'It will be,' the reporter opines, 'a spectacular explosion of light.'" Sam slapped the paper against his leg. "What better moment for van Drood to stage his show?"

⇥ ◈ ⇤

We spent the rest of the afternoon feverishly making our plans. Nathan, Omar, and Mr. Bellows pored over the blueprints of the Woolworth building, trying to determine where bombs would be placed and how they could be defused. Pythagoras and Nathan examined the leftover wires and watch gears to figure out what kind of device van Drood had built. Kid Marvel hurried back downtown to "get the lay of the land." The other Darklings flew off on a reconnaissance mission to examine the rooftop of the building. Helen and Dolores drew up a roster of who would be carried by which Darkling. Helen flew back to Blythewood with Oriole to collect our *Puppenfee* costumes so we could infiltrate the ballet corps.

"Ugh," Cam said as we changed in one of the bedrooms. "I hate to wear this thing again. How do we even know they'll be dancing *Die Puppenfee*?"

"The program says that the girls of Blythewood will take us to a magical toyshop in Mr. Woolworth's store," I told her. I had done my best to reassemble the burnt bits of programs to make sense of the evening's events. "And Herr Hofmeister has already used that music to control the girls."

"But doesn't Herr Hofmeister know he's going to die when the building explodes?" Helen said, frowning.

"Van Drood has him under his control. That's what van Drood does: he sucks your soul away." I shivered, remembering what it felt like to be missing even a tiny piece of my soul. "He hollows you out and then fills you with the *tenebrae*. When you're full of that darkness, you don't care if you live or die. All you feel is hate and envy and despair."

A few minutes later, Helen drew me away from the others to give me my repeater, which she'd carried for me on the boat. When she placed it in my hand she held my hand for a moment. "Before . . . when you spoke of being full of darkness . . . it sounded like you knew what that felt like. You've been so distant this year . . . I thought it was just your being head over heels with Raven, but it's not just that, is it?"

I shook my head, fighting back the tears that burned behind my eyes. "I'm sorry I haven't been a very good friend to you this year."

"Nor I to you if you didn't feel you could tell me what's been bothering you."

"It's not your fault," I insisted, stunned to think Helen would see my keeping a secret as *her* failure. "I've been afraid I would lose you if you knew the truth."

"Do you really think I'm so shallow that I wouldn't stand by you no matter what?"

I started to tell her that it wasn't her I doubted, but Sirena appeared to tell us that everyone was gathering in the ballroom to go over the plan one last time. When I looked back at Helen she was adjusting my costume, her face closed.

"Maybe I *am* shallow," she said, tugging at the silk and wire wings of my costume. "I'm actually jealous that you get to wear the fairy doll costume, and even more jealous that you look so good in it." She lifted her face and crooked her mouth into a wan smile. "Wings suit you."

⇥ ✦ ⇤

I let Helen and the other girls go on ahead and went to say goodbye to Raven. I found him sitting up on the edge of his bed, looking out at the river. Eirwyn and Gwynfor perched on the window ledge as if standing guard. Raven's tattered wings hung limply from his bandaged back. Wren had removed the broken feathers and imped in their place new feathers taken from her own wings and the wings of other Darklings. I saw Oriole's brown ones, Sirena's black-blue ones, and some of my gold and red. I'd plucked out so many Wren had told me I'd be bald if I didn't stop. Raven's wings looked now like a quilt patched from old scraps—and his face looked worse. One eye was swollen shut, his nose was crooked, and he had a livid gash running from his left cheekbone to his jaw. He no longer had the classic profile of a Grecian god. He looked like a used-up boxer, and I thought him all the handsomer for it.

"You look like a fairy," he said, when he saw me in my costume.

"You look a bit like a troll," I quipped back, sitting down gently on the bed so as not to jar his (three) broken ribs.

He laughed—then grimaced and clutched his ribs. "I guess this ridiculous getup means you're determined to go. I hate the idea of you flying into this alone."

Eirwyn squawked.

"See," I said. "I won't be alone. Eirwyn will be with me, and all your friends and mine. They've been working together all day. That's one good thing that's come out of this: the Council and the Elders will have to agree it's time to join forces."

"Unless you all die in a fiery inferno," he replied glumly. "Then the Order and the Darklings will probably blame each other and declare war."

"Well then," I said, "we'll just have to *not* die in a fiery inferno. Promise to be here when I get back?"

He lifted a limp and damaged wing. "I don't think I'm going anywhere."

I leaned into him, as carefully as I could, and found a patch of unbruised flesh in the crook of his neck to nuzzle. "Good," I said. "Me neither."

The Darklings flew on ahead and the rest of us crammed into my grandmother's Rolls, which Agnes had commandeered without my grandmother's knowledge, to go downtown. Helen spent the ride peering out the window, hoping to catch a glimpse of the Darklings.

"They're cloaked when they fly," I explained to her. "Besides, Raven says that humans never look up."

"I wonder if that will change when there are more planes in the air," Cam remarked.

"And taller buildings," Helen added.

"Yes," Dolores said. "If the Woolworth Building is a success there will be more like it, and taller and taller buildings until the whole city is full of them and we have to crane our necks to even see the sky."

Looking out the window at the tenements crowding the streets of lower Manhattan, I wondered what would happen to these noisy, teeming neighborhoods if men tore down everything to build their Cathedrals of Commerce. Where would the poor go? And where would the Darklings go if the world became so crowded?

"A fellow might need to take off for wider spaces if that happened."

It took me a moment to realize it had been Nathan who spoke. He'd been quiet all day, poring over the plans for the Woolworth Building. Seeing him look so studious, I'd wondered if he might be developing an interest in architecture.

"I can see you building things," I said to him.

He grinned at me—the first time I'd seen him smile since that day skating on the river.

"Actually," he said, "the part I found most interesting today was studying the explosives with Gus. I think I might have a future in blowing things up."

Before I could think of a response to this remarkable statement, we arrived at the Henry Street Settlement House. Miss Sharp had telephoned Miss Wald to ask if we could use the building tonight for a "union meeting." When I saw the outside of the settlement house, I thought that Miss Wald must have misunderstood. It appeared as though there already was a meeting going on there—some sort of ethnic dance group, from the looks of it. There were girls in colorful gauzy skirts and veils, and older women in gypsy scarves that glittered with gold coins. There was a rowdy group of Irishmen in green tweed jackets and a more somber contingent of Negro men and women eyeing the antics of the Irishmen warily. Marlin and the other Darklings stood in a close knot next to a group of dwarves, one of whom came over to open the car door for us. It was Kid Marvel.

"Whatcha waitin' for?" he cried with a wide grin. "An engraved invite? Everyone's here to do their part."

"Who exactly are these people?" Miss Corey asked, her eyes widening at one of the hootchy-kootchy girls.

"The madges, of course," Kid Marvel replied, waving his arms like the carnival showman he was.

He explained as we followed him into the house, which was even more crowded.

"When the word spread that the Darklings and the Order were working together against the Shadow Master, everyone wanted to help."

"But we're not even operating under the official sanction of the Order," Miss Corey whispered to Miss Sharp.

"We know that," a veiled woman said, stepping forward out of the crowd. It took me a second to recognize her as the hootchy-kootchy dancer we'd seen in Coney Island. She was wearing the same costume and exuded the same intoxicating jasmine perfume, but her bearing was now more regal than seductive as she addressed us. "We all have reasons not to trust the 'official sanction' of the Order."

She drew away her veil and a gasp went through the room. Beneath her veil was the face of a tawny cat. But that wasn't what I gasped at. There was a livid brand on her cheek.

"Who did that to you?" Miss Sharp demanded.

"Do you not recognize the rune?" the dancer asked, taking a step closer to Miss Sharp. I saw Mr. Bellows clutch his dagger and Miss Corey tried to step in front of Miss Sharp, but she pushed her away.

"It's one of ours," Miss Sharp said, her voice shaking. "It's a rune to dispel magic."

"Yes," the dancer purred. "I am Delilah, one of the handmaids of the goddess Bastet, revered in my country as the goddess of joy, perfume, and dance. My sisters and I are dedicated to peace, but because your Order confused our goddess with her warlike cousin Sekhmet they hunted us down and marked us with a rune to banish our magic."

"Then why ever would you want to help us?" Miss Corey asked.

A black man stepped forward. He was dressed in a dapper pin-striped suit with a bright yellow cravat, and carried a walking stick with a carved ivory rooster at the top. His head was completely shaved. When he moved I saw tattooed signs on his scalp, but they didn't look like the Order's runes. I heard a murmur go around the room, a reverent whisper of the name "Shango," and I recognized him as the "African tribesman" from Coney Island.

"We believe there are many good people in your Order," Shango began in a resonant voice that I felt vibrate in my belly. "Many of your people worked to free my people from slavery. The Order was meant to be a force for good, but it has become too mired in its own rivalries and hatreds. We believe it can become a force for good again."

"Aye," an Irishman said, raising his fist. "It's a gude sign ye've put aside your hatred of the Darklings. We want to be part of that!"

"And we want to fight the shadows," Delilah said. "My sisters have seen the shadows collecting in the cities—from the gambling hells to the mansions of the rich. The Shadow Master has even approached my sisters to recruit them to his side. He is amassing an army, and where there are armies, there will be war. We want to be on the side of good in that war, and we believe that if the Order and the Darklings can put aside their enmity to fight together, we will be victorious. Together."

The assembled crowd clamored their assent. Shango rapped his stick against the floor for quiet.

"What do you say?" he demanded in a booming baritone. "Will you have us as your compatriots?"

Miss Sharp looked from Mr. Bellows to Miss Corey. They both nodded to her. Then she looked to Marlin. He stood taller under her gaze and nodded also. Then she looked at me. I wasn't sure why my assent should matter, but I gave it to her in a firm nod. Miss Sharp turned back to Shango and Delilah.

"We can't guarantee what the rest of the Order will have to say when this is all done, but I can tell you this—if they won't have you, then I won't have them. It would be a great honor to stand by your side in tonight's battle and, should we survive, for the rest of my life."

A cheer rang out in the room that seemed to echo through the house and beyond. I felt a shiver go up my spine and through my wings, as if a spark had been kindled. When I looked around the room I saw that same spark in the eyes of my friends and new comrades. We had become stronger by this union. I only hoped that we were strong enough to defeat van Drood.

34

AN HOUR LATER I was flying on Sirena's back through the darkening sky toward the soaring tower of the Woolworth Building. It was the first time I'd seen the building with its carapace of scaffolding removed. It was truly majestic—a Gothic spire etched in black against the orange glow in the west, like a tower out of a fairy tale. As we got closer I made out the finely carved arched windows, the swooping buttresses, and the lacelike tracery of the pinnacles punctuating the sky—just like the great European cathedrals we studied in history class. And yet the man who'd built this Cathedral of Commerce had made his fortune on the nickels and dimes of people buying everyday necessities—sewing needles and dishcloths and buttons.

This tower celebrated a new spirit that made my heart soar. Even a girl like me, it seemed to say, who'd started out in a factory sewing shirtsleeves, could one day aspire to beauty and fineness. I could well understand why van Drood would plot to blow it up. The tower was all about hope, the one emotion a shadow-ridden creature like van Drood could not abide.

We landed on the topmost horizontal ledge below the peaked octagonal tower. We could see the rounded end of Manhattan Island and the Statue of Liberty standing in the harbor. The crowds in City Hall Park looked like a hive of swarming bees.

"If this blows up," Pythagoras remarked, "it will take out all these other buildings and kill most of those people."

"We shan't let it blow up!" Helen cried. "I'm sure Mr. Bellows and Nathan and those nice Irishmen are down in the engine room disarming the bomb right now. Our job is to get our friends out."

We had to break one of the arched glass windows to get inside. We left the hawks on the roof as lookouts and took the stairs down. From the program we knew the celebratory dinner was on the twenty-seventh floor—we were on the forty-third. Going down sixteen floors on foot was frustratingly slow after soaring through the sky. Helen and I were to go ahead to find out where the girls were being kept, and then I'd go back to report. We left the rest of our troop in the stairwell and entered the twenty-seventh floor.

We stepped into a carpeted hallway full of men in dark suits puffing on cigars and slapping each other on the back.

"Heigh ho!" a portly gentleman cried when he saw Helen and me. "What have we here? Are you little girls lost?"

"Oh, golly, sir," Helen responded in a high-pitched voice I barely recognized. "We're here to do a special dance for you gentlemen, but this building is so big we've forgotten how to get back to our dressing room. Do you know where it is?"

I was afraid that she'd given us away by overacting, but the portly gentleman was completely taken in.

"Well, I can't say I know where your dressing room is, little lady, but perhaps one of these waiters . . ." He snapped his fingers and a black-suited waiter carrying a silver tray of champagne glasses wheeled to a halt in front of him. "D'you know where the dancing girls are kept?" he asked, winking at the young man.

The waiter looked down his nose at Helen and me in our frilly costumes and sniffed as if we smelled bad. "You girls are not supposed to mingle with the guests. Follow me."

Helen simpered to the portly gentleman. "Thank you ever so much for your help, kind sir. I'll throw you a rose when we're dancing later."

"Helen," I muttered as we scurried to keep up with the fast-moving waiter, "don't you think you're laying it on a little thick?"

"These men," she said quietly in her normal voice, "expect us to act like simpletons. Look at them all." We were passing through a large dining hall decorated with palm trees and American flags. The room was full of men in black suits, gleaming white shirtfronts and white gardenias in their lapels. En masse they looked like a colony of penguins. "Puffed up like stuffed quails. So pleased with themselves for being rich and important enough to be invited to the biggest extravaganza of the year. It would serve them right if we took our girls out of here and let them all blow up."

"Helen!" I cried, shocked. A year ago she would have regarded this gathering as an opportunity to meet a husband. "You don't mean that!"

"Well, no, I don't suppose they deserve to die, but I would like to shake them out of their complacency. Look around you—what's missing from this scene?"

I took another look at the crowd of black-suited men. "Um . . . women?"

"Exactly. Not a single woman was invited to this gala, even though it's women spending their nickels and dimes that have gotten Mr. Woolworth where he is today. Oh look, there he is . . ." For a moment Helen's tone softened. "I think he's talking to Mr. Tesla. And is that Charles Dana Gibson? He once did my portrait." Helen sighed and I squeezed her shoulder.

Suddenly I didn't blame Helen for being angry. A year ago her father would have been one of these men, and it hurt her to see them all laughing and drinking as if the world was just the same, when her world had so utterly changed.

"You're absolutely right," I told Helen. "Things have got to change in this world. Let's go find our girls and get them out of this place."

We followed the stiff-backed waiter through plushly carpeted corridors to a closed door with a sign on it that read "Do not disturb—ladies dressing."

"As if we're exotic animals that have to be caged," Helen muttered.

The supercilious waiter rapped his knuckles once on the gilt door and without waiting for a reply pushed it open and stood stiffly aside to let us go by. "There," he said as we passed him. "Don't stray out of here again until it's time for your dance."

Helen trod on his foot as she went by, making him drop his tray. I repressed a giggle and yanked Helen into the dressing room before he could retaliate. We fell into a fug of perfume and talcum powder that turned our laughter into choking coughs.

"Hell's Bells!" Helen swore. "It smells like a French bordello in here."

Clearly that stuck-up waiter had taken us to the wrong room. These tarted-up women in scanty dresses couldn't be our girls. Most of them looked older. These must be the other girls who had been taken from the Hellgate Club.

But then out of the sea of bare shoulders, exposed cleavages, and rouged cheeks rose a familiar voice.

"Helen! Ava! Thank the Bells you're here!" A girl in a white off-the-shoulder blouse, tight blue bodice, and short red skirt pushed her way through the crowd. Only her voice identified her as Daisy. She lowered it now and leaned close to whisper in my ear. "Did you find him? I tried to leave you a message."

My heart leapt at Daisy's bravery. "Yes, he's going to be all right, thanks to you."

"Daisy Mildred Moffat, what on earth are you wearing?" Helen cried. "You look like a—"

"Patriotic shop girl?" another girl cried in an overly bright voice. I looked at her and recognized, beneath her garish makeup, Rue. "Yes, that's exactly what we are! At the last minute Herr Hofmeister changed the program, even though we had spent weeks learning the last one."

At the tone of annoyance that had crept into her voice, one of the girls looked up from sewing a frill onto a round pasteboard tower of giant hatboxes piled on top of each other.

"Turn that frown upside down, Miss Grumpy!" she told Rue. "Being flexible and able to roll with the punches is one of the qualities of a patriotic shop girl. Our job is not to wonder why, but to smile until we die."

"Yes, Beatrice," Rue replied. *Beatrice?* I peered at the painted face, trying to recognize Beatrice Jager. "I'll try to remember that. Go back to putting on those frills now; that last one is crooked."

Beatrice—it was, horribly, her—forgot her own advice and frowned. She peered down at the frill and then ripped it off.

"That should keep her busy for a while," Rue said, drawing us into a quiet corner. "We're programmed to do everything perfectly. If we make a single mistake—a misstep, a dropped stitch—we have to do it over and over again until it's perfect."

"I understand how you've avoided being programmed," Helen said to Rue, "but how have you, Daisy?"

"With this." She slipped out a piece of paper that had been folded into a tiny square. "It's Mr. Appleby's last letter to me after I broke off our engagement. I had it on me when I was taken. Whenever I feel myself slipping I read it over—or recite it. I have it memorized." She looked up while she recited the letter. "'Dearest Daisy,' he writes, 'It was with great disappointment and heartache that I read your last letter, but not surprise. I knew when you went to that fancy school back east you would find many opportunities beyond the plain and simple life I have to offer you here in Kansas City. I have only ever wanted the best for you. Part of me still hopes—foolishly, I suppose—that you will change your mind and come back to me. Know that if you ever do I will be waiting here for you. Your true and loving Ignatius Appleby.'"

"*Ignatius?*" Helen echoed.

"That's a lovely letter," I told Daisy. "What a fine man he must be."

"Yes," Daisy said, her eyes shining. "And he's waiting for me. That thought has kept me strong these last months—that and the firm belief that you two would come for us. You're not alone, though, are you?"

We quickly filled Daisy and Rue in on the entire mission. Rue was excited to hear that Etta was with us, Daisy that the Darklings had come.

"A league of Darklings and Blythewood girls," Daisy said. "Oh, I'm sorry I've missed those meetings! And is Mr. Bellows really downstairs disarming a bomb?" A cloud came over her face, which I thought might be concern for her favorite teacher but which lasted a little too long. She began silently mouthing the words of Mr. Appleby's letter again. When she finished she looked from Helen to me to Rue. "What were you saying?"

Helen and I looked at each other. Rue started waving her hands. "We told you Mr. Bellows was disarming a bomb," Helen began.

"There's no bomb, silly!" Daisy squeaked, while Rue tried to make her be quiet, but the other girls had heard and began echoing her. "No bomb, silly, no bomb, silly, no bomb, silly . . ."

"They do this whenever someone mentions the bomb," Rue explained.

"Only sparklers!" One of the girls—Susannah, I thought—came over to us holding two long tapered batons with wire wicks at each end. "See! For our big finale we'll twirl these." She demonstrated a complicated twirling maneuver that made me dizzy to watch.

"What's going on?" I asked Rue, but before she could answer there was a knock at the door in the five-part pattern we had agreed upon as a signal. I went to the door and opened it a crack. For a moment I thought it was the obnoxious waiter, but then I recognized Nathan in a waiter's suit, his fair hair greased and combed straight back. I grabbed his arm and pulled him in. "Have you found the bomb?" I asked.

"No bomb, silly," Daisy began again.

"Shut up!" Helen snapped at Daisy. I didn't blame her. The "no bomb, silly" chant was unnerving.

"She's right, though," Nathan said, staring at Daisy's cleavage. Helen punched him in the arm and he raised his eyes a few inches. "Sorry. We've searched the entire basement and Omar's mesmerized the whole staff downstairs. No one knows anything about a bomb."

"No bomb, silly," chanted the girls gluing red, white, and blue frills onto the giant hatbox.

"What's that?" Nathan asked, pointing at the giant hatbox.

"A cake, silly," one of the girls said. "A great big patriotic birthday cake to celebrate the birthday of Mr. Woolworth's great big wonderful building! Susannah is going to jump out of it and the rest of us are going to light our sparklers to look like birthday candles!"

"May I have a look inside?" Nathan asked the prattling girl with surprising gentleness.

The girl wagged a finger at him. "Uh-uh," she sang, "no one looks inside the cake before the big number. That would ruin the surprise."

"It's true that no one's been allowed to look inside," Rue said in a low voice.

"Let's find out," Nathan said to her, and then, in a louder voice, he addressed the girl. "Oh, but you see, I'm the, er, engineer and I just want to have a look to make sure there's enough room inside for Susannah. We wouldn't want anything to go wrong, would we?"

The girl cocked her head to the left and then to the right. "Nothing can go wrong," she said, in a low masculine voice that sent chills down my spine. Then she smiled and chirped in a feminine high-pitched voice, "Golly, I guess it's all right."

Nathan moved gingerly past the girl and through the crowd of girls gluing red, white, and blue frills onto the cardboard cake. As they moved away I made out the lettering on the sides. "Congratulations, Mr. Woolworth!" it read. "From the Girls of Blythewood."

Nathan carefully opened the top lid, which was made of flimsy paper. "See?" Susannah said. "I'll burst right through!"

"There's not a lot of room for you," Nathan said. "They've only given you the top layer. What's underneath . . . ?"

He reached his hand deep into the cake. I peered over his shoulder and watched him lift a plywood circle. Beneath it was a tangle of metal gears and wires attached to a bundle of sticks. It looked a bit like the inside of a clock, or . . .

"The bomb," Nathan whispered. "With enough dynamite to blow up the twenty-seventh floor. And once that's on fire—who knows? The whole building could go up."

35

"CAN YOU DEFUSE it?" Helen whispered.

"Maybe," he said, "but it will take time, and we need to get the girls out of here. Omar's out in the dining hall disguised as a guest. Go get him and bring him in here. And get Pythagoras—he might know how to defuse it."

I found Omar standing in the dining hall, looking regal in a yellow high-collared tunic and white turban, explaining to a stout man that he was the Maharaja Rana of Ramadan.

"Uh, your highness," I said, "you're wanted by the, er, king of Sweden," I improvised.

"Really, Gustaf is here?" the stout businessman asked, stroking his muttonchops. "I had heard that the archduke might also be putting in an appearance. Do give his highness my regards."

"It will be my honor," Omar said, bowing his way out of the dining room. I filled him in as we hurried down the hall. When we entered the dressing room, we found the Darklings already there. Oriole and Sirena, with Rue and Daisy's help, had drawn the girls over by the mirrors, where they were working through a dance number. Gus and Nathan were crouched beside the dismantled cake studying its lethal filling.

"I need you to get these girls out of here so I can concentrate," Nathan said without lifting his eyes from the bomb.

"Of course," Omar said. "I will introduce a counter-mesmerism to convince them that these gentlemen"—he indicated Buzz, Heron, Marlin, and Sparrow—"are their dancing partners. Come." He waved the four male Darklings to follow him. "Have you ever seen a grand jeté...?"

I sat down beside Nathan.

"You too, Ava. I need to know you're safe."

"I can leave at any time," I replied. "You know that."

I thought I saw him flinch. "All right, then make yourself useful and hold this lamp."

I lifted a goose-necked desk lamp and aimed the light at the tangle of wires Nathan was studying. I heard Omar telling the girls that Herr Hofmeister had introduced a new step to their routine. They were to perform a grand jeté, leaping into their partner's arms, and then hold an attitude and remain in it until their partners put them down again.

"It is very important that you keep your chin up and not look down," he told the girls in the singsong tone I recognized as his "suggestive" voice. I wanted to make that leap myself, but I blinked and focused on Nathan.

"You have very steady hands," I remarked.

"Yes," he dead-panned. "I am the soul of steadiness and reliability. A brick. A tower of strength—"

"You *are*," I said. "You've only convinced yourself otherwise because of Louisa."

"Who's Louisa?" Gus asked.

"His sister," I replied. "She was in Faerie and hasn't quite recovered from it."

"Oh," Gus said casually. "I came across a cure for that in one of the books in the library. When we're done with this I'll look it up for you . . . say, do you think this red wire is the one to cut? Or this blue one?"

Nathan stared at Gus. "You have a cure?" Then he looked down at the wires and frowned. I glanced behind me and saw Beatrice Jager take three dainty running steps and leap into Buzz's waiting arms. He soared out the window with her to a chorus of oohs and aahs from the other dancers who were lined up to take their grand jetés. Helen, Daisy, and Rue were standing at the open window applauding each dancer as she soared into the night.

I turned back to Nathan and Gus and saw their frozen faces.

"What's wrong . . . ?" I began, but then I followed their gazes up. They were looking at Herr Hofmeister—or rather, at the mouth of the gun he had pointed at Nathan's head.

"You will kindly please stop what you a doing," he bit off in chopped syllables. "That is a very important prop in tonight's performance."

"It's a bomb, Herr Hofmeister," I said. "It will kill you, too, when it explodes."

"I know very well what it is," he said. "It will be my grand finale, but I will die for a good cause. These men who look at me like dirt will remember me as the last face they see. I will be remembered—not as the ridiculous dancing master Herr Hofmeister, but by my real name, Aleksandar Zupan, Serbian patriot who died to liberate my country from the yoke of Austro-Hungarian oppression!"

"Serbian patriot? Austro-Hungary?" I echoed. "What does all that have to do with the Woolworth building?"

For a moment Herr Hofmeister looked confused. I almost felt sorry for him. Then he spit on the floor. "Archduke Franz Ferdinand is here tonight. When he dies, Russia will rally to our cause and there will be war."

"It's just a rumor that the archduke is here," I said, standing up. "Van Drood has made you believe that so you'll do his bidding."

"I do no man's bidding but my own!" Herr Hofmeister barked angrily.

"Can you get Omar to de-mesmerize him?" Nathan hissed. "This thing just started ticking."

But Omar was across the room, still shepherding our girls out of the window. He was motioning for Gus to come over to carry Susannah Dewsnap out the window. I couldn't interrupt.

"Of course it is ticking. Do you think I would rely on these silly girls to complete my plan? It is set to go off at seven-thirty when your American president pushes the button on his desk. The ignorant crowds will believe that their own president has blown up the building. Chaos will reign! Riots will ensue. In the coming days my manifesto will be found and read throughout the world. The Serbian nation will rise to power!"

"I don't think so, old chap," Nathan said, his eyes still on the mechanism of the bomb. "You've been had."

Herr Hofmeister looked like he was going to have an

apoplectic fit. I stepped closer to him, withdrawing the repeater from my pocket. When I depressed the stem it played a lilting lullaby that softened something in Herr Hofmeister's eyes. He lowered his gun.

"Van Drood has done this to you," I said. "Judicus van Drood. Perhaps you recall meeting him?"

"Yes," the dancing master said, furrowing his brow as if trying to recall something that had happened a long time ago. "A man came to see me in my humble garret in Paris, where I was living in exile. He told me he was a member of the Black Hand and said I could help to right the wrongs my country had suffered under the Austrian empire. He told me that the Order was supporting the Austrians in their crusade to crush my homeland and was responsible for the deaths of my family."

"He was lying to you," I said. "This is what van Drood does. He finds your vulnerable spot." I thought of what he had said to me in the fun house. "He told me that I was a monster, that my mother never loved me, that I would never belong." I noticed that Nathan, though his eyes were still on the bomb, had grown very still. He was listening to me. And so was Helen, who had come over from the window to stand beside me. All the other girls were gone.

"He drove a wedge between me and my friends because I would not trust them with the truth. But I know now that all the things he told me were lies."

"Were they, Ava?"

The words were in van Drood's voice, but they didn't come from Herr Hofmeister's mouth. I wheeled around and found myself looking into Nathan's dark gray eyes—hadn't they been a lighter gray before? He was still holding a pair of wire cutters to the one of the wires attached to the bomb, but he was looking up at me with a cold calculated look I'd never seen before on his face.

"No—"

"But yes, Ava, *dearling*, here we are again. Why shouldn't I take a younger, more handsome form, especially one so suited to me? After all, he is my son."

"That's a lie!" Helen cried out.

Nathan—or the *thing* inside Nathan—swiveled his head to stare at Helen. "Oh my dear, you have been so useful in helping me gain access to this young man. Watching you—his oldest friend—fall in love with a Darkling made him almost as vulnerable as watching the same thing happen to his beloved. Or didn't you know he loved Ava?"

"It doesn't matter to me if he loves Ava, but he's not your son. I've known Nathan since we were children. His father was Daniel Beckwith."

"I thought so, too, until your friend Ava suggested otherwise. Then I looked into the archives and found that old Daniel was away in Scotland on the relevant dates. India Beckwith changed Nathan's birth certificate so no one would know. She even fooled me!"

He leered in a way that made my blood run cold, precisely because I'd seen almost the same expression on Nathan's face before. The resemblance between the two was impossible to deny.

"It doesn't matter if you're Nathan's father!" I cried. "Blood means nothing compared with how a person is raised and whom he chooses as his friends and what he does. Nathan is a good man. He risked his life to save Louisa. He saved Ruth from the Hellgate Club."

I saw a flicker of light in Nathan's eyes—like the flash of a fish swimming through murky water—but when he spoke his voice was still van Drood's.

"All very valiant. But then why don't you love him, Ava? It's your not loving him that made him vulnerable to me. You have done this to him." He smiled a ghastly grin that stretched as wide as the funny-face sign at Coney Island. Smoke gushed out of his mouth. That flicker of light in Nathan's eyes had gone out. The thing in front of me was so revolting I wanted to run away from it, but Nathan was still in there somewhere.

"I *do* care for Nath—" I began, and then, stepping closer and kneeling by his side, I looked into those darkened eyes and spoke directly to the man I hoped was still there. "I do love you, Nathan."

"Let's see how much."

Van Drood's voice came from behind me. I whirled around to see Herr Hofmeister aiming his gun directly at Nathan's heart. I screamed and began to move, but before I could, something else flew between us—a flurry of ribbons and lace and blonde hair.

"Helen!" Nathan screamed, his own voice restored. He pushed me aside and leapt for her as she fell. A red rose was blooming on the white ruffled blouse of her costume. Herr Hofmeister was staring at Nathan and Helen, a startled look in his eyes. Because van Drood had left him? I wondered. But when I stood he raised his eyes to me and I saw that van Drood was still there. It was van Drood who looked surprised.

"I thought she didn't love him," he began. Helen's act had not only driven the shadows from Nathan, she had managed to confound the Shadow Master himself. There was a spark in his eyes, a chink of light like a tear in a blind in a darkened room. Just as weakness opened a wedge for the shadows, so strength must open a crack for the light.

I followed Nathan's gaze down to the bomb. When he had dropped the wire cutters they had severed the red wire.

"Nathan," I said, "that red wire . . . were you supposed to cut it?"

"I don't think so," he said. "What are we going to do?"

I looked at Helen and Nathan. I couldn't carry them both out of here—but I could carry the bomb. I picked up the metal box. I'd never flown carrying anything so heavy, but I'd just have to try. I carried it to the window.

"Ava, what are you doing?" I heard Helen's weak voice calling to me. I turned around.

"I'm sorry I didn't put more faith in you, Helen. You're the bravest girl I know. Take care of each other." I turned back to the window. The flimsy costume I was wearing was no match for my unfurling wings. I heard Helen's gasp and Nathan's voice.

"I knew that costume suited you," he said. "Wings of fire for a phoenix."

"It was you!" I said, half turning. "You sent me the dress."

But there wasn't time. The metal box in my hands was ticking away the seconds. I launched myself from the window into the open sky—and plummeted down. The bomb was too heavy. It was dragging me down toward the ground where thousands of people were waiting to see the Woolworth Building burst into incandescent light. Instead they would all die in a fiery inferno like the girls at the Triangle factory. I had to get the bomb out to sea.

I beat my wings as hard as I could, struggling to gain altitude. Little by little, I rose up into the sky. I could see the harbor lights to the south twinkling in the dusky twilight. I aimed in that direction, but with the weight of the bomb dragging me down, I'd never make it.

Suddenly it was as if the air around me lightened and a tailwind pushed me forward. I looked to my right and saw Raven flying beside me, his wing tips nearly touching mine. Ghosting me. Where his wing had been damaged, the new imped feathers—brown and gold and russet—had already taken root.

"I don't supposed you'd consider handing that thing over to me?" he shouted.

"Not on your life," I replied.

"Then we'd best make haste to the sea." He whistled a sharp note and I felt myself buoyed up. I looked to my left and saw Pythagoras. Then I heard Marlin's voice and saw him taking the lead. The fledglings were arraying themselves around me in a V formation, carving a wedge out of the air to make it easier for me to fly. Never mind that they'd all die if the bomb went off in the air. They flocked around me because they were my flock. I caught the thermals and soared. I'd never felt so free before, lifted by my friends.

"Ava. " Raven's voice reached me. "We're over the harbor! Bank a little to the right to avoid that tug boat."

I did. Then Marlin yelled, "Bombs away!" in a surprisingly gleeful voice and I dropped the bomb.

I heard its dull thud in the water below us and then, like an afterthought, the explosion. A great jet of water gushed upward and fiery trails of red, blue, gold, and green exploded around us. In the glow I saw Raven's face beaming. I looked to my right and Marlin's face was also lit up with excitement as the fireworks splashed across the sky.

"Boys." I heard Sirena's voice sigh on the wind. "They love blowing things up."

There was an unmistakable note of glee in her voice, though. The fireworks lighting up the harbor and the shining white spire of the Woolworth Building were spectacular. Helen would love them, I thought.

And then, thinking of Helen, I began to fall.

36

RAVEN CAUGHT ME and steered me back toward land.

"I have to find Helen," I told him. "She was shot."

I started flying toward the Woolworth Building, but Eirwyn intercepted our flight path, whistling sharply.

"Nathan's brought Helen back to Henry Street," Raven interpreted. I had understood a little of Eirwyn's language. *Wing-wounded* was the bit I'd caught.

We banked south toward the Henry Street House, skimming over the Lower East Side tenement rooftops. Only a few months ago I'd been running across these rooftops chasing Rue. Now they were packed with crowds spread out on blankets and kitchen chairs, picnicking, drinking homemade wine and ale, eating cold chicken, playing cards and singing and dancing—all to celebrate the lighting of the Woolworth Building. They had no idea how close they'd come to seeing it explode. Nor did most of them notice our cloaked wings passing over their heads. Only a few old women—babushka-wearing Jewish grandmothers, wizened Italian crones wrapped in black shawls—looked up as we passed and made signs with their crabbed fingers or spit over their shoulders.

On the roof of the Henry Street House, though, we were

greeted by an excited group: the rest of the Darklings and the girls they'd carried from the Woolworth Building—both the Blythewood girls and the other girls from the Hellgate Club—Kid Marvel and a boisterous crew of madges, Agnes and Mr. Greenfeder, Miss Sharp and Mr. Bellows, and a whole conflagration of lampsprites that lit up the roof like a Christmas tree.

They all burst into applause when we landed. Miss Sharp and Agnes stepped out of the crowd to greet us—but then halted, their eyes riveted on something just over my head that was casting a glow on their faces. I turned to see what they were looking at, afraid there'd been another bomb that had lit the Woolworth Building on fire, but found that it was me. My wings were glowing with a lambent flame.

I turned back to Agnes and Miss Sharp and met their gazes. The roof had grown silent. My friends from Blythewood—Cam and Beatrice and Dolores, Myrtilene and Etta and Susannah and Mary MacCrae—had come forward out of the crowd to stare at my wings. Mr. Bellows' mouth hung open. I hadn't seen him look so surprised since Miss Corey and Miss Sharp had kissed. I heard the madges murmur, "A phoenix!" and Cam Bennett whistle something under her breath and Myrtilene Montmorency say "I'll be—" before Susannah kicked her shin to quiet her.

It was my worst nightmare. I had been revealed to all my schoolmates. Would they turn on me now? Turn me in to the Council? Turn away in revulsion?

But then Dolores was stepping forward, holding her sister Beatrice's hand. She raised both their hands into the air. "Three cheers for Ava for getting rid of the bomb. Hip, hip—"

They all cheered me, the madges, too, Delilah spinning around in a hypnotic dance, the Irishmen breaking into a jig, the lampsprites fluttering up into the air like miniature firecrackers. It would have been perfect if I hadn't been missing three faces.

"Nathan and Daisy are with Helen," Miss Sharp whispered in my ear. "I think you'd better get down there."

The fire in my wings cooled at her words. I quickly told Raven where I was going and followed Miss Sharp inside and down the stairs to a room on the third floor. It was one of the rooms Miss Wald used to see patients. Miss Wald was there now with her black nurse's bag, sitting beside a narrow iron-framed cot. Helen lay in the bed, her face as white as the sheets and the bandages covering her chest. Nathan sat on the bed beside her, and Daisy stood, still wearing her patriotic shop girl costume, wringing her hands. When she saw me, Daisy ran to me and started whispering in my year. "She's not—"

"I thought we'd sworn off secrets," Helen interrupted in a weak voice.

"You're right," Daisy said, pulling me to the bed. "We've had enough secrets. They're all out now. Ava's half-Darkling— why, that's not so bad! And I'm engaged to Mr. Appleby—if he'll still have me. And Nathan's—"

"The son of the Shadow Master who's been filling my head with *tenebrae* for months," Nathan said, breaking into Daisy's bright, nervous chatter without taking his eyes off Helen.

"But you're free of them now," Daisy said, her eyes wide as silver dollars. "D'you know, Ava, after you left, Nathan carried Helen down twenty-seven flights of stairs because the elevators were all jammed with those awful men who kidnapped us? Don't worry, though, the madges rounded them up when they left the building and are holding them until Mr. Omar can de-mesmerize them—and then Nathan carried Helen all the way here and woke up Miss Wald and got her to get a doctor from Bellevue so they could remove the bullet from Helen's spine. She would have died otherwise!"

"Yes, Nathan saved me," Helen said, turning her head weakly in my direction.

"*You* saved *me*," Nathan said to Helen, squeezing her hand.

"Oh, pish," Helen replied. "I doubt that bullet would have hit you anyway. Herr Hofmeister was a terrible shot."

"That's not what I meant," Nathan began.

"Oh, but he is a terrible man," Daisy interrupted. "The madges have him in custody and are interrogating him. . . . "

Daisy chattered on about Herr Hofmeister, but Nathan and Helen weren't listening. They were looking into each other's eyes. Not with the moonstruck haze of lovers, but with the solemnity of soldiers after a battle. Helen had saved Nathan, not just by intercepting that bullet meant for him, but because her selfless action had banished the shadows from Nathan's soul. But were they gone for good? I studied Nathan. He was pale and drawn, his eyes sunk into his face, but those eyes were a clear gray again, and nothing moved in them besides concern for Helen.

And what about Helen?

"So they were able to get the bullet out?" I said, interrupting Daisy's chatter. "And Helen's going to be all right?"

Daisy's eyes immediately filled up with tears. Nathan lifted his head and looked from Daisy to me, silently mouthing the word "out." Daisy was getting to her feet.

"We should leave Helen to get some rest," she said, fleeing out the door. I followed her. As soon as we were in the hall Daisy burst into tears. Nathan followed, closing the door behind him and pulling us farther down the hall.

"What is it?" I cried.

"Helen is going to be fine," Nathan said in a steely voice that brooked no argument.

"It's just . . . the bullet that hit her spine . . ." Daisy sobbed. "She may never walk again."

"Oh," I said, feeling as if I'd been punched in the stomach.

"She *will* walk again," Nathan said through gritted teeth. "If I have to take her to every doctor in Europe." He glared at both of us, silver eyes flashing, as though daring us to contradict him. When we didn't, he nodded once, turned on his heel, and stomped back down the hall to Helen's room.

"The doctor says we won't know for months whether Helen will regain the use of her legs," Daisy said soberly. I realized now that her nervous, bright chatter had been to avoid the issue of Helen's condition. "Nathan won't hear it."

"Maybe it's what he needs," I said. "Someone to take care of . . ." I paused. His inability to help Louisa had driven a wedge into his soul that had let the shadows in. If Helen never recovered . . . I banished the thought from my head. "It will keep the shadows away," I said with more conviction than I felt. "Helen will make sure of it."

Daisy nodded and wiped her eyes. "If anyone can, it's Helen. And we'll be there to help her."

I squeezed Daisy's hand and turned to go back to Helen's room, but saw Raven and Marlin coming down from the roof. They looked worried.

"We have to go," Raven said, grabbing my arm.

"What's wrong?" I asked. "Are we under attack?"

"Not exactly," Raven answered.

I heard a commotion coming from downstairs. Voices raised. Miss Sharp shouting. Something breaking.

I ran down the stairs, Raven and Marlin at my heels. In the parlor I found Miss Sharp, Mr. Bellows, Agnes, and Miss Corey on one side of the room, and on the other, three women in black. I recognized them right away as the ladies who had interviewed me for admission to Blythewood. They still wore the same bird-crowned hats they had worn over a year ago. Didn't they know it was no longer popular to sport dead birds on millinery? But as they turned toward me, the stuffed crows came to life and flew straight for us. Raven and Marlin tried to beat them off, but they were too small and quick. I felt a stuffed bird's claws dig into my shoulder and suddenly couldn't move.

"Avaline Hall," Mrs. Ansonia van Hassel boomed, "I arrest you as an enemy of the Order."

"You can't arrest Avaline," Miss Sharp said. "She and the Darklings saved our girls today!"

"And they saved the Order from disgrace and shame," Agnes said. "The Council's been infiltrated by *tenebrae*."

"If the Woolworth Building had blown up, all your investments would have been destroyed," Mr. Greenfeder said.

"Silence!" Mrs. van Hassel screeched. "You will all face charges of consorting with the enemies of the Order!" Mrs. van

Hassel's face, already red, turned purple. Kid Marvel, Omar, Delilah, and all the other madges and lampsprites had appeared in the doorway and were crowding into the parlor.

"Mr. Bellows," Mrs. van Hassel called in a tremulous voice, "I charge you as a knight of the Order to defend us against these . . . these . . ."

"These good people?" Mr. Bellows asked, moving between the women from the Order and the crowd. Miss Corey and Miss Sharp went to stand on either side of him. Agnes and Mr. Greenfeder joined them. I felt a swelling of gratitude for my friends' loyalty, but I also didn't want to see anyone else get hurt tonight.

"I'll go with you if you release Raven and Marlin," I said. "And the other magicals. You can arrest me. Just leave my friends alone."

"Arrest a Hall! I don't think so!"

The voice came from behind the crowd of madges. I saw them edge apart at the sweep of an ivory walking stick to let my grandmother make her slow but stately way into the room.

"No one will be arresting my granddaughter, especially not you, Ansonia van Hassel. Who let those lecherous men into Blythewood? Who advised the Council to sink all the Order's money into the *Titanic*? And then, as if we hadn't learned our lesson, into the Woolworth Building?"

"Your granddaughter is a Darkling, Elvira," Mrs. van Hassel said.

My grandmother turned to look at me.

"It's true, Grandmother," I said, trying to meet her gaze

even though I was still held frozen by the stuffed crow's grip. "My father was a Darkling."

A tremor passed over my grandmother's face. Of course she would disown me now.

"So that was why poor Evie kept you hidden all those years," she said, her eyes glittering like the jet beads on her dress. "But wings or no wings, you're still a Hall." She snapped her fingers. The stuffed crow released its grip from my shoulder and fell lifeless to the floor. The ones holding Raven and Marlin collapsed as well.

"There will have to be an investigation and a special meeting of the Council, Elvira," Mrs. van Hassel began.

"Yes, there will," my grandmother replied, raising her lorgnette to her eyes and looking hard at Ansonia van Hassel. "I'll be interested to know what they make of your investment policies. And now, my granddaughter looks tired. It's time you came home, Avaline."

"But I can't leave Helen, Grandmother, or—" I looked around at the group in the parlor—Raven and Marlin, my teachers, Kid Marvel and Omar and all the madges. "Or my friends."

My grandmother looked around at the bedraggled group of schoolgirls and Darklings and magical beings and sighed. "Very well, then. I suppose Helen should be moved to our house anyway. Invite your friends along. We have plenty of room."

37

I WAS SO relieved that my grandmother had accepted that I was a Darkling and welcomed my friends into her house, I would have happily spent the rest of the spring waiting for the Council's meeting at the mansion on Fifth Avenue. But the next morning we received a wire from Dame Beckwith.

> Have heard reports of your bravery Stop Am very proud Stop Can you forgive an old woman for being so blind? Stop Gillie will be waiting at the station for the 5:02 train Stop

I took the telegram up to Helen's room, where Nathan was forcing toast and tea on her.

"For Bells' sake, Nathan, you don't have to feed me my toast. It's my legs that don't work, not my hands!"

"Oh good!" Daisy said, coming in. "Helen's feeling like herself this morning."

"I am always myself," she said to Daisy. "It was you who were someone else—" She halted as Nathan paled.

"Clearly I'm not needed here," he said, getting up.

"No, Nathan," I said. "You should see this, too. I've gotten a telegram from your mother."

I handed Nathan the telegram but Helen nimbly plucked it from his hands. A short tussle ensued, which I thought might result in them tearing the paper but ended with them leaning their heads together to read it.

"Oh, I'm so glad to hear Gillie's all right," Helen said. "Of course you must all go back."

"I'm not sure I can go back," I said. "Not with everyone knowing I'm a—"

"A hero," Helen said, looking at me with shining eyes. "You should have seen yourself flying out of that building with the bomb. You looked like Inez Milholland leading the suffrage parade on Washington!"

I smiled at Helen. "I'm sorry I didn't tell you earlier—and I'm glad you're able to accept what I am, but the others—"

"Can get stuffed if they don't!" Daisy cried.

"That's right," Nathan said gruffly. I looked at my friends.

"You three standing by me means the world to me, but I'm afraid it's not as simple as that. I'm half-Darkling. I owe something to them, too. I can't belong to the Order if they regard the Darklings as enemies."

"But they won't be able to after what's happened," Daisy said. "You heard what your grandmother said last night. There's going to be an investigation."

"Yes," Helen said, "when they see what the Darklings and madges did to save our girls they'll have to reconsider. They'll have to reconcile now. You might as well go to Blythewood until they finish the investigation and convene."

"But I want to stay here with you," I told Helen.

"Nathan can look after me," Helen said, looking impishly at Nathan. "I'll be up in a few weeks."

As usual it was difficult to argue with Helen's logic. I left for Blythewood that day, traveling by train with Daisy, Etta, and a dozen more girls—Dolores, Beatrice, Cam, Susannah, Mary, and Myrtilene among them. They crowded the train car and were so loud and raucous as they recounted the previous day's events that the conductor threatened to throw us off at Beacon if we didn't act like ladies.

"This, sir," Dolores Jager declaimed in a stentorian voice, "*is* how ladies behave."

Beatrice beamed at her newly vocal sister. "Papa will be so proud," she said, wiping tears from her eyes. "We averted an international crisis. Imagine what would have happened if that crazy man had assassinated the archduke!"

"It turned out the archduke wasn't even there," Dolores said modestly. "But it would have been a great loss if Mr. Tesla had died."

"Not to mention Mr. Gibson," Myrtilene averred. "There would have been no more Gibson Girls!" She patted her own upswept pouf.

I was amazed and heartened by the resiliency of my class-mates, but looking out the rain-splattered window at the fog-bound river (upon which I knew the changelings were traveling back to the Blythe Wood) I felt somehow removed from their gaiety. It wasn't that they knew what I was—they all professed delight and even jealousy (from Cam at least) that I possessed a pair of wings under my corset—but that I didn't feel as certain of the outcome of the Council meeting as they did. And I didn't like going back to Blythewood without Helen.

Some of my melancholy was dispelled by seeing Gillie at the station. He had brought the wagon to accommodate the crowd of girls and decked it out with violets and apple blossom boughs and a large purple-and-green banner that read "Hail the Conquering Heroines!"

The girls crowded in excitedly, shoving each other to make room for me, but when Gillie suggested I sit up front with him, I complied. I turned to him when he took his seat.

"You knew, didn't you."

His eyes turned a softer shade of green as he turned to me— the same spring green as the new leaves in the sycamore trees towering over River Road. Although it had rained all the way up on the train, the sky was blue here in Rhinecliff, and a soft breeze, sweet with the scent of apple blossom, wafted against my face. Looking into those bottomless green eyes—as deep and old as the forest—I realized what a silly question it was. A better one would have been what *didn't* Gillie know.

But he answered me with all seriousness. "I knew who your mother loved and why she went away. I saw the war going on inside you. I saw what ye were—but I didna see what ye would become. No one could see that. But I see you now. Your mother would be proud of you."

I felt tears sting my eyes, but before they could fall a breeze had caught them up and carried them away. Gillie made a soft clucking sound to the horses, but also, I thought, to me. It was the sound he made when he flew the hawks, to call them home.

Above us I heard Eirwyn and Gwynfor echoing him. As the wagon started down River Road I felt, for the moment at least, that I was home. Not because I was returning to Blythewood, but because I was sitting beside a friend—and really, what other sort of home was there?

In the weeks to come, though, the particulars of what I would call home remained uncertain. Dame Beckwith contrived to install a sense of normalcy and routine to the last weeks of the term. Our teachers rushed to cover the term's material. We worked hard to keep up with them. The ballroom was turned into a study hall, the mirrors taped over with diagrams and charts and timelines and color engravings of famous buildings and paintings we were supposed to memorize. Sometimes a girl might find herself humming a tune from *Die Puppenfee*, but then another girl would break into the Blythewood song, which began "Ring true, aim high!" and ended "Blythewood girls until we die!" sung to the tune of "La Marseillaise."

Once a week the Fledgling League met in the Ravencliffe boathouse—we used rowboats now that the river wasn't frozen—to compare notes on the progress of our Elders' meetings. Our Darkling friends informed us that their elders had been invited to the Council's meeting, and that the meeting was to be held at the Woolworth Building.

"I wonder why they chose that place?" Myrtilene asked. "I'd think it would give them all bad memories."

"I think it's a good sign," Beatrice said. "It's the place where the Darklings and Blythewood girls fought together. A symbol of our unity."

"And it has ripping good views!" Cam said.

I noticed that Raven was silent and thoughtful during the conversation.

On nights when there wasn't a league meeting, Raven and I flew to the Gunks together, wing tip to wing tip across the river. Some nights, we flew farther west over the Catskills and once as far as Lake Erie. Sometimes I wondered if we should keep flying west, far away from Blythewood and Ravencliffe, out to the Rockies, where Raven said there were great expanses of mountains where a Darkling could soar unobserved and even the humans didn't do things according to anyone's *old ways*. But we returned each night to watch the sun rise over the Hudson from our niche in the cliff. On one of those mornings I asked him what he thought about the choice of the Woolworth Building for the meeting of the Council and Darkling Elders.

"I think," he said, "that van Drood had his reasons for wanting to blow up that particular building and that we'll find out more at this meeting."

We hadn't talked about van Drood since Raven had been rescued from the dungeon at the Hellgate Club. When others mentioned him, his eyes would darken and he would turn away. Raven's wings had healed, his own feathers growing over the imped feathers, and his scars had faded, but I suspected there were scars he carried inside from his time in that pit that I couldn't see.

"When you were imprisoned," I said now, "did you . . . *hear* van Drood?"

He shuddered, feathers rustling, and looked away from me. "Yes. He was inside my head, telling me terrible things."

"That's what he does," I said. "He finds your weaknesses

and then uses them to open up a crack in your soul to let the shadows in. He told me that my mother was afraid of me turning into a monster and that my father knew about me when he abandoned me. He made me feel like I was a monster."

"And do you feel that way now?" he asked, still not looking at me. "Like a monster?"

"No," I said, squeezing his hand. "My friends have stood by me even knowing what I am. *Your* friends have stood by me. You—" I cradled my hand around his cheek and turned him to face me. "You risked your life to save my friends. You're not a monster—so how could I be one?"

In the first blush of dawn his skin was rosy and he looked very young. "He told me . . ." He swallowed and firmed his jaw. "He told me you loved Nathan."

I almost laughed. "Of all the things van Drood could have chosen, to pick something so—" I was going to say *petty*, but then I recalled what Dame Beckwith had said: *Evil often grows out of such petty jealousies and resentments.* Raven filled in the rest.

"True?"

"Don't be silly! I don't . . ." But I couldn't say it with complete honesty. I was picturing Nathan skating on the ice, Nathan at the helm of the *Half Moon* telling me he loved me, me telling Nathan I loved him while he was under van Drood's control . . . then Nathan carrying Helen down twenty-seven flights of stairs. "Nathan's with Helen," I said at last, even though I wasn't sure their bond was romantic. "And I love you." That was true, no matter what conflicted feelings I might have about Nathan.

"And I you," Raven said, folding his wings around me.

"That's what got me through those weeks in the pit listening to van Drood in my head. It didn't matter how much he tried to convince me you didn't love me. Remembering how much I loved you kept me whole. Van Drood failed, just as he failed to blow up the Woolworth Building, because your friends and mine wouldn't let their elders' differences divide them. I think that's why we're meeting there. Besides, the Elders are happy about meeting someplace high up. They like to be able to see what's coming." He cupped my face with his hand and looked at me solemnly. "And so do I."

Before I could ask what he meant, he stopped my mouth with a kiss so hard and urgent it kindled my wings into flames. They spread an orange-gold nimbus around us that rivaled the rising sun in the east.

38

IN SPITE OF Raven's compelling arguments, I was less pleased than he with the choice of meeting place. I knew that the Order had invested in the building and was afraid that their intent was to show off their wealth and power. I was also startled to learn that Uncle Taddie had been summoned to the meeting, and worried that the Council planned to use him as an example of the harm that came to humans through contact with the fairies. When I went to visit Miss Sharp at her aunts' home, she agreed, and was unsure if they could even get her uncle to leave Violet House. But when Taddie was shown a picture of the Woolworth Building he became very excited and determined to go. "It's just like the clock tower Papa designed!" he exclaimed.

Emmaline tried to explain that it wasn't exactly a clock tower—there wasn't even a clock in the tower—but Taddie insisted it was, and that it meant it was safe because clocks kept us safe. As if to illustrate his point of view, the clocks of Violet House began to chime the hour. Since Raven had fixed them, they chimed in synchronicity, each tune blending with the others into a symphony that, indeed, made me feel safe—both parts of me, Darkling and human. Uncle Taddie was right. Thaddeus

Sharp had designed the clocks to safeguard Violet House from all harm. It would be nice, I thought as I ate another scone, if the Woolworth Building had been designed to do the same.

»→ ✦ ←«

On the day of the meeting I traveled down to the city with Daisy and Etta and a dozen other girls. We had been told that we couldn't all attend the meeting, but everyone wanted to be there to lend their support and admire the view from the observatory.

"If Helen were here she'd wonder why they were all so anxious to see a view they nearly plummeted to their deaths from two months ago," Daisy remarked wistfully.

"I miss her, too," I said, squeezing Daisy's hand. "My grandmother says she's doing much better and she'll be there today."

"I know. She wrote to tell me. Nathan will be there, too. I think it's so wonderful how he's been taking care of her—and so romantic! Do you think they'll get married? If they wait until we graduate we could have a double ceremony."

"I doubt matters have progressed that far," I said, trying to curb my irritation. Since Mr. Appleby had taken Daisy back, after she'd written to explain that she'd been overtaxed with studying when she broke off their engagement, she'd talked of little else but wedding plans. It was beginning to wear on my nerves. But when I looked at her now I saw that despite her bright smile she had a worried look in her eyes. Even if the Council approved her marriage to Mr. Appleby, she might never be able to share the secrets of the Order with him. We'd all learned this year what the cost of keeping secrets was.

"We'll see," I told Daisy. "We don't even know what will come of this meeting. Our people might be at war. I hardly think it's time to be talking about marriage."

Daisy shrugged and turned to talk to Myrtilene about wedding customs in Savannah, and I looked out the window, hoping for a glimpse of the Darkling Elders flying to the city. Raven was flying with them, as well as my father, who was going to serve as an index to *A Darkness of Angels*. But I couldn't make out anything through the fog that I suspected was caused by the changelings traveling down to the city. They had been called to the meeting, too, to help decide the fate of Rue, who had been staying at Violet House with Ruth and pretending to be her cousin from Warsaw. I wished Raven could have ridden on the train with me.

My grandmother sent her limousine to the station to take us downtown, which was embarrassing, but the girls were delighted and all crammed in, Cam in front with Babson, whom she interrogated all the way downtown about Rolls-Royce engines. I barely got a word in edgewise to find out that he'd already brought Helen, Nathan, and my grandmother downtown earlier.

"Mrs. Hall wanted to be there first," Babson confided. "To make sure she got the best seat before Mrs. van Hassel."

"I hope she hasn't been overstraining herself with all this," I said.

"It's done her good," Babson replied. "She looks ten years younger. She's a fighter, your grandmother. Just like you."

I was heartened by Babson's belief in me, just as I had before the Montmorency ball ten months ago, but when we pulled up in front of the Woolworth Building I felt as intimidated as I had in front of the Montmorency mansion. It was such an imposing edifice. Entering the marble Gothic lobby I thought of what the press called it: the Cathedral of Commerce. What it felt like to me was a cathedral of power—the Order's power. Now I felt sure they had chosen this meeting place to intimidate the Darklings and the madges and put us all in our places.

But if that were their purpose, it hadn't worked on Kid Marvel. He was standing at the elevators in a shiny suit, crisp fedora, and a pink carnation boutonniere.

"There they are—the belles of Blythewood!" he cried out, twirling a walking stick like the Coney Island spieler he was. "Your chariot awaits." He waved us into an open elevator and hit the button with his cane. "The express takes you to the fifty-first floor in only one and three-quarter minutes. I've been going up and down in it all morning. It's one hell of a ride! Hold on to your hats, ladies!"

Some of the girls literally grabbed their hats. Having flown over this building, I felt sure that I need take no such precaution, but when the elevator rose swiftly up I wished I could hold on to my stomach to keep it from rising into my throat. I was relieved when the doors opened on the fifty-first floor.

"The observatory is just up the stairs, ladies," Kid announced like he owned the building. "Go give it a gawk. Not you, sister." He grabbed me by the elbow and steered me down a corridor. Daisy gave me a curious look, but I waved her on without me. Kid Marvel propelled me into a small room off the corridor. It was lavishly furnished with velvet couches and Persian rugs. It looked to be some sort of waiting room. At least the people in it all seemed to be waiting . . . for me.

Delilah approached me first. She was veiled but wearing a smart green baize jacket and skirt. "Miss Hall," she addressed me formally, with none of the frivolity of the hootchy-kootchy dancer I'd first met at Coney Island. "We are glad you are here. We would like a moment of your time to ask a favor of you."

"Of course," I said, looking around the room. I saw Omar and Shango and the other madges I'd met at the Henry Street House. At first I didn't notice the changelings until they shifted on the couches and I saw they had absorbed the rich red velvet and gold embroidery of the upholstery. Only Rue, sitting between Ruth and Etta, was in human form. "What can I do for you?"

"We would like you to speak for us," Delilah said.

"But isn't Omar representing you?" I asked. "That's what Dame Beckwith told me."

"Yes," Omar said. "I am honored to have been chosen as the representative of these good people. But we are concerned that my voice will not be enough to sway the tide of the Council's opinion."

"But you're the most convincing person I know," I blurted.

Omar smiled and inclined his head. "That is precisely the problem. The Council will think I am trying to mesmerize them, even though I have sworn not to use my hypnotic skills. But if one of their own should speak for us—"

"But I'm not one of their own," I protested. "I don't belong wholly to either the Order or the Darklings. I'm on trial here myself—they might exile me."

"We understand if you do not want to risk aligning yourself with us if you think it will hurt your standing—"

"No!" I cut in, appalled how he'd taken my words. "That's not it at all. I would be proud to stand beside any one of you. I just don't know how much help I will be."

"I think you underestimate your power," Delilah said softly. "You combine the best of both worlds—Darkling and human—and your experience has forged you into something wholly yourself: a phoenix, what my people call a Benu, the sun-bird, she who creates herself. We believe you can do whatever you set out to achieve, and if you speak for us, the Council will accept us."

"And if they do chuck you out," Kid Marvel added, "you'll always have a place with us."

I wondered if that meant at Coney Island. I smiled at Kid Marvel and gazed into Delilah's feline eyes. I didn't know if she was right about me, but I did know that I owed these people my life and the lives of my friends. "I would be honored to speak for you," I told them.

⋇→ ✦ ←⋇

I approached the meeting room feeling stronger than before, not just because of the madges' belief in me, but because I was no longer thinking only of myself. The madges were counting on me. My friends were counting on me. I straightened my spine, feeling the weight of my wings pull my shoulder blades back, raised my chin, and opened the door.

I was expecting some sort of conference room with a big long table, the opposing sides of Darklings and the Order arrayed on either side. Instead it was as if I had stepped inside a giant clock. Eight steeply sloping walls were clad in brass gears and bells shining in the bright light pouring through an open skylight. Even the floor was paved in brass. At the center was a raised disk, rimmed with a low bench on which sat Mrs. van Hassel flanked by Lucretia Fisk and Atalanta Jones, the other bird-hatted ladies from my admission interview; as well as Dame Beckwith, Professor Jager, my grandmother, and, surprisingly, Mrs. Calendar. The Darkling Elders were perched on ledges about the room. I recognized Merlinus, Wren and Gos. I also saw my father, who sat between Master Quill and Miss Corey. And Raven. I let out my breath when I saw him.

A short balding man, who looked familiar but whom I couldn't place, was standing in the center of the room holding a long bamboo cane in one hand and a folio in the other. Uncle Taddie was sitting cross-legged at his feet, rocking back and forth like a pendulum. When he saw me he jumped to his feet and excitedly waved me in.

"It's Papa's clock made huge!" he exclaimed, his eyes bulging. He was vibrating with excitement.

Actually, I realized, we were all vibrating. The entire room was moving, the gears clicking slowly but steadily, the central disk revolving in infinitesimal degrees. It made me feel a bit seasick. Mrs. van Hassel looked distinctly green.

"Yes, I see," I told Taddie. "It *is* a big clock. But where's its face? There's no clock on the outside of the building."

The short bald man pointed his cane to the ceiling—and

as he did, I recognized him. It was Mr. Humphreys, the clockmaker Raven was apprenticed to. I looked up and saw that the skylight was fitted with an iron grill that somewhat resembled a clock—or perhaps a compass. The circle's face was divided into quarters inside a brass ring, illustrating the sections of a globe. An arrow spun around the circumference. It reminded me of the game the nestlings played to choose who went first or got first choice of rooms. *Round and round the arrow goes...*

Suddenly a dozen or more gears clicked into place and struck the bells. I braced myself for a deafening peal, but the bells were silent. But their vibrations shook the entire room and rose up in the octagonal chamber and out the skylight. Closing my eyes I could feel the vibrations spreading out around the building—and farther, over the entire city, cloaking New York like a giant glass bell jar.

I opened my eyes when the vibrations ceased.

"What is it?" I asked.

"It's a protective shield designed by Mr. Humphreys," Dame Beckwith said, smiling at the old clockmaker.

"I couldn't have done it if my apprentice hadn't told me about the clocks in Violet House," Mr. Humphreys said, smiling at Raven.

"It was Uncle Taddie who gave me the idea," Raven said modestly. "He showed me how his father had made the clocks to protect the house. I told Mr. Humphreys about them, but I didn't know what he'd do."

"Mr. Humphreys told me," Dame Beckwith said, "and I referred him to Mr. Gilbert and Mr. Woolworth. We thought if the clocks could protect a house, then perhaps a larger version of them could protect a whole city."

"That's why van Drood wanted to destroy the building?" I said.

"Yes," Mrs. van Hassel said, "which we might have anticipated had anyone alerted the Council to this clock project."

"It was to be unveiled after the official opening ceremony," Dame Beckwith replied, glaring at Mrs. van Hassel. "Of course we didn't know that van Drood had found out about the clocks or had infiltrated Blythewood with the dancing master."

"It seems to me that if you ran your school properly such things would not happen," Mrs. van Hassel sniped back at Dame Beckwith.

"We all have our weaknesses."

The voice came from above, from the ledge where my father perched. He pushed himself off the ledge and glided to the center of the room, his wings rustling with the sound of paper. He looked at me as he spoke. "Van Drood uses our weaknesses against us, as a crack to let in the *tenebrae*. He used my own fears to convince me to leave my beloved and my child years ago instead of taking them with me into exile, and he's used our animosity against each other to make us weak. All these years he's plotted to destroy both of us: the Order for prohibiting his marriage to Evangeline, and the Darklings because of Evangeline's love for me. But what started as petty jealousy and resentment has grown into a hatred for all mankind—and Darklingkind and faykind. We are all at risk. Van Drood's ambitions have only grown with his hatred."

"It's true," Professor Jager said, rising from his seat. "The *tenebrae* have been gathering throughout Europe, seeding dissent and hatred in the Balkan States, infiltrating governments in Austria, France, England—even our brother school Hawthorn has been attacked this year. We believe that van Drood is planning a great war, one that will cause such turmoil and pain among mankind that his shadows will have dominion forever."

"Then we must stop him!" Mrs. van Hassel cried, rapping her cane on the brass floor. "The Order must stand strong, as it always has, to defeat the powers of evil. We must not allow ourselves to be compromised by Darklings and demons now of all times—"

"No!" Miss Corey slid down from her ledge in one graceful movement and came to stand beside my father. "Now of all times is exactly when we must join with the Darklings against the shadows. That's what Dame Alcyone knew and wrote about in her book. She foresaw there would come a time when the shadows would threaten to overcome the world and that the only hope was a joining between the Order and the Darklings. She wrote—" She turned to my father. "If you wouldn't mind, Mr. Falco."

"Not at all, Miss Corey," my father replied. He extended his wings until they filled the entire room. The illuminated pages of Dame Alcyone's book glimmered like peacock's eyes amidst his feathers. Miss Corey gently riffled through the pages until she found the place she was looking for, and then read aloud:

"And the shadow will fall between man and
Darkling and spread throughout the land, a

plague of shadows searching for their lost home. Out of the shards of the broken vessel a new light will shine—a phoenix born of Darkling and human, to drive the shadows away. Unless we two are joined, the third vessel will be broken and the shadows will prevail."

Mrs. van Hassel tsked. "That's all very . . . *florid*. How do we know it was really written by Dame Alcyone?"

"Because," Mrs. Calendar said in a reedy but clear voice, "that line—*Out of the shards of the broken vessel a new light will shine*—is part of the secret code of the Order. Only a member of the Order would know it."

Lucretia Fisk spoke up. "Junessa's right, you know. We learned that in codes and sigils senior year."

"That's all very well for you." Gos sneered from his perch. "How do we know this isn't a trick to entrap the Darklings?"

"Because," Wren replied, "we have a prophesy, too—that when a phoenix is fledged our curse will end."

"But who—" Gos began.

Raven and Miss Sharp and Miss Corey were all looking at me. I took off my cloak. Miss Janeway had made me a special shirtwaist and undergarment (corsets, she had told me, were on their way out) to allow my wings to unfold without tearing or burning my clothes. I spread them now, and heard the indrawn breath of Darkling and human alike. I felt the heat in my own face at being stared at, but then I remembered my promise.

"We've only talked about Darklings and humans," I said. "But we're nothing without the fairies and the other magicals who helped us defeat van Drood. We have to all join together."

As I waited for a reply I felt more exposed than I'd ever felt before. But then I looked around and saw that I was surrounded by glowing faces. It was the reflection of my wings in the brass walls bathing us all in a golden glow—a glow so strong it banished the shadows.

"I think that's only fair," Dame Beckwith said. "What do you say, Ansonia?"

Mrs. van Hassel looked like she wanted to say a lot of unpleasant things, but she only muttered, "I suppose beggars can't be choosers. I move to suspend all hostilities toward any magical beings who refrain from provoking us."

"I second the motion," my grandmother said.

"All in favor?" Professor Jager asked.

Everyone chimed in their agreement.

"Well then," Professor Jager said, "there are treaties to be drawn up!"

As he sat down on the bench with Master Quill, rubbing his hands together, I drew in my wings and a shadow passed over the skylight. I looked up, frightened it was a murder of shadow crows, but saw instead an enormous silvery balloon suspended above the tower.

"Ah, the dirigible is here," Mr. Humphreys declared. "Mr. Woolworth ordered it for us. You'd best hurry," he told Raven and me, "if you want to catch a ride back to Blythewood."

Raven looked at me and I grabbed his hand. "We have to," I said, "if only to see Cam's reaction."

He grinned and pulled me from the room, leaving behind the adults to their treaties and declarations. We passed Omar and Delilah as they were called inside the tower room and rushed up the spiral steps to the observatory deck where the giant silver-skinned dirigible was moored to the slender pinnacle of the tower. Cam was already on the plank laid down to the dirigible's door. A flock of Blythewood girls stood at the railing, their hair and ribbons tossing in the wind. I saw Nathan, hands in his pockets, chatting with a uniformed engineer. "I bet you want to talk to him, too," I said to Raven.

"I would like to know how they keep such an ungainly thing in the air."

I released his hand and watched him join Nathan and the engineer.

"If you don't watch out, those two will run off and join the British air force just so they can fly about in those dreadful machines." It was Helen. I turned around to find her in a wheelchair pushed by Daisy.

"Nathan's not going anywhere without you," Daisy said. "I saw the way he carried you up those stairs."

Helen smiled. "He has gotten quite remarkably strong carrying me about. I'm going to let him do it for a few more months while we visit Louisa in Vienna and I take a water cure."

"Let him?" Daisy and I asked together.

Helen peeked around us to make sure no one was watching, but everyone was gathered at the dirigible. Then she stood up.

"Helen!" Daisy cried. "You can—"

Helen clamped a hand over Daisy's mouth and then sat down, adjusting her skirt daintily over her boots.

"But why?" Daisy asked.

"To give Nathan a mission," I said. "One he can win. To keep the shadows at bay."

"Or maybe I just like being carried about," Helen replied airily. "But it does seem to be keeping Nathan's mind off his awful father, and when I make a miraculous recovery at Baden-Baden he'll think he saved me. Gus is coming, too, to try a cure on Louisa—oh, look! They're boarding. Daisy, do go ask Nathan to carry me aboard. I want to get a good seat."

Daisy ran toward Nathan, clutching her hat so it wouldn't get swept off in the wind. I turned back to Helen.

"What about Marlin?" I asked.

"What about him?" Helen asked, blinking her pretty blue eyes up at me.

"You love him, not Nathan."

"Do I?" Helen asked, tilting her head. "I suppose I do, but Nathan's my friend and he needs me. And besides—" She looked back toward the railing where Nathan and Raven had been joined by Buzz and Marlin and Cam and two more men in uniform. They were all laughing and smiling, but standing beneath the dirigible cast their faces in shadow. "I have a feeling that soon it's not going to matter much what we want for ourselves."

Helen's words struck a chill in my heart and seemed to echo in my head. I heard the words of the prophesy that Miss Corey had read—*Out of the shards of the broken vessel*—and I heard van Drood's last words to me: *I have what I need to destroy everything.* Was he talking about the Woolworth Building—or something even bigger? Did he mean the third vessel holding the last of the *tenebrae*? But how could van Drood know where it was?

Then I remembered flying with my father away from the *Titanic* . . . a crow tearing a page from the book. Could that page have told van Drood where to find the third vessel? And if it did, and van Drood was searching for it now . . .

Below us I could feel the gears of the tower clock revolving, moving us all toward the inevitable future in which we would all be tested.

But then Daisy turned and waved to us, her yellow ribbons streaming in the wind like medieval banners, and I felt my heart lift. Whatever was in store, I'd face it with my friends.

Hawthorn

❧

A Blythewood Novel

1

"HAVE YOU EVER wished you had a spell to stop time?"

I turned to my friend and roommate Helen van Beek. We had come to the edge of the Blythe Wood and she had turned to look back over the playing fields and gardens to the great stone castle of our school, Blythewood, glowing golden in the late afternoon sun. Four more girls and one boy were walking toward us. If the moment had been arrested it would have made a fine medieval tapestry, the lawns an emerald carpet stitched with a thousand bright flowers, the stones of the castle and the sleek heads of the girls picked out in gold thread, the boy's in silver marking him as a nobleman or fairy prince. *The Falconers*, it might have been called, since they each carried a falcon on their gauntleted hands.

The viewers of that tapestry might imagine the girls and the boy were discussing the fine points of falconry or courtly love, but they weren't.

"A Morane-Saulnier monoplane with a Gnome Omega 7 cylinder engine!" Cam's excited voice rose into the air, her little kestrel squawking as it attempted to keep its balance on her gesticulating hand. "That's what I'm going to fly when I get out of here next summer."

"You should see the hydro-aeroplanes they've got over in England now," Nathan remarked, excitement breaking through the pose of boredom he'd maintained since returning from Europe. "They can take off from ships now. I'm going to join the Royal Navy as soon as I graduate."

"No more chattering, Dianas," I called to the others, "we're on patrol."

"I thought I made it clear that I was not to be referred to as a Diana," Nathan drawled. "The male equivalent is Apollo."

"Diana or Apollo, we're all here to patrol the woods. Gillie found trow tracks at the edge of the Blythe Wood this morning. We need to scout the perimeter to make sure it hasn't gotten out."

"And what are we supposed to do if we find the trow?" Daisy asked.

"Kill it, of course," Cam said, patting her quiver of arrows.

Before Daisy could object—I knew she had a soft spot for all creatures of Faerie—I said, "Actually, Gillie says we should try to capture it. There's been an increase in fey activity in the woods lately—creatures straying out of the woods, ransacking local farmyards and orchards, even wandering into town. Gillie thinks something must be scaring them out of the woods."

"What's big enough to scare a trow?" Beatrice asked, raising an eyebrow.

"That's what we need to find out," I said. "Nathan and Cam, head toward the river. Bea, Dolores, Daisy, you take the eastern perimeter. Helen and I are going to go into the woods. If anyone finds any sign of the trow, whistle three times. Send your falcon if you need backup. Everybody clear?"

They all nodded, looking a little scared. Of the trow, I wondered, or me? Had I spoken too sharply to them? Well, I didn't have time to coddle them. We had a trow to find.

I turned to enter the woods with Helen close at my heels. As we passed from the bright sunshine of the lawn into the cool green shadows under the pines, I felt Eirwyn tense on my hand, her talons gripping so tightly I was afraid they'd pierce the thick leather of my glove.

Helen's peregrine squawked and darted from her glove.

"Frederica!" Helen cried as she watched the falcon rise into the trees. "Where do you think you're going?"

To a place where no one calls her by that ridiculous name, I began to say, but then my gyr launched herself from my hand and followed, uttering a high-pitched whistle.

"That's her hunting call," I told Helen. "Come on, they're tracking something."

I plunged into the woods. My wings itched to unfurl and follow Eirwyn and Frederica in the air, but I didn't want to leave Helen alone on the ground. Besides, it wasn't easy flying through the woods with a six-foot wing span, and the falcons were leading us into a denser part of the forest, where the trees grew so close together their branches interlaced overhead in a thick canopy that blocked out the sun. I couldn't see Eirwyn or Frederica ahead of us, but with my Darkling hearing I could hear Eirwyn's shrill hunting cry. I followed it into a copse of thorny shrubs that caught at my shirt sleeve and tugged at my skirt.

"Is it my imagination," Helen asked in a hushed whisper, "or do the trees seem to be moving closer together?"

I halted, my gloved hand raised to push aside a thorny branch, and turned back to look at Helen.

"The last time the woods acted to protect us, so we should be all right." I turned back and pulled the thorny branch away ... Uncovering the snarling face of a trow.

I screamed and let go of the branch, which slapped the trow across its thick overhanging brow. That only made it angrier. The creature opened its blue-lipped mouth and roared. Hot, rank breath blew into my face—it smelled like rotting meat and ashes.

Trows are naturally vegetarians in their indigenous habitat. The line from Miles Malmsbury's *Field Guide to the Lychnobious Peoples* wafted into my head. I'd have to tell him he was wrong—if I lived. I reached for the dagger strapped at my waist as the trow launched itself at me, but before I could unsheathe it I was slammed to the ground by what felt like the proverbial ton of bricks. Only bricks wouldn't have such bad breath, I thought staring up into two glazed eyes that appeared to be covered in some kind of film behind which dark shapes moved like fish swimming under ice.

I'd seen something like that before—

Then the ice shattered.

Black ooze poured out of its right eye and then the creature's weight collapsed on top of me. "Mnnn," it said, then mercifully rolled off me.

"Ava!" Helen was shouting into my face and shaking my arms. She was still grasping her bow with one hand. I turned my head and stared at the trow. One of Helen's arrows—all of hers were fletched with snow-white dove feathers which she deemed "smarter" than the dull brown ones the rest of us used—had gone straight through the back of its head and pierced its right eye. Black bile was oozing down its cheek.

"Y-you . . . you shot it."

"Don't start with Gillie's orders," Helen cried, her voice edging into hysteria. "That thing was going to eat you!"

"They're s-supposed to be veg . . . vegetarians," I stammered, struggling to my knees and kneeling over the trow.

Helen made a choking sound. "Well, this one's gone off his diet. He looks like he just finished a six course steak dinner at Delmonico's. Why, his fur . . . whatsit . . ." Helen gestured at the shaggy fur tunic the trow wore. ". . . doesn't fit him properly."

The trow's belly was indeed bulging out of his tunic and over his leather pants. It was disturbing to look at those clothes. This wasn't an animal—it was a person of sorts, one of the fey that had wandered out of Faerie into the Blythe Wood. Perhaps it had gotten lost and been scared. Its intact eye looked dazed.

No, not dazed—*glazed*. As if covered with ice. I leaned over to look more closely and saw something move beneath the opaque surface of the intact eye.

"Helen," I said, starting to get to my feet, "I think we'd better—"

Before I could finish the trow's left eye split open, releasing a spray of black ooze. Helen screamed and covered her face, shielding herself from the geyser that spewed out of the trow's eye—a geyser with feathers.

"Shadow crows!" I screamed, yanking Helen to her feet. "Run!"

I pushed Helen through a narrow opening in the brush into a clearing—a perfect circle surrounded by bushes covered in white flowers. I dimly had the thought that the woods had been leading us here all along, mocking our desire to stop time. There was no way to stop time. If you didn't take the future in hand it took you and yanked you where it wanted you to go. Then Helen and I were falling down a long dark tunnel into the vast unknown.

Acknowledgments

Thanks to my intrepid band of early readers—Sarah Alpert, Gary Feinberg, Wendy Gold, Juliet Harrison, Alisa Kwitney, Scott Silverman, Nora Slonimsky, and Ethel Wesdorp. Thanks to my daughter, Maggie, whose webcomic PennyDreadful (Pennydreadfulcomics.com) has been a continual inspiration in the creation of the Blythewood books.

There were a number of excellent books I relied on for source material: *Triangle* by David von Drehle, *A Fierce Discontent* by Michael McGerr, *The Lost Sisterhood* by Ruth Rosen, and especially *Good Old Coney Island* by Edo McCullough, for which I am indebted for some of the original language of the Coney Island spielers.

I am most grateful to the Hawthornden Castle Retreat for Writers, where much of this book was written, for granting me a perfect month of quiet and inspiration.

Thanks to my wonderful editor, Kendra Levin, for her Darkling editorial ear and for shepherding the Blythewood books into creation, and to Ken Wright, Vanessa Han, Nancy Brennan, and Janet Pascal at Penguin. Thanks to my agent, Robin Rue, and her assistant Beth Miller, at Writers House for believing in these books.

And, as always, I couldn't do any of this without the faith and love of my husband, Lee. You are my knight in shining armor.